I0565441

GERFAUT

BY

CHARLES DE BERNARD

Crowned by the French Academy

With a Preface by JULES
CLARETIE, of the French
Academy :: :: :: :: ::

WILDSIDE PRESS

COPYRIGHT 1905
BY
ROBERT ARNOT

COPYRIGHT 1910
BY
CURRENT LITERATURE PUBLISHING COMPANY

CHARLES DE BERNARD

IERRE - MARIE - CHARLES DE BERNARD DU GRAIL DE LA VILLETTE, better known by the name of Charles de Bernard, was born in Besançon, February 24, 1804. He came from a very ancient family of the Vivarais, was educated at the college of his native city, and studied for the law in Dijon and at Paris. He was awarded a prize by the *Jeux floraux* for his dithyrambics, *Une fête de Néron* in 1829. This first success in literature did not prevent him aspiring to the Magistrature, when the Revolution of 1830 broke out and induced him to enter politics. He became one of the founders of the *Gazette de Franche-Comté* and an article in the pages of this journal about *Peau de chagrin* earned him the thanks and the friendship of Balzac.

The latter induced him to take up his domicile in Paris and initiated him into the art of novel-writing. Bernard had published a volume of odes: *Plus Deuil que Joie* (1838), which was not much noticed, but a series of stories in the same year gained him the reputation of a genial *conteur*. They were collected under the title *Le Noeud Gordien*, and one of the tales, *Une Aventure du Magistrat,* was adapted by Sardou for his comedy *Pommes du voisin*. *Gerjaut*, his greatest work, crowned by the Academy, appeared also in 1838, then followed *Le Paravent*, another collection of novels (1839); *Les Ailes d'Icare* (1840); *La Peau du Lion* and *La Chasse aux Amants* (1841); *L'Ecueil* (1842); *Un Beau-père* (1845); and finally *Le Gentilhomme campagnard*, in 1847. Bernard died, only forty-eight years old, March 6, 1850.

Charles de Bernard was a realist, a pupil of Balzac. He surpasses his master, nevertheless, in energy and limpidity of composition. His style is elegant and cultured. His genius is most fully represented in a score or so of delightful tales rarely exceeding some sixty or seventy pages in length, but perfect in proportion, full of invention and originality, and saturated with the purest and pleasantest essence of the spirit which for six centuries in tableaux, farces, tales in prose and verse, comedies and correspondence, made French literature the delight and recreation of Europe. *Gerjaut* is considered De Bernard's greatest work. The plot turns on an attachment between a married woman and the hero of the story. The book has nothing that can justly offend, the incomparable sketches of Marillac and Mademoiselle de Corandeuil are admirable; Gerfaut and Bergenheim possess pronounced originality, and the author is, so to speak, incarnated with the hero of his romance.

The most uncritical reader can not fail to notice the success with which Charles de Bernard introduces people of rank and breeding into his stories. Whether

PREFACE

or not he drew from nature, his portraits of this kind are exquisitely natural and easy. It is sufficient to say that he is the literary Sir Joshua Reynolds of the post-revolution vicomtes and marquises. We can see that his portraits are faithful; we must feel that they are at the same time charming. Bernard is an amiable and spirited *conteur* who excels in producing an animated spectacle for a refined and selected public, whether he paints the ridiculousness or the misery of humanity.

The works of Charles de Bernard in wit and urbanity, and in the peculiar charm that wit and urbanity give, are of the best French type. To any elevation save a lofty place in fiction they have no claim; but in that phase of literature their worth is undisputed, and from many testimonies it would seem that those whom they most amuse are those who are best worth amusing.

These novels, well enough as they are known to professed students of French literature, have, by the mere fact of their age, rather slipped out of the list of books known to the general reader. The general reader who reads for amusement can not possibly do better than proceed to transform his ignorance of them into knowledge.

de l'Académie Française.

[vii]

CONTENTS

[ix]

CONTENTS

[x]

CONTENTS

CHAPTER XXI

GERFAUT

CHAPTER I

THE TRAVELLER

URING the first days of the month of September, 1832, a young man about thirty years of age was walking through one of the valleys in Lorraine originating in the Vosges mountains. A little river which, after a few leagues of its course, flows into the Moselle, watered this wild basin shut in between two parallel lines of mountains. The hills in the south became gradually lower and finally dwindled away into the plain. Alongside the plateau, arranged in amphitheatres, large square fields stripped of their harvest lay here and there in the primitive forest; in other places, innumerable oaks and elms had been dethroned to give place to plantations of cherry-trees, whose symmetrical rows promised an abundant harvest.

This contest of nature with industry is everywhere, but is more pronounced in hilly countries. The scene changed, however, as one penetrated farther, and little by little the influence of the soil gained ascend-

[1]

ancy. As the hills grew nearer together, enclosing the valley in a closer embrace, the clearings gave way to the natural obduracy of the soil. A little farther on they disappeared entirely. At the foot of one of the bluffs which bordered with its granite bands the highest plateau of the mountain, the forest rolled victoriously down to the banks of the river.

Now came patches of forest, like solid battalions of infantry; sometimes solitary trees appeared, as if distributed by chance upon the grassy slopes, or scaling the summit of the steepest rocks like a body of bold sharpshooters. A little, unfrequented road, if one can judge from the scarcity of tracks, ran alongside the banks of the stream, climbing up and down hills; overcoming every obstacle, it stretched out in almost a straight line. One might compare it to those strong characters who mark out a course in life and imperturbably follow it. The river, on the contrary, like those docile and compliant minds that bend to agreeable emergencies, described graceful curves, obeying thus the caprices of the soil which served as its bed.

At a first glance, the young man who was walking alone in the midst of this picturesque country seemed to have nothing remarkable in his dress; a straw hat, a blue blouse and linen trousers composed his costume. It would have been very natural to take him for an Alsatian peasant returning to his village through the Vosges's rough pathways; but a more attentive glance quickly dispelled this conjecture. There is something in the way in which a person wears the plainest costume which betrays the real man, no matter how he may be clothed. Thus, nothing could be more modest than this traveller's blouse, but the absence on collar and sleeves of the arabesques in white or red thread, the pride of all village dandies, was sufficient for one to realize that this was not a fancy costume.

His expressive, but not handsome face was dark, it is true, but it did not look as if wind or sun had contributed to its complexion; it seemed rather to have lost by a sedentary life something of the southern carnation, which had ended by blending these warmer tints into a dead uniform pallor. Finally, if, as one may suppose after different diagnoses, this person had the slightest desire to play the *rôle* of Tyrcis or Amintas, his white hand, as carefully cared for as a pretty woman's, would have been sufficient to betray him. It was evident that the man was above his costume; a rare thing! The lion's ears pierced the ass's skin this time.

It was three o'clock in the afternoon; the sky, which had been overcast all the morning, had assumed, within a few moments, a more sombre aspect; large clouds were rapidly moving from south to north, rolled one over another by an ominous wind. So the traveller, who had just entered the wildest part of the valley, seemed very little disposed to admire its fine vegetation and romantic sites. Impatient to reach the end of his journey, or fearing the approaching storm, he quickened his steps; but this pace was not kept long. At the end of a few moments, having crossed a small clearing, he found himself at the entrance of a lawn where the road divided in two directions, one continuing to skirt the river banks, the other, broader and better built, turning to the left into a winding ravine.

Which of these two roads should he follow? He did not know. The profound solitude of the place made him fear that he might not meet any one who could direct him, when the sound of a psalm vigorously chanted reached his ears from the distance. Soon it became more distinct, and he recognized the words, *In exitu Israel de Egypto*, sung at the top of the lungs by a voice so shrill that it would have irritated the larynx of any of the sopranos at the Opera. Its vibrating but sharp tones resounded so clearly in the dead silence of the forest that a number of stanzas were finished before the pious musician came in sight. At last a drove of cattle appeared through the trees which bordered the road on the left, walking with a slow, grave step; they were driven by a little shepherd about nine or ten years of age, who interrupted his song from time to time to reassemble the members of his flock with heavy blows from his whip, thus uniting temporal cares with those of a spiritual nature with a coolness which the most important personages might have envied him.

"Which of these roads leads to Bergenheim?" called out the traveller when they were near enough to speak to each other.

"Bergenheim!" repeated the child, taking off his cotton cap, which was striped like a rainbow, and adding a few words in an unintelligible Gallo-Germanic *patois*.

GERFAUT

"You are not French, then?" asked the stranger, in a disappointed tone.

The shepherd raised his head proudly and replied:

"I am Alsatian, not French!"

The young man smiled at this trait of local patriotism so common then in the beautiful province by the Rhine; then he thought that pantomime might be necessary, so he pointed with his finger first at one road, then at the other:

"There or there, Bergenheim?" asked he.

The child, in his turn, pointed silently with the tip of his whip to the banks of the river, designating, at some distance on the other side, a thicket of woods behind which a slight column of smoke was rising.

"The deuce!" murmured the stranger, "it seems that I have gone astray; if the château is on the other side, where can I establish my ambuscade?"

The shepherd seemed to understand the traveller's embarrassment. Gazing at him with his intelligent blue eyes, he traced, with the tip of his toe in the middle of the road, a furrow across which he rounded his whip like the arch of a bridge; then he pointed a second time up the river.

"You are an honor to your country, young fellow," exclaimed the stranger; "there is the material in you to make one of Cooper's redskins." As he said these words he threw a piece of money into the child's cap and walked rapidly away in the direction indicated.

The Alsatian stood motionless for a few moments with one hand in his blond hair and his eyes fastened upon the piece of silver which shone like a star in the

[5]

bottom of his cap; when the one whom he considered as a model of extraordinary generosity had disappeared behind the trees, he gave vent to his joy by heavy blows from his whip upon the backs of the cattle, then he resumed his way, singing in a still more triumphant tone: *Montes exultaverunt ut arites*, and jumping higher himself than all the hills and rams in the Bible.

The young man had not walked more than five minutes before he recognized the correctness of the directions he had received. The ground which he had passed over was a field covered with clumps of low trees; it was easy to see by its disc-like shape that it had been formed by successive alluvia, at the expense of the other shore, which had been incessantly worn away by the stream. This sort of flat, level peninsula was crossed in a straight line by the road, which deviated from the river at the point where the two roads came together again, like the cross and string of a bow at its extremity. The trees, becoming thinner, revealed a perspective all the more wonderful as it was unexpected. While the eye followed the widening stream, which disappeared in the depths of a mountainous gorge, a new prospect suddenly presented itself on the right upon the other shore.

A second valley, smaller than the first and in measure its vassal, formed an amphitheatre the crest of which was bordered by a fringe of perpendicular rocks as white as dried bones. Under this crown, which rendered it almost inaccessible, the little valley was resplendent in its wealth of evergreen trees, oaks with their knotty branches, and its fresh green turf.

GERFAUT

Taken as a whole, it was a foundation worthy of the picturesque edifice which met one's eye in the foreground, and at which the traveller gazed with extreme interest.

At the junction of the two valleys stood an enormous building, half manorial, half monastic in appearance. The shore formed, at this point, for an extent of several hundred feet, a bluff whose edge plunged vertically into the river. The château and its outbuildings rested upon this solid base. The principal house was a large parallelogram of very old construction, but which had evidently been almost entirely rebuilt at the beginning of the sixteenth century. The stones, of grayish granite which abounds in the Vosges, were streaked with blue and violet veins, and gave the façade a sombre aspect, increased by the scarcity of windows, some of which were *à la Palladio*, others almost as narrow as loop-holes. An immense roof of red tile, darkened by rain, projected several feet over the whole front, as is still to be seen in old cities in the North. Thanks to this projecting weather-board, the apartments upon the upper floor were shaded from the sun's rays, like those persons who have weak eyes and who protect them from a strong light by wearing a green shade.

The view which this melancholy dwelling presented from the place where the traveller had first seen it, was one which made it appear to the best advantage; it seemed, from this point, to come immediately out of the river, built as it was upon the very curb of the bluffs, at this place at least thirty feet high. This elevation, added to that of the building, effaced the lack of proportion of the roof and gave to the whole a most imposing appearance; it seemed as if the rocks were a part of the building to which it served as foundation, for the stones had ended by assuming the same color, and it would have been difficult to discover the junction of man's work and that of nature, had it not been outlined by a massive iron balcony running across the entire length of the first story, whence one could enjoy the pleasure of line-fishing. Two round towers with pointed roofs stood at each corner of the façade and seemed to gaze with proud satisfaction at their own reflection in the water.

A long line of sycamore-trees skirted the banks of the river, beginning from the foot of the château, and forming the edge of a park which extended to the back of the double valley. A little wooden bridge connected this sort of avenue with the road the traveller had just passed over; but the latter did not seem disposed to profit by this silent invitation to which large raindrops gave more emphasis. He was so absorbed in his meditation that, to arouse him, it needed the sound of a gruff voice behind him uttering these words:

"That is what I call an ugly castle! It is hardly as good as our common country houses around Marseilles."

The stranger turned quickly around and found himself face to face with a man wearing a gray cap and carrying his coat upon his shoulder, as workmen do in the South. He held in his hand a knotty stick which had been recently cut. The newcomer had a swarthy complexion, harsh features, and deep-set eyes which gave his face an ugly, false expression.

"I said an ugly castle," continued he. "However, the cage is made for the bird."

"It seems, then, that you do not like its master?" said the traveller.

"The master!" repeated the workman, seizing hold of his stick with a threatening air, "Monsieur le Baron de Bergenheim, as they say! He is rich and a nobleman, and I am only a poor carpenter. Well, then, if you stay here a few days, you will witness a comical ceremony; I shall make this brigand repent."

"Brigand!" exclaimed the stranger, in a surprised tone. "What has he done to you?"

"Yes, brigand! you may tell him so from me. But, by the way," continued the workman, surveying his companion from head to foot with a searching, defiant air, "do you happen to be the carpenter who is coming from Strasbourg? In that case, I have a few words to say to you. Lambernier does not allow any one to take the bread out of his mouth in that way; do you understand?"

The young man seemed very little moved by this declaration.

"I am not a carpenter," said he, smiling, "and I have no wish for your work."

"Truly, you do not look as if you had pushed a plane very often. It seems that in your business one does not spoil one's hands. You are a workman about as much as I am pope."

CHARLES DE BERNARD

This remark made the one to whom it was addressed feel in as bad a humor as an author does when he finds a grammatical error in one of his books.

"So you work at the château, then," said he, finally, to change the conversation.

"For six months I have worked in that shanty," replied the workman; "I am the one who carved the new woodwork, and I will say it is well done. Well, this great wild boar of a Bergenheim turned me out of the house yesterday as if I had been one of his dogs."

"He doubtless had his reasons."

"I tell you, I will crush him—reasons! Damn it! They told him I talked too often with his wife's maid and quarrelled with the servants, a pack of idlers! Did he not forbid my putting my foot upon his land? I am upon his land now; let him come and chase me off; let him come, he will see how I shall receive him. Do you see this stick? I have just cut it in his own woods to use it on himself!"

The young man no longer listened to the workman; his eyes were turned toward the castle, whose slightest details he studied, as if he hoped that in the end the stone would turn into glass and let him see the interior. If this curiosity had any other object than the architecture and form of the building it was not gratified. No human figure came to enliven this sad, lonely dwelling. All the windows were closed, as if the house were uninhabited. The baying of dogs, probably imprisoned in their kennel, was the only sound which came to break the strange silence, and the distant thunder, with its dull rumbling, repeated by the echoes, responded plaintively, and gave a lugubrious character to the scene.

"When one speaks of the devil he appears," said the workman, suddenly, with an emotion which gave the lie to his recent bravado; "if you wish to see this devil incarnate of a Bergenheim, just turn your head. Good-by."

At these words he leaped a ditch at the left of the road and disappeared in the bushes. The stranger also seemed to feel an impression very like that of Lambernier's as he saw a man on horseback advancing on a gallop. Instead of waiting for him, he darted into the field which descended to the river, and hid behind a group of trees.

The Baron, who was not more than thirty-three years of age, had one of those energetic, handsome faces whose type seems to belong particularly to old military families. His bright, blond hair and clear, blue eyes contrasted strongly with his ruddy complexion; his aspect was severe, but noble and imposing, in spite of his negligent dress, which showed that indifference to matters of personal attire which becomes habitual with country lords. His tall figure was beginning to grow stout, and that increased his athletic appearance. He sat very erect in his saddle, and from the way in which he straightened out his long legs against the sides of his beast, one suspected that he could, if necessary, repeat the Marshal de Saxe's feats of skill. He stopped his horse suddenly at the very spot which the two men had just vacated and called out in a voice which would startle a regiment of cuirassiers:

"Here, Lambernier!"

The carpenter hesitated a moment, at this imperative call, between the fear which he could not overcome and shame at fleeing from a single man in the presence of a witness; finally this last feeling triumphed. He returned to the edge of the road without saying a word, and stationed himself in an insolent way face to face with the Baron, with his hat drawn down over his ears, and grasped through precaution the knotty stick which served him as a weapon.

"Lambernier," said the master of the castle, in a severe tone, "your account was settled yesterday; was it not paid in full? Is anything due you?"

"I ask nothing of you," replied the workman, brusquely.

"In that case, why are you wandering about my place when I forbade you?"

"I am upon the highway, nobody can prevent me from passing there."

"You are upon my land, and you came out of my woods," replied the Baron, emphasizing his words with the firmness of a man who would permit no violation of his rights as a landowner.

"The ground upon which I walk is mine," said the workman, in his turn, as he struck the end of his stick upon the ground as if to take possession. This gesture attracted Bergenheim's attention, and his eyes flashed with a sudden light at the sight of the stick which Lambernier held.

"You scoundrel!" he exclaimed, "you probably regard my trees also as your own. Where did you cut that stick?"

"Go and find out," said the workman, accompanying his reply with a flourish of the stick.

The Baron coolly dismounted, threw the bridle over his horse's neck, walked up to the workman, who had taken the position of a practised pugilist to receive him, and, without giving him time to strike, he disarmed him with one hand by a blow which would have been sufficient to uproot the beech rod before it was metamorphosed into a club; with the other hand he seized the man by the collar and gave him a shaking that it was as impossible to struggle against as if it had been caused by a steam-engine. Obeying this irresistible force, in spite of his kicking, Lambernier described a dozen circles around his adversary, while the latter set these off with some of the hardest blows from green wood that ever chastised an insolent fellow. This gymnastic exercise ended by a sleight-of-hand trick, which, after making the carpenter pirouette for the last time, sent him rolling head-first into a ditch, the bottom of which, fortunately for him, was provided with a bed of soft mud. When the punishment was over, Bergenheim remounted his horse as tranquilly as he had dismounted it, and continued his way toward the château.

The young man, in the midst of the thicket where he was concealed, had lost no detail of this rural scene. He could not help having a feeling of admiration for this energetic representative of the feudal ages who, with no fear of any court of justice or other *bourgeois* inventions, had thus exerted over his own domains the summary justice in force in Eastern countries.

"France has thrashed Gaul," said he, smiling to himself; "if all our men had this Bergenheim's iron fist many things determined upon to-day might be called in question. If I ever have the slightest difficulty with this Milo de Crotona, he may be sure I shall not choose pugilism as my mode of discussion."

The storm now burst forth in all its fury. A dark curtain covered the whole valley, and the rain fell in torrents. The Baron put spurs to his horse, crossed the bridge and, entering the sycamore avenue, was soon out of sight. Without paying any attention to Lambernier, who was uttering imprecations at the bottom of the ditch, into which he was sinking deeper and deeper, the stranger went to seek a less illusive shelter than the trees under which he had taken his position; but at this moment his attention was attracted to one side of the castle. A window, or rather a glass door, just then opened upon the balcony, and a young woman in a rose-colored *negligée* appeared upon the dark façade. It would be impossible to imagine anything more fresh or charming than this apparition at such a moment. Leaning upon the balustrade, the young woman rested her face upon a hand which was as white as a lily, and her finger smoothed with a mechanical caress the ringlets of chestnut hair that lay upon her forehead, while her large brown eyes gazed into the depths of the clouds from which the lightning was flashing, and with which they vied in brilliancy. A poet would have said it was Miranda evoked by the tempest.

The stranger parted the branches before him to get a better view; at the same instant he was blinded by a terrible flash which lighted the whole valley and was immediately followed by a terrific crash. When he opened his eyes the château which he believed to be at the bottom of the river stood still upright, solemn, and firm as before; but the lady in the rose-colored gown had disappeared.

CHAPTER II

THE appearance of the room into which the lady had precipitately entered, when startled by the thunder, corresponded with the edifice to which it belonged. It was a very large room, longer than it was wide, and lighted by three windows, the middle one of which opened from top to bottom like a door and led out upon the balcony. The woodwork and ceiling were in chestnut, which time had polished and a skilful hand had ornamented with a profusion of allegorical figures. The beauty of this work of art was almost entirely concealed by a very remarkable decoration which covered every side of the room, consisting of one of the most glorious collections of family portraits which a country château of the nineteenth century could offer.

The first of these portraits hung opposite the windows at the right of the entrance door and was that of a chevalier in full armor, whose teeth gleamed from under his long moustache like those of an untamed tiger. Beginning with this formidable figure, which bore the date 1247, forty others of about the same dimensions were placed in order according to their dates. It seemed as if each period had left its mark upon those of the personages it had seen live and die, and had left something of its own character there.

There were more gallant cavaliers cut after the same pattern as the first. Their stern, harsh faces, red beards, and broad, square military shoulders told that by sword-thrusts and broken lances they had founded the nobility of their race. An heroic preface to this family biography! A rough and warlike page of the Middle Ages! After these proud men-of-arms came several figures of a less ferocious aspect, but not so imposing. In these portraits of the fifteenth century beards had disappeared with the sword. In those wearing caps and velvet toques, silk robes and heavy gold chains supporting a badge of the same metal, one recognized lords in full and tranquil possession of the fiefs won by their fathers, landowners who had degenerated a little and preferred mountain life in a manor to the chances of a more hazardous existence. These pacific gentlemen were, for the most part, painted with the left hand gloved and resting upon the hip; the right one was bare, a sort of token of disarmament which one might take for a painter's epigram. Some of them had allowed their favorite dogs to share the honors of the picture. All in this group indicated that this branch of the family had many points of resemblance with the more illustrious faces. It was the period of idle kings.

A half dozen solemn personages with gold-braided hats and long red robes bordered with ermine, and wearing starched ruffles, occupied one corner of the

parlor near the windows. These worthy advisers of
the Dukes of Lorraine explained the way in which
the masters of the château had awakened from the
torpor in which they had been plunged for several generations, in order to participate in the affairs of their
country and enter a more active sphere.

Here the portraits assumed the proportions of history.
Did not this branch, descended from warlike stock,
seem like a fragment taken from the European annals?
Was it not a symbolical image of the progress of civilization, of regular legislation struggling against bar-
baric customs? Thanks to these respectable coun-
sellors and judges, one might reverse the motto: *Non
solum toga*, in favor of their race. But it did not
seem as if these bearded ancestors looked with much
gratitude upon this parliamentary flower added to
their feudal crest. They appeared to look down from
the height of their worm-eaten frames upon their en-
robed descendants with that disdainful smile with
which the peers of France used to greet men of law
the first time they were called to sit by their side, after
being for so long a time at their feet.

In the space between the windows and upon the
remaining woodwork was a crowd of military men,
with here and there an Abbé with cross and mitre,
a Commander of Malta, and a solemn Canon, sterile
branches of this genealogical tree. Several among
the military ones wore sashes and plumes of the colors of Lorraine; others, even before the union of this
province to France, had served the latter country;
there were lieutenant-colonels of infantry and cavalry;

some dressed in blue coats lined with buff serge and little round patches of black plush, which served as the uniform for the dragoons of the Lorraine legion.

Last of all was a young man with an agreeable face, who smiled superciliously from under a vast wig of powdered hair; a rose was in the buttonhole of his green cloth pelisse with orange facings, a red sabre-cache hung against his boots a little lower than the hilt of his sabre. The costume represented a sprightly officer of the Royal Nassau hussars. The portrait was hung on the left of the entrance door and only separated by it from his great-grandfather of 1247, whom he might have assisted, had these venerable portraits taken some night a fancy to descend from their frames to execute a dance such as Hoffmann dreamed.

These two persons were the *alpha* and the *omega* of this genealogical tree, the two extreme links of the chain—one, the root buried in the sands of time; the other, the branch which had blossomed at the top. Fate had created a tragical resemblance between these two lives, separated by more than five centuries. The chevalier in coat-of-mail had been killed in the battle of the Mansourah during the first crusade of St. Louis. The young man with the supercilious smile had mounted the scaffold during the Reign of Terror, holding between his lips a rose, his usual decoration for his coat. The history of the French nobility was embodied in these two men, born in blood, who had died in blood.

Large gilded frames of Gothic style surrounded all

[19]

these portraits. At the right, on the bottom of each picture was painted a little escutcheon having for its crest a baronial coronet and for supports two wild men armed with clubs. The field was red; with its three bulls' heads in silver, it announced to people well versed in heraldic art that they had before them the lineaments of noble and powerful lords, squires of Reisnach-Bergenheim, lords of Reisnach in Suabia, barons of the Holy Empire, lords of Sapois, Labresse, Gerbamont, etc., counts of Bergenheim, the latter title granted them by Louis XV, chevaliers of Lorraine, etc., etc., etc.

This ostentatious enumeration was not needed in order to recognize the kindred of all these noble personages. Had they been mingled with other portraits, a careful observer would have promptly distinguished and reunited them, so pronounced were the family features common to them all. The furniture of the room was not unworthy of these proud defunct ones. High-backed chairs and enormous armchairs, dating from the time of Louis XIII; more modern sofas, which had been made to harmonize with the older furniture, filled the room. They were covered with flowered tapestry in thousands of shades, which must have busied the white hands of the ladies of the house for two or three generations past.

The row of portraits was interrupted on one side by a large fireplace of grayish granite, which was too high for one to hang a mirror above or to place ornaments upon its mantel. Opposite was an ebony console inlaid with ivory, upon which was placed one of those elegant clocks whose delicate and original chased work has not been eclipsed by any modern workmanship. Two large Japanese vases accompanied it; the whole was reflected in an antique mirror which hung above the console; its edges were bevelled, doubtless in order to cause one to admire the thickness of the glass.

It would be impossible to imagine a stronger contrast than that of this Gothic room with the lady in the rose-colored gown who had just entered it so precipitately. The fire upon the hearth threw a warm light over the old portraits, and it was heightened by the heavy, red damask curtains which hung by the windows. The light sometimes softened, sometimes revivified by some sudden flash of the flames, glanced over the scowling faces and red beards, enlivening the eyes and giving a supernatural animation to those lifeless canvases. One would have said that the cold, grave faces looked with curiosity at the young woman with graceful movements and cool garments, whom Aladdin's genii seemed to have transported from the most elegant boudoir on the Chaussée-d'Antin, and thrown, still frightened, into the midst of this strange assembly.

"You are crazy, Clémence, to leave that window open!" said at this moment an old voice issuing from an armchair placed in a corner near the fireplace.

The person who broke the charm of this silent scene was a woman of sixty or seventy years of age, according to the gallantry of the calculator. It was easy to judge that she was tall and thin as she lay, rather than sat, in her chair with its back lowered

[21] ·

down. She was dressed in a yellowish-brown gown. A false front as black as jet, surmounted by a cap with poppy-colored ribbons, framed her face. She had sharp, withered features, and the brilliancy of her primitive freshness had been converted into a blotched and pimpled complexion which affected above all her nose and cheek-bones, but whose ardor had been dimmed only a trifle by age. There was something about the whole face as crabbed, sour, and unkind as if she had daily bathed it in vinegar. One could read old maid in every feature! Besides, a slight observation of her ways would have destroyed all lingering doubt in this respect.

A large, coffee-colored pug-dog was lying before the fire. This interesting animal served as a footstool for his mistress, stretched in her easy-chair, and recalled to mind the lions which sleep at the foot of chevaliers in their Gothic tombs. As a pug-dog and an old maid pertain to each other, it was only necessary, in order to divine this venerable lady's state, to read the name upon the golden circlet which served as a collar for the dog: "Constance belongs to Mademoiselle de Corandeuil."

Before the younger lady, who was leaning upon the back of a chair, seeming to breathe with difficulty, had time to reply, she received a second injunction.

"But, aunt," said she, at last, "it was a horrible crash! Did you not hear it?"

"I am not so deaf as that yet," replied the old maid. "Shut that window; do you not know that currents of air attract lightning?"

Clémence obeyed, dropping the curtain to shut out the flashes of lightning which continued to dart through the heavens; she then approached the fireplace.

"Since you are so afraid of lightning," said her aunt; "which, by the way, is perfectly ridiculous in a Corandeuil, what induced you to go out upon the balcony? The sleeve of your gown is wet. That is the way one gets cold; afterward, there is nothing but an endless array of syrups and drugs. You ought to change your gown and put on something warmer. Who would ever think of dressing like that in such weather as this?"

"I assure you, aunt, it is not cold. It is because you have a habit of always being near the fire——"

"Ah! habit! when you are my age you will not hint at such a thing. Now, everything goes wonderfully well; you never listen to my advice—you go out in the wind and rain with that flighty Aline and your husband, who has no more sense than his sister; you will pay for it later. Open the curtains, I pray; the storm is over, and I wish to read the *Gazette*."

The young woman obeyed a second time and stood with her forehead pressed against the glass. The distant rumbling of the thunder announced the end of the storm; but a few flashes still traversed the horizon.

"Aunt," said she, after a moment's silence, "come and look at the Montigny rocks; when the lightning strikes them they look like a file of silver columns or a procession of ghosts."

"What a romantic speech," growled the old lady, never taking her eyes from her paper.

"I assure you I am not romantic the least in the world," replied Clémence. "I simply find the storm a distraction, and here, you know, there is no great choice of pleasures."

"Then you find it dull?"

"Oh, aunt, horribly so!" At these words, pronounced with a heartfelt accent, the young woman dropped into an armchair.

Mademoiselle de Corandeuil took off her eye-glasses, put the paper upon the table and gazed for several moments at her pretty niece's face, which was tinged with a look of deep melancholy. She then straightened herself up in her chair, and, leaning forward, asked in a low tone:

"Have you had any trouble with your husband?"

"If so, I should not be so bored," replied Clémence, in a gay tone, which she repented immediately, for she continued more calmly:

"No, aunt; Christian is kind, very kind; he is very much attached to me, and full of good-humor and attentions. You have seen how he has allowed me to arrange my apartments to suit myself, even taking down the partition and enlarging the windows; and yet, you know how much he clings to everything that is old about the house. He tries to do everything for my pleasure. Did he not go to Strasbourg the other day to buy a pony for me, because I thought Titania was too skittish? It would be impossible to show greater kindness."

"Your husband," suddenly interrupted Mademoiselle de Corandeuil, for she held the praise of others in sovereign displeasure, "is a Bergenheim like all the Bergenheims present, past, and future, including your little sister-in-law, who appears more as if she had been brought up with boys than at the 'Sacred Heart.' He is a worthy son of his father there," said she, pointing to one of the portraits near the young Royal-Nassau officer; "and he was the most brutal, unbearable, and detestable of all the dragoons in Lorraine; so much so that he got into three quarrels at Nancy in one month, and at Metz, over a game of checkers, he killed the poor Vicomte de Megrigny, who was worth a hundred of him and danced so well! Some one described Bergenheim as being 'proud as a peacock, as stubborn as a mule, and as furious as a lion!' Ugly race! ugly race! What I say to you now, Clémence, is to excuse your husband's faults, for it would be time lost to try to correct them. However, all men are alike; and since you are Madame de Bergenheim, you must accept your fate and bear it as well as possible. And then, if you have your troubles, you still have your good aunt to whom you can confide them and who will not allow you to be tyrannized over. I will speak to your husband."

Clémence saw, from the first words of this tirade, that she must arm herself with resignation; for anything which concerned the Bergenheims aroused one of the hobbies which the old maid rode with a most complacent spite; so she settled herself back in her chair like a person who would at least be comfortable while she listened to a tiresome discourse, and busied herself during this lecture caressing with the tip of a very shapely foot the top of one of the andirons.

"But, aunt," said she at last, when the tirade was over, and she gave a rather drawling expression to her voice, "I can not understand why you have taken this idea into your head that Christian renders me unhappy. I repeat it, it is impossible that one should be kinder to me than he, and, on my side, I have the greatest respect and friendship for him."

"Very well, if he is such a pearl of husbands, if you live so much like turtle-doves—and, to tell the truth, I do not believe a word of it—what causes this *ennui* of which you complain and which has been perfectly noticeable for some time? When I say *ennui*, it is more than that; it is sadness, it is grief? You grow thinner every day; you are as pale as a ghost; just at this moment, your complexion is gone; you will end by being a regular fright. They say that it is the fashion to be pale nowadays; a silly notion, indeed, but it will not last, for complexion makes the woman."

The old lady said this like a person who had her reasons for not liking pale complexions, and who gladly took pimples for roses.

Madame de Bergenheim bowed her head as if to acquiesce in this decision, and then resumed in her drawling voice:

"I know that I am very unreasonable, and I am often vexed with myself for having so little control over my feelings, but it is beyond my strength. I have a tired sensation, a disgust for everything, something which I can not overcome. It is an inexplicable physical and moral languor, for which, for this reason, I see no remedy. I am weary and I suffer; I am sure it will end in my being ill. Sometimes I wish I were dead. However, I have really no reason to be unhappy. I suppose I am happy—I ought to be happy."

"Truly, I can not understand in the least the women of to-day. Formerly, upon exciting occasions, we had a good nervous attack and all was over; the crisis passed, we became amiable again, put on rouge and went to a ball. Now it is languor, *ennui*, stomach troubles—all imagination and humbug! The men are just as bad, and they call it spleen! Spleen! a new discovery, an English importation! Fine things come to us from England; to begin with, the constitutional government! All this is perfectly ridiculous. As for you, Clémence, you ought to put an end to such childishness. Two months ago, in Paris, you did not have any of the rest that you enjoy here. I had serious reasons for wishing to delay my departure; my apartment to refurnish, my neuralgia which still troubles me—and Constance, who had just been in the hands of the doctor, was hardly in a condition to travel, poor creature! You would listen to nothing; we had to submit to your caprices, and now——"

"But, aunt, you admitted yourself that it was the proper thing for me to do, to join my husband. Was it not enough, and too much, to have left him to pass the entire winter alone here while I was dancing in Paris?"

"It was very proper, of course, and I do not blame you. But why does the very thing you so much desired two months ago bore you so terribly now? In Paris you talked all the time of Bergenheim, longed only for Bergenheim, you had duties to fulfil, you wished to be with your husband; you bothered and wore me out with your conjugal love. When back at Bergenheim, you dream and sigh for Paris. Do not shake your head; I am an old aunt to whom you pay no heed, but who sees clearly yet. Will you do me the favor to tell me what it is that you regret in Paris at this time of the year, when there are no balls or parties, and not one human being worth visiting, for all the people you know are in the country? Is it because——"

Mademoiselle de Corandeuil did not finish her sentence, but she put a severity into these three words which seemed to condense all the quintessence of prudery that a celibacy of sixty years could coagulate in an old maid's heart.

Clémence raised her eyes to her aunt's face as if to demand an explanation.

It was such a calm, steady glance that the latter could not help being impressed by it.

"Well," said she, softening her voice, "there is no necessity for putting on such queenly airs; we are here alone, and you know that I am a kind aunt to you. Now, then, speak freely—have you left anything or any person in Paris, the remembrance of which makes your sojourn here more tiresome than it really is? Any of your adorers of the winter?"

"What an idea, aunt! Did I have any adorers?" exclaimed Madame de Bergenheim, quickly, as if try-

ing to conceal by a smile the rosy flush that mounted
to her cheeks.

"And what if you should have some, child?" continued the old maid, to whom curiosity lent an unaccustomed coaxing accent to her voice, "where would
be the harm? Is it forbidden to please? When one
is of good birth, must one not live in society and hold
one's position there? One need not bury one's self
in a desert at twenty-three years of age, and you really
are charming enough to inspire love; you understand,
I do not say, to experience it; but when one is young
and pretty conquests are made almost unwittingly.
You are not the first of the family to whom that has
happened; you are a Corandeuil. Now, then, my good
Clémence, what troubled heart is pining for you in
Paris? Is it Monsieur de Mauleon?"

"Monsieur de Mauleon!" exclaimed the young
woman, bursting into laughter; "he, a heart! and a
troubled one, too! Oh, aunt, you do him honor! Monsieur de Mauleon, who is past forty-five years old
and wears stays! an audacious man who squeezes his
partners' hands in the dance and looks at them with
passionate glances! Oh! Monsieur de Mauleon!"

Mademoiselle de Corandeuil sanctioned by a slight
grimace of her thin lips her niece's burst of gayety,
when, with one hand upon her heart, she rolled her
sparkling eyes in imitation of the languishing air of
her unfortunate adorer.

"Perhaps it is Monsieur d'Arzenac?"

"Monsieur d'Arzenac is certainly very nice; he has
perfect manners; it may be that he did not disdain to

chat with me; on my side, I found his conversation very entertaining; but you may rest assured that he did not think of me nor I of him. Besides, you know that he is engaged to marry Mademoiselle de la Neuville."

"Monsieur de Gerfaut?" continued Mademoiselle de Corandeuil, with the persistency with which aged people follow an idea, and as if determined to pass in review all the young men of their acquaintance until she had discovered her niece's secret.

The latter was silent a moment before replying.

"How can you think of such a thing, aunt?" said she at last, "a man with such a bad reputation, who writes books that one hardly dares read, and plays that it's almost a sin to witness! Did you not hear Madame de Pontivers say that a young woman who cared for her reputation would permit his visits very rarely?"

"Madame de Pontivers is a prude, whom I can not endure, with her show of little grimaces and her pretentious, outrageous mock-modesty. Did she not take it into her head this winter to constitute me her chaperon? I gave her to understand that a widow forty years old was quite old enough to go about alone! She has a mania for fearing that she may be compromised. The idea of turning up her nose at Monsieur de Gerfaut! What presumption! He certainly is too clever ever to solicit the honor of being bored to death in her house; for he *is* clever, very clever. I never could understand your dislike for him, nor your haughty manner of treating him; especially, during the latter part of our stay in Paris."

GERFAUT

"One is not mistress of one's dislikes or affections, aunt. But to reply to your questions, I will say that you may rest assured that none of these gentlemen, nor any of those whom you might name, has the slightest effect upon my state of mind. I am bored because it probably is my nature to need distractions, and there are none in this deserted place. It is an involuntary disagreeableness, for which I reproach myself and which I hope will pass away. Rest assured, that the root of the evil does not lie in my heart."

Mademoiselle de Corandeuil understood by the cold and rather dry tone in which these words were spoken that her niece wished to keep her secret, if she had one; she could not prevent a gesture of anger as she saw her advances thus repelled, but felt that she was no wiser than when she began the conversation. She manifested her disappointment by pushing the dog aside with her foot—the poor thing was perfectly innocent!—and in a cross tone, which was much more familiar than her former coaxing one, she continued:

"Very well, since I am wrong, since your husband adores you and you him, since, to sum it all up, your heart is perfectly tranquil and free, your conduct is devoid of common-sense, and I advise you to change it. I warn you that all this hypochondria, paleness, and languor are caprices which are very disagreeable to others. There is a Provence proverb which says: *Vaillance de Blacas, prudence de Pontevez, caprice de Corandeuil.* If there was not such a saying, it should be created for you, for you have something incomprehensible enough in your character to make a saint swear. If anybody should know you, it is I, who brought you up. I do not wish to reproach you, but you gave me trouble enough; you were a most wayward, capricious, and fantastic creature, a spoiled child——"

"Aunt," interrupted Clémence, with heightened color in her pale cheeks, "you have told me of my faults often enough for me to know them, and, if they were not corrected, it was not your fault, for you never spared me scoldings. If I had not been so unfortunate as to lose my mother when I was a baby, I should not have given you so much trouble."

Tears came into the young woman's eyes, but she had enough control over herself to keep them from streaming down her burning cheeks. Taking a journal from the table, she opened it, in order to conceal her emotion and to put an end to this conversation, which had become painful to her. Mademoiselle de Corandeuil, on her side, carefully replaced her eye-glasses upon her nose, and, solemnly stretching herself upon her chair, she turned over the leaves of the *Gazette de France*, which she had neglected so long.

Silence reigned for some moments in the room. The aunt apparently read the paper very attentively. Her niece sat motionless, with her eyes fastened upon the yellow cover of the last number of *La Mode*, which had chanced to fall into her hands. She aroused herself at last from her revery and carelessly turned over the leaves of the review in a manner which showed how little interest she felt in it. As she turned the first page a surprised cry escaped her, and her eyes were fastened upon the pamphlet with eager curiosity. Upon the frontispiece, where the Duchesse de Berry's coat-of-arms is engraved, and in the middle of the shield, which was left empty at this time by the absence of the usual *fleurs de lys*, was sketched with a pencil a bird whose head was surmounted by a baron's coronet.

Curious to know what could have caused her niece so much surprise, Mademoiselle de Corandeuil stretched out her neck and gazed for an instant upon the page without seeing, at first, anything extraordinary, but finally her glance rested upon the armorial bearings, and she discovered the new feature added to the royal Bourbon coat-of-arms.

"A cock!" exclaimed she, after a moment's reflection; "a cock upon Madame's shield! What can that mean, *bon Dieu!* and it is not engraved nor lithographed; it is drawn with a pencil."

"It is not a cock, it is a crowned gerfaut," said Madame de Bergenheim.

"A gerfaut! How do you know what a gerfaut is? At Corandeuil, in your grandfather's time, there was a falconry, and I have seen gerfauts there, but you— I tell you it is a cock, an old French cock; ugly thing! What you take for a coronet—and it really does resemble one—is a badly drawn cock's comb. How did this horrid creature come to be there? I should like to know if such pretty tricks are permitted at the post-office. People protest against the *cabinet noir*, but it is a hundred times worse if one is permitted to outrage with impunity peaceable families in their own homes. I mean to find out who has played this trick. Will you be so kind as to ring the bell?"

"It really is very strange!" said Madame de Bergenheim, pulling the bell-rope with a vivacity which showed that she shared, if not the indignation, at least the curiosity of her aunt.

A servant in green livery appeared.

"Who went to Remiremont yesterday for the newspapers?" asked Mademoiselle de Corandeuil.

"It was Père Rousselet, Mademoiselle," replied the servant.

"Where is Monsieur de Bergenheim?"

"Monsieur le Baron is playing billiards with Mademoiselle Aline."

"Send Leonard Rousselet here."

And Mademoiselle de Corandeuil settled herself back in her chair with the dignity of a chancellor about to hold court.

CHAPTER III

HE servants in the castle of Bergen-
heim formed a family whose mem-
bers were far from living in harmony.
The Baron managed his household
himself, and employed a large number of day-laborers, farm servants,
and kitchen-girls, whom the liveried
servants treated with great disdain.
The rustics, on their side, resisted these privileged
lackeys and called them "coxcombs" and "Parisians,"
sometimes accompanying these remarks with the most
expressive blows. Between these tribes of sworn enemies a third class, much less numerous, found themselves in a critical position; these were the two servants
brought by Mademoiselle de Corandeuil. It was
fortunate for them that their mistress liked large,
vigorous men, and had chosen them for their broad,
military shoulders; but for that it would have been
impossible for them to come out of their daily quarrels safe and sound.

The question of superiority between the two house-
holds had been the first apple of discord; a number of
personal quarrels followed to inflame them. They
fought for their colors the whole time; the Bergenheim livery was red, the Corandeuil green. There

were two flags; each exalted his own while throwing
that of his adversaries in the mud. *Greenhorn* and
crab were jokes; *cucumber* and *lobster* were insults.

Such were the gracious terms exchanged every day
between the two parties. In the midst of this civil
war, which was carefully concealed from their mas-
ters' eyes, whose severity they feared, lived one rather
singular personage. Leonard Rousselet, Père Rousselet, as he was generally called, was an old peasant who, disheartened with life, had made various
efforts to get out of his sphere, but had never succeeded
in doing so. Having been successively hair-dresser,
sexton, school-teacher, nurse, and gardener, he had
ended, when sixty years old, by falling back to the
very point whence he started. He had no particular
employment in M. de Bergenheim's house; he went
on errands, cared for the gardens, and doctored the
mules and horses; he was a tall man, about as much
at ease in his clothing as a dry almond in its shell.
A long, dark, yellow coat usually hung about the
calves of his legs, which were covered with long, blue
woollen stockings, and looked more like vine-poles
than human legs; a conformation which furnished
daily jokes for the other servants, to which the old
man deigned no response save a disdainful smile,
grumbling through his teeth, "Menials, peasants without education." This latter speech expressed the
late gardener's scorn, for it had been his greatest grief
to pass for an uneducated man; and he had gathered
from his various conditions a singularly dignified and
pretentious way of speaking.

GERFAUT

In spite of his self-confidence, it was not without some emotion that Leonard Rousselet responded to this call to appear in the drawing-room before the person he most feared in the château. His bearing showed this feeling when he presented himself at the drawing-room door, where he stood as grave and silent as Banquo's ghost. Constance arose at sight of this fantastic figure, barked furiously and darted toward a pair of legs for which she seemed to share the irreverence of the liveried servants; but the texture of the blue stocking and the flesh which covered the tibia were rather too hard morsels for the dowager's teeth; she was obliged to give up the attack and content herself with impotent barks, while the old man, who would gladly have given a month's wages to break her jaw with the tip of his boot, caressed her with his hand, saying, "Softly, pretty dear! softly, pretty little creature!" in a hypocritical tone.

This courtier-like conduct touched the old lady's heart and softened the severe look upon her face.

"Stop your noise, Constance," said she, "lie down beside your mistress. Rousselet, come nearer."

The old man obeyed, walking across the floor with reverential bows, and taking a position like a soldier presenting arms.

"You were the one," said Mademoiselle de Corandeuil, "who was sent to Remiremont yesterday? Did you perform all the commissions that were given you?"

"It is not among the impossibilities, Mademoiselle, that I may have neglected some of them," replied

[37]

the old man, fearing to compromise himself by a positive affirmative.

"Tell us, then, what you did."

Leonard wiped his nose behind his hat, like a well-bred orator, and, balancing himself upon his legs in a way not at all Bourbonic, he said:

"I went to the city that morning myself because Monsieur le Baron had said the night before that he should hunt to-day, and that the groom was to help Monsieur le Baron drive a wild boar out of the Corne woods. I reached Remiremont; I went to the butcher's; I purchased five kilogrammes of dressed goods——"

"Of dressed goods at the butcher's!" exclaimed Madame de Bergenheim.

"I would say ten pounds of what uneducated people call pork," said Rousselet, pronouncing this last word in a strangled voice.

"Pass over these details," said Mademoiselle de Corandeuil. "You went to the post-office."

"I went to the post-office, where I put in letters for Mademoiselle, Madame, Monsieur le Baron, and one from Mademoiselle Aline for Monsieur d'Artigues."

"Aline writing to her cousin! Did you know that?" said the old aunt, turning quickly toward her niece.

"Certainly; they correspond regularly," replied Clémence with a smile which seemed to say that she saw no harm in it.

The old maid shook her head and protruded her under lip, as much as to say: We will attend to this another time.

GERFAUT

Madame de Bergenheim, who was out of patience at this questioning, began to speak in a quick tone which was a contrast to her aunt's solemn slowness.

"Rousselet," said she, "when you took the news-papers out of the office, did you notice whether the wrappers were intact, or whether they had been opened?"

The good man half concealed his face in his cravat at this precise questioning, and it was with embarrass-ment that he replied, after a moment's hesitation:

"Certainly, Madame—as to the wrappers—I do not accuse the postmaster——"

"If the journals were sealed when you received them, you are the only one who could have opened them."

Rousselet straightened himself up to his full height, and, giving to his nut-cracker face the most dignified look possible, he said in a solemn tone:

"With due deference to you, Madame, Leonard Rousselet is well known. Fifty-seven years old on Saint-Hubert's day, I am incapable of opening news-papers. When they have been read at the château and they send me with them to the curé, I do not say—perhaps on my way—it is a recreation—and then the curé is Jean Bartou, son of Joseph Bartou, the tile-maker. But to read the newspaper before my mas-ters have done so! Never! Leonard Rousselet is an old man incapable of such baseness. Baptized when a child; fifty-seven years on Saint-Hubert's day."

"When you speak of your pastor, do so in a more becoming manner," interrupted Mademoiselle de Corandeuil, although she herself in private did not speak of the plebeian priest in very respectful terms. But if Joseph Bartou's son was always the son of Joseph Bartou to her, she meant that he should be Monsieur le Curé to the peasants.

Madame de Bergenheim had not been much affected by Père Rousselet's harangue, and shook her head impatiently, saying in an imperative tone:

"I am certain that the newspapers have been opened by you, or by some person to whom you have given them, and I wish to know at once by whom."

Rousselet dropped his pose of a Roman senator; passing his hand behind his ears, a familiar gesture with people when in embarrassing positions, he continued less emphatically:

"I stopped on my way back at La Fauconnerie, at the Femme-sans-Tête Inn."

"And what were you doing in a tavern?" interrupted Mademoiselle de Corandeuil severely. "You know it is not intended that the servants in this house should frequent taverns and such low places, which are not respectable and corrupt the morals of the lower classes."

"Servants! lower classes! Old aristocrat!" growled Rousselet secretly; but, not daring to show his ill humor, he replied in a bland voice:

"If Mademoiselle had gone the same road that I did, with the same conveyance, she would know that it is a rather thirsty stretch. I stopped at the Femme-sans-Tête to wash the dust down my parched throat. Whereupon Mademoiselle Reine—the daughter of Madame Gobillot, the landlady of the inn—Mademoiselle Reine asked me to allow her to look at the yellow-journal in which there are fashions for ladies; I asked her why; she said it was so that she might see how they made their bonnets, gowns, and other finery in Paris. The frivolity of women!"

Mademoiselle de Corandeuil threw herself back in her chair and gave way to an access of hilarity in which she rarely indulged.

"Mademoiselle Gobillot reading *La Mode!* Mademoiselle Gobillot talking of gowns, shawls, and cashmeres! Clémence, what do you say to that? You will see, she will be ordering her bonnets from Herbault! Ha! ha! This is what is called the progress of civilization, the age of light!"

"Mademoiselle Gobillot," said Clémence, fixing a penetrating glance upon the old man, "was not the only one who looked at *La Mode.* Was there no other person in the tavern who saw it?"

"Madame," replied Rousselet, forced from his last refuge, "there were two young men taking their refection, and one of them wore a beard no longer than a goat's. Madame will pardon me if I allow myself to use this vulgar expression, but Madame wished to know all."

"And the other young man?"

"The other had his facial epidermis shaved as close as a lady's or mine. He was the one who held the journal while his comrade was smoking outside the door."

Madame de Bergenheim made no further inquiries, but fell into a profound revery. With eyes fixed upon the last number of *La Mode*, she seemed to study the slightest lines of the sketch that had been made thereon, as if she hoped to find a solution to the mystery. Her irregular breathing, and the bright flush which tinged her usually pale cheeks, would have denoted to an eye-witness one of those tempests of the heart, the physical manifestations of which are like those of a fever. The pale winter flower dying under the snow had suddenly raised its drooping head and recovered its color; the melancholy against which the young woman had so vainly struggled had disappeared as if by enchantment. A little bird surmounted by a coronet, the whole rather badly sketched, was the strange talisman that had produced this change.

"They were commercial travellers," said the old aunt; "they always pretend to know everything. One of them, doubtless, when reading the well-known name of Monsieur de Bergenheim upon the wrapper, sketched the animal in question. These gentlemen of industry usually have a rather good education! But this is giving the affair more importance than it merits. Leonard Rousselet," said she, raising her voice as a judge does in court when pronouncing his charge, "you were wrong to let anything addressed to your master leave your hands. We will excuse you this time, but I warn you to be more careful in future; when you go to Madame Gobillot's, you may say to Mademoiselle Reine, from me, that if she wishes to read *La Mode* I shall be delighted to procure a subscriber to one of our journals. You may retire now."

GERFAUT

Without waiting for this invitation to be repeated, Rousselet backed out of the room like an ambassador leaving the royal presence, escorted by Constance acting as master of ceremonies. Not having calculated the distance, he had just bumped against the door, when it suddenly opened and a person of extreme vivacity bounded into the middle of the room.

It was a very young and *petite* lady, whose perfectly developed form predicted an inclination to stoutness in the future. She belonged to the Bergenheim family, if one could credit the resemblance between her characteristic features and several of the old portraits in the room; she wore a dark-brown riding-habit, a gray hat perched on one side, showing on the left a mass of very curly, bright blond hair. This coiffure and the long green veil, floating at each movement like the plume in a helmet, gave a singularly easy air to the fresh face of this pretty amazon, who brandished, in guise of a lance, a billiard cue.

"Clémence," she exclaimed, "I have just beaten Christian; I made the red ball, I made the white, and then the double stroke; I made all! Mademoiselle, I have just beaten Christian two games; is it not glorious? He made only eighteen points in a single game. Père Rousselet, I have just beaten Christian! Do you know how to play billiards?"

"Mademoiselle Aline, I am absolutely ignorant of the game," replied the old man, with as gracious a smile as was possible, while he tried to recover his equilibrium.

"You are needed no longer, Rousselet," said Mademoiselle de Corandeuil; "close the door as you go out."

When she had been obeyed, the old maid turned gravely toward Aline, who was still dancing about the room, having seized her sister-in-law's hands in order to force her to share her childish joy.

"Mademoiselle," said she in a severe tone, "is it the custom at the 'Sacred Heart' to enter a room without greeting the persons who are in it, and to jump about like a crazy person? a thing that is never permitted even in a peasant's house."

Aline stopped short in the midst of her dance and blushed a trifle; she caressed the pug dog, instead of replying, for she knew as well as Rousselet that it was the surest way of softening the old maid's heart. The cajolery was lost this time.

"Do not touch Constance, I beg of you," exclaimed the aunt, as if a dagger had been raised against the object of her love, "do not soil this poor beast with your hands. What dreadful thing have you on your fingers? Have you just come out of an indigo bag?"

The young girl blushed still deeper and gazed at her pretty hands, which were really a little daubed, and began to wipe them with an embroidered handkerchief which she took from her pocket.

"It was the billiards," she said, in a low voice, "it is the blue chalk they rub the cue with in order to make good shots and caroms."

"Make good shots! Caroms! Will you be so good as to spare us your slang speeches," continued Ma-

demoiselle de Corandeuil, who seemed to become
more crabbed as the young girl's confusion increased.
"What a fine education for a young lady! and one
who has just come from the 'Sacred Heart'! One that
has taken five prizes not fifteen days ago! I really do
not know what to think of those ladies, your teachers!
And now I suppose you are going to ride. Billiards
and horses, horses and billiards! It is fine! It is admirable!"

"But, Mademoiselle," said Aline, raising her large
blue eyes, which were on the verge of tears, "it is
vacation now, and there is no wrong in my playing a
game of billiards with my brother; we have no billiards at the 'Sacred Heart,' and it is such fun! It
is like riding; the doctor said that it would be very
healthful for me, and Christian hoped that it might
make me grow a little."

As she said these words, the young girl glanced into
the mirror in order to see whether her brother's hopes
had been realized; for her small stature was her sole
anxiety. But this glance was as quick as a flash, for
she feared that the severe old maid would make this
act of coquetry serve as the text for another sermon.

"You are not my niece, and I am thankful for it,"
continued the old lady. "I am too old to begin another education; thank goodness, one is quite enough!
I have no authority over you, and your conduct is your
brother's concern. The advice which I give you is
entirely disinterested; your amusements are not such
as seem to me proper for a young girl of good birth.
It may be possible that it is the fashion to-day, so I

will say no more about it; but there is one thing more serious, upon which I should advise you to reflect. In my youth, a young lady never was allowed to write letters except to her father and mother. Your letters to your cousin d'Artigues are inconsiderate—do not interrupt me—they are inconsiderate, and I should advise you to mend your ways."

Mademoiselle de Corandeuil arose, and, as she had found an opportunity to read three sermons in one forenoon, she could not say, like Titus, "I have wasted my morning." She left the room with a majestic step, escorted by her dog and satisfied with herself, bestowing an ironical curtsey on the young girl, which the latter did not think it necessary to return.

"How hateful your aunt is!" exclaimed Mademoiselle de Bergenheim to her sister-in-law, when they were alone. "Christian says that I must pay no attention to her, because all women become like her if they never marry. As for myself, I know very well that if I am an old maid I shall try not to hurt others' feelings—I, inconsiderate! When she can think of nothing more to say, she scolds me about my cousin. It is hardly worth while, for what we write about! Alphonse wrote of nothing, in his last letter, but of the partridge he had shot and his hunting costume; he is such a boy! But why do you not say something? You sit there speechless; are you angry with me, too?"

She approached Clémence and was about to seat herself in her lap, when the latter arose to avoid this loving familiarity.

"So you really have beaten Christian," said she, in

a listless tone; "are you going for a ride now? Your habit is very becoming."

"Truly? oh! I am so glad!" replied the young girl, planting herself before the glass to look at her pretty figure. She pulled down her waist, adjusted the folds of the skirt of her dress and arranged her veil, placed her hat on her head with a little more jaunty air, turned three quarters around to get a better view of her costume; in one word, she went through the co-quettish movements that all pretty women learn upon entering society. On the whole, she seemed very well pleased with her examination, for she smiled and showed a row of small teeth which were as white as milk.

"I am sorry now," said she, "that I did not send for a black hat; my hair is so light that gray makes me look ugly. Do you not think so? Why do you not reply, Clémence? One can not get a word out of you to-day; is it because you have your neuralgia?"

"I have a trifle of it," said Madame de Bergenheim, in order to give some pretext for her preoccupation.

"Now, then, you ought to come with us for a ride; the fresh air will do you good. Look how fine the weather is now; we will have a good gallop. Will you? I will help you put on your habit, and in five minutes you will be ready. Listen, I hear them in the yard now. I am going to tell Christian to have your horse saddled; come."

Aline took her sister-in-law by the hand, led her into the next room and opened the window to see what was going on outside, where the cracking of whips and several voices were to be heard. A servant was walking up and down the yard leading a large horse which he had just brought from the stable; the Baron was holding a smaller one, which bore a lady's saddle, while he carefully examined all the buckles. As he heard the window open above his head, he turned and bowed to Clémence with much chivalrous gallantry.

"You still refuse to go with us?" he asked.

"Is Aline going to ride Titania," replied Madame de Bergenheim, making an effort to speak; "I am sure the mare will end by playing her some trick."

The young girl, who had a fancy for Titania because the skittish creature had the attraction of forbidden fruit, nudged her sister with her elbow, and made a little grimace.

"Aline is afraid of nothing," said the Baron; "we will enlist her with the hussars as soon as she leaves the 'Sacred Heart.' Come, Aline."

The young girl kissed the Baroness, gathered up her skirt, and in a few moments was in the yard patting the neck of her dear brown mare.

"Up with you!" said Christian, taking his sister's foot in one hand while he raised her with the other, placing her in the saddle as easily as he would a six-year-old child. Then he mounted his large horse, saluted his wife, and the couple, starting at a trot, soon disappeared down the avenue, which began at the gate of the courtyard.

As soon as they were out of sight, Clémence went to her room, took a shawl from her bed, and went rapidly down a secret stairway which led into the gardens.

CHAPTER IV

THE GALLANT IN THE GARDEN

MADAME de Bergenheim's apartments occupied the first floor of the wing on the left side of the house. On the ground floor were the library, a bathroom, and several guest-chambers. The large windows had a modern look, but they were made to harmonize with the rest of the house by means of grayish paint. At the foot of this façade was a lawn surrounded by a wall and orange-trees planted in tubs, forming a sort of English garden, a sanctuary reserved for the mistress of the castle, and which brought her, as a morning tribute, the perfume of its flowers and the coolness of its shade.

Through the tops of the fir-trees and the tulip-trees, which rose above the group of smaller shrubs, the eye could follow the winding river until it finally disappeared at the extremity of the valley. It was this picturesque view and a more extensive horizon which had induced the Baroness to choose this part of the Gothic manor for her own private apartments.

After crossing the lawn, the young woman opened a gate concealed by shrubs and entered the avenue by the banks of the river. This avenue described a curve around the garden, and led to the principal entrance

4 [49]

of the château. Night was approaching, the country-
side, which had been momentarily disturbed by the
storm, had resumed its customary serenity. The
leaves of the trees, as often happens after a rain,
looked as fresh as a newly varnished picture. The
setting sun cast long shadows through the trees, and
their interlaced branches looked like a forest of boa-
constrictors.

Clémence advanced slowly under this leafy dome,
which became darker and more mysterious every
moment, with head bent and enveloped in a large
cashmere shawl which fell in irregular folds to the
ground. Madame de Bergenheim had one of those
faces which other women would call not at all remarkable, but which intelligent men ardently admire. At the first glance she seemed hardly pretty;
at the second, she attracted involuntary admiration;
afterward, it was difficult to keep her out of one's
thoughts. Her features, which taken separately might
seem irregular, were singularly harmonious, and, like
a thin veil which tempers a too dazzling light, softened
the whole expression. Her light chestnut hair was
arranged about the temples in ingenious waves; while
her still darker eyebrows gave, at times, an imposing
gravity to her face. The same contrast was to be
found in the mouth; the short distance which separated it from the nose would indicate, according to
Lavater, unusual energy; but the prominent under-
lip impregnated her smile with enchanting voluptu-
ousness. Her rather clear-cut features, the exceeding
brilliancy of her brown eyes, which seemed like dia-

monds set in jet, would, perhaps, have given to the whole rather too strong a character had not these eyes when veiled given to their dazzling rays a glamour of indescribable softness.

The effect produced by this face might be compared to that of a prism, every facet of which reflects a different color. The ardor burning under this changeable surface, which, through some sudden cause, betrayed its presence, was so deeply hidden, however, that it seemed impossible to fathom it completely. Was she a coquette, or simply a fashionable lady, or a devotee? In one word, was she imbued with the most egotistical pride or the most exalted love? One might suppose anything, but know nothing; one remained undecided and thoughtful, but fascinated, the mind plunged into ecstatic contemplation such as the portrait of Monna Lisa inspires. An observer might have perceived that she had one of those hearts, so finely strung, from which a clever hand might make incomparable harmonies of passion gush; but perhaps he would be mistaken. So many women have their souls only in their eyes!

Madame de Bergenheim's revery rendered the mysterious and impenetrable veil which usually enveloped her countenance more unfathomable yet. What sentiment made her bend her head and walk slowly as she meditated? Was it the *ennui* of which she had just complained to her aunt? Was it pure melancholy? The monotonous ripple of the stream, the singing of the birds in the woods, the long golden reflections under the trees, all seemed to unite in filling the soul with sadness; but neither the murmuring water, the singing birds, nor the sun's splendor was paid any attention to by Madame de Bergenheim; she gave them neither a glance nor a sigh. Her meditation was not revery, but thought; not thoughts of the past, but of the present. There was something precise and positive in the rapid, intelligent glance which flashed from her eyes when she raised them; it was as if she had a lucid foresight of an approaching drama.

A moment after she had passed over the wooden bridge which led from the avenue, a man wearing a blouse crossed it and followed her. Hearing the sound of hurried steps behind her, she turned and saw, not two steps from her, the stranger who, during the storm, had vainly tried to attract her attention. There was a moment's silence. The young man stood motionless, trying to catch his breath, which had been hurried, either by emotion or rapid walking. Madame de Bergenheim, with head thrown back and widely opened eyes, looked at him with a more agitated than surprised look.

"It is you," exclaimed he, impulsively, "you whom I had lost and now find again!"

"What madness, Monsieur!" she replied, in a low voice, putting out her hand as if to stop him.

"I beg of you, do not look at me so! Let me gaze at you and assure myself that it is really you—I have dreamed of this moment for so long! Have I not paid dear enough for it? Two months passed away from you—from heaven! Two months of sadness, grief, and unhappiness! But you are pale! Do you suffer, too?"

"Much, at this moment."

"Clémence!"

"Call me Madame, Monsieur de Gerfaut," she interrupted, severely.

"Why should I disobey you? Are you not my lady, my queen?"

He bent his knee as a sign of bondage, and tried to seize her hand, which she immediately withdrew. Madame de Bergenheim seemed to pay very little attention to the words addressed her; her uneasy glances wandered in every direction, into the depths of the bushes and the slightest undulations of the ground. Gerfaut understood this pantomime. He glanced, in his turn, over the place, and soon discovered at some distance a more propitious place for such a conversation as theirs. It was a semicircular recess in one of the thickets in the park. A rustic seat under a large oak seemed to have been placed there expressly for those who came to seek solitude and speak of love.` From there, one could see the approach of danger, and, in case of alarm, the wood offered a secure retreat. The young man had had enough experience in gallant strategies to seize the advantage of this position, and wended his steps in that direction while continuing to converse. It may be that instinct which, in a critical situation, makes us follow mechanically an unknown impulse; it may be that the same idea of prudence had also struck her, for Madame de Bergenheim walked beside him.

"If you could understand what I suffered," said he, "when I found that you had left Paris! I could not discover at first where you had gone; some spoke of Corandeuil, others of Italy. I thought, from this hasty departure and the care you took to conceal your abiding-place, that you were fleeing from me. Oh! tell me that I was mistaken; or, if it is true that you wished to separate yourself from me, say that this cruel resolve had left your mind, and that you will pardon me for following you! You will pardon me, will you not? If I trouble or annoy you, lay the blame entirely upon my love, which I can not restrain, and which drives me at times to do the most extravagant things; call it reckless, insane love, if you will; but believe it to be true and devoted!"

Clémence replied to this passionate tirade by simply shaking her head as a child does who hears the buzzing of a wasp and fears its sting; then, as they reached the bench, she said with affected surprise:

"You have made a mistake, this is not your road; you should have gone over the bridge."

There was a little palpable insincerity in these words; for if the road which they had taken did not lead to the bridge, neither did it lead to the château, and the mistake, if there was one, was mutual.

"Listen to me, I beg of you," replied the lover, with a supplicating glance, "I have so many things to say to you! I beg of you, grant me one moment."

"Afterward, will you obey me?"

"Only a few words, and I will then do all that you wish."

GERFAUT

She hesitated a moment; then, her conscience doubtless lulled by this promise, she seated herself and made a gesture for M. de Gerfaut to do likewise. The young man did not make her repeat this invitation, but hypocritically seated himself on the farther end of the seat.

"Now, talk reasonably," she said, in a calm tone. "I suppose that you are on your way to Germany or Switzerland, and as you passed near me you wished to favor me with a call. I ought to be proud of this mark of respect from a man so celebrated as you are, although you are rather hiding your light under this garb. We are not very strict as to dress in the country, but, really, yours is quite unceremonious. Tell me, where did you find that head-dress?"

These last words were spoken with the careless, mocking gayety of a young girl.

Gerfaut smiled, but he took off his cap. Knowing the importance that women attach to little things, and what an irreparable impression an ugly cravat or unblacked boots might produce in the most affecting moments, he did not wish to compromise himself by a ridiculous head-gear. He passed his hand through his hair, pushing it back from his large, broad forehead, and said softly:

"You know very well that I am not going to Germany or Switzerland, and that Bergenheim is the end of my journey, as it has been its aim."

"Then will you be so good as to tell me what your intention was in taking such a step, and whether you have realized how strange, inconsiderate, and in every way extravagant your conduct is?"

"I have realized it; I know it. You were here, I came because there is a loadstone within you, that is my heart's sole attraction, and I must follow my heart. I came because I wanted to see your beautiful eyes again, to be intoxicated by your sweet voice, because to live away from you is impossible for me; because your presence is as necessary to my happiness as air to my life; because I love you. That is why I came. Is it possible that you do not understand me, that you will not pardon me?"

"I do not wish to believe that you are speaking seriously," said Clémence, with increased severity. "What sort of an idea can you have of me, if you think I will allow such conduct? And then, even if I were foolish enough for that—which I never shall be —to what would it lead? You know perfectly well that it is impossible for you to come to the castle, as you are not acquainted with Monsieur de Bergenheim, and I certainly shall not introduce you to him. My aunt is here, and she would persecute me the whole day long with questions! *Mon Dieu!* how you disturb me! how unhappy you make me!"

"Your aunt never goes out, so she will not see me, unless I am officially received at the château, and then there could be no danger."

"But the servants she brought with her, and mine, who have seen you in her house! I tell you, the whole thing is as perilous as it is crazy, and you will make me die of fright and chagrin."

"If one of those servants should chance to meet me, how could he ever recognize me in this costume?

Do not fear, I shall be prudent! I would live in a log cabin, if necessary, for the joy of seeing you occasionally."

Madame de Bergenheim smiled disdainfully.

"That would be quite pastoral," she replied; "but I believe that such disguises are seldom seen now except upon the stage. If this is a scene out of a play, which you wish to rehearse in order to judge its effect, I warn you that it is entirely lost upon me, and that I consider the play itself very ill-timed, improper, and ridiculous. Besides, for a man of talent and a romantic poet you have not exhibited any very great imagination. It is a classical imitation, nothing better. There is something like it in mythology, I believe. Did not Apollo disguise himself as a shepherd?"

Nothing more is to be feared by a lover than a witty woman who does not love or loves but half; he is obliged to wear velvet gloves in all such sentimental controversies; he owes it to himself out of propriety first, out of prudence afterward. For it is not a question of taking part in a conversation for the simple pleasure of brilliant repartee; and while he applies himself carefully to play his part well, he feels that he has been dexterously cut to pieces with a well-sharpened knife.

Gerfaut indulged in these unpleasant reflections while gazing at Madame de Bergenheim. Seated upon the bench as proudly as a queen upon her throne, with shining eyes, scornful lips, and arms tightly folded under her cashmere shawl, with that haughty gesture familiar to her, the young woman looked as invulnerable under this light wrap as if she had been covered with Ajax's shield, formed, if we can credit Homer, of seven bulls' hides and a sheet of brass.

After gazing at this scornful face for a moment, Gerfaut glanced at his coarse blouse, his leggings, and muddy boots. His usual dainty ways made the details of this costume yet more shocking to him, and he exaggerated this little disaster. He felt degraded and almost ridiculous. The thought took away for a moment his presence of mind; he began mechanically to twirl his hat in his hands, exactly as if he had been Père Rousselet himself. But instead of being hurtful to him, this awkwardness served him better than the eloquence of Rousseau or the coolness of Richelieu. Was it not a genuine triumph for Clémence to reduce a man of his recognized talent, who was usually anything but timid, to this state of embarrassment? What witty response, what passionate speech could equal the flattery of this poet with bent head and this expression of deep sadness upon his face?

Madame de Bergenheim continued her raillery, but in a softer tone.

"This time, instead of staying in a cabin, the god of poetry has descended to a tavern. Have you not established your general headquarters at La Fauconnerie?"

"How did you know that?"

"By the singular visiting-card that you drew in *La Mode*. Do I not know your coat-of-arms? An expressive one, as my aunt would say."

At these words, which probably referred to some

letters, doubtless read without very much anger, since they were thus recalled, Gerfaut took courage.

"Yes," said he, "I am staying at La Fauconnerie; but I can not stay there any longer, for I think your servants make the tavern their pleasure-ground. I must come to some decision. I have two propositions to submit to you: the first is, that you will allow me to see you occasionally; there are numerous promenades about here; you go out alone, so it would be very easy."

"Let us hear the second," said Clémence, with a shrug of the shoulders.

"If you will not grant my first, I beg of you to persuade your aunt that she is ill and to take her with you to Plombières or Baden. The season is not very far advanced; there, at least, I should be able to see you."

"Let us end this folly," said the Baroness; "I have listened patiently to you; now, in your turn, listen to me. You will be sensible, will you not? You will leave me and go. You will go to Switzerland, and return to the Montanvert, where you met me for the first time, which I shall always remember, if you, yourself, do not make it painful for me to do so. You will obey me, Octave, will you not? Give me this proof of your esteem and friendship. You know very well that it is impossible for me to grant what you ask; believe me, it is painful to me to be forced to refuse you. So, say farewell to me; you shall see me again next winter in Paris. Adieu!"

She arose and extended her hand; he took it, but,

thinking to profit by the emotion betrayed by Madame de Bergenheim's voice, he exclaimed in a sort of transport:

"No! I will not wait until next winter to see you. I was about to submit to your will; if you repulse me I will consult only myself; if you repulse me, Clémence, I warn you that to-morrow I shall be in your house, seated at your table and admitted to your drawing-room."

"You?"

"I!"

"To-morrow?"

"To-morrow."

"And how will you do it, pray?" said she, defiantly.

"That is my secret, Madame," he replied, coldly.

Although her curiosity was greatly aroused, Clémence felt that it would be beneath her to ask any more questions. She replied with an affectation of mocking indifference:

"Since I am to have the pleasure of seeing you to-morrow, I hope you will permit me to leave you to-day. You know that I am not well, and it is showing me very little attention to allow me to stand here in this wet grass."

She raised her skirt a trifle and extended her foot, showing her slipper, which was really covered with pearly drops of rain. Octave threw himself quickly upon his knees, and, taking a silk handkerchief from his pocket, began to wipe away all traces of the storm. His action was so rapid that Madame de Bergenheim stood for a moment motionless and speechless, but

when she felt her foot imprisoned in the hand of the
man who had just declared war against her, her surprise gave place to a mingled feeling of impatience and
anger. She drew her foot back with a sudden movement, but unfortunately the foot went one way and
the slipper another. A fencing-master, who sees his
foil carried ten steps away from him by a back stroke,
could not feel more astonishment than that felt by
Madame de Bergenheim. Her first movement was to
place her foot, so singularly undressed, upon the
ground; an instinctive horror of the damp, muddy
walk made her draw it quickly back. She stood thus
with one foot lifted; the movement which she had
started to make threw her off her balance and as she
was about to fall she extended her hand to find some
support. This support proved to be Octave's head,
for he still remained upon his knees. With the usual
presumption of lovers, he believed that he had the
right to give her the assistance which she seemed to
ask for, and passed his arm about the slender waist
which was bent toward him.

Clémence drew herself up at once, and with frowning brow regained her coolness, standing upright upon one foot, like Cupid in the painting by Gérard;
like him, also, she seemed about to fly away, there was
so much airy lightness in her improvised attitude.

Many puerile incidents and ridiculous events occur
in life, which it would render impossible for the most
imperturbable of mandarins to struggle against in order to preserve his gravity. When Louis XIV, this
king so expert in courtly ways, dressed his hair alone

behind his curtains before presenting himself to the eyes of his courtiers, he feared that this disarray of costume might compromise even his royal majesty. So, upon such authority, if one looks upon a complete head of hair as indispensable to the dignity of manhood, the same reasoning should exist for the covering of one's feet.

In less than a second, Madame de Bergenheim comprehended that in such circumstances prudish airs would fail of their effect. Meanwhile, the agreeable side of her position operated within her; she felt unable to keep up the show of anger that she had wished to assume. The involuntary smile upon her lips smoothed her forehead as a ray of sun dissipates a cloud. Thus, disposed to clemency by reflection or fascination, it was in a very sweet and coaxing voice that she said:

"Octave, give me my slipper."

Gerfaut gazed at the lovely face bent toward him with an expression of childish entreaty, then he glanced with an irresolute air at the trophy which he held in his hand. This slipper, which was as small as Cinderella's, was not green, but gray, the lining was of rose-colored silk, and the whole was so pretty, coquettish, and dainty that it seemed impossible its owner could be vexed with him if he examined it closely.

"I will give it back to you," said he, at last, "on condition that you will allow me to put it on for you."

"As to that, certainly not," said she, in a sharp

tone; "I should much prefer to leave it with you and return home as I am."

Gerfaut shook his head and smiled incredulously.

"Think of your delicate lungs and of this terrible mud?"

Clémence drew her foot suddenly back under her skirt, concealing it entirely from the sight of the young man, who gazed at it more than she thought proper. Then she exclaimed, with the obstinacy of a spoiled child:

"Very well! I will return hopping on one foot; I could hop very well when I was young, I should be able to do so now."

To give more weight to this observation, she took two little jumps with a grace and sprightliness worthy of Mademoiselle Taglioni.

Octave arose.

"I have had the pleasure of seeing you waltz," said he; "but I admit that I shall be pleased to witness a new dance, and one executed for me alone."

As he said these words, he pretended to conceal the innocent object of this dispute in his blouse. The pretty dancer saw by this that a compromise would be necessary. Recourse to concessions is often as fatal to women as to kings; but what can one do when every other exit is closed? Obliged by absolute necessity to accept the conditions imposed upon her, Clémence wished at least to cover this defeat with sufficient dignity, and escape from an awkward position with the honors of war.

"Get down upon your knees, then," she said,

[63]

haughtily, "and put on my slipper, since you exact it, and let this end this ridiculous scene. I think you should be too proud to regard a maid's privilege as a favor."

"As a favor which a king would envy," replied Gerfaut, in a voice as tender as hers had been disdainful. He put one knee on the ground, placed the little slipper upon the other and seemed to await his enemy's pleasure. But the latter found a new subject for complaint in the pedestal offered her, for she said with increased severity:

"On the ground, Monsieur; and let that end it."

He obeyed, without a reply, after giving her a reproachful glance by which she was as much moved as by his silent obedience. She put out her foot with a more gracious air, and thrust it into the slipper. To be a correct historian, we must admit that this time she left it in the hands which softly pressed it longer than was strictly necessary. When Octave had fastened it with skill but with no haste, he bent his head and pressed his lips to the openwork stocking, through which he could catch a glimpse of white, satiny skin.

"My husband!" exclaimed Madame de Bergenheim, as she heard the clatter of horses' hoofs at the end of the avenue; and without adding a word she fled rapidly toward the château. Gerfaut arose from his position no less rapidly and darted into the woods. A rustling of branches which he heard a few steps from him made him uneasy at first, for he feared that an invisible witness had been present at this imprudent interview; but he was soon reassured by the silence which reigned about him.

After the Baron and his sister had passed, he crossed the avenue and soon disappeared over the winding road on the other side of the bridge.

CHAPTER V

LEAGUE below the castle of Bergen-
heim, the village of La Fauconnerie
was situated, at the junction of several valleys the principal of which,
by means of an unfrequented road,
opened communications between Lorraine and upper Alsatia. This position had been one of some impor-
tance in the Middle Ages, at the time when the Vosges
were beset with partisans from the two countries, always ready to renew border hostilities, the everlasting
plague of all frontiers. Upon a cliff overlooking the
village were situated the ruins which had given the
village its name; it owed it to the birds of prey [falcons,
in French: *faucons*], the habitual guests of the perpendicular rocks. To render proper justice to whom
it belongs, we should add that the proprietors of La
Fauconnerie had made it a point at all times to justify
this appellation by customs more warlike than hos-
pitable; but for some time the souvenirs of their feudal
prowess had slept with their race under the ruins of
the manor; the château had fallen without the ham-
let extending over its ruins; from a *bourg* of some
importance La Fauconnerie had come down to a small

village, and had nothing remarkable about it but the melancholy ruins of the château.

It would be impossible to imagine anything more miserably prosaic than the houses that bordered the road, in regular order; their one story with its thatched roof blackened by rain; the sorry garden surrounded by a little low wall and presenting as vegetables patches of cabbage and a few rows of beans, gave an idea of the poverty of its inhabitants. Save the church, which the Bishop of St.-Die had caused to be built, and the manse that had naturally shared this fortunate privilege, only one house rose above the condition of a thatched cottage; this was the tavern called La Femme-sans-Tête, and kept by Madame Gobillot, an energetic woman, who did not suggest in the least the name of her establishment, "The Headless Woman."

A large sign shared, with the inevitable bunch of juniper, the honor of decorating the entrance and justified an appellation one might have regarded as disrespectful to the fair sex. The original design had been repainted in dazzling colors by the artist charged with restoring the church. This alliance of the profane with the sacred had, it is true, scandalized the parish priest, but he did not dare say a word too much, as Madame Gobillot was one of his most important parishioners. A woman in a rose-colored dress and large panniers, standing upon very high-heeled shoes, displayed upon this sign the rejuvenated costume of 1750; an enormous green fan, which she held in her hand, entirely concealed her face, and it was through this caprice of the painter that the tavern came to have the name it bore.

At the right of this original figure was painted, in a very appetizing manner, a pie out of whose crust peeped a trio of woodcocks' heads. A little farther, upon a bed of water-cresses, floated a sort of marine monster, carp or sturgeon, trout or crocodile. The left of the sign was none the less tempting; it represented a roast chicken lying upon its back with its head under its wing, and raising its mutilated legs in the air with a piteous look; it had for its companion a cluster of crabs, of a little too fine a red to have been freshly caught. The whole was interspersed with bottles and glasses brimful of wine. There were stone jugs at each extremity, the sergeants of the rear-rank of this gastronomic platoon, whose corks had blown out and were still flying in space, while a bubbling white foam issued from their necks and fell majestically over their sides after describing a long parabola. A misleading sign, indeed!

A remorseful conscience, or a desire to protect herself from all reproach of mendacity on the part of the customers, had made the owner of the inn place a wire cupboard upon the sill of one of the windows near the door; in which receptacle were some eggs on a plate, a bit of bread with which David might have loaded his sling, a white glass bottle filled with a liquid of some color intended to represent kirsch, but which was in reality only water. This array gave a much more correct idea of the resources of the establishment and formed a menu like an anchorite's repast, and even this it was difficult for the kitchen's resources to maintain.

A carriage-gate led into the yard and to the stables, cart-drivers being the principal *habitués* of the place; another entrance, the one which was crowned with the fantastic sign, was flanked by two stone seats and opened directly into the kitchen, which also served as parlor for the guests. A fireplace with an enormous mantel, under which a whole family might warm themselves, occupied the middle of one side of the room. There was a large oven in one corner which opened its huge mouth, the door partly hiding the shovels and tongs employed in its service. Two or three thoroughly smoked hams, suspended from the beams, announced that there was no fear of a famine before the gastronomic massacres of Middlemas. Opposite the window, a large, polished oak dresser displayed an array of large flowered plates and little octagon-shaped glasses. A huge kitchen kettle and some wooden chairs completed the furniture of the room.

From the kitchen one passed into another room, where a permanent table surrounded by benches occupied its entire length. The wall paper, once green, was now a dirty gray; it was embellished by half a dozen black frames representing the story of Prince Poniatowski, who shares the honor of decorating village inns with Paul and Virginia and Wilhelm Tell. On the upper floor—for this aristocratic dwelling had a second story—several sleeping-rooms opened upon a long corridor, at the end of which was a room with two beds in it. This room was very neat and clean, and was destined for any distinguished guests whose unlucky star led them into this deserted country.

That evening the inn presented an unaccustomed lively appearance; the long seats, each side of the door, were occupied by rustics stripping hemp, by some village lads, and three or four cart-drivers smoking short pipes as black as coal. They were listening to two girls who were singing in a most mournful way a song well known to all in this country:

"Au château de Belfort
Sont trois jolies filles, etc."

The light from the hearth, shining through the open door, left this group in the shadow and concentrated its rays upon a few faces in the interior of the kitchen. First, there was Madame Gobillot in person, wearing a long white apron, her head covered with an immense cap. She went from oven to dresser, and from dresser to fireplace with a very important air. A fat little servant disappeared frequently through the dining-room door, where she seemed to be laying the cover for a feast. With that particular dexterity of country girls, she made three trips to carry two plates, and puffed like a porpoise at her work, while the look of frightened amazement showed upon her face that every fibre of her intelligence was under unaccustomed tension. Before the fire, and upon the range, three or four stewpans were bubbling. A plump chicken was turning on the spit, or, rather, the spit and its victim were turned by a bright-looking boy of about a dozen years, who with one hand turned the handle and with the other, armed with a large cooking-ladle, basted the roast.

But the two principal persons in this picture were a young country girl and a young man seated opposite her, who seemed busily engaged in making her portrait. One would easily recognize, from the airs and elegance of the young woman, that she was the daughter of the house, Mademoiselle Reine Gobillot, the one whose passion for fashion-plates had excited Mademoiselle de Corandeuil's anger. She sat as straight and rigid upon her stool as a Prussian corporal carrying arms, and maintained an excessively gracious smile upon her lips, while she made her bust more prominent by drawing back her shoulders as far as she could.

The young painter, on the contrary, was seated with artistic abandon, balancing himself upon a two-legged chair with his heels resting against the mantel; he was dressed in a black velvet coat, and a very small Tam O'Shanter cap of the same material covered the right side of his head, allowing a luxuriant crop of brown hair to be seen upon the other side. This head-dress, accompanied by long moustaches and a pointed beard covering only his chin, gave the stranger's face the mediæval look he probably desired. This travelling artist was sketching in an album placed upon his knees, with a freedom which indicated perfect confidence in his own talents. A cigar, skilfully held in one corner of his mouth, did not prevent him from warbling between each puff some snatches of Italian

airs of which he seemed to possess a complete réper-
toire. In spite of this triple occupation he sustained
a conversation with the ease of a man who, like Cæsar,
could have dictated to three secretaries at once if necessary.

> "Dell' Assiria, ai semidei
> Aspirar——"

"I have already asked you not to purse up your
mouth so, Mademoiselle Reine; it gives you a Watteau air radically *bourgeois*."

"What sort of air does it give me?" she asked,
anxiously.

"A Watteau, Régence, Pompadour air. You have
a large mouth, and we will leave it natural, if you
please."

"I have a large mouth!" exclaimed Reine, blushing with anger; "how polite you are!"

And she pinched up her lips until she reduced
them to nearly the size of Montmorency cherries.

"Stop this vulgar way of judging of art, queen of my
heart. Learn that there is nothing more appetizing
than a large mouth. I do not care for rosebud
mouths!"

"If it is the fashion!" murmured the young girl, in
a pleased tone, as she spread out horizontally her
vermillion lips, which might have extended from ear
to ear, not unlike—if we can credit that slanderer,
Bussy-Rabutin—the amorous smile of Mademoiselle
de la Vallière.

"Why did you not let me put on my gold necklace?

That would have given my portrait a smarter look.
Sophie Mitoux had hers painted with a coral comb
and earrings. How shabby this style is!"

"I beg of you, my good Reine, let me follow my
own fancy; an artist is a being of inspiration and
spontaneity. Meanwhile, you make your bust too
prominent; there is no necessity for you to look as if
you had swallowed a whale. *L'art n'est pas fait pour
toi, tu n'en as pas besoin.* Upon my word, you have
a most astonishing bust; a genuine Rubens."

Madame Gobillot was an austere woman, though
an innkeeper, and watched over her daughter with
particular care, lest any ill-sounding or insiduous expression should reach her child's ear. Considering the
company which frequented the house, the task was
not easy. So she was shocked at the young man's
last words, and although she did not quite understand
his meaning, for that very reason she thought she
scented a concealed poison more dangerous for Mademoiselle Reine than the awful words used by the
drivers. She dared not, however, show her displeasure to a customer, and one who seemed disposed to
spend money freely; and, as usual in such circumstances, she vented her displeasure upon the persons
immediately under her charge.

"Hurry now, Catherine! Will you never finish setting the table? I told you before to put on the Bri-
tannia; these gentlemen are used to eating with silver.
Listen to me when I am talking to you. Who washed
these glasses? What a shame! You are as afraid of
water as a mad-dog. And you! what are you staring

[73]

at that chicken for, instead of basting it? If you let it burn you shall go to bed without any supper. If it is not provoking!" she continued, in a scolding tone, visiting her stewpans one after another, "everything is dried up; a fillet that was as tender as it could be will be scorched! This is the third time that I have diluted the gravy. Catherine! bring me a dish. Now, then, make haste."

"One thing is certain," interrupted the artist, "that Gerfaut is making a fool of me. I do not see what can have become of him. Tell me, Madame Gobillot, are you certain that an amateur of art and the picturesque, travelling at this hour, would not be eaten by wolves or plundered by robbers in these mountains?"

"Our mountains are safe, Monsieur," replied the landlady, with offended dignity; "except for the pedler who was assassinated six months ago and whose body was found in the Combe-aux-Renards——"

"And the driver who was stopped three weeks ago in the Fosse," added Mademoiselle Reine; "the thieves did not quite kill him, but he is still in the hospital at Remiremont."

"Oh! that is enough to make one's hair stand on end! This is worse than the forest of Bondy! Truly, if I knew what direction my friend took this morning, I would follow him with my pistols."

"Here is Fritz," said Madame Gobillot. "He met a stranger in the woods who gave him ten sous for telling him the way to Bergenheim. From his description, it seems that it must be the gentleman you speak of. Tell us about it, Fritz."

The child related in his Alsatian *patois* his meeting of the afternoon, and the artist was convinced that it was Gerfaut he had met.

"He must be wandering in the valley," said he, "dreaming about our play. But did you not say something about Bergenheim? Is there a village near here by that name?"

"There is a château of that name, Monsieur, and it is about a league from here as you go up the river."

"And does this château happen to belong to the Baron de Bergenheim—a large, blond, good-looking fellow, with rather reddish moustache?"

"That's the picture of its owner, only that the Baron does not wear a moustache now, not since he left the service. Do you know him, Monsieur?"

"Yes, I know him! Speaking of service, I once rendered him one which was of some account. Is he at the castle?"

"Yes, Monsieur, and his lady also."

"Ah! his wife, too. She was a Mademoiselle de Corandeuil, of Provence. Is she pretty?"

"Pretty," said Mademoiselle Gobillot, pursing up her lips, "that depends upon tastes. If a person likes a face as white as a ghost, she is. And, then, she is so thin! It certainly can not be very difficult to have a slender waist when one is as thin as that."

"Not everybody can have rosy cheeks and a form like an enchantress," said the painter, in a low voice, as he looked at his model in a seductive manner.

"There are some people who think that Monsieur's

sister is prettier than Madame," observed Madame Gobillot.

"O mother! how can you say that?" exclaimed Reine with a disdainful air. "Mademoiselle Aline! A child of fifteen! She certainly is not wanting in color; her hair is such a blond, such a red, rather! It looks as if it were on fire."

"Do not say anything against red hair, I beg of you," said the artist, "it is an eminently artistic shade, which is very popular."

"With some it may be so, but with Christians! It seems to me that black hair——"

"When it is long and glossy like yours, it is wonderful," said the young man, darting another killing glance. "Madame Gobillot, would you mind closing that door? One can not hear one's self think here. I am a little critical, so far as music is concerned, and you have two sopranos outside who deafen me with their shrieks."

"It is Marguerite Mottet and her sister. Since our curé has taken to teaching them, they bore us to death, coming here and singing their fine songs. One of these days I shall notify them to leave."

As she said these words, Madame Gobillot went to close the door in order to please her guest; as soon as her back was turned, the latter leaned forward with the boldness of a Lovelace and imprinted a very loving kiss upon the rosy cheek of Mademoiselle Reine, who never thought of drawing back until the offence was committed.

The sole witness to this incident was the little

kitchen drudge, whose blue eyes had been fastened upon the artist's moustache and beard for some time. They seemed to plunge him into a deep admiration. But at this unexpected event his amazement was so complete that he dropped his spoon into the ashes.

"Eh! mein herr, do you wish to go to bed without your supper, as has been promised you?" said the young man, while the beautiful Reine was trying to recover her countenance. "Now, then, sing us a little song instead of staring at me as if I were a giraffe. Your little cook has a nice voice, Madame Gobillot. Now, then, mein herr, give us a little German *lied*. I will give you six kreutzers if you sing in tune, and a flogging if you grate upon my ears."

He arose and put his album under his arm.

"And my portrait?" exclaimed the young girl, whose cheek was still burning from the kiss she had just received.

The painter drew near her, smiling, and said in a mysterious tone:

"When I make a portrait of a pretty person like you, I never finish it the first day. If you will give me another sitting in the morning before your mother arises I promise to finish this sketch in a way that will not be displeasing to you."

Mademoiselle Reine saw that her mother was watching her, and walked away with no reply save a glance which was not discouraging.

"Now, then! You droll little fellow!" exclaimed the artist, as he whirled on one foot; "triple time; one, two, begin."

CHARLES DE BERNARD

The child burst into an Alsatian song in a high, ringing voice.

"Wait a moment! What devilish key are you singing that in?—La, la, la, la; mi, in E major, key of four sharps. By Jove, my little man! here is a fellow who sings B's and C's away up in the clouds; an E sharp, too!" he continued, with astonishment, while the singer made a hold upon the keynote an octave higher in a voice as clear as a crystal.

The artist threw into the fire the cigar which he had just lighted, and began pacing the kitchen floor, paying no more attention to Mademoiselle Reine, who felt a little piqued at seeing herself neglected for a kitchen drudge.

"A rare voice," said he, as he took a great stride; "*per Bacco*, a very rare voice. Added to that, he sings very deep; two octaves and a half, a clear, ringing tone, the two registers are well united. He would make an admirable *primo musico*. And the little fellow has a pretty face, too. After supper I will make him wash his face, and I will sketch it. I am sure that in less than a year's study, he could make his début with the greatest success. By Jove! I have an idea! Why does not that Gerfaut return? Now, then, he would do very well for 'Pippo' in *La Gazza*, or for Gemma in *Wilhelm Tell*. But we must have a *rôle* for him to make his début in. What subject could we take properly to introduce a child's part? Why does not that d—— Gerfaut come? A child, girl or boy; a boy part would be better. Daniel, of course; *viva* Daniel! *The Chaste Suzannah*, opera in three acts. Madame Begrand would be fine as Suzannah. By Jove! if Meyerbeer would only take charge of the score! That falls to him by right as a compatriot. Then, that would give him an opportunity to break lances with Mehul and Rossini. If that fool of a Gerfaut would only come! Let us see what would be the three characters: Soprano, Suzannah; contralto, David; the old men, two basses; as for the tenor, he would be, of course, Suzannah's husband. There would be a superb entrance for him upon his return from the army, *cavatina guerriera con cori.* Oh! that terrible Gerfaut! the wolves must have devoured him. If he were here, we would knock off the thing between our fruit and cheese.

Just at that moment the door opened suddenly.

"Is supper ready?" asked a deep voice.

"Eh, here he is, the dear friend!

   "O surprise extrême!
   Grand Dieu! c'est lui-même—

alive and in the flesh."

"And hungry," said Gerfaut, as he dropped into a chair near the fire.

"Would you like to compose an opera in three acts, *The Chaste Suzannah*, music by Meyerbeer?"

"I should like some supper first. Madame Gobillot, I beseech you, give me something to eat. Thanks to your mountain air, I am almost starved."

"But, Monsieur, we have been waiting two hours for you," retorted the landlady, as she made each stewpan dance in succession.

"That is a fact," said the artist; "let us go into the dining-room, then.

"Già la mensa e preparata."

"While supping, I will explain my plans to you. I have just found a Daniel in the ashes——"

"My dear Marillac, drop your Daniel and Suzannah," replied Gerfaut, as he sat down to the table; "I have something much more important to talk to you about."

CHAPTER VI

HILE the two friends are devouring
to the very last morsel the feast pre-
pared for them by Madame Gobillot,
it may not be out of place to explain
in a few words the nature of the
bonds that united these two men.

The Vicomte de Gerfaut was one of
those talented beings who are the veri-
table champions of an age when the lightest pen weighs
more in the social balance than our ancestors' heaviest
sword. He was born in the south of France, of one of
those old families whose fortune had diminished each
generation, their name finally being almost all that they
had left. After making many sacrifices to give their
son an education worthy of his birth, his parents did
not live to enjoy the fruits of their efforts, and Gerfaut became an orphan at the time when he had just
finished his law studies. He then abandoned the
career of which his father had dreamed for him, and
the possibilities of a red gown bordered with ermine.
A mobile and highly colored imagination, a passionate
love for the arts, and, more than all, some intimacies
contracted with men of letters, decided his vocation
and launched him into literature.

6   [81]

CHARLES DE BERNARD

The ardent young man, without a murmur or any misgivings, drank to the very dregs the cup poured out to neophytes in the harsh career of letters by editors, theatrical managers, and publishers. With some, this course ends in suicide, but it only cost Gerfaut a portion of his slender patrimony; he bore this loss like a man who feels that he is strong enough to repair it. When his plans were once made, he followed them up with indefatigable perseverance, and became a striking example of the irresistible power of intelligence united to will-power. Reputation, for him, lay in the unknown depths of an arid and rocky soil; he was obliged, in order to reach it, to dig a sort of artesian well. Gerfaut accepted this heroic labor; he worked day and night for several years, his forehead, metaphorically, bathed in a painful perspiration alleviated only by hopes far away. At last the untiring worker's drill struck the underground spring over which so many noble ones breathlessly bend, although their thirst is never quenched. At this victorious stroke, glory burst forth, falling in luminous sparks, making this new name—his name—flash with a brilliancy too dearly paid for not to be lasting.

At the time of which we speak, Octave had conquered every obstacle in the literary field. With a versatility of talent which sometimes recalled Voltaire's "proteanism," he attacked in succession the most difficult styles. Besides their poetic value, his dramas had this positive merit, the highest in the theatre world: they were money-makers; so the managers greeted him with due respect, while collaborators swarmed

about him. The journals paid for his articles in their
weight in gold; reviews snatched every line of his yet
unfinished novels; his works were illustrated by Por-
ret and Tony Johannot—the masters of the day—
and shone resplendent behind the glass cases in the
Orléans gallery. Gerfaut had at last made a place
for himself among that baker's dozen of writers who
call themselves, and justly, too, the field-marshals of
French literature, of which Chateaubriand was then
commander-in-chief.

What was it that had brought such a person a hundred leagues from the opera balcony, to put on a
pretty woman's slipper? Was the fair lady one of
those caprices, so frequent and fleeting in an artist's
thoughts, or had she given birth to one of those sentiments that end by absorbing the rest of one's life?

The young man seated opposite Gerfaut was, phys-
ically and morally, as complete a contrast to him as
one could possibly imagine. He was one of the kind
very much in request in fashionable society. There
is not a person who has not met one of these worthy
fellows, destined to make good officers, perfect mer-
chants, and very satisfactory lawyers, but who, unfortunately, have been seized with a mania for notoriety.
Ordinarily they think of it on account of somebody
else's talent. This one is brother to a poet, another
son-in-law to a historian; they conclude that they
also have a right to be poet and historian in their turn.
Thomas Corneille is their model; but we must admit
that very few of our writers reach the rank attained
by Corneille the younger.

CHARLES DE BERNARD

Marillac was train-bearer to Gerfaut, and was rewarded for this bondage by a few bribes of collaboration, crumbs that fall from the rich man's table. They had been close friends since they both entered the law school, where they were companions in folly rather than in study. Marillac also had thrown himself into the arena of literature; then, different fortunes having greeted the two friends' efforts, he had descended little by little from the *rôle* of a rival to that of an inferior. Marillac was an artist, talent accepted, from the tip of his toes to the sole of his boots, which he wished to lengthen by pointed toes out of respect for the Middle Ages; for he excelled above all things in his manner of dressing, and possessed, among other intellectual merits, the longest moustache in literature.

If he had not art in his brain, to make up for it he always had its name at his tongue's end. Vaudeville writing or painting, poetry or music, he dabbled in all these, like those horses sold as good for both riding and driving, which are as bad in the saddle as in front of a tilbury. He signed himself "Marillac, man of letters"; meanwhile, aside from his profound disdain for the *bourgeois*, whom he called vulgar, and for the French Academy, to which he had sworn never to belong, one could reproach him with nothing. His *penchant* for the picturesque in expression was not always, it is true, in the most excellent taste, but, in spite of these little oddities, his unfortunate passion for art, and his affection for the Middle Ages, he was a brave, worthy, and happy fellow, full of good qualities, very much devoted to his friends, above all to

[84]

Gerfaut. One could, therefore, pardon him for being a pseudo-artist.

"Will your story be a long one?" said he to the playwright, when Catherine had conducted them after supper to the double-bedded room, where they were to pass the night.

"Long or short, what does it matter, since you must listen to it?"

"Because, first, I would make some grog and fill my pipe; otherwise, I would content myself with a cigar."

"Take your pipe and make your grog."

"Here!" said the artist, running after Catherine, "don't rush downstairs so. You are wanted. Fear nothing, interesting maid; you are safe with us; but bring us a couple of glasses, brandy, sugar, a bowl, and some hot water."

"They want some hot water," cried the servant, rushing into the kitchen with a frightened look; "can they be ill at this hour?"

"Give the gentlemen what they want, you little simpleton!" replied Mademoiselle Reine; "they probably want to concoct some of their Paris drinks."

When all the articles necessary for the grog were on the table, Marillac drew up an old armchair, took another chair to stretch his legs upon, replaced his cap with a handkerchief artistically knotted about his head, his boots with a pair of slippers, and, finally, lighted his pipe.

"Now," said he, as he seated himself, "I will listen without moving an eyelid should your story last, like the creation, six days and nights."

CHARLES DE BERNARD

Gerfaut took two or three turns about the room with the air of an orator who is seeking for a beginning to a speech.

"You know," said he, "that Fate has more or less influence over our lives, according to the condition of mind in which we happen to be. In order that you may understand the importance of the adventure I am about relating to you, it will be necessary for me to picture the state of mind which I was in at the time it happened; this will be a sort of philosophical and psychological preamble."

"Thunder!" interrupted Marillac, "if I had known that, I would have ordered a second bowl."

"You will remember," continued Gerfaut, paying no attention to this pleasantry, "the rather bad attack of spleen which I had a little over a year ago?"

"Before your trip to Switzerland?"

"Exactly."

"If I remember right," said the artist, "you were strangely cross and whimsical at the time. Was it not just after the failure of our drama at the Porte Saint-Martin?"

"You might also add of our play at the Gymnase."

"I wash my hands of that. You know very well that it only went as far as the second act, and I did not write one word in the first."

"And hardly one in the second. However, I take the catastrophe upon my shoulders; that made two perfect failures in that d——d month of August."

"Two failures that were hard to swallow," replied Marillac. "We can say, for our consolation, that there never were more infamous conspiracies against us, above all, than at the Gymnase. My ears ring with the hisses yet! I could see, from our box, a little villain in a dress coat, in one corner of the pit, who gave the signal with a whistle as large as a horse-pistol. How I would have liked to cram it down his throat!" As he said these words, he brought his fist down upon the table, and made the glasses and candles dance upon it.

"Conspiracy or not, this time they judged the play aright. I believe it would be impossible to imagine two worse plays; but, as Brid' Oison says, 'These are things that one admits only to himself'; it is always disagreeable to be informed of one's stupidity by an ignorant audience that shouts after you like a pack of hounds after a hare. In spite of my pretension of being the least susceptible regarding an author's vanity of all the writers in Paris, it is perfectly impossible to be indifferent to such a thing—a hiss is a hiss. However, vanity aside, there was a question of money which, as I have a bad habit of spending regularly my capital as well as my income, was not without its importance. It meant, according to my calculation, some sixty thousand francs cut off from my resources, and my trip to the East was indefinitely postponed.

"They say, with truth, that misfortunes never come singly. You know Mélanie, whom I prevented from making her *début* at the Vaudeville? By taking her away from all society, lodging her in a comfortable manner and obliging her to work, I rendered her a valuable service. She was a good girl, and, aside from her love for the theatre and a certain indolence that was not without charm, I did not find any fault in her and grew more attached to her every day. Sometimes after spending long hours with her, a fancy for a retired life and domestic happiness would seize me. Gentlemen with brains are privileged to commit foolish acts at times, and I really do not know what I might have ended in doing, had I not been preserved from the danger in an unexpected manner.

"One evening, when I arrived at Mélanie's, I found the bird had flown. That great ninny of a Férussac, whom I never had suspected, and had introduced to her myself, had turned her head by making capital out of her love for the stage. As he was about to leave for Belgium, he persuaded her to go there and dethrone Mademoiselle Prévost. I have since learned that a Brussels banker revenged me by taking this Hélène of the stage away from Férussac. Now she is launched and can fly with her own wings upon the great highway of bravos, flowers, guineas——"

"And wreck and ruin," added Marillac. "Here's to her health!"

"This triple disappointment of pride, money, and heart did not cause, I hope you will believe me, the deep state of melancholy into which I soon fell; but the malady manifested itself upon this occasion, for it had been lurking about me for a long time, as the dormant pain of a wound is aroused if one pours a caustic upon its surface.

"There is some dominant power in each individual which is developed at the expense of the other facul-

ties, above all when the profession one chooses suits
his nature. The vital powers thus condensed man-
ifest themselves externally, and gush out with an
abundance which would become impossible if all the
faculties were used alike, and if life filtered away, so
to speak. To avoid such destruction, and concentrate
life upon one point, in order to increase the action,
is the price of talent and individuality. Among ath-
letes, the forehead contracts according as the chest
enlarges; with men of thought, it is the brain which
causes the other organs to suffer, insatiable vampire,
exhausting at times the last drop of blood in the body
which serves as its victim. This vampire was my
torturer.

"For ten years I had crowded romance upon poetry,
vaudeville upon drama, literary criticism upon leader;
I proved, through my own self, in a physical way, the
phenomena of the absorption of the senses by intelligence. Many times, after several nights of hard work,
the chords of my mind being too violently stretched,
they relaxed and gave only indistinct harmony. Then,
if I happened to resist this lassitude of nature de-
manding repose, I felt the pressure of my will exhausting the sources at the very depths of my being.
It seemed to me that I dug out my ideas from the
bottom of a mine, instead of gathering them upon the
surface of the brain. The more material organs came
to the rescue of their failing chief. The blood from
my heart rushed to my head to revive it; the muscles
of my limbs communicated to the fibres of the brain
their galvanic tension. Nerves turned into imagina-

tion, flesh into life. Nothing has developed my materialistic beliefs like this decarnation of which I had such a sensible, or rather visible perception.

"I destroyed my health with these psychological experiments, and the abuse of work perhaps shortened my life. When I was thirty years old my face was wrinkled, my cheeks were pallid, and my heart blighted and empty. For what result, *grand Dieu!* For a fleeting and fruitless renown!

"The failure of my two plays warned me that others judged me as I judged myself. I recalled to mind the Archbishop of Granada, and I thought I could hear Gil Blas predicting the failure of my works. We can not dismiss the public as we can our secretary; meanwhile, I surrendered to a too severe justice in order to decline others' opinions. A horrible thought suddenly came into my mind; my artistic life was ended, I was a worn-out man; in one word, to picture my situation in a trivial but correct manner, I had reached the end of my rope——

"I could not express to you the discouragement that I felt at this conviction. Mélanie's infidelity was the crowning touch. It was not my heart, but my vanity which had been rendered more irritable by recent disappointments. This, then, was the end of all my ambitious dreams! I had not enough mind left, at thirty years of age, to write a vaudeville or to be loved by a grisette!

"One day Doctor Labanchie came to see me.

"'What are you doing there' said he, as he saw me seated at my desk.

" 'Doctor,' said I, reaching out my hand to him, 'I believe that I am a little feverish.'

" 'Your pulse is a little rapid,' said he, after making careful examination, 'but your fever is more of imagination than of blood.'

"I explained to him my condition, which was now becoming almost unendurable. Without believing in medicine very much, I had confidence in him and knew him to be a man who would give good advice.

" 'You work too much,' said he, shaking his head. 'Your brain is put to too strong a tension. This is a warning nature gives you, and you will make a mistake if you do not follow it. When you are sleepy, go to bed; when you are tired, you must have rest. It is rest for your brain that you now need. Go into the country, confine yourself to a regular and healthy diet: vegetables, white meat, milk in the morning, a very little wine, but, above all things, no coffee. Take moderate exercise, hunt—and avoid all irritating thoughts; read the *Musée des familles* or the *Magasin Pittoresque*. This *régime* will have the effect of a soothing poultice upon your brain, and before the end of six months you will be in your normal condition again.'

" 'Six months!' I exclaimed. 'You wretch of a doctor, tell me, then, to let my beard and nails grow like Nebuchadnezzar. Six months! You do not know how I detest the country, partridges, rabbits and all. For heaven's sake, find some other remedy for me.'

" 'There is homœopathy,' said he, smiling. 'Hahnemann is quite the fashion now.'

CHARLES DE BERNARD

" 'Let us have homœopathy!'

" 'You know the principles of the system: '*Similia similibus!*' If you have fever, redouble it; if you have smallpox, be inoculated with a triple dose. So far as you are concerned, you are a little used up and *blasé*, as we all are in this Babylon of ours; have recourse, then, as a remedy, to the very excesses which have brought you into this state. Homœopathize yourself morally. It may cure you, it may kill you; I wash my hands of it.'

"The doctor was joking, I said to myself after he had left. Does he think that passions are like the Wandering Jew's five sous, that there is nothing to do but to put your hand in your pocket and take them out at your convenience when necessary. However, this idea, strange as it seemed, struck me forcibly. I decided to try it.

"The next day at seven o'clock in the evening, I was rolling along the road to Lyons. Eight days later, I was rowing in a boat on Lake Geneva. For a long time I had wanted to go to Switzerland, and it seemed as if I could not have chosen a better time. I hoped that the fresh mountain air and the soft pure breezes from the lakes would communicate some of their calm serenity to my heart and brain.

"There is something in Parisian life, I do not know what, so exclusive and hardening, that it ends by making one irresponsive to sensations of a more simple order.

" 'My kingdom for the gutter in the Rue du Bac!' I exclaimed with Madame de Staël from the height of the Coppet terrace. The spectacle of nature interests only contemplative and religious minds powerfully. Mine was neither the one nor the other. My habits of analysis and observation make me find more attraction in a characteristic face than in a magnificent landscape; I prefer the exercising of thought to the careless gratification of ecstasy, the study of flesh and soul to earthly horizons, of human passions to a perfectly pure atmosphere.

"I met at Geneva an Englishman, who was as morose as myself. We vented our spleen in common and were both bored together. We travelled thus through the Oberland and the best part of Valais; we were often rolled up in our travelling robes in the depths of the carriage, and fast asleep when the most beautiful points of interest were in sight.

"From Valais we went to Mont-Blanc, and one night we arrived at Chamounix——"

"Did you see any idiots in Valais?" suddenly interrupted Marillac, as he filled his pipe the second time.

"Several, and they were all horrible."

"Do you not think we might compose something with an idiot in it? It might be rather taking."

"It would not equal Caliban or Quasimodo; will you be so kind as to spare me just now these efforts of imagination, and listen to me, for I am reaching the interesting part of my story?"

"God be praised!" said the artist, as he puffed out an enormous cloud of smoke.

"The next day the Englishman was served with tea in his bedroom, and when I asked him to go to the

CHARLES DE BERNARD

Mer de Glace he turned his head toward the wall; so, leaving my phlegmatic companion enveloped in bedclothes up to his ears, I started alone for the Montanvert.

"It was a magnificent morning, and small parties of travellers, some on foot, others mounted, skirted the banks of the Arve or climbed the sides of the mountain. They looked like groups of mice in the distance, and this extreme lessening in size made one comprehend, better than anything else, the immense proportions of the landscape. As for myself, I was alone: I had not even taken a guide, this was too favorite a resort for tourists, for the precaution to be necessary. For a wonder, I felt rather gay, with an elasticity of body and mind which I had not felt in some time. I courageously began climbing the rough pathway which led to the *Mer de Glace*, aiding myself with a long staff, which I had procured at the inn.

"At every step I breathed with renewed pleasure the fresh, pure, morning air; I gazed vaguely at the different effects of the sun or mist, at the undulations of the road, which sometimes rose almost straight up in the air, sometimes followed a horizontal line, while skirting the open abyss at the right. The Arve, wending its course like a silvery ribbon, seemed at times to recede, while the ridges of the perpendicular rocks stood out more plainly. At times, the noise of a falling avalanche was repeated, echo after echo. A troupe of German students below me were responding to the voice of the glaciers by a chorus from *Oberon*. Following the turns in the road, I could see through the fir-trees, or, rather, at my feet, their long Teutonic frock-coats, their blond beards, and caps about the size of one's fist. As I walked along, when the path was not too steep, I amused myself by throwing my stick against the trunks of the trees which bordered the roadside; I remember how pleased I was when I succeeded in hitting them, which I admit was not very often.

"In the midst of this innocent amusement, I reached the spot where the reign of the Alpine plants begins. All at once I saw, above me, a rock decked with rhododendrons; these flowers looked like tufts of oleanders through the dark foliage of the fir-trees, and produced a charming effect. I left the path in order to reach them sooner, and when I had gathered a bouquet, I threw my staff and at the same time uttered a joyous cry, in imitation of the students, my companions on this trip.

"A frightened scream responded to mine. My staff in its flight had crossed the path and darted into an angle in the road. At that same moment, I saw a mule's head appear with ears thrown back in terror, then the rest of its body, and upon its back a lady ready to fall into the abyss. Fright paralyzed me. All aid was impossible on account of the narrowness of the road, and this stranger's life depended upon her coolness and the intelligence of her beast. Finally the animal seemed to regain its courage and began to walk away, lowering its head as if it could still hear the terrible whistle of the javelin in his ears. I slipped from the rock upon which I stood and seized the mule by the bridle, and succeeded in getting them out of a bad position. I led the animal in this way for some distance, until I reached a place where the path was broader, and danger was over.

"I then offered my apologies to the person whose life I had just compromised by my imprudence, and for the first time took a good look at her. She was young and well dressed; a black silk gown fitted her slender form to perfection; her straw hat was fastened to the saddle, and her long chestnut hair floated in disorder over her pale cheeks. As she heard my voice, she opened her eyes, which in her fright she had instinctively closed; they seemed to me the most beautiful I had ever seen in my life.

"She looked at the precipice and turned away with a shudder. Her glance rested upon me, and then upon the rhododendrons which I held in my hand.

"The frightened expression on her face was replaced immediately by one of childish curiosity.

"'What pretty flowers!' she exclaimed, in a fresh, young voice. "Are those rhododendrons, Monsieur?'

"I presented her my bouquet without replying; as she hesitated about taking it, I said:

"'If you refuse these flowers, Madame, I shall not believe that you have pardoned me.'

"By this time, the persons who were with her had joined us. There were two other ladies, three or four men mounted upon mules, and several guides. At the word rhododendron, a rather large, handsome fellow, dressed in a pretentious style, slipped from his mule and climbed the somewhat steep precipice in quest of the flowers which seemed to be so much in favor. When he returned, panting for breath, with an enormous bunch of them in his hand, the lady had already accepted mine.

" 'Thank you, Monsieur de Mauléon,' said she, with a rather scornful air; 'offer your flowers to these ladies.' Then, with a slight inclination of the head to me, she struck her mule with her whip, and they rode away.

"The rest of the company followed her, gazing at me as they passed, the big, fashionable fellow especially giving me a rather impertinent glance. I did not try to pick a quarrel with him on account of this discourteous manifestation. When the cavalcade was at some distance, I went in search of my stick, which I found under a tree on the edge of the precipice; then I continued climbing the steep path, with my eyes fastened upon the rider in the black silk gown, her hair flying in the wind and my bouquet in her hand.

"A few moments later, I reached the pavilion at the Montanvert, where I found a gay company gathered together, made up principally of English people. As for myself, I must admit the frivolous, or, rather mundane, bent of my tastes; the truly admirable spectacle presented to my eyes interested me much less than the young stranger, who at this moment was descending with the lightness of a sylph the little road which led to the *Mer de Glace*.

"I do not know what mysterious link bound me to this woman. I had met many much more beautiful, but the sight of them had left me perfectly indifferent. This one attracted me from the first. The singular circumstances of this first interview, doubtless, had something to do with the impression. I felt glad to see that she had kept my bouquet; she held it in one hand, while she leaned with the other upon a staff somewhat like my own. The two other ladies, and even the men had stopped on the edge of the ice.

Monsieur de Mauléon wished to fulfil his duties as escort, but at the first crevasse he had also halted without manifesting the slightest desire to imitate the chamois. The young woman seemed to take a malicious pleasure in contemplating her admirer's prudent attitude, and, far from listening to the advice he gave her, she began to run upon the ice, bounding over the crevasses with the aid of her stick. I was admiring her lightness and thoughtlessness, but with an uneasy feeling, when I saw her suddenly stop. I instinctively ran toward her. An enormous crevasse of great depth lay at her feet, blue at its edges and dark in its depths. She stood motionless before this frightful gulf with hands thrown out before her in horror, but charmed like a bird about to be swallowed by a serpent. I knew the irresistible effect upon nervous temperaments of this magnetic attraction toward an abyss. I seized her by the arm, the suddenness of the movement made her drop her staff and flowers, which fell into the depths of the chasm.

"I tried to lead her away, but after she had taken a few steps, I felt her totter; she had grown pale; her eyes were closed. I threw my arm about her, in order to support her and turned her face toward the north; the cold air striking her revived her, and she soon opened her beautiful brown eyes. I do not know what sudden tenderness seized me then, but I pressed this lovely creature within my grasp, and she remained in my arms unresistingly. I felt that I loved her already.

"She remained for a moment with her languishing eyes fixed on mine, making no response, perhaps not even having heard me. The shouts of her party, some of whom were coming toward her, broke the charm. With a rapid movement, she withdrew from my embrace, and I offered her my arm, just as if we were in a drawing-room and I was about to lead her out for a dance; she took it, but I did not feel elated at this, for I could feel her knees waver at every step. The smallest crevasse, which she had crossed before with such agility, now inspired her with a horror which I could divine by the trembling of her arm within mine. I was obliged to make numerous détours in order to avoid them, and thus prolonged the distance, for which I was not sorry. Did I not know that when we reached our destination, the world, that other *sea of ice*, was going to take her away from me, perhaps forever? We walked silently, occasionally making a few trivial remarks, both deeply embarrassed. When we reached the persons who awaited her, I said, as she disengaged my arm:

" 'You dropped my flowers, Madame; will it be the same with your memory of me?'

"She looked at me, but made no reply. I loved this silence. I bowed politely to her and returned to the pavilion, while she related her adventure to her friends; but I am quite sure she did not tell *all* the details.

"The register for travellers who visit the Montan-vert is a mixture of all nationalities, and no tourist refuses his tribute; modest ones write down their names only. I hoped in this way to learn the name of the young traveller, and I was not disappointed. I soon saw the corpulent Monsieur de Mauléon busily writing his name upon the register in characters worthy of Monsieur Prudhomme; the other members of the little party followed his example. The young woman was the last to write down her name. I took the book in my turn, after she had left, and with apparent composure I read upon the last line these words, writ-ten in a slender handwriting:

"Baroness Clémence de Bergenheim."

CHAPTER VII

"HE Baroness de Bergenheim!" exclaimed Marillac. "Ah! I understand it all now, and you may dispense with the remainder of your story. So this was the reason why, instead of visiting the banks of the Rhine as we agreed, you made me leave the route at Strasbourg under the pretext of walking through the picturesque sites of the Vosges. It was unworthy of you to abuse my confidence as a friend. And I allowed myself to be led by the nose to within a mile of Bergenheim!"

"Peace," interrupted Gerfaut; "I have not finished. Smoke and listen.

"I followed Madame de Bergenheim as far as Geneva. She had gone there from here with her aunt, and had availed herself of this journey to visit Mont Blanc. She left for her home the next day without my meeting her again; but I preserved her name, and it was not unknown to me. I had heard it spoken in several houses in the Faubourg Saint-Germain, and I knew that I should certainly have an opporutnity of meeting her during the winter.

"So I remained at Geneva, yielding to a sensation

as new as it was strange. It first acted upon my brain whose ice I felt melting away, and its sources ready to gush forth. I seized my pen with a passion not unlike an access of rage. I finished in four days two acts of a drama that I was then writing. I never had written anything more vigorous or more highly colored. My unconstrained genius throbbed in my arteries, ran through my blood, and bubbled over as if it wished to burst forth. My hand could not keep even with the course of my imagination; I was obliged to write in hieroglyphics.

"Adieu to the empty reveries brought about by spleen, and to the meditations *à la Werther!* The sky was blue, the air pure, life delightful—my talent was not dead.

"After this first effort, I slackened a little! Madame de Bergenheim's face, which I had seen but dimly during this short time, returned to me in a less vaporous form; I took extreme delight in calling to mind the slightest circumstances of our meeting, the smallest details of her features, her toilette, her manner of walking and carrying her head. What had impressed me most was the extreme softness of her dark eyes, the almost childish tone of her voice, a vague odor of heliotrope with which her hair was perfumed; also the touch of her hand upon my arm. I sometimes caught myself embracing myself in order to feel this last sensation again, and then I could not help laughing at my thoughts, which were worthy of a fifteen-year-old lover.

"I had felt so convinced of my powerlessness to love,

that the thought of a serious passion did not at first enter my mind. However, a remembrance of my beautiful traveller pervaded my thoughts more and more, and threatened to usurp the place of everything else. I then subjected myself to a rigid analysis; I sought for the exact location of this sentiment whose involuntary yoke I already felt; I persuaded myself, for some time yet, that it was only the transient excitement of my brain, one of those fevers of imagination whose fleeting titillations I had felt more than once.

"But I realized that the evil, or the good—for why call love an evil?—had penetrated into the most remote regions of my being, and I realized the energy of my struggle like a person entombed who tries to extricate himself. From the ashes of this volcano which I had believed to be extinct, a flower had suddenly blossomed, perfumed with the most fragrant of odors and decked with the most charming colors. Artless enthusiasm, faith in love, all the brilliant array of the fresh illusions of my youth returned, as if by enchantment, to greet this new bloom of my life; it seemed to me as if I had been created a second time, since I was aided by intelligence and understood its mysteries while tasting of its delights. My past, in the presence of this regeneration, was nothing more than a shadow at the bottom of an abyss. I turned toward the future with the faith of a Mussulman who kneels with his face toward the East—I loved!

"I returned to Paris, and applied to my friend Casorans, who knows the Faubourg Saint-Germain from Dan to Beersheba.

CHARLES DE BERNARD

" 'Madame de Bergenheïm,' he said to me, 'is a very popular society woman, not very pretty, perhaps, rather clever, though, and very amiable. She is one of our coquettes of the old nobility, and with her twenty-four carats' virtue she always has two sufferers attached to her chariot, and a third on the waiting-list, and yet it is impossible for one·to find a word to say against her behavior. Just at this moment, Mauléon and d'Arzenac compose the team; I do not know who is on the waiting-list. She will probably spend the winter here with her aunt, Mademoiselle de Corandeuil, one of the hatefullest old women on the Rue de Varennes. The husband is a good fellow who, since the July revolution, has lived upon his estates, caring for his forests and killing wild boars without troubling himself much about his wife.'

"He then told me which houses these ladies frequented, and left me, saying with a knowing air:

" 'Take care, if you intend to try the power of your seductions upon the little Baroness; whoever meddles with her smarts for it!'

"This information from a viper like Casorans satisfied me in every way. Evidently the place was not taken; impregnable, that was another thing.

"Before Madame de Bergenheim's return, I began to show myself assiduously at the houses of which my friend had spoken. My position in the Faubourg Saint-Germain is peculiar, but good, according to my opinion. I have enough family ties to be sustained by several should I be attacked by many, and this is the essential point. It is true that, thanks to my

works, I am regarded as an atheist and a Jacobin;
aside from these two little defects, they think well
enough of me. Besides, it is a notorious fact that I
have rejected several offers from the present government, and refused last year the *croix d'honneur;* this
makes amends and washes away half my sins. Finally,
I have the reputation of having a certain knowledge
of heraldry, which I owe to my uncle, a confirmed
hunter after genealogical claims. This gains me a
respect which makes me laugh sometimes, when I
see people who detest me greet me as cordially as the
Curé of Saint-Eustache greeted Bayle, for fear that
I might destroy their favorite saint. However, in this
society, I am no longer Gerfaut of the Porte-Saint-
Martin, but I am the Vicomte de Gerfaut. Perhaps,
with your *bourgeois* ideas, you do not understand——"

"*Bourgeois!*" exclaimed Marillac, bounding from his
seat, "what are you talking about? Do you wish that
we should cut each other's throats before breakfast
to-morrow? *Bourgeois!* why not grocer? I am an
artist—don't you know that by this time?"

"Don't get angry, my dear fellow; I meant to say
that in certain places the title of a Vicomte has still a
more powerful attraction than you, with your artistic
but plebeian ideas, would suppose in this year of our
Lord 1832."

"Well and good. I accept your apology."

"A vicomte's title is a recommendation in the eyes
of people who still cling to the baubles of nobility,
and all women are of this class. There is something,
I know not what, delicate and knightly in this title,

which suits a youngish bachelor. Duke above all titles is the one that sounds the best. Molière and Regnard have done great harm to the title of marquis. Count is terribly *bourgeois*, thanks to the senators of the empire. As to a Baron, unless he is called Montmorency or Beaufremont, it is the lowest grade of nobility; vicomte, on the contrary, is above reproach; it exhales a mixed odor of the old *régime* and young France; then, don't you know, our Chateaubriand was a vicomte.

"I departed from my subject in speaking of nobility. I accidentally turned over one day to the article upon my family in the *Dictionnaire de Saint-Allais;* I found that one of my ancestors, Christophe de Gerfaut, married, in 1569, a Mademoiselle Yolande de Corandeuil.

"'O my ancestor! O my ancestress!' I exclaimed, 'you had strange baptismal names; but no matter, I thank you. You are going to serve me as a grappling iron; I shall be very unskilful if at the very first meeting the old aunt escapes Christophe.'

"A few days later I went to the Marquise de Chameillan's, one of the most exclusive houses in the noble Faubourg. When I enter her drawing-room, I usually cause the same sensation that Beelzebub would doubtless produce should he put his foot into one of the drawing-rooms in Paradise. That evening, when I was announced, I saw a certain undulation of heads in a group of young women who were whispering to one another; many curious eyes were fastened upon me, and among these beautiful eyes were two more

beautiful than all the others: they were those of my
bewitching traveller.

"I exchanged a rapid glance with her, one only;
after paying my respects to the mistress of the house,
I mingled with a crowd of men, and entered into conversation with an old peer upon some political question, avoiding to look again toward Madame de Bergenheim.

"A moment later, Madame de Chameillan came to
ask the peer to play whist; he excused himself, he
could not remain late.

" 'I dare not ask you to play with Mademoiselle de
Corandeuil,' said she, turning toward me; 'besides, I
understand too well that it is to my interest and the
pleasure of these ladies, not to exile you to a whist
table.'

"I took the card which she half offered me with an
eagerness which might have made her suppose that
I had become a confirmed whist expert during my
voyage.

"Mademoiselle de Corandeuil certainly was the ugly,
crabbed creature that Casorans had described; but
had she been as frightful as the witches in *Macbeth*
I was determined to make her conquest. So I began
playing with unusual attention. I was her partner,
and I knew from experience the profound horror
which the loss of money inspires in old women. Thank
heaven, we won! Mademoiselle de Corandeuil, who
has an income of one hundred thousand francs, was
not at all indifferent to the gain of two or three louis.
She, therefore, with an almost gracious air, congratu-

lated me, as we left the table, upon my manner of playing.

" 'I would willingly contract an alliance, offensive and defensive with you,' said she to me.

" 'The alliance is already contracted, Mademoiselle,' said I, seizing the opportunity.

" 'How is that, Monsieur?' she replied, raising her head with a dignified air, as if she were getting ready to rebuke some impertinent speech.

"I also gravely straightened up and gave a feudal look to my face.

" 'Mademoiselle, I have the honor of belonging to your family, a little distantly, to be sure; that is what makes me speak of an alliance between us as a thing already concluded. One of my ancestors, Christophe de Gerfaut, married Mademoiselle Yolande de Corandeuil, one of your great-grandaunts, in 1569.'

" 'Yolande is really a family name,' replied the old lady, with the most affable smile that her face would admit; 'I bear it myself. The Corandeuils, Monsieur, never have denied their alliances, and it is a pleasure for me to recognize my relationship with such a man as you. We address by the title of cousin relatives as far back as 1300.'

" 'I am nearer related to you by three centuries,' I replied, in my most insinuating voice; 'may I hope that this good fortune will authorize me to pay my respects to you?'

"Mademoiselle de Corandeuil replied to my *tartuferie* by granting me permission to call upon her. My attention was not so much absorbed in our conversation that I did not see in a mirror, during this time, the interest with which Madame de Bergenheim watched my conversation with her aunt; but I was careful not to turn around, and I let her take her departure without giving her a second glance.

"Three days later, I made my first call. Madame de Bergenheim received my greeting like a woman who had been warned and was, therefore, prepared. We exchanged only one rapid, earnest glance, that was all. Availing myself of the presence of other callers, numerous enough to assure each one his liberty, I began to observe, with a practised eye, the field whereon I had just taken my position.

"Before the end of the evening, I recognized the correctness of Casorans's information. Among all the gentlemen present I found only two professed admirers: Monsieur de Mauléon, whose insignificance was notorious, and Monsieur d'Arzenac, who appeared at first glance as if he might be more to be feared. D'Arzenac, thanks to an income of ten thousand livres, beside being a man of rank, occupies also one of the finest positions that one could desire; he is not unworthy of his name and his fortune. Irreproachable in morals as in manners; sufficiently well informed; of an exquisite but reserved politeness; understanding perfectly the ground that he is walking upon; making also more advances than is customary among the pachas of modern France, he was, without doubt, the flower of the flock in Mademoiselle de Corandeuil's drawing-room. In spite of all these advantages, an attentive examination showed me that his passion was hopeless. Madame de Bergenheim received his attentions very kindly—too kindly. She usually listened to him with a smile in which one could read gratitude for the devotion he lavished upon her. She willingly accepted him as her favorite partner in the galop, which he danced to perfection. His success stopped there.

"At the end of several days, the ground having been carefully explored and the admirers, dangerous and otherwise, having been passed in review, one after another, I felt convinced that Clémence loved nobody.

" 'She shall love me,' said I, on the day I reached this conclusion. In order to formulate in a decisive manner the accomplishment of my desire, I relied upon the following propositions, which are to me articles of faith.

"No woman is unattainable, except when she loves another. Thus, a woman who does not love, and who has resisted nine admirers, will yield to the tenth. The only question for me was to be the tenth. Here began the problem to be solved.

"Madame de Bergenheim had been married only three years; her husband, who was good-looking and young, passed for a model husband; if these latter considerations were of little importance, the first was of great weight. According to all probability, it was too soon for any serious attack. Without being beautiful, she pleased much and many; a second obstacle, since sensibility in women is almost always developed in inverse ratio to their success. She had brains; she was wonderfully aristocratic in all her tastes.

Last, being very much the fashion, sought after and
envied, she was under the special surveillance of pious
persons, old maids, retired beauties in one word, all
that feminine mounted police, whose eyes, ears, and
mouths seem to have assumed the express mission
of annoying sensitive hearts while watching over the
preservation of good morals.

"This mass of difficulties, none of which escaped
me, traced as many lines upon my forehead as if I
had been commanded to solve at once all the propositions in Euclid. *She shall love me!* these words
flashed unceasingly before my eyes; but the means to
attain this end? No satisfactory plan came to me.
Women are so capricious, deep, and unfathomable!
It is, with them, the thing soonest done which is soonest ended! A false step, the least awkwardness, a
want of intelligence, a quarter of an hour too soon or
too late! One thing only was evident: it needed a
grand display of attractions, a complete plan of gallant
strategy; but, then, what more?

"That earthly paradise of the Montanvert was far
from us, where I had been able in less time than it
would take to walk over a quadrille, to expose her to
death, to save her afterward, and finally to say to her:
'I love you!' Passion in drawing-rooms is not allowed those free, dramatic ways; flowers fade in the
candle-light; the oppressive atmosphere of balls and
fêtes stifles the heart, so ready to dilate in pure mountain air. The unexpected and irresistible influence of
the glacier would have been improper and foolish in
Paris. There, an artless sympathy, stronger than

social conventions, had drawn us to each other—
Octave and Clémence. Here, she was the Baroness
de Bergenheim, and I the Vicomte de Gerfaut. I
must from necessity enter the ordinary route, begin
the romance at the first page, without knowing how
to connect the prologue with it.

"What should be my plan of campaign?

"Should I pose as an agreeable man, and try to captivate her attention and good graces by the minute
attentions and delicate flattery which constitute what
is classically called paying court? But D'Arzenac had
seized this *rôle*, and filled it in such a superior way
that all competition would be unsuccessful. I saw
where this had led him. It needed, in order to inflame this heart, a more active spark than foppish
gallantry; the latter flatters the vanity without reaching the heart.

"There was the passionate method—ardent, burning, fierce love. There are some women upon whom
convulsive sighs drawn from the depths of the stomach,
eyebrows frowning in a fantastic manner, and eyes
in which only the whites are to be seen and which seem
to say: 'Love me, or I will kill you!' produce a pro-
digious effect. I had myself felt the power of this
fascination while using it one day upon a soft-hearted
blond creature who thought it delightful to have a
Blue-Beard for a lover. But the drooping corners of
Clémence's mouth showed at times an ironical expression which would have cooled down even an
Othello's outbursts.

" 'She has brains, and she knows it,' said I to my-

[112]

self; 'shall I attack her in that direction?' Women rather like such a little war of words; it gives them an opportunity for displaying a mine of pretty expressions, piquant pouts, fresh bursts of laughter, graceful peculiarities of which they well know the effect. Should I be the Benedict to this Beatrice? But this by-play would hardly fill the prologue, and I very much wished to reach the epilogue.

"I passed in review the different routes that a lover might take to reach his end; I recapitulated every one of the more or less infallible methods of conquering female hearts; in a word, I went over my tactics like a lieutenant about to drill a battalion of recruits. When I had ended I had made no farther advance than before.

" 'To the devil with systems!' exclaimed I; 'I will not be so foolish as wilfully to adopt the *rôle* of *roué* when I feel called upon to play the plain *rôle* of true lover. Let those who like play the part of Lovelace! As for myself, I will love; upon the whole, that is what pleases best.' And I jumped headlong into the torrent without troubling myself as to the place of landing.

"While I was thus scheming my attack, Madame de Bergenheim was upon her guard and had prepared her means of defence. Puzzled by my reserve, which was in singular contrast with my almost extravagant conduct at our first meeting, her woman's intelligence had surmised, on my part, a plan which she proposed to baffle. I was partly found out, but I knew it and thus kept the advantage.

8 [113]

CHARLES DE BERNARD

"I could not help smiling at the Baroness's clever coquetry, when I decided to follow the inspirations of my heart, instead of choosing selfish motives as my guide. Every time I took her hand when dancing with her, I expected to feel a little claw ready to pierce the cold glove. But, while waiting for the scratch, it was a very soft, velvety little hand that was given me; and I, who willingly lent myself to her deception, did not feel very much duped. It was evident that the sort of halo which my merited or un-merited reputation had thrown over me had made me appear to her as a conquest of some value, a victim upon whom one could lavish just enough flowers in order to bring him to the sacrificial altar. In order to wind the first chain around my neck, Mauléon and D'Arzenac, *e tutti quanti*, were sacrificed for me without my soliciting, even by a glance, this general disband-ment. I could interpret this discharge. I saw that the fair one wished to concentrate all her seductions against me, so as to leave me no means of escape; people neglect the hares to hunt for the deer. You must excuse my conceit.

"This conduct wounded me at first, but I afterward forgave her, when a more careful examination taught me to know this adorable woman's character. Co-quetry was with her not a vice of the heart or of an unscrupulous mind; having nothing better to do, she enjoyed it as a legitimate pastime, without giving it any importance or feeling any scruples. Like all women, she liked to please; her success was sweet to her vanity; perhaps flattery turned her head at

times, but in the midst of this tumult her heart remained in perfect peace. She found so little danger
for herself in the game she played that it did not seem
to her that it could be very serious for others. Genuine
love is not common enough in Parisian parlors for a
pretty woman to conceive any great remorse at pleasing without loving.

"Madame de Bergenheim was thus, ingenuously,
unsuspectingly, a matchless coquette. Never having
loved, not even her husband, she looked upon her
little intriguing as one of the rights earned on the
day of her marriage, the same as her diamonds and
cashmeres. There was something touching in the
sound of her voice and in her large, innocent eyes
which she sometimes allowed to rest upon mine, without thinking to turn them away, and which said, 'I
have never loved.' As for myself, I believed it all;
one is so happy to believe!

"Far from being annoyed at the trap she laid for
me, I, on the contrary, ran my head into it and presented my neck to the yoke with a docility which
must have amused her, I think; but I hoped not to
bear it alone. A coquette who coolly flaunts her tri-
umphs to the world resembles those master-swimmers
who, while spectators are admiring the grace of their
poses, are struck by an unexpected current; the per-
former is sometimes swept away and drowned without
his elegant strokes being of much service to him.
Throw Célimène into the current of genuine passion
—I do not mean the brutality of Alceste—I will wager
that coquetry will be swept away by love. I had such

faith in mine that I thought to be able to fix the moment when I should call myself victorious and sure of being obeyed.

"You know that sadness and *ennui* were considered etiquette last winter, in a certain society, which was thrown into mourning by the July revolution. Reunions were very few; there were no balls or *soirées;* dancing in drawing-rooms to the piano was hardly permissible, even with intimate friends. When once I was installed in Mademoiselle de Corandeuil's drawing-room upon a friendly footing, this cessation of worldly festivities gave me an opportunity to see Clémence in a rather intimate way.

"It would take too long to tell you now all the thousand and one little incidents which compose the history of all passions. Profiting by her coquetry, which made her receive me kindly in order to make me expiate my success afterward, my love for her was soon an understood thing between us; she listened to me in a mocking way, but did not dispute my right to speak. She ended by receiving my letters, after being constrained to do so through a course of strategies in which, truly, I showed incredible invention. I was listened to and she read my letters; I asked for nothing more.

"My love, from the first, had been her secret as well as mine; but every day I made to sparkle some unexpected facet of this prism of a thousand colors. Even after telling her a hundred times how much I adored her, my love still had for her the attraction of the unknown. I really had something inexhaustible in my heart, and I was sure, in the end, to intoxicate her with this philtre, which I constantly poured out and which she drank, while making sport of it like a child.

"One day I found her thoughtful and silent. She did not reply to me with her usual sprightliness during the few moments that I was able to talk with her; the expression of her eyes had changed; there was something deeper and less glowing in their depths; instead of dazzling me by their excessive splendor, as had often happened to me before, they seemed to soften as they rested on mine; she kept her eyelids a trifle lowered, as if she were tired of being gazed at by me. Her voice, as she spoke, had a low, soft sound, a sort of inexplicable something which came from the very depths of her soul. She never had looked at me with that glance or spoken to me in that tone before. Upon that day I knew that she loved me.

"I returned to my home unutterably happy, for I loved this woman with a love of which I believed myself incapable.

"When I met Madame de Bergenheim again, I found her completely changed toward me; an icy gravity, an impassible calm, an ironical and disdainful haughtiness had taken the place of the delicious abandon of her former bearing. In spite of my strong determination to allow myself to love with the utmost candor, it was impossible for me to return to that happy age when the frowning brows of the beautiful idol to whom we paid court inspired us with the resolve to drown ourselves. I could not isolate myself from my past experiences. My heart was rejuvenated, but my head remained old. I was, therefore, not in the least discouraged by this change of humor, and the fit of anger which it portended.

" 'Now,' said I to myself, 'there is an end to coquetry, it is beaten on all sides; it is gone, never to return. She has seen that the affair is a little too deep for that, and the field not tenable. She will erect barriers in order to defend herself and will no longer attack.' Thus we pass from the period of amiable smiles, sweet glances, and half-avowals to that of severity and prudery, while waiting for the remorse and despair of the *dénouement*. I am sure that at this time she called to her help all her powers of resistance. From that day she would retreat behind the line of duty, conjugal fidelity, honor, and all the other fine sentiments which would need numbering after the fashion of Homer. At the first attack, all this household battalion would make a furious *sortie;* should I succeed in overthrowing them and take up my quarters in the trenches, there would then be a gathering of the reserve force, and boiling oil or tar would rain upon my head, representing virtue, religion, heaven, and hell."

"A sort of conjugal earthquake," interrupted Marillac.

"I calculated the strength and approximate duration of these means of defence. The whole thing appeared to me only a question of time, a few days or weeks at most—so long on the husband's account, so long on the father confessor's account. I deserved to be boxed on the ears for my presumption; I was.

"A combat is necessary in order to secure a victory. In spite of all my efforts and ruses, it was not possible for me to fight this combat; I did not succeed, in spite of all my challenges, in shattering, as I expected, this virtuous conjugal fortress. Madame de Bergenheim still persisted in her systematic reserve, with incredible prudence and skill. During the remainder of the winter, I did not find more than one opportunity of speaking to her alone. As I was a permanent fixture every evening in her aunt's parlors, she entered them only when other guests were there. She never went out alone, and in every place where I was likely to meet her I was sure to find a triple rampart of women erected between us, through which it was impossible to address one word to her. In short, I was encountering a desperate resistance; and, yet, she loved me! I could see her cheeks gradually grow pale; her brilliant eyes often had dark rings beneath them, as if sleep had deserted her. Sometimes, when she thought she was not observed, I surprised them fastened upon me; but she immediately turned them away.

"She had been coquettish and indifferent; she was now loving but virtuous.

"Spring came. One afternoon I went to call upon Mademoiselle de Corandeuil, who had been ill for several days. I was received, however, probably through some mistake of the servants. As I entered the room I saw Madame de Bergenheim; she was alone at her embroidery, seated upon a divan. There were several vases of flowers in the windows, whose curtains only permitted a soft, mysterious light to penetrate the room. The perfume from the flowers, the sort of obscurity, the solitude in which I found her, overcame me for a moment; I was obliged to pause in order to quiet the beating of my heart.

"She arose as she heard my name announced; without speaking or laying down her work, she pointed to a chair and seated herself; but instead of obeying her, I fell upon my knees before her and seized her hands, which she did not withdraw. It had been impossible for me to say another word to her before, save 'I love you!' I now told her of all my love. Oh! I am sure of it, my words penetrated to the very depth of her heart, for I felt her hands tremble as they left mine. She listened without interrupting me or making any reply, with her face bent toward me as if she were breathing the perfume of a flower. When I begged her to answer me, when I implored her for one single word from her heart, she withdrew one of her hands, imprisoned within mine, and placed it upon my forehead, pushing back my head with a gesture familiar to women. She gazed at me thus for a long time; her eyes were so languishing under their long lashes, and their languor was so penetrating, that I closed mine, not being able to endure the fascination of this glance any longer.

"A shiver which ran over her and which went through me also, like an electric shock, aroused me. When I opened my eyes I saw her face bathed in tears. She drew back and repelled me. I arose impetuously, seated myself by her side and took her in my arms.

" 'Am I not a wretched, unhappy woman?' said she, and fell upon my breast, sobbing.

" 'Madame la Comtesse de Pontiviers,' announced the servant, whom I would willingly have assassinated, as well as the visiting bore who followed in his footsteps.

"I never saw Madame de Bergenheim in Paris again. I was obliged to go to Bordeaux the next day, on account of a lawsuit which you know all about. Upon my return, at the end of three weeks, I found she had left. I finally learned that she had come to this place, and I followed her. That is the extent of my drama.

"Now you know very well that I have not related this long story to you for the sole pleasure of keeping you awake until one o'clock in the morning. I wanted to explain to you that it was really a serious thing for me, so that you might not refuse to do what I wish to ask of you."

"I think I understand what you are aiming at," said Marillac, rather pensively.

"You know Bergenheim; you will go to see him to-morrow. He will invite you to pass a few days with him; you will stay to dinner. You will see Mademoiselle de Corandeuil, in whose presence you will speak my name as you refer to our journey; and before night, my venerable cousin of 1569 shall send me an invitation to come to see her."

"I would rather render you any other service than

this," replied the artist, walking up and down the room in long strides. "I know very well that in all circumstances bachelors should triumph over husbands, but that does not prevent my conscience from smiting me. You know that I saved Bergenheim's life?"

"Rest assured that he runs no very great danger at present. Nothing will result from this step save the little enjoyment I shall take in annoying the cruel creature who defied me to-day. Is it agreed?"

"Since you insist upon it. But then, when our visit is ended, shall we go to work at our drama or upon *The Chaste Suzannah* opera in three acts? For, really, you neglected art terribly for the sake of your love affairs."

"*The Chaste Suzannah* or the whole Sacred History we shall put into vaudeville, if you exact it. Until to-morrow, then."

"Until to-morrow."

CHAPTER VIII

T was three o'clock in the afternoon; the drawing-room of the Château de Bergenheim presented its usual aspect and occupants. The fire on the hearth, lighted during the morning, was slowly dying, and a beautiful autumn sun threw its rays upon the floor through the half-opened windows. Mademoiselle de Corandeuil, stretched on the couch before the fireplace with Constance at her feet, was reading, according to her habit, the newspapers which had just arrived. Madame de Bergenheim seemed very busily occupied with a piece of tapestry in her lap; but the slow manner in which her needle moved, and the singular mistakes she made, showed that her mind was far away from the flowers she was working. She had just finished a beautiful dark lily, which contrasted strangely with its neighbors, when a servant entered.

"Madame," said he, "there is a person here inquiring for Monsieur le Baron de Bergenheim."

"Is Monsieur de Bergenheim not at home?" asked Mademoiselle de Corandeuil.

"Monsieur has gone to ride with Mademoiselle Aline."

"Who is this person?"

"It is a gentleman; but I did not ask his name."

"Let him enter."

Clémence arose at the servant's first words and threw her work upon a chair, making a movement as if to leave the room; but after a moment's reflection, she resumed her seat and her work, apparently indifferent as to who might enter.

"Monsieur de Marillac," announced the lackey, as he opened the door a second time.

Madame de Bergenheim darted a rapid glance at the individual who presented himself, and then breathed freely again.

After setting to rights his coiffure *à la Perinet*, the artist entered the room, throwing back his shoulders. Tightly buttoned up in his travelling redingote, and balancing with ease a small gray hat, he bowed respectfully to the two ladies and then assumed a pose *à la Van Dyke*.

Constance was so frightened at the sight of this imposing figure that, instead of jumping at the newcomer's legs, as was her custom, she sheltered herself under her mistress's chair, uttering low growls; at first glance the latter shared, if not the terror, at least the aversion of her dog. Among her numerous antipathies, Mademoiselle de Corandeuil detested a beard. This was a common sentiment with all old ladies, who barely tolerated moustaches: "Gentlemen did not wear them in 1780," they would say.

Marillac's eyes turned involuntarily toward the portraits, and other picturesque details of a room which was worthy the attention of a connoisseur; but he felt that the moment was not opportune for indulging in artistic contemplation, and that he must leave the dead for the living.

"Ladies," said he, "I ought, first of all, to ask your pardon for thus intruding without having had the honor of an introduction. I hoped to find here Monsieur de Bergenheim, with whom I am on very intimate terms. I was told that he was at the château."

"My husband's friends do not need to be presented at his house," said Clémence; "Monsieur de Bergenheim probably will return soon." And with a gracious gesture she motioned the visitor to a seat.

"Your name is not unknown to me," said Mademoiselle de Corandeuil in her turn, having succeeded in calming Constance's agitation. "I remember having heard Monsieur de Bergenheim mention you often."

"We were at college together, although I am a few years younger than Christian."

"But," exclaimed Madame de Bergenheim, struck by some sudden thought, "there is more than a college friendship between you. Are you not, Monsieur, the person who saved my husband's life in 1830?"

Marillac smiled, bowed his head, and seated himself. Mademoiselle de Corandeuil herself could not but graciously greet her nephew's preserver, had he had a moustache as long as that of the Shah of Persia, who ties his in a bow behind his neck.

After the exchange of a few compliments, Madame de Bergenheim, with the amiability of a mistress of

the house who seeks subjects of conversation that
may show off to best advantage the persons she re-
ceives, continued:

"My husband does not like to talk of himself, and
never has told us the details of this adventure, in
which he ran such great danger. Will you be kind
enough to gratify our curiosity on this point?"

Marillac, among his other pretensions, had that of
being able to relate a story in an impressive manner.
These words were as pleasing to his ears as the request for a song is to a lady who requires urging,
although she is dying to sing.

"Ladies," said he, crossing one leg over the other
and leaning upon one arm of his chair, "it was on the
twenty-eighth of July, 1830; the disastrous decrees had
produced their effects; the volcano which——"

"Pardon me, Monsieur, if I interrupt you," said
Mademoiselle de Corandeuil, quickly; "according to
my opinion, and that of many others, the royal decrees
you speak of were good and necessary. The only mistake of Charles Tenth was not to have fifty thousand
men around Paris to force their acceptance. I am
only a woman, Monsieur, but if I had had under my
command twenty cannon upon the quays, and as many
upon the boulevards, I assure you that your tricolored
flag never should have floated over the Tuileries."

"Pitt and Cobourg!" said the artist between his
teeth, as, with an astonished air, he gazed at the old
lady; but his common-sense told him that republican-
ism was not acceptable within this castle. Besides,
remembering the mission with which he was charged,

he did not think his conscience would feel much hurt if he made a little concession of principles and manœuvred diplomatically.

"Madame," replied he, "I call the decrees disastrous when I think of their result. You will certainly admit that our situation to-day ought to make everybody regret the causes which brought it about."

"We are exactly of the same opinion regarding that point, Monsieur," said Mademoiselle de Corandeuil, resuming her serenity.

"The open volcano beneath our feet," continued Marillac, who still stuck to his point, "warned us by deep rumblings of the hot lava which was about to gush forth. The excitement of the people was intense. Several engagements with the soldiers had already taken place at different points. I stood on the Boulevard Poissonnière, where I had just taken my luncheon, and was gazing with an artist's eye upon the dramatic scene spread out before me. Men with bare arms and women panting with excitement were tearing up the pavements or felling trees. An omnibus had just been upset; the rioters added cabriolets, furniture, and casks to it; everything became means of defence. The crashing of the trees as they fell, the blows of crowbars on the stones, the confused roaring of thousands of voices, the Marseillaise sung in chorus, and the irregular cannonading which resounded from the direction of the Rue Saint-Denis, all composed a strident, stupefying, tempestuous harmony, beside which Beethoven's *Tempest* would have seemed like the buzzing of a bee.

CHARLES DE BERNARD

"I was listening to the roaring of the people, who were gnawing at their chains before breaking them, when my eyes happened to fall upon a window of a second-floor apartment opposite me. A man about sixty years of age, with gray hair, a fresh, plump face, an honest, placid countenance, and wearing a mouse-colored silk dressing-gown, was seated before a small, round table. The window opened to the floor, and I could see him in this frame like a full-length portrait. There was a bowl of coffee upon the table, in which he dipped his roll as he read his journal. I beg your pardon, ladies, for entering into these petty details, but the habit of writing——"

"I assure you, Monsieur, your story interests me very much," said Madame de Bergenheim, kindly.

"A King Charles spaniel, like yours, Mademoiselle, was standing near the window with his paws resting upon it; he was gazing with curiosity at the revolution of July, while his master was reading his paper and sipping his coffee, as indifferent to all that passed as if he had been in Pekin or New York.

" 'Oh, the calm of a pure, sincere soul!' I exclaimed to myself, at the sight of this little tableau worthy of Greuze; 'oh, patriarchal philosophy! in a few minutes perhaps blood will flow in the streets, and here sits a handsome old man quietly sipping his coffee.' He seemed like a lamb browsing upon a volcano."

Marillac loved volcanoes, and never lost an opportunity to bring one in at every possible opportunity.

"Suddenly a commotion ran through the crowd; the people rushed in every direction, and in an instant the boulevard was empty. Plumes waving from high caps, red- and-white flags floating from the ends of long lances, and the cavalcade that I saw approaching through the trees told me the cause of this panic. A squadron of lancers was charging. Have you ever seen a charge of lancers?"

"Never!" said both of the ladies at once.

"It is a very grand sight, I assure you. Fancy, ladies, a legion of demons galloping along upon their horses, thrusting to the right and left with long pikes, whose steel points are eighteen inches long. That is a charge of lancers. I beg you to believe that I had shown before this the mettle there was in me, but I will not conceal from you that at this moment I shared with the crowd the impression which the coming of these gentlemen made. I had only time to jump over the sidewalk and to dart up a staircase which ran on the outside of a house, every door being closed. I never shall forget the face of one of those men who thrust the point of a lance at me, long enough to pierce through six men at once. I admit that I felt excited then! The jinn having passed——"

"The—what?" asked Mademoiselle de Corandeuil, who was not familiar with Eastern terms.

"I beg a thousand pardons, it was a poetical reminiscence. The lancers, having rushed through the boulevard like an avalanche, a laggard rider, a hundred steps behind the others, galloped proudly by, erect in his stirrups and flourishing his sword. Suddenly the report of a gun resounded, the lancer reeled backward, then forward, and finally fell upon his

9 [129]

horse's neck; a moment later he turned in his saddle and lay stretched upon the ground, his foot caught in the stirrup; the horse, still galloping, dragged the man and the lance, which was fastened to his arm by a leather band."

"How horrible!" said Clémence, clasping her hands.

Marillac, much pleased with the effect of his narration, leaned back in his chair and continued his tale with his usual assurance.

"I looked to the neighboring roofs to discover whence came this shot; as I was glancing to the right and left I saw smoke issuing through the blinds of the room on the second floor, which had been closed at the approach of the lancers.

" 'Good God!' I exclaimed; 'it must be this handsome old man in the mouse-colored silk dressing-gown who amuses himself by firing upon the lancers, as if they were rabbits in a warren!'

"Just then the blinds were opened, and the strange fellow with the unruffled countenance leaned out and gazed with a smiling face in the direction the horse was taking, dragging his master's body after him. The patriarch had killed his man between two sips of his coffee."

"And that is the cowardly way in which members of the royal guard were assassinated by the 'heroes' of your glorious insurrection!" exclaimed Mademoiselle de Corandeuil, indignantly.

"When the troops had passed," Marillac continued, "the crowd returned, more excited and noisy than ever. Barricades were erected with wonderful rapidity; two of those were on the boulevard close to the place where I was. I saw a horseman suddenly bound over the first; he wore a tuft of red-and-white feathers in his hat. I saw that it was a staff officer, doubtless carrying some despatch to headquarters. He continued his way, sabre in its sheath, head erect, proud and calm in the midst of insulting shouts from the crowd; stones were thrown at him and sticks at his horse's legs; he looked as if he were parading upon the Place du Carrousel.

"When he reached the second barricade, he drew his horse up, as if it were merely a question of jumping a hurdle in a steeplechase. Just then I saw the window on the first floor open again. 'Ah! you old rascal!' I exclaimed. The report of a gun drowned my voice; the horse which had just made the leap, fell on his knees; the horseman tried to pull him up, but after making one effort the animal fell over upon his side. The ball had gone through the steed's head."

"It was that poor Fidèle that I gave your husband," said Mademoiselle de Corandeuil, who was always very sentimental in the choice of names she gave to animals.

"He merited his name, Mademoiselle, for the poor beast died for his master, for whom the shot was intended. Several of those horrible faces, which upon riot days suddenly appear as if they came out of the ground, darted toward the unhorsed officer. I, and several other young men who were as little disposed as myself to allow a defenceless man to be slaughtered, ran toward him. I recognized Christian as I approached; his right leg was caught under the horse, and he was trying to unsheath his sword with his left hand. Sticks and stones were showered at him. I drew out the sword, which his position prevented him from doing, and exclaimed as I waved it in the air: 'The first rascal who advances, I will cut open like a dog.'

"I accompanied these words with a flourish which kept the cannibals at a distance for the time being.

"The young fellows who were with me followed my example. One took a pickaxe, another seized the branch of a tree, while others tried to release Christian from his horse. During this time the crowd increased around us; the shouts redoubled: 'Down with the ordinances!—These are disguised gendarmes! *Vive la liberté!*—We must kill them! Let's hang the spies to the lamp-posts!'

"Danger was imminent, and I realized that only a patriotic harangue would get us out of the scrape. While they were releasing Christian, I jumped upon Fidèle so as to be seen by all and shouted:

" '*Vive la liberté!*'

" '*Vive la liberté!*' replied the crowd.

" 'Down with Charles Tenth! Down with the ministers! Down with the ordinances!'

" 'Down!' shouted a thousand voices at once.

"You understand, ladies, this was a sort of bait, intended to close the mouths of these brutes.

" 'We are all citizens, we are all Frenchmen,' I continued; 'we must not soil our hands with the blood of one of our disarmed brothers. After a victory there are no enemies. This officer was doing his duty in fulfilling his chief's commands; let us do ours by dying, if necessary, for our country and the preservation of our rights.'

" '*Vive la liberté! vive la liberté!*' shouted the crowd. 'He is right; the officer was doing his duty. It would be assassination!' exclaimed numerous voices.

" 'Thanks, Marillac,' said Bergenheim to me, as I took his hand to lead him away, availing ourselves of the effect of my harangue; 'but do not press me so hard, for I really believe that my right arm is broken; only for that, I should ask you to return me my sword that I might show this rabble that they can not kill a Bergenheim as they would a chicken.'

" 'Let him cry: *Vive la Charte!*' roared out a man, with a ferocious face.

" 'I receive orders from nobody,' Christian replied, in a very loud voice, as he glared at him with eyes which would have put a rhinoceros to flight."

"Your husband is really a very brave man," said Mademoiselle de Corandeuil, addressing Clémence.

"Brave as an old warrior. This time he pushed his courage to the verge of imprudence; I do not know what the result might have been if the crowd had not been dispersed a second time by the approach of the lancers, who were returning through the boulevard. I led Bergenheim into a café; fortunately, his arm was only sprained."

Just at this moment Marillac's story was interrupted by a sound of voices and hurried steps. The door opened suddenly, and Aline burst into the room with her usual impetuosity.

"What has happened to you, Aline?" exclaimed Madame de Bergenheim, hurrying to her sister's side. The young girl's riding-habit and hat were covered with splashes of mud.

"Oh, nothing," replied the young girl, in a broken voice; "it was only Titania, who wanted to throw me into the river. Do you know where Rousselet is? They say it is necessary to bleed him; and he is the only one who knows how to do it."

"Whom do you mean, child? Is my husband wounded?" asked Clémence, turning pale.

"No, not Christian; it is a gentleman I do not know; only for him I should have been drowned. *Mon Dieu!* can not Rousselet be found?"

Aline left the room in great agitation. They all went over to the windows that opened out into the court, whence the sound of voices seemed to arise, and where they could hear the master's voice thundering out his commands. Several servants had gone to his assistance: one of them held Titania by the bridle; she was covered with foam and mud, and was trembling, with distended nostrils, like a beast that knows it has just committed a wicked action. A young man was seated upon a stone bench, wiping away blood which streamed from his forehead. It was Monsieur de Gerfaut.

At this sight Clémence supported herself against the framework of the window, and Marillac hurriedly left the room.

GERFAUT

Père Rousselet, who had at last been found in the kitchen, advanced majestically, eating an enormous slice of bread and butter.

"Good heavens! have you arrived at last?" exclaimed Bergenheim. "Here is a gentleman this crazy mare has thrown against a tree, and who has received a violent blow on the head. Do you not think it would be the proper thing to bleed him?"

"A slight phlebotomy might be very advantageous in stopping the extravasation of blood in the frontal region," replied the peasant, calling to his aid all the technical terms he had learned when he was a hospital nurse.

"Are you sure you can do this bleeding well?"

"I'll take the liberty of saying to Monsieur le Baron that I phlebotomized Perdreau last week and Mascareau only a month ago, without any complaint from them."

"Indeed! I believe you," sneered the groom, "both are on their last legs."

"I am neither Perdreau nor Mascareau," observed the wounded man with a smile.

Rousselet drew himself up at full height, with the dignity of a man of talent who scorns to reply to either criticism or mistrust.

"Monsieur," said Gerfaut, turning to the Baron, "I am really causing you too much trouble. This trifle does not merit the attention you give it. I do not suffer in the least. Some water and a napkin are all that I need. I fancy that I resemble an Iroquois

Indian who has just been scalped; my pride is really
what is most hurt," he added, with a smile, "when I
think of the grotesque sight I must present to the
ladies whom I notice at the window."

"Why, it is Monsieur de Gerfaut!" exclaimed Mademoiselle de Corandeuil, toward whom he raised his
eyes.

Octave bowed to her with a gracious air. His
glance wandered from the old lady to Clémence, who
did not seem to have the strength to leave the window. M. de Bergenheim, after hurriedly greeting
Marillac, finally yielded to the assurance that a sur-
geon was unnecessary, and conducted the two friends
to his own room, where the wounded man could find
everything that he needed.

"What the devil was the use in sending me as ambassador, since you were to make such a fine entrance
upon the stage?" murmured Marillac in his friend's
ear.

"Silence!" replied the latter as he pressed his hand;
"I am only behind the scenes as yet."

During this time Clémence and her aunt had led
Aline to her room.

"Now, tell us what all this means?" said Mademoiselle de Corandeuil, while the young girl was changing her dress.

"It was Christian's fault," replied Aline. "We
were galloping along beside the river when Titania
became frightened by the branch of a tree. 'Do not
be afraid!' exclaimed my brother. I was not in the
least frightened; but when he saw that my horse was

about to run away, he urged his on in order to join me. When Titania heard the galloping behind her she did run away in earnest; she left the road and started straight for the river. Then I began to be a little frightened. Just fancy, Clémence, I bounded in the saddle at each leap, sometimes upon the mare's neck, sometimes upon the crupper; it was terrible! I tried to withdraw my foot from the stirrup as Christian had told me to do; but just then Titania ran against the trunk of a tree, and I rolled over with her. A gentleman, whom I had not seen before, and who, I believe, actually jumped out of the ground, raised me from the saddle, where I was held by something, I do not know what; then that naughty Titania threw him against the tree as he was helping me to my feet, and when I was able to look at him his face was covered with blood. Christian rushed on the scene, and, when he saw that I was not badly hurt, he ran after Titania and beat her! Oh! how he beat her! *Mon Dieu!* how cruel men are! It was in vain for me to cry for mercy; he would not listen to me. Then we came home, and, since this gentleman is not badly wounded, it seems that my poor dress has fared worst of all."

The young girl took her riding-habit from the chair as she said these words, and could not restrain a cry of horror when she saw an enormous rent in it.

"*Mon Dieu!*" she exclaimed, as she showed it to her sister-in-law. It was all that she had strength to articulate.

Mademoiselle de Corandeuil took the skirt in her turn, and looked at it with the practised eye of a person who had made a special study of little disasters of the toilet and the ways of remedying them.

"It is in the fullness," said she, "and by putting in a new breadth it will never be seen."

Aline, once convinced that the evil could be repaired, soon recovered her serenity.

When the three ladies entered the drawing-room they found the Baron and his two guests chatting amicably. Gerfaut had his forehead tied up with a black silk band which gave him a slight resemblance to Cupid with his bandage just off his eyes. His sparkling glance showed that blindness was not what there was in common between him and the charming little god. After the first greetings, Mademoiselle de Corandeuil, who was always strict as to etiquette, and who thought that Titania had been a rather unceremonious master of ceremonies between her nephew and M. de Gerfaut, advanced toward the latter in order to introduce them formally to each other.

"I do not think," said she, "that Monsieur de Bergenheim has had the honor of meeting you before to-day; allow me then to present you to him. Baron, this is Monsieur le Vicomte de Gerfaut, one of my relatives."

When Mademoiselle de Corandeuil was in good humor, she treated Gerfaut as a relative on account of their family alliance of 1569. At this moment the poet felt profoundly grateful for this kindness.

"Monsieur has presented himself so well," said Christian frankly, "that your recommendation, my dear aunt, in spite of the respect I have for it, will not add to my gratitude. Only for Monsieur de Gerfaut, here is a madcap little girl whom we should be obliged to look for now at the bottom of the river."

As he said these words, he passed his arm about his sister's waist and kissed her tenderly, while Aline was obliged to stand upon the tips of her toes to reach her brother's lips.

"These gentlemen," he continued, "have agreed to sacrifice for us the pleasure of the Femme-sans-Tête, as well as Mademoiselle Gobillot's civilities, and establish their headquarters in my house. They can pursue their picturesque and romantic studies from here just as well; I suppose, Marillac, that you are still a determined dauber of canvas?"

"To tell the truth," replied the poet, "art absorbs me a great deal."

"As to myself, I never succeeded in drawing a nose that did not resemble an ear and *vice versa*. But for that worthy Baringnier, who was kind enough to look over my plans, I ran a great risk of leaving Saint Cyr without a graduating diploma. But seriously, gentlemen, when you are tired of sketching trees and tumbledown houses, I can give you some good boar hunting. Are you a hunter, Monsieur de Gerfaut?"

"I like hunting very much," replied the lover, with rare effrontery.

The conversation continued thus upon the topics that occupy people who meet for the first time. When the Baron spoke of the two friends installing themselves at the château, Octave darted a glance at Madame de Bergenheim, as if soliciting a tacit approbation of his conduct; but met with no response. Clémence, with a gloomy, sombre air fulfilled the duties that politeness imposed upon her as mistress of the house. Her conduct did not change during the rest of the evening, and Gerfaut no longer tried by a single glance to soften the severity she seemed determined to adopt toward him. All his attentions were reserved for Mademoiselle de Corandeuil and Aline, who listened with unconcealed pleasure to the man whom she regarded as her saviour; for the young girl's remembrance of the danger which she had run excited her more and more.

After supper Mademoiselle de Corandeuil proposed a game of whist to M. de Gerfaut, whose talent for the game had made a lasting impression upon her. The poet accepted this diversion with an enthusiasm equal to that he had shown for hunting, and quite as sincere too. Christian and his sister—a little gamester in embryo, like all of her family—completed the party, while Clémence took up her work and listened with an absent-minded air to Marillac's conversation. It was in vain for the latter to call art and the Middle Ages to his aid, using the very quintessence of his brightest speeches—success did not attend his effort. After the end of an hour, he had a firm conviction that Madame de Bergenheim was, everything considered, only a woman of ordinary intelligence and entirely unworthy of the passion she had inspired in his friend.

"Upon my soul," he thought, "I would a hundred times rather have Reine Gobillot for a sweetheart. I must take a trip in that direction to-morrow."

When they separated for the night, Gerfaut, bored

by his evening and wounded by his reception from Clémence, which, he thought, surpassed anything he could have expected of her capricious disposition, addressed to the young woman a profound bow and a look which said:

"I am here in spite of you; I shall stay here in spite of you; you shall love me in spite of yourself."

Madame de Bergenheim replied by a glance none the less expressive, in which a lover the most prone to conceit could read:

"Do as you like; I have as much indifference for your love as disdain for your presumption."

This was the last shot in this preliminary skirmish.

CHAPTER IX

GERFAUT, THE WIZARD

HERE are some women who, like the heroic Curé Merino, need but one hour's sleep. A nervous, irritable, subtle organization gives them a power for waking, without apparent fatigue, refused to most men. And yet, when a strong emotion causes its corrosive waters to filtrate into the veins of these impressionable beings, it trickles there drop by drop, until it has hollowed out in the very depths of their hearts a lake full of trouble and storms.

Then, in the silence of night and the calm of solitude, insomnia makes the rosy cheeks grow pale and dark rings encircle the most sparkling eyes. It is in vain for the burning forehead to seek the cool pillow; the pillow grows warm without the forehead cooling. In vain the mind hunts for commonplace ideas, as a sort of intellectual poppy-leaves that may lead to a quiet night's rest; a persistent thought still returns, chasing away all others, as an eagle disperses a flock of timid birds in order to remain sole master of its prey. If one tries to repeat the accustomed prayer, and invoke the aid of the Virgin, or the good angel who watches at the foot of young girls' beds, in order

[142]

to keep away the charms of the tempter, the prayer is only on the lips, the Virgin is deaf, the angel sleeps! The breath of passion against which one struggles runs through every fibre of the heart, like a storm over the chords of an Æolian harp, and extorts from it those magic melodies to which a poor, troubled, and frightened woman listens with remorse and despair; but to which she listens, and with which at last she is intoxicated, for the allegory of Eve is an immortal myth, that repeats itself, through every century and in every clime.

Since her entrance into society, Madame de Bergenheim had formed the habit of keeping late hours. When the minute details of her toilette for the night were over, and she had confided her beautiful body to the snowy sheets of her couch, some new novel or fashionable magazine helped her wile away the time until sleep came to her. Christian left his room, like a good country gentleman, at sunrise; he left it either for the chase or to oversee workmen, who were continually being employed upon some part of his domain. Ordinarily, he returned only in time for dinner, and rarely saw Clémence except between that time and supper, at the conclusion of which, fatigued by his day's work, he hastened to seek the repose of the just. Husband and wife, while living under the same roof, were thus almost completely isolated from each other; night for one was day for the other.

By the haste with which Clémence shortened her preparations for the night, one would have said that she must have been blessed with an unusually sleepy sensation. But when she lay in bed, with her head under her arm, like a swan with his neck under his wing, and almost in the attitude of Correggio's Magdalen, her eyes, which sparkled with a feverish light, betrayed the fact that she had sought the solitude of her bed in order to indulge more freely in deep meditation.

With marvelous fidelity she went over the slightest events of the day, to which by a constant effort of will-power, she had seemed so indifferent. First, she saw Gerfaut with his face covered with blood, and the thought of the terrible sensation which this sight caused her made her heart throb violently. She then recalled him as she next saw him, in the drawing-room by her husband's side, seated in the very chair that she had left but a moment before. This trifling circumstance impressed her; she saw in this a proof of sympathetic understanding, a sort of gift of second sight which Octave possessed, and which in her eyes was so formidable a weapon. According to her ideas, he must have suspected that this was her own favorite chair and have seized it for that reason, just as he would have loved to take her in his arms.

For the first time, Clémence had seen together the man to whom she belonged and the man whom she regarded somewhat as her property. For, by one of those arrangements with their consciences of which women alone possess the secret, she had managed to reason like this: "Since I am certain always to belong to Monsieur de Bergenheim only, Octave can certainly belong to me." An heterodoxical syllogism, whose two

premises she reconciled with an inconceivable sub-
tlety. A feeling of shame had made her dread this
meeting, which the most hardened coquette could never
witness without embarrassment. A woman, between
her husband and her lover, is like a plant one sprinkles
with ice-cold water while a ray of sunlight is trying to
comfort it. The sombre and jealous, or even tranquil
and unsuspecting, face of a husband has a wonderful
power of repression. One is embarrassed to love
under the glance of an eye that darts flashes as bright
as steel; and a calm, kindly look is more terrible yet,
for all jealousy seems tyrannical, and tyranny leads to
revolt; but a confiding husband is like a victim strangled in his sleep, and inspires, by his very calmness,
the most poignant remorse.

The meeting of these two men naturally led Clémence to a comparison which could but be to Christian's
advantage. Gerfaut had nothing remarkable about him
save an intelligent, intensely clever air; there was a
thoughtful look in his eyes and an archness in his smile,
but his irregular features showed no mark of beauty;
his face wore an habitually tired expression, peculiar to those people who have lived a great deal in a
short time, and it made him look older than Christian,
although he was really several years younger. The
latter, on the contrary, owed to his strong constitution,
fortified by country life, an appearance of blooming
youth that enhanced his noble regularity of features.

In a word, Christian was handsomer than his rival,
and Clémence exaggerated her husband's superiority
over her lover. Not being able to find the latter awk-

ward or insignificant, she tried to persuade herself that
he was ugly. She then reviewed in her mind all M.
de Bergenheim's good qualities, his attachment and
kindness to her, his loyal, generous ways; she recalled
the striking instance that Marillac had related of his
bravery, a quality without which there is no hope
of success for a man in the eyes of any woman. She
did all in her power to inflame her imagination and
to see in her husband a hero worthy of inspiring the
most fervent love. When she had exhausted her efforts toward such enthusiasm and admiration, she
turned round, in despair, and, burying her head in her
pillow, she sobbed:

"I cannot, I cannot love him!"

She wept bitterly for a long while. As she recalled
her own severity in the past regarding women whose
conduct had caused scandal, she employed in her turn
the harshness of her judgment in examining her own
actions. She felt herself more guilty than all the
others, for her weakness appeared less excusable to
her. She felt that she was unworthy and contempti-
ble, and wished to die that she might escape the shame
that made her blush scarlet, and the remorse that
tortured her soul.

How many such unhappy tears bathe the eyes of
those who should shed only tears of joy! How many
such sighs break the silence of the night! There are
noble, celestial beings among women whom remorse
stretches out upon its relentless brasier, but in the
midst of the flames that torture them the heart pal-
pitates, imperishable as a salamander. Is it not hu-

man fate to suffer? After Madame de Bergenheim
had given vent, by convulsive sobs and stifled sighs,
to her grief for this love which she could not tear from
her breast, she formed a desperate resolution. From
the manner in which M. de Gerfaut had taken possession of the château the very first day, she recognized
that he was master of the situation. The sort of in-
fatuation which Mademoiselle de Corandeuil seemed
to have for him, and Christian's courteous and hos-
pitable habits, would give him an opportunity to prolong his stay as long as he desired. She thus compared
herself to a besieged general, who sees the enemy
within his ramparts.

"Very well! I will shut myself up in the fortress!"
said she, smiling in spite of herself in the midst of her
tears. "Since this insupportable man has taken possession of my drawing-room, I will remain in my own
room; we will see whether he dares to approach that!"

She shook her pretty head with a defiant air, but
she could not help glancing into the room which was
barely lighted with a night lamp. She sat up and
listened for a moment rather anxiously, as if Octave's
dark eyes might suddenly glisten in the obscurity.
When she had assured herself that all was tranquil,
and that the throbbing of her heart was all that disturbed the silence, she continued preparing her plan
of defense.

She decided that she would be ill the next day and
keep to her bed, if necessary, until her persecutor
should make up his mind to beat a retreat. She solemnly pledged herself to be firm, courageous, and in-

flexible; then she tried to pray. It was now two o'clock in the morning. For some time Clémence remained motionless, and one might have thought that at least she was asleep. Suddenly she arose. Without stopping to put on her dressing-gown, she lighted a candle by the night-lamp, pushed the bolt of her door and then went to the windows, the space between them forming a rather deep projection on account of the thickness of the walls. A portrait of the Duke of Bordeaux hung there; she raised it and pressed a button concealed in the woodwork. A panel opened, showing a small empty space. The shelf in this sort of closet contained only a rosewood casket. She opened this mysterious box and took from it a package of letters, then returned to her bed with the eagerness of a miser who is about to gaze upon his treasures.

Had she not struggled and prayed? Had she not offered upon the tyrannical altar of duty as an expiation, tears, pale cheeks and a tortured soul? Had she not just taken a solemn vow, in the presence of God and herself, which should protect her against her weakness? Was she not a virtuous wife, and had she not paid dearly enough for a moment of sad happiness? Was it a crime to breathe for an instant the balmy air of love through the gratings of this prison-cell, the doors of which she had just locked with her own hand? Admirable logic for loving hearts, which, not being able to control their feelings, suffer in order to prove themselves less guilty, and clothe themselves in haircloth so that each shudder may cause a pain that condones the sin!

· Being at peace with herself, she read as women read who are in love; leaning her head upon her hand, she drew out the letters, one by one, from her bosom where she had placed them. She drank with her heart and eyes the poison these passionate words contained; she allowed herself to be swayed at will by these melodies which lulled but did not benumb. When one of those invincible appeals of imploring passion awoke all the echoes of her love, and ran through her veins with a thrill, striking the innermost depths of her heart, she threw herself back and imprinted her burning lips upon the cold paper. With one letter pressed to her heart, and another pressed to her lips, she gave herself up completely, exclaiming in an inaudible voice: "I love thee! I am thine!"

The next morning, when Aline entered her sister-in-law's room, according to her usual custom, the latter was not obliged to feign the indisposition she had planned; the sensations of this sleepless night had paled her cheeks and altered her features; it would have been difficult to imagine a more complete contrast than that between these two young women at this moment. Clémence, lying upon her bed motionless and white as the sheet which covered her, resembled Juliet sleeping in her tomb; Aline, rosy, vivacious, and more petulant than usual, looked very much the madcap Mademoiselle de Corandeuil had reproached her with being. Her face was full of that still childish grace, more lovely than calm, more pleasing than impressive, which makes young girls so charming to the eye but less eloquent to the heart;

for are they not fresh flowers more rich in coloring than in perfume?

Clémence could hardly stifle a sigh as she gazed at those rosy cheeks, those sparkling eyes, that life so full of the rich future. She recalled a time when she was thus, when grief glided over her cheeks without paling them, when tears dried as they left her eyes; she also had had her happy, careless days, her dreams of unalloyed bliss.

Aline, after presenting her face like a child who asks for a kiss, wished to tease her as usual, but, with a tired gesture, her sister-in-law begged for mercy.

"Are you ill?" asked the young girl anxiously, as she seated herself upon the edge of the bed.

Madame de Bergenheim smiled, a forced smile.

"Thank me for my poor health," said she, "for it obliges you to do the honors; I shall doubtless not be able to go down to dinner, and you must take my place. You know that it tires my aunt to have to trouble herself about others."

Aline made a little grimace as she replied:

"If I thought you were speaking seriously, I would go and get into my own bed at once!"

"Child! will you not in your turn be mistress of a home? Is it not necessary for you to become accustomed to it? It is an excellent opportunity, and, with my aunt as a guide, you are sure to acquit yourself well."

These last words were spoken rather maliciously, for the young woman knew that of all the possible mentors, Mademoiselle de Corandeuil was the one whom Aline dreaded most.

"I beg of you, my kind sister," replied the girl, clasping her hands, "do not be ill to-day. Is it the neuralgia of the day before yesterday you are suffering from? Do be a good sister, and get up and come and take a walk in the park; the fresh air will cure you, I am sure of it——"

"And I shall not be obliged to preside at the dinner-table, you would add; is it not so? You selfish girl!"

"I am afraid of Monsieur de Gerfaut," said the child, lowering her voice.

When she heard pronounced this name, so deeply agitating her, Madame de Bergenheim was silent for a moment; at last she said:

"What has Monsieur de Gerfaut done to you? Is it not downright ungrateful to be afraid of him so soon after the service he has rendered you?"

"No, I am not ungrateful," replied the young girl quickly. "I never shall forget that I owe my life to him, for certainly, but for him, I should have been dragged into the river. But he has such black, piercing eyes that they seem to look into your very soul; and then, he is such a brilliant man! I am all the time afraid of saying something that he may laugh at. You know, some people think I talk too much; but I shall never dare open my mouth in his presence. Why do some persons' eyes make such an impression upon one?"

Clémence lowered her own beautiful eyes and made no reply.

"His friend, Monsieur Marillac, does not frighten me one bit, in spite of his big moustache. Tell me, does not this Monsieur de Gerfaut frighten you a little too?"

"Not at all, I assure you," replied Madame de Bergenheim, trying to smile. "But," she continued, in order to change the conversation, "how fine you look! You have certainly some plan of conquest. What! a city gown at nine o'clock in the morning, and hair dressed as if for a ball?"

"Would you like to know the compliment your aunt just paid me?"

"Some little jest of hers, I suppose?"

"You might say some spiteful remark, for she is the hatefulest thing! She told me that blue ribbons suited red hair very badly and advised me to change one or the other. Is it true that my hair is red?"

Mademoiselle de Bergenheim asked this question with so much anxiety that her sister-in-law could not repress a smile.

"You know that my aunt delights in annoying you," said she. "Your hair is very pretty, a bright blond, very pleasant to the eye; only Justine waves it a little too tight; it curls naturally. She dresses your hair too high; it would be more becoming to you if she pushed it back from your temples a little than to wave it as much as she does. Come a little nearer to me."

Aline knelt before Madame de Bergenheim's bed, and the latter, adding a practical lesson to verbal advice, began to modify the maid's work to suit her own taste.

"It curls like a little mane," said the young girl, as she saw the trouble her sister-in-law had in succeeding; "it was my great trouble at the Sacred Heart. The sisters wished us to wear our hair plain, and I always had a terrible time to keep it in place. However, blond hair looks ugly when too plainly dressed, and Monsieur de Gerfaut said yesterday that it was the shade he liked best."

"Monsieur de Gerfaut told you he liked blond hair best!"

"Take care; you are pulling my hair! Yes, blond hair and blue eyes. He said that when speaking of Carlo Dolci's Virgin, and he said she was of the most beautiful Jewish type; if he intended it as a compliment to me, I am very much obliged to him. Do you think that my eyes are as blue as that of the painted Virgin's. Monsieur de Gerfaut pretends that there is a strong resemblance."

Madame de Bergenheim withdrew her hand so quickly that she pulled out half a dozen or more hairs from her sister-in-law's head, and buried herself up to the chin in the bedclothes.

"Oh! Monsieur de Gerfaut knows how to pay very pretty compliments!" she said. "And you doubtless are very well pleased to resemble Carlo Dolci's Madonna?"

"She is very pretty!—and then it is the Holy Virgin, you know—Ah! I hear Monsieur de Gerfaut's voice in the garden."

The young girl arose quickly and ran to the window, where, concealed behind the curtains, she could see what was going on outside without being seen herself.

"He is with Christian," she continued. "There, they are going to the library. They must have just taken a long walk, for they are bespattered with mud. If you could only see what a pretty little cap Monsieur de Gerfaut has on!"

"Truly, he will turn her head," thought Madame de Bergenheim, with a decided feeling of anger; then she closed her eyes as if she wished to sleep.

Gerfaut had, in fact, just returned from paying his respects to the estate. He had followed his host, who, under the pretext of showing him several picturesque sights, promenaded him, in the morning dew, through the lettuce in the kitchen garden and the underbrush in the park. But he knew through experience that all was not roses in a lover's path; watching in the snow, climbing walls, hiding in obscure closets, imprisonment in wardrobes, were more disagreeable incidents than a quiet *tête-à-tête* with a husband.

He listened, therefore, complacently enough to Bergenheim's prolix explanations, interested himself in the planting of trees, thought the fields very green, the forests admirable, the granite rocks more beautiful than those of the Alps, went into ecstasies over the smallest vista, advised the establishment of a new mill on the river, which, being navigable for rafts, might convey lumber to all the cities on the Moselle, and thus greatly increase the value of the owner's woods. They fraternized like Glaucus and Diomede; Gerfaut hoping, of course, to play the part of the Greek, who, according to Homer, received in return for a common iron armor a gold one of inestimable value. There is always such a secret mental reservation in the lover's mind when associating with the husband of his inamorata.

When he entered the room of his wife, whose indisposition had been reported to him, Christian's first words were:

"This Monsieur de Gerfaut appears to be a very excellent fellow, and I shall be delighted if he will stay with us a while. It is too bad that you are ill. He is a good musician, as well as Marillac; you might have sung together. Try to get better quickly and come down to dinner."

"I can not really tell him that Monsieur de Gerfaut has loved me for more than a year," said Madame de Bergenheim to herself.

A moment later, Mademoiselle de Corandeuil appeared, and with a prim air seated herself beside the bed.

"Perhaps you think that I am fooled by this indisposition. I see plainly that you wish to be impolite to Monsieur de Gerfaut, for you can not endure him. It seems to me, however, that a relative of your family ought to be treated with more respect by you, above all, when you know how much I esteem him. This is unheard-of absurdity, and I shall end by speaking to your husband about it; we shall see if his intervention will not have more effect than mine."

"You shall not do that, aunt," Clémence interrupted, sitting up in bed and trying to take her aunt's hand.

"If you wish that your discourteous conduct should rest a secret between us, I advise you to get rid of your neuralgia this very day. Now, you had better decide immediately——"

"This is genuine persecution," exclaimed Madame de Bergenheim, falling back upon her bed when the old lady had departed. "He has bewitched everybody! Aline, my aunt, and my husband; to say nothing of myself, for I shall end by going mad. I must end this, at any price." She rang the bell violently.

"Justine," said she to her maid, "do not let any one enter this room under any pretext whatsoever, and do not come in yourself until I ring; I will try to sleep."

Justine obeyed, after closing the blinds. She had hardly gone out when her mistress arose, put on her dressing-gown and slippers with a vivacity which betokened anger; she then seated herself at her desk and began to write rapidly, dashing her pen over the satiny paper without troubling herself as to blots. The last word was ended with a dash as energetically drawn as the Napoleonic flourish.

When a young man who, according to custom, begins to read the end of his letters first finds an arabesque of this style at the bottom of a lady's letter, he ought to arm himself with patience and resignation before he reads its contents.

CHAPTER X

PLOTS

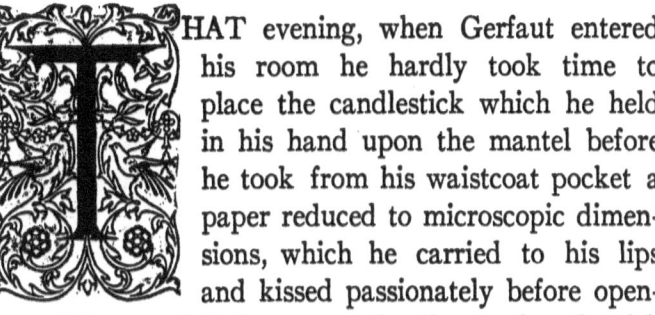THAT evening, when Gerfaut entered his room he hardly took time to place the candlestick which he held in his hand upon the mantel before he took from his waistcoat pocket a paper reduced to microscopic dimensions, which he carried to his lips and kissed passionately before opening. His eyes fell first upon the threatening flourish of the final word; this word was: *Adieu!*

"Hum!" said the lover, whose exaltation was sensibly cooled at this sight.

He read the whole letter with one glance of the eye, darting to the culminating point of each phrase as a deer bounds over ledges of rocks; he weighed the plain meaning as well as the innuendoes of the slightest expression, like a rabbi who comments upon the Bible, and deciphered the erasures with the patience of a seeker after hieroglyphics, so as to detach from them some particle of the idea they had contained. After analyzing and criticising this note in all its most imperceptible shades, he crushed it within his hand and began to pace the floor, uttering from time to time some of those exclamations which the *Dictionnaire de*

CHARLES DE BERNARD

l'Académie has not yet decided to sanction; for all lovers resemble the *lazzaroni* who kiss San-Gennaro's feet when he acts well, but who call him *briconne* as soon as they have reason to complain of him. However, women are very kind, and almost invariably excuse the stones that an angry lover throws at them in such moments of acute disappointment, and willingly say with the indulgent smile of the Roman emperor: "I feel no wound!"

In the midst of this paroxysm of furious anger, two or three knocks resounded behind the woodwork.

"Are you composing?" asked a voice like that of a ventriloquist; "I am with you."

A minute later, Marillac appeared upon the threshold, in his slippers and with a silk handkerchief tied about his head, holding his candlestick in one hand and a pipe in the other; he stood there motionless.

"You are fine," said he, "you are magnificent, fatal and accursed—You remind me of Kean in *Othello*.—

"Have you pray'd to-night, Desdemona?"

Gerfaut gazed at him with frowning brows, but made no reply.

"I will wager that it is the last scene in our third act," replied the artist, placing his candlestick upon the mantel; "it seems that it is to be very tragic. Now listen! I also feel the poetical afflatus coming over me, and, if you like, we will set about devouring paper like two boa-constrictors. Speaking of serpents, have you a rattle? Ah, yes! Here is the bell-rope. I was about to say that we would have a bowl of coffee. Or rather, I will go into the kitchen myself; I am very good friends with Marianne, the cook; besides, the motto of the house of Bergenheim is *liberté, libertas.* Coffee is my muse; in this respect, I resemble Voltaire——"

"Marillac!" exclaimed Gerfaut, as the artist was about to leave the room. The artist turned, and meekly retraced his steps.

"You will be so good as to do me the favor of returning to your room," said Gerfaut. "You may work or you may sleep, just as you like; between us, you would do well to sleep. I wish to be alone."

"You say that as if you meditated an attempt upon your illustrious person. Are you thinking of suicide? Let us see whether you have some concealed weapon, some poisoned ring. Curse upon it! the poison of the Borgias! Is the white substance in this china bowl, vulgarly called sugar, by some terrible chance infamous arsenic disguised under the appearance of an honest colonial commodity?"

"Be kind enough to spare your jokes," said Octave, as his friend poked about in all the corners of the room with an affectation of anxiety, "and, as I can not get rid of you, listen to my opinion: if you think that I brought you here for you to conduct yourself as you have for the last two days, you are mistaken."

"What have I done?"

"You left me the whole morning with that tiresome Bergenheim on my hands, and I verily believe he made me count every stick in his park and every frog in his pond. To-night, when that old witch of Endor pro-

posed her infernal game of whist, to which it seems I
am to be condemned daily, you excused yourself upon
the pretext of ignorance, and yet you play as good a
game as I."

"I can not endure whist at twenty sous a point."

"Do I like it any better?"

"Well, you are a nice fellow! You have an object in
view which should make you swallow all these disagreeable trifles as if they were as sweet as honey. Is
it possible you would like me to play Bertrand and
Raton? I should be Raton the oftener of the two!"

"But, really, what did you do all day?"

Marillac posed before the mirror, arranged his ker-
chief about his head in a more picturesque fashion,
twisted his moustache, puffed out, through the corner
of his mouth, a cloud of smoke, which surrounded his
face like a London fog, then turned to his friend and
said, with the air of a person perfectly satisfied with
himself:

"Upon my faith, my dear friend, each one for himself and God for us all! You, for example, indulge in
romantic love-affairs; you must have titled ladies.
Titles turn your head and make you exclusive. You
make love to the aristocracy; so be it, that is your
own concern. As for me, I have another system; I
am, in all matters of sentiment, what I am in politics: I want republican institutions."

"What is all that nonsense about?"

"Let me tell you. I want universal suffrage, the
cooperation of all citizens, admission to all offices,
general elections, a popular government, in a word,

a sound, patriotic *hash*. Which means regarding women that I carry them *all* in my heart, that I recognize between them no distinction of caste or rank. Article First of my set of laws: all women are equal in love, provided they are young, pretty, admirably attractive in shape and carriage, above all, not too thin."

"And what of equality?"

"So much the worse. With this eminently liberal and constitutional policy, I intend to gather all the flowers that will allow themselves to be gathered by me, without one being esteemed more fresh than another, because it belongs to the nobility, or another less sweet, because plebeian. And as field daisies are a little more numerous than imperial roses, it follows that I very often stoop. That is the reason why, at this very moment, I am up to my ears in a little rustic love affair:

Simple et naïve bergerette, elle règne——"

"Stop that noise; Mademoiselle de Corandeuil's room is just underneath."

"I will tell you then, since I must give an account of myself, that I went into the park to sketch a few fir-trees before dinner; they are more beautiful of their kind than the ancient Fontainebleau oaks. That is for art. At dinner, I dined nobly and well. To do the Bergenheims justice, they live in a royal manner. That is for the stomach. Afterward I stealthily ordered a horse to be saddled and rode to La Fauconnerie in a trice, where I presented the expression of

my adoration to Mademoiselle Reine Gobillot, a minor
yet, but enjoying her full rights already. That is for
the heart."

"Indeed!"

"No sarcasm, if you please; not everybody can
share your taste for princesses, who make you go a
hundred leagues to follow them and then upon your
arrival, only give you the tip of a glove to kiss. Such
intrigues are not to my fancy.

> *Je suis sergent,*
> *Brave——"*

"Again, I say, will you stop that noise? Don't you
know that I have nobody on my side at present but
this respectable dowager on the first floor below? If
she supposes that I am making all this racket over her
head we shall be deadly enemies by to-morrow."

> "*Zitto, zitto, piano, piano,*
> *Senza strepito e rumore,*"

replied Marillac, putting his finger to his lips and
lowering his voice. "What you say is a surprise to
me. From the way in which you offered your arm to
Madame de Bergenheim to lead her into the drawing-
room after supper, I thought you understood each
other perfectly. As I was returning, for I made it my
duty to offer my arm to the old lady—and you say that
I do nothing for you—it seemed to me that I noticed
a meeting of hands—You know that I have an eagle
eye. She slipped a note into your hand as sure as my
name is Marillac."

GERFAUT

Gerfaut took the note which he held crumpled up in his hand, and held it in the flame of one of the candles. The paper ignited, and in less than a second nothing of it remained but a few dark pieces which fell into ashes upon the marble mantel.

"You burn it! You are wrong," said the artist; "as for me, I keep everything, letters and hair. When I am old, I shall have the letters to read evenings, and shall weave an allegorical picture with the hair. I shall hang it before my desk, so as to have before me a souvenir of the adorable creatures who furnished the threads. I will answer for it that there will be every shade in it from that of Camille Hautier, my first love, who was an albino, to this that I have here."

As he spoke, he took out of his pocket a small parcel from which he drew a lock of coal-black hair, which he spread out upon his hand.

"Did you pull this hair from Titania's mane?" asked Gerfaut, as he drew through his fingers the more glossy than silky lock, which he ridiculed by this ironical supposition.

"They might be softer, I admit," replied Marillac negligently; and he examined the lock submitted to this merciless criticism as if it were simply a piece of goods, of the fineness of whose texture he wished to assure himself.

"You will admit at least that the color is beautiful, and the quantity makes up for the quality. Upon my word, this poor Reine has given me enough to make a pacha's banner. Provincial and primitive simplicity! I know of one woman in particular who never gave an adorer more than seven of her hairs; and yet, at the end of three years, this cautious beauty was obliged to wear a false front. All her hair had disappeared.

"Are you like me, Octave? The first thing I ask for is one of these locks. Women rather like this sort of childishness, and when they have granted you that, it is a snare spread for them which catches them."

Marillac took the long, dark tress and held it near the candle; but his movement was so poorly calculated that the hair caught fire and was instantly destroyed.

"A bad sign," exclaimed Gerfaut, who could not help laughing at his friend's dismayed look.

"This is a day of *autos-da-fé*," said the artist, dropping into a chair; "but bah! small loss; if Reine asks to see this lock, I will tell her that I destroyed it with kisses. That always flatters them, and I am sure it will please this little field-flower. It is a fact that she has cheeks like rosy apples! On my way back I thought of a vaudeville that I should like to write about this. Only I should lay the scene in Switzerland and I should call the young woman Betty or Kettly instead of Reine, a name ending in 'Y' which would rhyme with Rutly, on account of local peculiarities. Will you join in it? I have almost finished the scenario. First scene—Upon the rising of the curtain, harvesters are discovered——"

"Will you do me the favor of going to bed?" interrupted Gerfaut.

"Chorus of harvesters:

GERFAUT

*Déjà l'aurore
Qui se colore—"*

"If you do not leave me alone, I will throw the contents of this water-pitcher at your head."

"I never have seen you in such a surly temper. It looks indeed as if your divinity had treated you cruelly."

"She has treated me shamefully!" exclaimed the lover, whose anger was freshly kindled at this question; "she has treated me as one would treat a barber's boy. This note, which I just burned, was a most formal, unpleasant, insolent dismissal. This woman is a monster, do you understand me?"

"A monster! your angel, a monster!" said Marillac, suppressing with difficulty a violent outburst of laughter.

"She, an angel? I must say that she is a demon—This woman——"

"Do you not adore her?"

"I hate her, I abhor her, she makes me shudder. You may laugh, if you like!"

As he said these words, Gerfaut struck a violent blow upon the table with his fist.

"You forget that Mademoiselle de Corandeuil's room is just beneath us," said the artist, in a teasing way.

"Listen to me, Marillac! Your system with women is vulgar, gross, and trivial. The daisies which you gather, the maidens from whom you cut handfuls of hair excellent for stuffing mattresses, your rustic beauties with cheeks like rosy apples are conquests worthy of counter-jumpers in their Sunday clothes. That is

[165]

nothing but the very lowest grade of love-making, and yet you are right, a thousand times right, and wonderfully wise compared with me."

"You do me too much honor! So, then, you are not loved?"

"Truly, I had an idea I was, or, if I was not loved to-day, I hoped to be to-morrow. But you are mistaken as to what discourages me. I simply fear that her heart is narrow. I believe that she loves me as much as she is able to love; unfortunately, that is not enough for me."

"It certainly seems to me that, so far, she has not shown herself madly in love with you."

"Ah, madly! Do you know many women who love madly with their hearts and souls? You talk like a college braggart. There are conquerors like yourself who, if we are to believe them, would devour a whole convent at their breakfast. These men excite my pity. As for me, really, I have always felt that it was most difficult to make one's self really loved. In these days of prudery, almost all women of rank appear *frappé à la glace*, like a bottle of champagne. It is necessary to thaw them first, and there are some of them whose shells are so frigid that they would put out the devil's furnace. They call this virtue; I call it social servitude. But what matters the name? the result is the same."

"But, really, are you sure that Madame de Bergenheim loves you?" asked Marillac, emphasizing the word "love" so strongly as to attract his friend's attention.

"Sure? of course I am!" replied the latter. "Why do you ask me?"

"Because, when you are not quite so angry, I want to ask you something." He hesitated a moment. "If you learned that she cares more for another than for you, what would you do?"

Gerfaut looked at him and smiled disdainfully.

"Listen!" said he, "you have heard me storm and curse, and you took this nonsense for genuine hatred. My good fellow! do you know why I raved in such a manner? It was because, knowing my temperament, I felt the necessity of getting angry and giving vent to what was in my heart. If I had not employed this infallible remedy, the annoyance which this note caused me would have disturbed my nerves all night, and when I do not sleep my complexion is more leaden than usual and I have dark rings under my eyes."

"Fop!"

"Simpleton!"

"Why simpleton?"

"Do you take me for a dandy? Do you not understand why I wish to sleep soundly? It is simply because I do not wish to appear before her with a face like a ghost. That would be all that was needed to encourage her in her severity. I shall take good care that she does not discover how hard her last thrust has hit me. I would give you a one-hundred-franc note if I could secure for to-morrow morning your alderman's face and your complexion à la *Teniers*."

"Thanks, we are not masquerading just at present.

Nevertheless, all that you have said does not prove in the slightest that she loves you."

"My dear Marillac, words may have escaped me in my anger which have caused you to judge hastily. Now that I am calm and that my remedy has brought back my nervous system to its normal state, I will explain to you my real position. She is my Galatea, I her Pygmalion. 'An allegory as old as the world,' you are about to say; old or not, it is my true story. I have not yet broken the marble—virtue, education, propriety, duty, prejudices—which covers the flesh of my statue; but I am nearing my goal and I shall reach it. Her desperate resistance is the very proof of my progress. It is a terrible step for a woman to take, from No to Yes. My Galatea begins to feel the blows from my heart over her heart and she is afraid —afraid of the world, of me, of her husband, of herself, of heaven and hell. Do you not adore women who are afraid of everything? She, love another! never! It is written in all eternity that she shall be mine. What did you wish to say to me?"

"Nothing, since you are so sure of her."

"Sure—more than of my eternal life! But I wish to know what you mean."

"But you won't be told. Just a suspicion that came to me; something that was told to me the other day; a conjecture so vague that it would be useless to dwell upon it."

"I am not good at guessing enigmas," said Octave, in a dry tone.

"We will speak of this again to-morrow."

"As you like," replied the lover, with somewhat affected indifference. "If you wish to play the part of Iago with me, I warn you I am not disposed to jealousy."

"To-morrow, I tell you, I shall enlighten myself as to this affair; whatever the result of my inquiries may be, I will tell you the truth. After all, it was nothing but woman's gossip."

"Very well, take your time. But I have another favor to ask of you. To-morrow I shall try to persuade the ladies to take a walk in the park. Mademoiselle de Corandeuil will probably not go; you must do me the favor of sticking to Bergenheim and the little sister, and gradually to walk on ahead of us, in such a way as to give me an opportunity of speaking with this cruel creature alone for a few moments; for she has given me to understand that I shall not succeed in speaking with her alone under any circumstances, and it is absolutely necessary that I should do so."

"There will be one difficulty in the way, though—they expect about twenty persons at dinner, and all her time will probably be taken up with her duties as hostess."

"That is true," exclaimed Gerfaut, jumping up so suddenly that he upset his chair.

"You still forget that Mademoiselle de Corandeuil's room is beneath us."

"The devil is playing her hand!" exclaimed the lover, as he paced the room in long strides. "I wish that during the night he would wring the neck of all these visitors. Now, then, she has her innings. To-day and to-morrow this little despot's battle of Ligny will be fought and won; but the day after to-morrow, look out for her Waterloo!"

"Good-night, my Lord Wellington," said Marillac, as he arose and took up his candlestick.

"Good-night, Iago! Ah! you think you have annoyed me with your mysterious words and melodramatic reticence?"

"To-morrow! to-morrow!" replied the artist as he left the room.

> "Ce secret-là
> Se trahira."

CHAPTER XI

A QUARREL

HE next morning, before most of the inhabitants of the château had thought of leaving their beds, or at least their rooms, a man, on horseback, and alone, took his departure through a door opening from the stable-yard into the park. He wore a long travelling redingote trimmed with braid and fur, rather premature clothing for the season, but which the sharp cold air that was blowing at this moment made appear very comfortable. He galloped away, and continued this pace for about three-quarters of a mile, in spite of the unevenness of the road, which followed a nearly straight line over hilly ground. It would have been difficult to decide which to admire more, the horse's limbs or the rider's lungs; for the latter, during this rapid ride, had sung without taking breath, so to speak, the whole overture to *Wilhelm Tell*. We must admit that the voice in which he sang the *andante* of the Swiss mountaineer's chorus resembled a reed pipe more than a hautboy; but, to make amends when he reached the *presto*, his voice, a rather good bass, struck the horse's ears with such

force that the latter redoubled his vigor as if this melody had produced upon him the effect of a trumpet sounding the charge on the day of battle.

The traveller, whom we have probably recognized by his musical feat, concluded his concert by stopping at the entrance to some woods which extended from the top of the rocks to the river, breaking, here and there, the uniformity of the fields. After gazing about him for some time, he left the road and, entering the woods on the right, stopped at the foot of a large tree. Near this tree was a very small brook, which took its source not far away and descended with a sweet murmur to the river, making a narrow bed in the clayey ground which it watered. Such was the modesty of its course that a little brighter green and fresher grass a few feet away from it were the only indications of its presence. Nothing was wanting to make this an idyllic place for a rendezvous, neither the protecting shade, the warbling of birds in the trees, the picturesque landscape surrounding it, nor the soft grass.

After dismounting from his steed and tying him to the branches of an oak, thus conforming to the time-honored custom of lovers, the cavalier struck his foot upon the ground three or four times to start the circulation in his legs, and then drew from his pocket a very pretty Breguet watch.

"Ten minutes past eight," said he; "I am late and yet I am early. It looks as if the clocks at La Fauconnerie were not very well regulated." He walked up and down with a quick step whistling with a vengeance:

GERFAUT

"Quand je quittai la Normandie—
J'attends—j'attends—"

a refrain which the occasion brought to his mind.
When this pastime was exhausted he had recourse to
another, the nature of which proved that if the expected beauty had not punctuality for a virtue, she was
not one of those little exacting creatures always ready
to faint or whose delicate nerves make them intolerant of
their lovers' imperfections.   Plunging his hand into one
of the pockets in his redingote, the waiting cavalier drew
out a sealskin case filled with Havana cigars, and, light-
ing one, began to smoke, while continuing his promenade.

But at the end of a few moments this palliative, like
the first, had exhausted its effect.

"Twenty-five minutes past eight!" exclaimed Marillac, as he looked at his watch a second time; "I should
like to know what this little miniature rose takes me
for?   It was hardly worth the trouble of overstraining
this poor horse, who looks as wet as if he had come out
of the river.   It is enough to give him inflammation of
the lungs.   If Bergenheim were to see him sweating
and panting like this in this bleak wind, he would give
me a sound blowing-up.   Upon my word, it is becoming comical!   There are no more young girls!   I shall
see her appear presently as spruce and conceited as if
she had been playing the finest trick in the world.   It
will do for once; but if we sojourn in these quarters
some time yet, she must be educated and taught to
say, 'If you please' and 'Thanks.'   Ah! ha! she has
no idea what sort of man she is dealing with!   Half
past eight!   If she is not here in five minutes I shall

[173]

go to La Fauconnerie and raise a terrible uproar. I will break every bit of crockery there is in the Femme-sans-Tête with blows from my whip. What can I do to kill time?" He raised his head quickly, as he felt himself suddenly almost smothered under a shower of dust. This was a fatal movement for him, for his eyes received part of the libation destined for his hair. He closed them with a disagreeable sensation, after seeing Mademoiselle Reine Gobillot's fresh, chubby face, her figure prim beyond measure in a lilac-and-green plaid gingham dress, and carrying a basket on her arm, a necessary burden to maidens of a certain class who play truant.

"What sort of breeding is this?" exclaimed Maril-lac, rubbing his eyes; "you have made me dance attendance for an hour and now you have blinded me. I do not like this at all, you understand."

"How you scold me, just for a little pinch of dust!" replied Reine, turning as red as a cherry as she threw the remainder of the handful which she had taken from a mole-heap close by them.

"It is because it smarts like the devil," replied the artist, in a milder tone, for he realized the ridiculousness of his anger; "since you have hurt me, try at least to ease the pain; they say that to blow in the eye will cure it."

"No. I'll do nothing of the kind—I don't like to be spoken to harshly."

The artist arose at once as he saw the young girl make a movement as if to go; he put his arm about her waist and half forced her to sit beside him.

"The grass is damp and I shall stain my dress," said she, as a last resistance.

A handkerchief was at once spread upon the ground, in lieu of a carpet, by the lover, who had suddenly become very polite again.

"Now, my dear Reine," continued he, "will you tell me why you come so late? Do you know that for an hour I have been tearing my hair in despair?"

"Perhaps the dust will make it grow again," she replied, with a malicious glance at Marillac, whose head was powdered with brown dust as if a tobacco-box had been emptied upon it.

"Naughty girl!" he exclaimed, laughing, although his eyes looked as if he were crying; and, acting upon the principle of retaliation less odious in love than in war, he tried to snatch a kiss to punish her.

"Stop that, Monsieur Marillac! you know very well what you promised me."

"To love you forever, you entrancing creature," said he, in the voice of a crocodile that sighs to attract his prey.

Reine pursed up her lips and assumed important airs, but, in order to obey the feminine instinct which prescribes changing the subject of conversation after too direct an avowal, with the firm intention of returning to it later through another channel, she said:

"What were you doing just as I arrived? You were so busy you did not hear me coming. You were so droll; you waved your arms in the air and struck your forehead as you talked."

"I was thinking of you."

[175]

"But it was not necessary, in order to do that, to strike your head with your fist. It must have hurt you."

"Adorable woman!" exclaimed the artist, in a passionate tone.

"*Mon Dieu!* how you frighten me. If I had known I would not have come here at all. I must go away directly."

"Leave me already, queen of my heart! No! do not expect to do that; I would sooner lose my life——"

"Will you stop! what if some one should hear you? they might be passing," said Reine, gazing anxiously about her. "If you knew how frightened I was in coming! I told mamma that I was going to the mill to see my uncle; but that horrid old Lambernier met me just as I entered the woods. What shall I do if he tells that he saw me? This is not the road to the mill. It is to be hoped that he has not followed me! I should be in a pretty plight!"

"You can say that you came to gather berries or nuts, or to hear the nightingale sing; Mother Gobillot will not think anything of it. Who is this Lambernier?"

"You know—the carpenter. You saw him at our house the other day."

"Ah! ah!" said Marillac, with interest, "the one who was turned away from the château?"

"Yes, and they did well to do it, too; he is a downright bad man."

"He is the one who told you something about Madame de Bergenheim. Tell me the story. Your mother interrupted us yesterday just as you began telling it to me.—What was it that he said?"

"Oh! falsehoods probably. One can not believe anything that he says."

"But what did he tell you?"

"What difference does it make to you what is said about the Baroness?" replied the young girl, rather spitefully, as she saw that Marillac was not occupied in thinking of her exclusively.

"Pure curiosity. He told you then that he would tell the Baron what he knew, and that the latter would give him plenty of money to make him keep silent?"

"It makes no difference what he told me. Ask him if you wish to know. Why did you not stay at the château if you can think only of the Baroness? Are you in love with her?"

"I am in love with you, my dear. [The devil take me if she is not jealous now! How shall I make her talk?] I am of the same opinion as you," he replied, in a loud voice, "that all this talk of Lambernier's is pure calumny."

"There is no doubt about it. He is well known about the place; he has a wicked tongue and watches everything that one does or says in order to report it at cross-purposes. *Mon Dieu!* suppose he should make some story out of his seeing me enter these woods!"

"Madame de Bergenheim," continued the artist, with affectation, "is certainly far above the gossip of a scoundrel of this kind."

Reine pursed up her lips, but made no reply.

"She has too many good qualities and virtues for people to believe anything he says."

"Oh, as to that, there are hypocrites among the Parisian ladies as well as elsewhere," said the young girl, with a sour look.

"Bless me!" thought Marillac, "we have it now. I'd wager my last franc that I'll loosen her tongue."

"Madame de Bergenheim," he replied, emphasizing each word, "is such a good woman, so sensible and so pretty!"

"*Mon Dieu!* say that you love her at once, then— that'll be plain talk," exclaimed Reine, suddenly disengaging herself from the arm which was still about her waist. "A great lady who has her carriages and footmen in livery is a conquest to boast of! While a country girl, who has only her virtue——"

She lowered her eyes with an air of affected modesty, and did not finish her sentence.

"A virtue which grants a rendezvous at the end of three days' acquaintance, and in the depths of the woods! That is amusing!" thought the artist.

"Still, you will not be the first of the fine lady's lovers," she continued, raising her head and trying to conceal her vexation under an ironical air.

"These are falsehoods."

"Falsehoods, when I tell you that I know what I am speaking about! Lambernier is not a liar."

"Lambernier is not a liar?" repeated a harsh, hoarse voice, which seemed to come from the cavity of the tree under which they were seated. "Who has said that Lambernier was a liar?"

At the same moment, the carpenter in person suddenly appeared upon the scene. He stood before the amazed pair with his brown coat thrown over his shoulders, as usual, and his broad-brimmed gray hat pulled down over his ears, gazing at them with his deep, ugly eyes and a sardonic laugh escaping from his lips.

Mademoiselle Reine uttered a shriek as if she had seen Satan rise up from the ground at her feet; Marillac rose with a bound and seized his whip.

"You are a very insolent fellow," said he, in his ringing bass voice. "Go your way!"

"I receive no such orders," replied the workman, in a tone which justified the epithet which had just been bestowed upon him; "we are upon public ground, and I have a right to be here as well as you."

"If you do not take to your heels at once," said the artist, becoming purple with rage, "I will cut your face in two."

"Apples are sometimes cut in two," said Lambernier, sneeringly advancing his face with an air of bravado. "My face is not afraid of your whip; you can not frighten me because you are a gentleman and I am a workman! I snap my fingers at *bourgeois* like——"

This time he did not have time to finish his comparison; a blow from the whip cut him in the face and made him reel in spite of himself.

"By heaven!" he exclaimed, in a voice like thunder, "may I lose my name if I do not polish you off well!"

He threw his coat on the grass, spat in his hands

and rubbed them together, assuming the position of an athlete ready for a boxing-bout.

Mademoiselle Gobillot, arose, trembling with fright at this demonstration, and uttered two or three inarticulate cries; but, instead of throwing herself between the combatants in the approved style, she ran away as fast as she could.

Although the weapons of the adversaries were not of a nature to spill blood upon the turf, there was something warlike about their countenances which would have done honor to ancient paladins. Lambernier squatting upon his legs, according to the rules of pugilism, and with his fists on a level with his shoulders, resembled, somewhat, a cat ready to bound upon its prey. The artist stood with his body thrown backward, his legs on a tension, his chin buried up to his moustache in the fur collar of his coat, with whip lowered, watching all his adversary's movements with a steady eye. When he saw the carpenter advancing toward him, he raised his arm and gave him on the left side a second lash from his whip, so vigorously applied that the workman beat a retreat once more, rubbing his hands and roaring:

"Thunder! I'll finish you——"

He put his hands in his trousers' pockets and drew out one of those large iron compasses such as carpenters use, and opened it with a rapid movement. He then seized it in the centre and was thus armed with a sort of double-pointed stiletto, which he brandished with a threatening gesture.

Marillac, at this sight, drew back a few paces, passed

his whip to his left hand and, arming himself with his Corsican poniard, placed himself in a position of defence.

"My friend," said he, with perfect deliberation, "my needle is shorter than yours, but it pricks better. If you take one step nearer me, if you raise your hand, I will bleed you like a wild boar."

Seeing the firm attitude of the artist, whose solid figure seemed to denote rather uncommon vigor, and whose moustache and sparkling eyes gave him a rather formidable aspect at this moment; above all, when he saw the large, sharp blade of the poniard, Lambernier stopped.

"By the gods!" exclaimed Marillac, who saw that his bold looks had produced their effect, "you are a Provençal, and I a Gascon. You have a quick hand, comrade——"

"But, by Jove! you are the one who has the quick hand; you struck me with your whip as if I had been a horse. You have put my eye almost out. Do you imagine that I am well provided for like yourself and have nothing to do but to flirt with girls? I need my eyes in order to work, by God! Because you are a *bourgeois* and I am a workman——"

"I am not more of a *bourgeois* than you," replied the artist, rather glad to see his adversary's fury exhaust itself in words, and his attitude assume a less threatening character; "pick up your compass and return to your work. Here," he added, taking two five-franc pieces from his pocket. "You were a little boorish and I a little hasty. Go and bathe your eyes with a glass of wine."

CHARLES DE BERNARD

Lambernier scowled and his eyes darted ugly, hateful glances. He hesitated a moment, as if he were thinking what he had better do, and was weighing his chances of success in case of a hostile resolve. After a few moments' reflection, prudence got the better of his anger. He closed his compass and put it in his pocket, but he refused the silver offered him.

"You are generous," said he, with a bitter smile; "five francs for each blow of the whip! I know a good many people who would offer you their cheek twelve hours of the day at that price. But I am not one of that kind; I ask nothing of nobody."

"If Leonardo da Vinci could have seen this fellow's face just now," thought the artist, "he would not have had to seek so long for his model for the face of Judas. Only for my poniard, my fate would have been settled. This man was ready to murder me.

"Listen, Lambernier," said he, "I was wrong to strike you, and I would like to atone for it. I have been told that you were sent away from the château against your will. I am intimate enough with Monsieur de Bergenheim to be useful to you; do you wish me to speak to him for you?"

The carpenter stood motionless in his place, with his eyes fixed upon his adversary while the latter was preparing his horse to mount, eyes which seemed filled with hatred to their very depths. His face suddenly changed its expression and became abjectly polite when he heard himself addressed anew. He shook his head two or three times before replying.

"Unless you are the very devil," he said, "I defy

you to make this gentleman say yes when he has once said no. He turned me away like a dog; all right. Let them laugh that win. It was that old idiot of a Rousselet and that old simpleton of a coachman of Mademoiselle de Corandeuil's who told tales about me. I could tell tales also if I liked."

"But what motive could they have to send you away?" continued Marillac, "you are a clever workman. I have seen your work at the château; there are some rooms yet unfinished; there must have been some very grave reason for their not employing you just at the moment when they needed you most."

"They said that I talked with Mademoiselle Justine, and Madame caused me to be discharged. She is mistress there, is she not? But I am the one to make her repent for it."

"And how can you make her repent for it?" asked the artist, whose curiosity, left ungratified by Mademoiselle Reine, was growing more and more excited, "what can you have in common with Madame la Baronne?"

"Because she is a lady and I am a workman, you mean? All the same, if I could only whisper two or three words in her ear, she would give me more gold than I have earned since I worked at the château, I am sure of it."

"By the powers! if I were in your place, I would say those words to her this very day."

"So as to be thrown out by that band of idle fellows in their red coats. None of that for me. I have my own scheme; let them laugh that win!"

As he repeated this proverb, the workman uttered his usual sardonic laugh.

"Lambernier," said the artist, in a serious tone, "I have heard of certain very strange speeches that you have made within the last few days. Do you know that there is a punishment by law for those who invent calumnies?"

"Is it a calumny, when one can prove what he says?" replied the carpenter, with assurance.

"What is it that you undertake to prove?" exclaimed Marillac, suddenly.

"Eh! you know very well that if Monsieur le Baron ——" he did not continue, but with a coarse gesture he finished explaining his thoughts.

"You can prove this?"

"Before the courts, if necessary."

"Before the courts would not amount to very much for you; but if you will cease this talk and never open your mouth about all this, whatever it may be, and will give to me, and me only, this proof of which you speak, I will give you ten napoleons."

For a moment Lambernier gazed at the artist with a singularly penetrating glance.

"So you have two sweethearts, then—one from the city and one from the country, a married woman and this poor girl," said he, in a jeering tone; "does little Reine know that she is playing second fiddle?"

"What do you mean to insinuate?"

"Oh! you are more clever than I."

The two men looked at each other in silence, trying to read each other's thoughts.

"This is a lover of Madame de Bergenheim," thought Lambernier, with the barefaced impudence of his kind; "if I were to tell him what I know, my vengeance would be in good hands, without my taking the trouble to commit myself."

"Here is a sneaking fellow who pretends to be deucedly strong in diplomacy," said Marillac to himself; "but he is revengeful and I must make him explain himself."

"Ten napoleons are not to be found every day," continued the carpenter, after a moment's silence; "you may give them to me, if you like, in a week."

"You will be able to prove to me, then, what you have said," replied Marillac, with hesitation, blushing in spite of himself at the part he was playing at that moment, upon the odious side of which he had not looked until now. "Bah!" said he to himself, in order to quiet his conscience, "if this rascal really knows anything it is much better that I should buy the secret than anybody else. I never should take advantage of it, and I might be able to render the lady a service. Is it not a gentleman's sworn duty to devote himself to the defence of an imprudent beauty who is in danger?"

"I will bring you the proof you want," said the carpenter.

"When?"

"Meet me Monday at four o'clock in the afternoon at the cross-roads near the corner of the Corne woods."

"At the end of the park?"

"Yes, a little above the rocks."

"I will be there. Until then, you will not say a word to anybody?"

"That is a bargain, since you buy the goods I have for sale——"

"Here is some money to bind the trade," replied the artist. And he handed him the silver pieces he still held in his hand; Lambernier took them this time without any objections, and put them in his pocket.

"Monday, at four o'clock!"

"Monday, at four o'clock!" repeated Marillac, as he mounted his horse and rode away in great haste as if eager to take leave of his companion. He turned when he reached the road, and, looking behind him, saw the workman standing motionless at the foot of the tree.

"There is a scamp," thought he, "whose ball and chain are waiting for him at Toulon or Brest, and I have just concluded a devilish treaty with him. Bah! I have nothing to reproach myself with. Of two evils choose the least; it remains to be seen whether Gerfaut is the dupe of a coquette or whether his love is threatened with some catastrophe; at all events, I am his friend, and I ought to clear up this mystery and put him on his guard."

"Ten francs to-day, and ten napoleons Monday," said Lambernier as, with an eye in which there was a mixture of scorn and hatred, he watched the traveller disappear. "I should be a double idiot to refuse. But this does not pay for the blows from your whip, you puppy; when we have settled this affair of the fine lady, I shall attend to you."

CHAPTER XII

HE visitors referred to in the conversation between the two friends arrived at the castle at an early hour, according to the custom in the country, where they dine in the middle of the day. Gerfaut saw from his chamber, where he had remained like Achilles under his tent, half a dozen carriages drive one after another up the avenue, bringing the guests announced by Marillac. Little by little the company scattered through the gardens in groups; four or five young girls under Aline's escort hurried to a swing, to which several good-natured young men attached themselves, and among them Gerfaut recognized his Pylades. During this time Madame de Bergenheim was doing the honors of the house to the matrons, who thought this amusement too youthful for their age and preferred a quiet walk through the park. Christian, on his side, was explaining methods of improvements to gentlemen of agricultural and industrial appearance, who seemed to listen to him with great interest. Three or four others had taken possession of the billiard-table, while the more venerable among the guests had remained in the parlor with Mademoiselle de Corandeuil.

CHARLES DE BERNARD

"Have you a pair of clean trousers?" asked Maril-lac, hastily entering his friend's room as the first bell rang for dinner. An enormous green stain upon one of his knees was all the explanation necessary on this subject.

"You lose no time," said Gerfaut, as he opened a drawer in his closet. "Which of these rustic beauties has had the honor of seeing you on your knees at her feet?"

"It was that confounded swing! Silly invention! To sacrifice one's self to please little girls! If I am ever caught at it again I'll let you know! Your self-ish method is a better one. By the way, Madame de Bergenheim asked me, with a rather sly look, whether you were ill and whether you would not come down to dinner?"

"Irony!"

"It seemed like it. The lady smiled in a decidedly disagreeable manner. I am not timid, but I would rather write a vaudeville in three acts than to be obliged to make a declaration to her if she had that impish smile on her lips. She has a way of protruding her under lip—ugh! do you know you are terribly slender? Will you let me cut the band of your trousers? I never could dance with my stomach compressed in this manner."

"What about this secret you were to reveal to me?" Gerfaut interrupted, with a smile which seemed to de-note perfect security.

Marillac looked at his friend with a grave counte-nance, then began to laugh in an embarrassed manner.

GERFAUT

"We will leave serious matters until to-morrow," he replied. "The essential thing to-day is to make ourselves agreeable. Madame de Bergenheim asked me a little while ago whether we would be kind enough to sing a few duets? I accepted for us both. I do not suppose that the inhabitants of this valley have often heard the duet from *Mosé* with the embellishments *à la* Tamburini—

> "*Palpito a quello aspetto,*
> '*Gemo nel suo dolor.*'

Would you prefer that or the one from *Il Barbiere?* although that is out of date, now."

"Whatever pleases you, but do not split my head about it in advance. I wish that music and dancing were at the bottom of the Moselle."

"With all my heart, but not the dinner. I gave a glance into the dining-room; it promises to be very fine. Now, then, everybody has returned to the house; to the table!"

The time has long since passed when Paris and the province formed two regions almost foreign to each other. To-day, thanks to the rapidity of communication, and the importations of all kinds which reach the centre from the circumference without having time to spoil on the way, Paris and the rest of France are only one immense body excited by the same opinions, dressed in the same fashions, laughing at the same *bon mot*, revolutionized by the same opinions.

Provincial customs have almost entirely lost their peculiarities; a drawing-room filled with guests is the same everywhere. There are sometimes exceptions, however. The company gathered at the Bergenheim château was an example of one of those heterogeneous assemblies which the most exclusive mistress of a mansion can not avoid if she wishes to be neighborly, and in which a duchess may have on her right at the table the village mayor, and the most elegant of ladies a corpulent justice of the peace who believes he is making himself agreeable when he urges his fair neighbor to frequent potations.

Madame de Bergenheim had discovered symptoms of haughty jealousy among her country neighbors, always ready to feel themselves insulted and very little qualified to make themselves agreeable in society. So she resolved to extend a general invitation to all those whom she felt obliged to receive, in order to relieve herself at once of a nuisance for which no pleasure could prove an equivalent. This day was one of her duty days.

Among these ladies, much more gorgeously than elegantly attired, these healthy young girls with large arms, and feet shaped like flat-irons, ponderous gentlemen strangled by their white cravats and puffed up in their frock-coats, Gerfaut, whose nervous system had been singularly irritated by his disappointment of the night before, felt ready to burst with rage. He was seated at the table between two ladies, who seemed to have exhausted, in their toilettes, every color in the solar spectrum, and whose coquettish instincts were aroused by the proximity of a celebrated writer. But their simperings were all lost; the one for whom they

were intended bore himself in a sulky way, which fortunately passed for romantic melancholy; this rendered
him still more interesting in the eyes of his neighbor
on the left, a plump blonde about twenty-five years
old, fresh and dimpled, who doted upon Lord Byron,
a common pretension among pretty, buxom women
who adore false sentimentality.

With the exception of a bow when he entered the
drawing-room, Octave had not shown Madame de
Bergenheim any attention. The cold, disdainful,
bored manner in which he patiently endured the
pleasures of the day exceeded even the privilege for
boorish bearing willingly granted to gentlemen of
unquestionable talent. Clémence, on the contrary,
seemed to increase in amiability and liveliness. There
was not one of her tiresome guests to whom she did not
address some pleasant remark, not one of those vulgar,
pretentious women to whom she was not gracious and
attentive; one would have said that she had a particular desire to be more attractive than usual, and that
her lover's sombre air added materially to her good
humor.

After dinner they retired to the drawing-room where
coffee was served. A sudden shower, whose drops
pattered loudly against the windows, rendered impossible all plans for amusement out of doors. Gerfaut soon noticed a rather animated conversation taking place between Madame de Bergenheim, who was
somewhat embarrassed as to how to amuse her guests
for the remainder of the afternoon, and Marillac, who,
with his accustomed enthusiasm, had constituted him-

self master of ceremonies. A moment later, the drawing-room door opened, and servants appeared bending
under the burden of an enormous grand piano which
was placed between the windows. At this sight, a
tremor of delight ran through the group of young girls,
while Octave, who was standing in one corner near the
mantel, finished his Mocha with a still more melancholy air.

"Now, then!" said Marillac, who had been extremely busy during these preparations, and had spread
a dozen musical scores upon the top of the piano, "it
is agreed that we shall sing the duet from *Mosè*. There
are two or three little boarding-school misses here
whose mothers are dying for them to show off. You
understand that we must sacrifice ourselves to encourage them. Besides, a duet for male voices is the thing
to open a concert with."

"A concert! has Madame de Bergenheim arranged
to pasture us in this sheepfold in order to make use of
us this evening?" replied Gerfaut, whose ill-humor increased every moment.

"Five or six pieces only, afterward they will have a
dance. I have an engagement with your diva; if
you wish for a quadrille and have not yet secured your
number, I should advise you to ask her for it now, for
there are five or six dandies who seem to be terribly
attentive to her. After our duet I shall sing the trio
from *La Dame Blanche*, with those young ladies who
have eyes as round as a fish's, and apricot-colored
gowns on—those two over there in the corner, near
that pretty blonde who sat beside you at table and

ogled you all the time. She had already bored me to death! I do not know whether I shall be able to hit my low 'G' right or not. I have a cataclysm of charlotte-russe in my stomach. Just listen:

'*A cette complaisance!—*'"

Marillac leaned toward his friend and roared in his ear the note supposed to be the "G" in question.

"Like an ophicleide," said Gerfaut, who could not help laughing at the importance the artist attached to his display of talent.

"In that case I shall risk my great run at the end of the first solo. Two octaves from 'E' to 'E'! Zuchelli was good enough to give me a few points as to the time, and I do it rather nicely."

"Madame would like to speak to Monsieur," said a servant, who interrupted him in the midst of his sentence.

"*Dolce, soave amor,*" warbled the artist, softly, as he responded to the call from the lady of the house, trying to fix in his mind that run, which he regarded as one of the most beautiful flowers in his musical crown.

Everybody was seated, Madame de Bergenheim sat at the piano and Marillac stood behind her. The artist selected one of the scores, spread it out on the rack, turned down the corners so that during the execution he might not be stopped by some refractory leaf, coughed in his deep bass voice, placed himself in such a manner as to show the side of his head which he thought would produce the best effect upon the audience, then gave a knowing nod to Gerfaut, who still stood gloomy and isolated in a far corner.

"We trespass upon your kindness too much, Monsieur," said Madame de Bergenheim to him, when he had responded to this mute invitation; and as she struck a few chords, she raised her dark, brown eyes to his. It was the first glance she had given him that day; from coquetry, perhaps, or because sorrow for her lover had softened her heart, or because she felt remorse for the extreme harshness of her note the night before, we must admit that this glance had nothing very discouraging in it. Octave bowed, and spoke a few words as coldly polite as he would have spoken to a woman sixty years of age.

Madame de Bergenheim lowered her eyes and endeavored to smile disdainfully, as she struck the first bars of the duet.

The concert began. Gerfaut had a sweet, clear, tenor voice which he used skilfully, gliding over dangerous passages, skipping too difficult ones which he thought beyond his execution, singing, in fact, with the prudence of an amateur who can not spend his time studying runs and chromatic passages four hours daily. He sang his solo with a simplicity bordering upon negligence, and even substituted for the rather complicated passage at the end a more than modest ending.

Clémence, for whom he had often sung, putting his whole soul into the performance, was vexed with this affectation of indifference. It seemed to her as if he ought, for her sake, to make more of an effort in her drawing-room, whatever might be their private quarrel; she felt it was a consideration due to her and to which his numerous homages had accustomed her. She entered this new grievance in a double-entry book, which a woman always devotes to the slightest actions of the man who pays court to her.

Marillac, on the contrary, was grateful to his friend for this indifference of execution, for he saw in it an occasion to shine at his expense. He began his solo *E il ciel per noi sereno*, with an unusual tension of the larynx, roaring out his low notes. Except for the extension being a little irregular and unconnected, he did not acquit himself very badly in the first part. When he reached his final run, he took a long breath, as if it devolved upon him to set in motion all the windmills in Montmartre, and started with a majestic fury; the first forty notes, while they did not resemble Mademoiselle Grisi's pearly tones, ascended and descended without any notable accident; but at the last stages of the descent, the singer's breath and voice failed him at the same moment, the "A" came out weak, the "G" was stifled, the "F" resembled the buzzing of a bee, and the "E" was absent!

Zuchelli's run was like one of those Gothic staircases which show an almost complete state of preservation upon the upper floor, but whose base, worn by time, leaves a solution of continuity between the ground and the last step.

Madame de Bergenheim waited the conclusion of this dangerous run, not thinking to strike the final chord; the only sound heard was the rustling of the dilettante's beard, as his chin sought his voice in vain in the depths of his satin cravat, accompanied by applause from a benevolent old lady who had judged of the merit of the execution by the desperate contortions of the singer.

"D——n that charlotte-russe!" growled the artist, whose face was as red as a lobster.

The rest of the duet was sung without any new incident, and gave general satisfaction.

"Madame, your piano is half a tone too low," said the basso, with a reproachful accent.

"That is true," replied Clémence, who could not restrain a smile; "I have so little voice that I am obliged to have my piano tuned to suit it. You can well afford to pardon me for my selfishness, for you sang like an angel."

Marillac bowed, partly consoled by this compliment, but thinking to himself that a hostess's first duty was to have her piano in tune, and not to expose a bass singer to the danger of imperilling his low "E" before an audience of forty.

"Madame, can I be of any more service to you?" asked Gerfaut, as he leaned toward Madame de Bergenheim, with one of his coldest smiles.

"I do not wish to impose further upon your kindness, Monsieur," said she, in a voice which showed her secret displeasure.

The poet bowed and walked away.

Then Clémence, upon general request, sang a romance with more taste than brilliancy, and more method than expression. It seemed as if Octave's icy manner had reacted upon her, in spite of the efforts she had made at first to maintain a cheerful air. A singular oppression overcame her; once or twice she feared her voice would fail her entirely. When she finished, the compliments and applause with which she was overwhlemed seemed so insupportable to her that it was with difficulty she could restrain herself from leaving the room. While exasperated by her weakness, she could not help casting a glance in Octave's direction. She could not catch his eye, however, as he was busy talking with Aline. She felt so lonely and deserted at this moment, and longed so for this glance which she could not obtain, that tears of vexation filled her eyes.

"I was wrong to write him as I did," thought she; "but if he really loved me, he would not so quickly resign himself to obeying me!"

A woman in a drawing-room resembles a soldier on a breastwork; self-abnegation is the first of her duties; however much she may suffer, she must present as calm and serene a countenance as a warrior in the hour of danger, and fall, if necessary, upon the spot, with death in her heart and a smile upon her lips. In order to obey this unwritten law, Madame de Bergenheim, after a slight interruption, seated herself at the piano to accompany three or four young girls who were each to sing in turn the songs that they had been drilled on for six months.

Marillac, who had gone to strengthen his stomach with a glass of rum, atoned for his little mishap, in the trio from *La Dame Blanche*, and everything went smoothly. Finally, to close this concert (may heaven preserve us from all exhibitions of this kind!), Aline was led to the piano by her brother, who, like all people who are not musical, could not understand why one should study music for years if not from love for the art. Christian was fond of his little sister and very proud of her talents. The poor child, whose courage had all disappeared, sang in a fresh, trembling little voice, a romance revised and corrected at her boarding-school. The word love had been replaced by that of friendship, and to repair this slight fault of prosody, the extra syllable disappeared in a hiatus which would have made Boileau's blond wig stand on end. But the Sacred Heart has a system of versification of its own which, rather than allow the dangerous expression to be used, let ultra-modesty destroy poetry!

This sample of sacred music was the final number of the concert; after that, they began dancing, and Gerfaut invited Aline. Whether because he wished to struggle against his ill-humor, or from kindness of heart because he understood her emotion, he began to talk with the young girl, who was still blushing at her success. Among his talents, Octave possessed in a peculiar degree that of adapting his conversation to the age, position, and character of his companions. Aline listened with unconcealed pleasure to her partner's words; the elasticity of her step and a sort of general trembling made her seem like a flower swaying to the breeze, and revealed the pleasure which his conversation gave her. Every time her eyes met Octave's penetrating glance they fell, out of instinctive modesty. Each word, however indifferent it might be, rang in her ears sweet and melodious; each contact with his hand seemed to her like a tender pressure.

Gerfaut experienced a feeling of melancholy as he noticed how this fresh, innocent rose brightened up at each word he uttered, and he thought:

"She would love me as I want to be loved, with all her heart, mind, and soul. She would kneel before my love as before an altar, while this coquette——"

He glanced in the direction where Madame de Bergenheim was dancing with Marillac, and met her gaze fixed full upon him. The glance which he received was rapid, displeased, and imperious. It signified clearly: "I forbid you to speak thus to your partner."

Octave, at that moment, was not disposed to obedience. After glancing over the quadrille, as if it were by mere chance that his eyes had met Clémence's, he turned toward Aline and redoubled his amiability

A moment later, he received, not directly, but through the medium of the mirror—that so often indiscreet confidant—a second glance more sombre and threatening than before.

"Very good," said he, to himself, as he led the young girl to her seat; "we are jealous. That alters the situation. I know now where the ramparts are the weakest and where to begin my attack."

No other incident marked the day. The guests left at nightfall, and the society was reduced to the usual members of the household. Octave entered his room after supper, humming an Italian air, evidently in such good spirits that his friend was quite surprised.

"I give it up, I can not understand your conduct," said the latter; "you have been as solemn as an owl all day, and now here you are as gay as a lark; have you had an understanding?"

"I am more vexed than ever."

"And you enjoy being so?"

"Very much."

"Ah! you are playing 'who loses wins!'"

"Not exactly; but as my good sentiments lead to nothing, I hope to conduct myself in such a disagreeable way as to force this capricious creature to adore me."

"The devil! that is clever. Besides, it is a system as good as any other. Women are such extraordinary creatures!"

"Woman," said Octave, "resembles a pendulum, whose movement is a continual reaction; when it moves to the right, it has to go to the left in order to return to the right again, and so on. Suppose virtue is on one side and love on the other, and the feminine balance between them, the odds are that, having moved to the right in a violent manner, it will return none the less energetically to the left; for the longer a vibration has been, the greater play the contrary vibration has. In order to hasten the action of this pendulum I am about to attach to it—to act as extra balance-weight—a little anguish which I ought to have employed sooner."

"Why make her suffer, since you believe that she loves you?"

"Why? Because she drives me to it. Do you fancy

that I torture her willingly; that I take pleasure in seeing her cheeks grow pale from insomnia and her eyes show traces of tears? I love her, I tell you; I suffer and weep with her. But I love her, and I must make sure of her love. If she will leave but a road full of brambles and sharp stones for me to reach her, must I give up the struggle just because I run the risk by taking her with me, of wounding her charming feet? I will cure them with my kisses!"

"Listen to me! I am not in love; I am an artist. If I have some peculiar ideas, it is not my fault. And you, in your character of docile lover, have you decided to yield?"

"Morally."

"Very well! after all, you are right. The science of love resembles those old signs upon which one reads: 'Here, hair is dressed according to one's fancy.' If this angel wishes her hair pulled, do it for her."

CHAPTER XIII

SOME men in society marry too soon, a great number too late, a small and fortunate proportion at an opportune time. Young men in the country, of good family, are usually established in marriage by their parents as early as possible. When the family council finds an heiress who answers all the conditions of the programme laid out, they begin by giving the victim his cue. Provided the young lady has not a positively crooked nose, arms too red, and too uncouth a waist—sometimes even notwithstanding these little misfortunes—the transaction is concluded without any difficulty.

Clémence and Christian should be placed in the first rank of privileged couples of this kind. The most fastidious old uncle or precise old dowager could not discover the slightest pretense for criticism. Age, social position, wealth, physical endowments, all seemed united by a chance as rare as fortunate. So Mademoiselle de Corandeuil, who had very high pretensions for her niece, made no objection upon receiving the first overtures. She had not, at this time, the antipathy for her future nephew's family which developed later. The Bergenheims were in her eyes very well-born gentleman.

A meeting took place at the Russian Embassy. Bergenheim came in uniform; it was etiquette to do so, as the minister of war was present; but at the same time, of course, there was a little vanity on his part, for his uniform showed off his tall, athletic figure to the best advantage. Christian was certainly a very handsome soldier; his moustache and eyebrows were of a lighter tint than his complexion, and gave him that martial air which pleases women. Clémence could find no reason for a refusal. The way in which she had been brought up by her aunt had not rendered her so happy but that she often desired to change her situation. Like the greater number of young girls, she consented to become a wife so as not to remain a maiden; she said yes, so as not to say no.

As to Christian, he was in love with his wife as nine out of ten cavalry officers know how to love, and he seemed perfectly satisfied with the sentiment that he received in return for this sudden affection. A few successes with young belles, for whom an epaulette has an irresistible attraction, had inspired Baron de Bergenheim with a confidence in himself the simplicity of which excused the conceit. He persuaded himself that he pleased Clémence because she suited him exactly.

There are singers who pretend to read music at sight; give them a score by Glück—"I beg your pardon," they will say, "my part is written here in the key of 'C' and I sing only in the key of 'G'!" How many men do not know even the key of 'G' in matters of love! Unfortunately for him, Bergenheim was one of that number. After three years of married life, he had not divined the first note in Clémence's character. He decided in his own mind, at the end of a few months, that she was cold, if not heartless. This discovery, which ought to have wounded his vanity, inspired him, on the contrary, with a deeper respect for her; insensibly this reserve reacted upon himself, for love is a fire whose heat dies out for want of fuel, and its cooling off is more sudden when the flame is more on the surface than in the depths.

The revolution of 1830 stopped Christian's career, and gave further pretexts for temporary absences which only added to the coolness which already existed between husband and wife. After handing in his resignation, the Baron fixed his residence at his château in the Vosges mountains, for which he shared the hereditary predilection of his family. His tastes were in perfect harmony with this dwelling, for he had quickly become the perfect type of a country gentleman, scorning the court and rarely leaving his ancestral acres. He was too kind-hearted to exact that his wife should share his country tastes and retired life. The unlimited confidence which he had in her, a loyalty which never allowed him to suppose evil or suspect her, a nature very little inclined to jealousy, made him allow Clémence the greatest liberty. The young woman lived at will in Paris with her aunt, or at Bergenheim with her husband, without a suspicious thought ever entering his head. Really, what had he to fear? What wrong could she reproach him with? Was he not full of kindness and attention toward her? Did he not leave her mistress of her own fortune, free to do as she liked, to gratify every caprice? He thus lived upon his faith in the marriage contract, with unbounded confidence and old-fashioned loyalty.

According to general opinion, Madame de Bergenheim was a very fortunate woman, to whom virtue must be so easy that it could hardly be called a merit. Happiness, according to society, consists in a box at the Opera, a fine carriage, and a husband who pays the bills without frowning. Add to the above privileges, a hundred thousand francs' worth of diamonds, and a woman has really no right to dream or to suffer. There are, however, poor, loving creatures who stifle under this happiness as if under one of those leaden covers that Dante speaks of; they breathe, in imagination, the pure, vital air that a fatal instinct has revealed to them; they struggle between duty and desire; they gaze, like captive doves and with a sorrowful eye, upon the forbidden region where it would be so blissful to soar; for, in fastening a chain to their feet, the law did not bandage their eyes, and nature gave them wings; if the wings tear the chain asunder, shame and misfortune await them! Society will never forgive the heart that catches a glimpse of the joys it is unacquainted with; even a brief hour in that paradise has to be expiated by implacable social damnation and its everlasting flames.

CHAPTER XIV

GERFAUT'S ALLEGORY

THERE almost always comes a moment when a woman, in her combat against love, is obliged to call falsehood to the help of duty. Madame de Bergenheim had entered this terrible period, in which virtue, doubting its own strength, does not blush to resort to other resources. At the moment when Octave, a man of experience, was seeking assistance in exciting her jealousy, she was meditating a plan of defence founded upon deceit. In order to take away all hope from her lover, she pretended a sudden affection for her husband, and in spite of her secret remorse she persisted in this *rôle* for two days; but during the night her tears expiated her treachery. Christian greeted his wife's virtuous coquetry with the gratitude and eagerness of a husband who has been deprived of love more than he likes. Gerfaut was very indignant at the sight of this perfidious manœuvre, the intention of which he immediately divined; and his rage wanted only provocation to break out in full force.

One evening they were all gathered in the drawing-room with the exception of Aline, whom a reprimand from Mademoiselle de Corandeuil had exiled to her room. The old lady, stretched out in her chair, had decided to be unfaithful to her whist in favor of conversation. Marillac, leaning his elbows upon a round table, was negligently sketching some political caricatures, at that time very much the fashion, and particularly agreeable to the Legitimist party. Christian, who was seated near his wife, whose hand he was pressing with caressing familiarity, passed from one subject to another, and showed in his conversation the overwhelming conceit of a happy man who regards his happiness as a proof of superiority.

Gerfaut, standing, gazed gloomily at Clémence, who leaned toward her husband and seemed to listen eagerly to his slightest word. Bergenheim was a faithful admirer of the classics, as are all country gentlemen, who introduce a sentiment of propriety into their literary opinions and prefer the ancient writers to the modern, for the reason that their libraries are much richer in old works than in modern books. The Baron unmercifully sacrificed Victor Hugo and Alexandre Dumas, whom he had never read, upon the altar of Racine and Corneille, of which he possessed two or three editions, and yet it would have embarrassed him to recite half a dozen verses from them. Marillac boldly defended the cause of contemporary literature, which he considered as a personal matter, and poured out a profusion of sarcastic remarks in which there was more wit than good taste.

"The gods fell from Olympus, why should they not also fall from Parnassus?" said the artist, finally, with a triumphant air. "Say what you will, Bergenheim, your feeble opposition will not prevail against the instincts of the age. The future is ours, let me tell you, and we are the high priests of the new religion; is it not so, Gerfaut?"

At these words, Mademoiselle de Corandeuil shook her head, gravely.

"A new religion!" said she; "if this pretension should be verified you would only be guilty of heresy, and, without allowing myself to be taken in, I can understand how elevated minds and enthusiastic hearts might be attracted by the promises of a deceptive Utopia; but you, gentlemen, whom I believe to be sincere, do you not see to what an extent you delude yourselves? What you call religion is the most absolute negation of religious principles; it is the most distressing impiety ornamented with a certain sentimental hypocrisy which has not even the courage frankly to proclaim its principles."

"I swear to you, Mademoiselle, that I am religious three days out of four," replied Marillac; "that is something; there are some Christians who are pious only on Sunday."

"Materialism is the source from which modern literature takes its inspiration," continued the old lady; "and this poisonous stream not only dries up the thoughts which would expand toward heaven, but also withers all that is noble in human sentiment. To-day, people are not content to deny God, because they are not pure enough to comprehend Him; they disown even the weakness of the heart, provided they have an exalted and dignified character. They believe no longer in love. All the women that your fashionable writers tell us about are vulgar and sometimes unchaste creatures, to whom formerly a gentleman would have blushed to give one glance or to offer a supper. I say this for your benefit, Monsieur de Gerfaut, for in this respect you are far from being irreproachable; and I could bring forth your books to support my theory. If I accuse you of atheism, in love, what have you to say in reply?"

Carried away by one of those impulsive emotions which men of imagination can not resist, Octave arose and said:

"I should not deny such an accusation. Yes, it is a sad thing, but true, and only weak minds recoil from the truth: reality exists only in material objects; all the rest is merely deception and fancy. All poetry is a dream, all spiritualism a fraud! Why not apply to love the accommodating philosophy which takes the world as it is, and does not throw a savory fruit into the press under the pretext of extracting I know not what imaginary essence? Two beautiful eyes, a satin skin, white teeth, and a shapely foot and hand are of such positive and inestimable value! Is it not unreasonable, then, to place elsewhere than in them all the wealth of love? Intellect sustains its owner, they say; no, intelligence kills. It is thought that corrupts sensation and causes suffering where, but for that, joy would reign supreme.

"Thought! accursed gift! Do we give or ask a thought of the rose whose perfume we breathe? Why

14   [209]

not love as we breathe? Would not woman, considered simply as a perfectly organized vegetation, be the queen of creation? Why not enjoy her perfume as we bend before her, leaving her clinging to the ground where she was born and lives? Why tear her from the earth, this flower so fresh, and have her wither in our hands as we raise her up like an offering? Why make of so weak and fragile a creature a being above all others, for whom our enthusiasm can find no name, and then discover her to be but an unworthy angel?

"Angel! yes, of course, but an angel of the Earth, not of Heaven; an angel of flesh, not of light! By dint of loving, we love wrongly. We place our mistress too high and ourselves too low; there is never a pedestal lofty enough for her, according to our ideas. Fools! Oh! reflection is always wise, but desire is foolish, and our conduct is regulated by our desire. We, above all, with our active, restless minds, *blasé* in many respects, unbelieving in others and disrespectful in the remainder, soar over life as over an impure lake, and look at everything with contempt, seeking in love an altar before which we can humble our pride and soften our disdain.

"For there is in every man an insurmountable need to fall on his knees before no matter what idol, if it remains standing and allows itself to be adored. At certain hours, a prayer-bell rings in the depth of the heart, the sound of which throws him upon his knees as it cries: 'Kneel!' And then the very being who ignores God in His churches and scorns kings upon their thrones, the being who has already exhausted the hollow idols of glory and fame, not having a temple to pray in, makes a fetich for himself in order to have a divinity to adore, so as not to be alone in his impiety, and to see, above his head when he arises, something that shall not be empty and vacant space. This man seeks a woman, takes all that he has, talent passion, youth, enthusiasm, all the wealth of his heart, and throws them at her feet like the mantle that Raleigh spread out before Elizabeth, and he says to this woman: 'Walk, O my queen; trample under your blessed feet the heart of your adoring slave!' This man is a fool, is he not? For when the queen has passed, what remains upon the mantle? Mud!''

Gerfaut accompanied these words with such a withering glance that the one for whom they were intended felt her blood freeze in her veins, and withdrew the hand her husband had kept till then in his; she soon arose and seated herself at the other side of the table, under the pretext of getting nearer the lamp to work, but in reality in order to withdraw from Christian's vicinity. Clémence had expected her lover's anger, but not his scorn; she had not strength to endure this torture, and the conjugal love which had, not without difficulty, inflamed her heart for the last few days, fell to ashes at the first breath of Octave's indignation.

Mademoiselle de Corandeuil greeted the Vicomte's words indulgently; for, from consummate pride, she separated herself from other women.

"So then," said she, "you pretend that if to-day love is painted under false and vulgar colors, the fault is the model's, not the artist's."

"You express my thought much better than I could have done it myself," said Gerfaut, in an ironical tone; "where are the angels whose portraits are called for?"

"They are in our poetical dreams," said Marillac, raising his eyes to the ceiling with an inspired air.

"Very well! tell us your dreams then, instead of copying a reality which it is impossible for you to render poetic, since you yourselves see it without illusions."

Gerfaut smiled bitterly at this suggestion, artlessly uttered by the Baron.

"My dreams," he replied, "I should tell them to you poorly indeed, for the first blessing of the awakening is forgetfulness, and to-day I am awake. However, I remember how I allowed myself to be once overcome by a dream that has now vanished, but still emits its luminous trail in my eyes. I thought I had discovered, under a beautiful and attractive appearance, the richest treasure that the earth can bestow upon the heart of man; I thought I had discovered a soul, that divine mystery, deep as the ocean, ardent as a flame, pure as air, glorious as heaven itself, infinite as space, immortal as eternity! It was another universe, where I should be king. With what ardent and holy love I attempted the conquest of this new world, but, less fortunate than Columbus, I met with shipwreck instead of triumph."

Clémence, at this avowal of her lover's defeat, threw him a glance of intense contradiction, then lowered her eyes, for she felt her face suffused with burning blushes.

GERFAUT

When he entered his room that night, Gerfaut went straight to the window. He could see in the darkness the light which gleamed in Clémence's room.

"She is alone," said he to himself; "certainly heaven protects us, for in the state of exasperation I am in, I should have killed them both."

CHAPTER XV

DECLARATION OF WAR

AR from rejoicing at this moment in the triumph he had just obtained, Gerfaut fell into one of those attacks of disenchantment, during which, urged on by some unknown demon, he unmercifully administered to himself his own dreaded sarcasm. Being unable to sleep, he arose and opened his window again, and remained with his elbows resting upon the sill for some time. The night was calm, numberless stars twinkled in the heavens, the moon bathed with its silvery light the tops of the trees, through which a monotonous breeze softly rustled. After gazing at this melancholy picture of sleeping nature, the poet smiled disdainfully, and said to himself:

"This comedy must end. I can not waste my life thus. Doubtless, glory is a dream as well as love; to pass the night idiotically gazing at the moon and stars is, after all, as reasonable as to grow pale over a work destined to live a day, a year, or a century! for what renown lasts longer than that? If I were really loved, I should not regret those wasted hours; but is it true that I am loved? There are moments when I recover my coolness and clearness of mind, a degree of self-possession incompatible with the enthusiasm of genuine passion; at other times, it is true, a sudden agitation renders me powerless and leaves me as weak as a child. Oh, yes, I love her in a strange manner; the sentiment that I feel for her has become a study of the mind as well as an emotion of the heart, and that is what gives it its despotic tenacity; for a material impression weakens and gradually dies out, but when an energetic intelligence is brought to bear upon it, it becomes desperate. I should be wrong to complain. Passion, a passive sentiment! This word has a contradictory meaning for me. I am a lover as Napoleon was an emperor: nobody forced the crown upon him, he took it and crowned himself with his own hand. If my crown happens to be a thorny one, whom can I accuse? Did not my brow crave it?

"I have loved this woman of my own choosing, above all others; the choice made, I have worked at my love as I would at a cherished poem; it has been the subject of all my meditations, the fairy of all my dreams, for more than a year. I have not had a thought in which I have not paid her homage. I have devoted my talents to her; it seemed to me that by loving and perpetually contemplating her image, I might at last become worthy of painting it. I was conscious of a grand future, if only she had understood me; I often thought of Raphael and his own Fornarina. There is a throne vacant in poetry; I had dreamed of this throne in order to lay it at Clémence's feet. Oh! although this may never be more than a dream, this dream has given me hours of incomparable happiness! I should be ungrateful to deny it.

"And yet this love is only a fictitious sentiment; I realize it to-day. It is not with her that I am in love, it is with a woman created by my imagination, and whom I see clearly within this unfeeling marble shape. When we have meditated for a long time, our thoughts end by taking life and walking by our side. I can now understand the allegory of Adam taking Eve from his own substance; but flesh forms a palpitating flesh akin to itself; the mind creates only a shadow, and a shadow can not animate a dead body. Two dead bodies can not make a living one; a body without a soul is only a cadaver—and she has no soul."

Gerfaut sat motionless for some time with his face buried in his hands; suddenly he raised his head and burst into harsh laughter.

"Enough of this soaring in the clouds!" he exclaimed; "let us come down to earth again. It is permissible to think in verse, but one must act in prose, and that is what I shall do to-morrow. This woman's caprices, which she takes for efforts of virtue, have made of me a cruel and inexorable man; I have begged in vain for peace; if she wishes war, very well, so be it, she shall have war."

CHAPTER XVI

OR several days, Gerfaut followed, with unrelenting perseverance, the plan which he had mapped out in that eventful night. The most exacting woman could but appear satisfied with the politeness he displayed toward Madame de Bergenheim, but nothing in his conduct showed the slightest desire for an explanation. He was so careful of every look, gesture, and word of his, that it would have been impossible to discover the slightest difference in his actions toward Mademoiselle de Corandeuil, and the manner in which he treated Clémence. His choicest attentions and most particular efforts at amiability were bestowed upon Aline. He used as much caution as cunning, in his little game, for he knew that in spite of her inclination to be jealous, Madame de Bergenheim would never believe in a sudden desertion, and that she would surely discover the object of his ruse, if he made the mistake of exaggerating it in the least.

While renouncing the idea of a direct attack, he did not work with any less care to fortify his position. He redoubled his activity in widening the breach be-

[217]

tween the old aunt and the husband, following the principles of military art, that one should become master of the exterior works of a stronghold before seriously attacking its ramparts.

It was, in a way, by reflection that Octave's passion reached Clémence. Every few moments she learned some detail of this indirect attack, to which it was impossible for her to raise any objections.

"Monsieur de Gerfaut has promised to spend a fortnight longer with us," said her aunt to her, in a jeering tone.

"Really, Gerfaut is very obliging," said her husband, in his turn; "he thinks it very strange that we have not had a genealogical tree made to put in the drawing-room. He pretends that it is an indispensable complement to my collection of family portraits, and he offers to do me the favor of assuming charge of it. It seems, from what your aunt tells me, that he is very learned in heraldry. Would you believe it, he spent the whole morning in the library looking over files of old manuscripts? I am delighted, for this will prolong his stay here. He is a very charming fellow; a Liberal in politics, but a gentleman at heart. Marillac, who is a superb penman, undertakes to make a fair copy of the genealogy and to illuminate the crests. Do you know, we can not find my great-grandmother Cantelescar's coat-of-arms? But, my darling, it seems to me that you are not very kindly disposed toward your cousin Gerfaut."

Madame de Bergenheim, when these remarks and various others of a similar nature came up, tried to change the conversation, but she felt an antipathy for her husband bordering upon aversion. For lack of intelligence is one of the faults women can pardon the least; they look upon a confidence which is lulled into security by faith in their honor, and a blindness which does not suspect the possibility of a fall, as positive crimes.

"Look at these pretty verses Monsieur de Gerfaut has written in my album, Clémence," said Aline, in her turn. During vacation, among her other pleasures forbidden her at the Sacred Heart, the young girl had purchased a superbly bound album, containing so far but two ugly sketches in sepia, one very bad attempt in water-colors, and the verses in question. She called this "my album!" as she called a certain little blank book, "my diary!" To the latter she confided every night the important events of the day. This book had assumed such proportions, during the last few days, that it threatened to reach the dimensions of the Duchesse d'Abrantès' *mémoires*, but if the album was free to public admiration, nobody ever saw the diary, and Justine herself never had been able to discover the sanctuary that concealed this mysterious manuscript.

Aline was not so pleasantly received as the others, and Madame de Bergenheim hardly concealed the ill-humor her pretty sister-in-law's beaming face caused her every time Octave's name was mentioned.

The latter's diplomatic conduct was bearing fruit, and his expectations were being fulfilled with a precision which proved the correctness of his calculations.

CHARLES DE BERNARD

In the midst of all the contradictory sentiments of fear, remorse, vexation, love, and jealousy, Clémence's head was so turned, at times, that she did not know what she did want. She found herself in one of those situations when a woman of a complex and mobile character whom all sensations impress, passes, with surprising facility, from one resolve to another entirely opposed to it. After being frightened beyond measure by her lover's presence in her husband's house, she ended by becoming accustomed to it, and then by ridiculing her first terror.

"Truly," she thought, at times, "I was too silly thus to torment myself and make myself ill; I was wanting in self-respect to mistrust myself to such an extent, and to see danger where there was none. He can not expect to make himself so very formidable while scrawling this genealogical tree. If he came one hundred leagues from Paris for that, he really does not merit such severe treatment."

Then, having thus reassured herself against the perils of her position, without realizing that to fear danger less was to embolden love, she proceeded to examine her lover's conduct.

"He seems perfectly resigned," she said, to herself; "not one word or glance for two days! Since he resigns himself so easily, he might, it seems to me, obey me entirely and go away; or, if he wishes to disobey me, he might do it in a less disagreeable manner. For really, his manner is almost rude; he might at least remember that I am his hostess, and that he is in my house. I do not see what pleasure he can take in talking to this little girl. I wager that his only object is to annoy me! He deceives himself most assuredly; it is all the same to me! But Aline takes all this seriously! She has become very coquettish, the last few days! It certainly is very wrong for him to try to turn this child's head. I should like to know what he would say to justify himself."

Thus, little by little, she mentally reached the point to which Octave wished to bring her. The desire for an explanation with him, which she dared not admit to herself at first from a feeling of pride, became greater from day to day, and at last Octave himself could not have longed more ardently for an interview. Now that Octave seemed to forget her, she realized that she loved him almost to adoration. She reproached herself for her harshness toward him more than she had ever reproached herself for her weakness. Her antipathy for all that did not concern him increased to such a degree that the most simple of household duties became odious to her. It seemed to her that all the people about her were enemies bent upon separating her from happiness, for happiness was Octave; and this happiness, made up of words, letters, glances from him, was lost!

The evening of the fourth day, she found this torture beyond her strength.

"I shall become insane," she thought; "to-morrow I will speak to him."

Gerfaut was saying to himself, at nearly the same moment: "To-morrow I will have a talk with her." Thus, by a strange sympathy, their hearts seemed to understand each other in spite of their separation. But what was an irresistible attraction in Clémence was only a determination resulting from almost a mathematical calculation on her lover's part. By the aid of this gift of second sight which intelligent men who are in love sometimes possess, he had followed, degree by degree, the variations of her heart, without her saying one word; and in spite of the veil of scorn and indifference with which she still had the courage to shield herself, he had not lost a single one of the tortures she had endured for the last four days. Now he thought that he had discovered enough to allow him to risk a step that, until then, he would have deemed dangerous; and with the egotism common to all men, even the best of lovers, he trusted in the weakness born of sorrow.

The next day a hunting party was arranged with some of the neighbors. Early in the morning, Bergenheim and Marillac started for the rendezvous, which was at the foot of the large oak-tree where the artist's *tête-à-tête* had been so cruelly interrupted. Gerfaut refused to join them, under the pretence of finishing an article for the *Revue de Paris*, and remained at home with the three ladies. As soon as dinner was ended, he went to his room in order to give a semblance of truth to his excuse.

He had been busying himself for some time trimming a quill pen at the window, which looked out upon the park, when he saw in the garden, directly beneath him, Constance's forefeet and nose; soon the dog jumped upon the sill in order to warm herself in the sun.

GERFAUT

"The old lady has entered her sanctuary," thought Gerfaut, who knew that it was as impossible to see Constance without her mistress as St.-Roch without his dog.

A moment later he saw Justine and Mademoiselle de Corandeuil's maid starting off, arm in arm, as if they were going for a promenade. Finally, he had hardly written half a page, when he noticed Aline opposite his window, with a straw hat upon her head and a watering-pot in her hand. A servant carried a bucket of water and placed it near a mass of dahlias, which the young girl had taken under her protection, and she at once set about her work with great zeal.

"Now," said Gerfaut, "let us see whether the place is approachable." And closing his desk, he stealthily descended the stairs.

After crossing the vestibule on the first floor, and a small gallery decorated with commonplace pictures, he found himself at the library door. Thanks to the genealogical tree which he had promised to compile, he possessed a key to this room, which was not usually open. By dint of preaching about the danger in certain reading for young girls, Mademoiselle de Corandeuil had caused this system of locking-up, especially designed to preserve Aline from the temptation of opening certain novels which the old lady rejected *en masse*. "Young girls did not read novels in 1780," she would say. This put an end to all discussion and cut short the protestations of the young girl, who was brought up exclusively upon a diet of Le Ragois and Mentelle's geography, and such solid mental food.

CHARLES DE BERNARD

Several large books and numerous manuscripts were spread out upon the table in the library, together with a wide sheet of Holland paper, upon which was sketched the family tree of the Bergenheims. Instead of going to work, however, Gerfaut locked the door, and then went across the room and pressed a little knob which opened a small door no one would have noticed at first.

Leather bands representing the binding of books, like those which covered the rest of the walls, made it necessary for one to be informed of the existence of this secret exit in order to distinguish it from the rest of the room. This door had had a singular attraction for Gerfaut ever since the day he first discovered it. After silently opening it, he found himself in a small passage at the end of which was a small spiral staircase leading to the floor above. A cat creeping to surprise a bird asleep could not have walked more stealthily than he, as he mounted the stairs.

When he crossed the last step, he found himself in a small room, filled with wardrobes, lighted by a small glass door covered with a muslin curtain. This door opened into a little parlor which separated Madame de Bergenheim's private sitting-room from her sleeping-apartment. The only window was opposite the closet and occupied almost the whole of the woodwork, the rest of which was hung with pearl-gray stuff with lilac figures upon it. A broad, low divan, covered with the same material as the hanging, occupied the space in front of the window. It was the only piece of furniture, and it seemed almost impossible to introduce even one chair more.

GERFAUT

The blinds were carefully closed, as well as the double curtains, and they let in so little light that Octave had to accustom himself to the obscurity before he could distinguish Madame de Bergenheim through the muslin curtains and the glass door. She was lying upon the divan, with her head turned in his direction and a book in her hand. He first thought her asleep, but soon noticed her gleaming eyes fastened upon the ceiling.

"She is not asleep, she does not read, then she is thinking of me!" said he to himself, by a logical deduction he believed incontestable.

After a moment's hesitation, seeing that the young woman remained motionless, Gerfaut tried to turn the handle of the door as softly as possible so as to make his entrance quietly. The bolt had just noiselessly slipped in the lock when the drawing-room door suddenly opened, a flood of light inundated the floor, and Aline appeared upon the threshold, watering-pot in hand.

The young girl stopped an instant, for she thought her sister-in-law was asleep; but, meeting in the shade Clémence's sparkling eyes, she entered, saying in a fresh, silvery voice:

"All my flowers are doing well; I have come to water yours."

Madame de Bergenheim made no reply, but her eyebrows contracted slightly as she watched the young girl kneel before a superb datura. This almost imperceptible symptom, and the rather ill-humored look, foretold a storm. A few drops of water falling upon

15

the floor gave her the needed pretext, and Gerfaut, as much in love as he was, could not help thinking of the fable of the wolf and the lamb, when he heard the lady of his thoughts exclaim, in an impatient tone:

"Let those flowers alone; they do not need to be watered. Do you not see that you are wetting the floor?"

Aline turned around and looked at the scolder for a moment; then, placing her watering-pot upon the floor, she darted toward the divan like a kitten that has just received a blow from its mother's paw and feels authorized to play with her. Madame de Bergenheim tried to rise at this unexpected attack; but before she could sit up, she was thrown back upon the cushions by the young girl, who seized both her hands and kissed her on each cheek.

"Good gracious! how cross you have been for the last few days!" cried Aline, pressing her sister's hands. "Are you going to be like your aunt? You do nothing but scold now. What have I done? Are you vexed with me? Do you not love me any longer?"

Clémence felt a sort of remorse at this question, asked with such a loving accent; but her jealousy she could not overcome. To make up for it, she kissed her sister-in-law with a show of affection which seemed to satisfy the latter.

"What are you reading?" asked the young girl, picking up the book which had fallen to the floor in their struggle—"*Notre Dame de Paris*. That must be interesting! Will you let me read it? Oh! do! will you?"

"You know very well that my aunt has forbidden you to read novels."

"Oh! she does that just to annoy me and for no other reason. Do you think that is right? Must I remain an idiot, and never read anything but history and geography the rest of my life? As if I did not know that Louis Thirteenth was the son of Henri Fourth, and that there are eighty-six departments in France. You read novels. Does it do you any harm?"

Clémence replied in a rather imperative tone, which should have put an end to the discussion:

"When you are married you can do as you like. Until then you must leave your education in the hands of those who are interested in you."

"All my friends," replied Aline with a pout, "have relatives who are interested in them, at least as much as your aunt is in me, and they do not prevent their reading the books they like. There is Claire de Saponay, who has read all of Walter Scott's novels, *Maleck-Adel*, *Eugénie* and *Mathilde*—and I do not know how many more; Gessner, Mademoiselle de Lafayette— she has read everything; and I—they have let me read *Numa Pompilius* and *Paul and Virginia*. Isn't that ridiculous at sixteen years of age?"

"Do not get excited, but go into the library and get one of Walter Scott's novels; but do not let my aunt know anything about it."

At this act of capitulation, by which Madame de Bergenheim doubtless wished to atone for her disagreeableness, Aline made one joyous bound for the glass door. Gerfaut had barely time to leave his post of observation and to conceal himself between two wardrobes, under a cloak which was hanging there, when the young girl made her appearance, but she paid no attention to the pair of legs which were but imperfectly concealed. She bounded down the stairs and returned a moment later with the precious volumes in her hand.

"*Waverley, or, Scotland Sixty Years Ago*," said she, as she read the title. "I took the first one on the shelf, because you are going to lend them all to me, one by one, are you not? Claire says that a young girl can read Walter Scott, and that his books are very nice."

"We shall see whether you are sensible," replied Clémence, smiling; "but, above all things, do not let my aunt see these books, for I am the one who would get the scolding."

"Do not worry; I will go and hide them in my room."

She went as far as the door, then stopped and came back a few steps.

"It seems," said she, "that Monsieur de Gerfaut worked in the library yesterday, for there are piles of books on the table. It is very kind of him to be willing to make this tree, is it not? Shall we both be in it? Do they put women in such things? I hope your aunt will not be there; she is not one of our family."

Clémence's face clouded again at the name of Gerfaut.

"I know no more about it than you," she replied, a little harshly.

"The reason I asked is because there are only pictures of men in the drawing-room; it is not very polite on their part. I should much prefer that there should be portraits of our grandmothers; it would be so amusing to see the beautiful dresses that they wore in those days rather than those old beards which frighten me. But perhaps they do not put young girls in genealogical trees," she continued, in a musing tone.

"You might ask Monsieur de Gerfaut; he wishes to please you too much to refuse to tell you," said Clémence, with an almost ironical smile.

"Do you think so?" asked Aline, innocently. "I should never dare to ask him."

"You are still afraid of him, then?"

"A little," replied the young girl, lowering her eyes, for she felt her face flush.

This symptom made Madame de Bergenheim more vexed than ever, and she continued, in a cutting, sarcastic tone:

"Has your cousin d'Artigues written you lately?"

Mademoiselle de Bergenheim raised her eyes and looked at her for a moment with an indifferent air:

"I don't know," she said, at last.

"What! you do not know whether you have received a letter from your cousin?" continued Clémence, laughing affectedly.

"Ah! Alphonse—no, that is, yes; but it was a long time ago."

"How cold and indifferent you are all of a sudden to this dear Alphonse! You do not remember, then, how you wept at his departure, a year ago, and how vexed you were with your brother who tried to tease you about this beautiful affection, and how you swore that you would never have any other husband than your cousin?"

"I was a simpleton, and Christian was right. Alphonse is only one year older than I! Think of it, what a fine couple we should make! I know that I am not very sensible, and so it is necessary that my husband should be wise enough for both. Christian is nine years older than you, is he not?"

"Do you think that is too much?" asked Madame de Bergenheim.

"Quite the contrary."

"What age should you like your husband to be?"

"Oh!—thirty," replied the young girl, after a slight hesitation.

"Monsieur de Gerfaut's age?"

They gazed at each other in silence. Octave, who, from his place of concealment heard the whole of this conversation, noticed the sad expression which passed over Clémence's face, and seemed to provoke entire confidence. The young girl allowed herself to be caught by this appearance of interest and affection.

"I will tell you something," said she, "if you will promise never to tell a soul."

"To whom should I repeat it? You know that I am very discreet as to your little secrets."

"It is because this might be perhaps a great secret," continued Aline.

Clémence took her sister-in-law's hand, and drew her down beside her.

GERFAUT

"You know," said Aline, "that Christian has promised to give me a watch like yours, because I do not like mine. Yesterday, when we were out walking, I told him I thought it was very unkind of him not to have given it to me yet. Do you know what he replied?—It is true that he laughed a little—'It is hardly worth while buying you one now; when you are the Vicomtesse de Gerfaut, your husband will give you one.'"

"Your brother was joking at your expense; how could you be such a child as not to perceive it?"

"I am not such a child!" exclaimed Aline, rising with a vexed air; "I know what I have seen. They were talking a long time together in the drawing-room last evening, and I am sure they were speaking of me."

Madame de Bergenheim burst into laughter, which increased her sister-in-law's vexation, for she was less and less disposed to be treated like a young girl.

"Poor Aline!" said the Baroness, at last; "they were talking about the fifth portrait; Monsieur de Gerfaut can not find the name of the original among the old papers, and he thinks he did not belong to the family. You know, that old face with the gray beard, near the door."

The young girl bent her head, like a child who sees her naughty sister throw down her castle of cards.

"And how do you know?" said she, after a moment's reflection. "You were at the piano. How could you hear at the other end of the room what Monsieur de Gerfaut was saying?"

It was Clémence's turn to hang her head, for it

seemed to her that the girl had suspected the constant attention which, under an affectation of indifference, never allowed her to lose one of Octave's words. As usual, she concealed her embarrassment by redoubling her sarcasm.

"Very likely," said she, "I was mistaken, and you may be right after all. What day shall we have the honor of saluting Madame la Vicomtesse de Gerfaut?"

"I foolishly told you what I imagined, and you at once make fun of me," said Aline, whose round face lengthened at each word, and passed from rose-color to scarlet; "is it my fault that my brother said this?"

"I do not think it was necessary for him to speak of it, for you to think a great deal about the matter."

"Very well; must one not think of something?"

"But one should be careful of one's thoughts; it is not proper for a young girl to think of any man," replied Clémence, with an accent of severity which would have made her aunt recognize with pride the pure blood of the Corandeuils.

"I think it is more proper for a young girl to do so than for a married woman."

At this unexpected retort, Madame de Bergenheim lost countenance and sat speechless before the young maiden, like a pupil who has just been punished by his teacher.

"Where the devil did the little serpent get that idea?" thought Gerfaut, who was very ill at ease between the two wardrobes where he was concealed.

Seeing that her sister-in-law did not reply to her, Aline took this silence from confusion for an expression of bad temper, and at once became angry in her turn.

"You are very cross to-day," said she; "good-by, I do not want your books."

She threw the volumes of *Waverley* upon the sofa, picked up her watering-pot and went out, closing the door with a loud bang. Madame de Bergenheim sat motionless with a pensive, gloomy air, as if the young girl's remark had changed her into a statue.

"Shall I enter?" said Octave to himself, leaving his niche and putting his hand upon the door-knob. "This little simpleton has done me an infinite wrong with her silly speeches. I am sure that she is cruising with full sails set upon the stormy sea of remorse, and that those two rosebuds she is gazing at now seem to her like her husband's eyes."

Before the poet could make up his mind what to do, the Baroness arose and left the room, closing the door almost as noisily as her sister-in-law had done.

Gerfaut went downstairs, cursing, from the very depths of his heart, boarding-school misses and sixteen-year-old hearts. After walking up and down the library for a few moments, he left it and started to return to his room. As he passed the drawing-room, loud music reached his ear; chromatic fireworks, scales running with the rapidity of the cataract of Niagara, extraordinary arpeggios, hammering in the bass with a petulance and frenzy which proved that the *furie française* is not the exclusive right of the stronger sex. In this jumble of grave, wild, and sad notes, Gerfaut recognized, by the clearness of touch and brilliancy of some of the passages, that this improvisation could not come from Aline's unpractised fingers. He understood that the piano must be at this moment Madame de Bergenheim's confidant, and that she was pouring out the contradictory emotions in which she had indulged for several days; for, to a heart deprived of another heart in which to confide its joys and woes, music is a friend that listens and replies.

Gerfaut listened for some time in silence, with his head leaning against the drawing-room door. Clémence wandered through vague melodies without fixing upon any one in particular. At last a thought seemed to captivate her. After playing the first measures of the romance from *Saul*, she resumed the motive with more precision, and when she had finished the *ritornello* she began to sing, in a soft, veiled voice,

"Assisa al piè d'un salice——"

Gerfaut had heard her sing this several times, in society, but never with this depth of expression. She sang before strangers with her lips; now it all came from her heart. At the third verse, when he believed her to be exalted by her singing and the passion exhaled in this exquisite song, the poet softly entered, judging it to be a favorable moment, and enough agitated himself to believe in the contagion of his agitation.

The first sight which met his eyes was Mademoiselle de Corandeuil stretched out in her armchair, head thrown back, arms drooping and letting escape by way

of accompaniment a whistling, crackling, nasal melody.
The old maid's spectacles hanging on the end of her
nose had singularly compromised the harmony of her
false front. The *Gazette de France* had fallen from
her hands and decorated the back of Constance, who,
as usual, was lying at her mistress's feet.

"Horrible old witch!" said Gerfaut to himself.
"Decidedly, the Fates are against me to-day." However, as both mistress and dog were sleeping soundly,
he closed the door and tiptoed across the floor.

Madame de Bergenheim had ceased to sing, but her
fingers still continued softly to play the motive of the
song. As she saw Octave approaching her, she leaned
over to look at her aunt, whom she had not noticed to
be asleep, as the high back of her chair was turned
toward her. Nobody sleeps in a very imposing manner, but the old lady's profile, with her false front
awry, was so comical that it was too much for her
niece's gravity. The desire to laugh was, for the moment, stronger than respect for melancholy; and
Clémence, through that necessity for sympathy peculiar to acute merriment, glanced involuntarily at Octave, who was also smiling. Although there was nothing sentimental in this exchange of thoughts, the latter
hastened to profit by it; a moment more, and he was
seated upon a stool in front of the piano, at her left
and only a few inches from her.

"How can a person sleep when you are singing?"

The most embarrassed freshman could have turned
out as bright a speech as this; but the eloquence of
it lay less in the words than in the expression. The

ease and grace with which Octave seated himself, the elegant precision of his manner, the gracious way in which he bent his head toward Clémence, while speaking, showed a great aptitude in this kind of conversation. If the words were those of a freshman, the accent and pose were those of a graduate.

The Baroness's first thought was to rise and leave the room, but an invincible charm held her back. She was not mistress enough of her eyes to dare to let them meet Octave's; so she turned them away and pretended to look at the old lady.

"I have a particular talent for putting my aunt to sleep," said she, in a gay tone; "she will sleep until evening, if I like; when I stop playing, the silence awakens her."

"I beg of you, continue to play; never awaken her," said Gerfaut; and, as if he were afraid his wish would not be granted, he began to pound in the bass without being disturbed by the unmusical sounds.

"Do not play discords," said Clémence, laughing; "let us at least put her to sleep in tune."

She was wrong to say *us;* for her lover took this as complicity for whatever might happen. *Us,* in a *tête-à-tête,* is the most traitorous word in the whole language.

It may be that Clémence had no great desire that her aunt should awaken; perhaps she wished to avoid a conversation; perhaps she wished to enjoy in silence the happiness of feeling that she was still loved, for since he had seated himself beside her Octave's slightest action had become a renewed avowal. Madame

de Bergenheim began to play the Duke of Reich-
stadt's Waltz, striking only the first measure of the
accompaniment, in order to show her lover where to
put his fingers.

The waltz went on. Clémence played the air and
Octave the bass, two of their hands remaining unoccupied—those that were close to each other. Now,
what could two idle hands do, when one belonged to
a man deeply in love, the other to a young woman who
for some time had ill-treated her lover and exhausted
her severity? Before the end of the first part, the
long unoccupied, tapering fingers of the treble were
imprisoned by those of the bass, without the least dis-
turbance in the musical effect—and the old aunt slept
on!

A moment later, Octave's lips were fastened upon
this rather trembling hand, as if he wished to imbibe,
to the very depths of his soul, the soft, perfumed tis-
sue. Twice the Baroness tried to disengage herself,
twice her strength failed her. It was beginning to be
time for the aunt to awaken, but she slept more soundly than ever; and if a slight indecision was to be noticed in the upper hand, the lower notes were struck
with an energy capable of metamorphosing Mademoiselle de Corandeuil into a second Sleeping Beauty.

When Octave had softly caressed this hand for a
long time, he raised his head in order to obtain a new
favor. This time Madame de Bergenheim did not
turn away her eyes, but, after looking at Octave for
an instant, she said to him in a coquettish, seductive
way:

CHARLES DE BERNARD

"Aline?"

The mute glance which replied to this question was such an eloquent denial that all words were superfluous. His sweet, knowing smile betrayed the secret of his duplicity; he was understood and forgiven. There was at this moment no longer any doubt, fear, or struggle between them. They did not feel the necessity of any explanation as to the mutual suffering they had undergone; the suffering no longer existed. They were silent for some time, happy to look at each other, to be together and alone—for the old aunt still slept. Not a sound was to be heard; one would have said that sleep had overcome the two lovers also. Suddenly the charm was broken by a terrible noise, like a trumpet calling the guilty ones to repentance.

CHAPTER XVII

HAD a cannon-ball struck the two lovers in the midst of their ecstasy it would have been less cruel than the sensation caused by this horrible noise. Clémence trembled and fell back in her chair, frozen with horror. Gerfaut rose, almost as frightened as she; Mademoiselle de Corandeuil, aroused from her sleep, sat up in her chair as suddenly as a Jack-in-a-box that jumps in one's face when a spring is touched. As to Constance, she darted under her mistress's chair, uttering the most piteous howls.

One of the folding-doors opposite the window opened; the bell of a hunting-horn appeared in the opening, blown at full blast and waking the echoes in the drawing-room. The curtain of the drama had risen upon a parody, a second incident had changed the pantomime and sentiments of the performers. The old lady fell back in her chair and stopped up her ears with her fingers, as she stamped upon the floor; but it was in vain for her to try to speak, her words were drowned by the racket made by this terrible instrument. Clémence also stopped her ears. After running in her terror, under every chair in the room, Constance, half wild, darted, in a fit of despair, through the partly opened door. Gerfaut finally began to laugh heartily as if he thought it all great fun, for M. de Bergenheim's purple face took the place of the trumpet and his hearty laugh rang out almost as noisily.

"Ah! ha! you did not expect that kind of accompaniment," said the Baron, when his gayety had calmed a little; "this is the article that you were obliged to write for the *Revue de Paris*, is it? Do you think that I am going to leave you to sing Italian duets with Madame while I am scouring the woods? You must take me for a very careless husband, Vicomte. Now, then, right about face! March! Do me the kindness to take a gun. We are going to shoot a few hares in the Corne woods before supper."

"Monsieur de Bergenheim," exclaimed the old lady, when her emotion would allow her to speak, "this is indecorous—vulgar—the conduct of a common soldier —of a cannibal! My head is split open; I am sure to have an awful neuralgia in a quarter of an hour. It is the conduct of a herdsman."

"Do not think of your neuralgia, my dear aunt," replied Christian, whose good-humor seemed aroused by the day's sport; "you are as fresh as a rosebud—and Constance shall have some hares' heads roasted for her supper."

At this moment a second uproar was heard in the courtyard; a horn was evidently being played by an amateur, accompanied by the confused yelps and barks of a numerous pack of hounds; the whole was mingled with shouts of laughter, the cracking of whips, and clamors of all kinds. In the midst of this racket, a cry, more piercing than the others, rang out, a cry of agony and despair.

"Constance!" exclaimed Mademoiselle de Corandeuil, in a falsetto voice full of terror; she rushed to one of the windows and all followed her.

The spectacle in the courtyard was as noisy as it was picturesque. Marillac, seated upon a bench, was blowing upon a trumpet, trying to play the waltz from *Robert-le-Diable* in a true infernal manner. At his feet were seven or eight hunters and as many servants encouraging him by their shouts. The Baron's pack of hounds, of great renown in the country, was composed of about forty dogs, all branded upon their right thighs with the Bergenheim coat-of-arms. From time immemorial, the château's dogs had been branded thus with their master's crest, and Christian, who was a great stickler for old customs, had taken care not to drop this one. This feudal sign had probably acted upon the morals of the pack, for it was impossible to find, within twenty leagues, a collection of more snarly terriers, dissolute hounds, ugly bloodhounds, or more quarrelsome greyhounds. They were perfect hunters, but it seemed as if, on account of their being dogs of quality, all vices were permitted them.

In the midst of this horde, without respect for law or order, the unfortunate Constance had found herself after crossing the ante-chamber, vestibule, and outside steps, still pursued by the sounds from Christian's

16 [241]

huge horn. An honest merchant surprised at the turn of the road by a band of robbers would not have been greeted any better than the poodle was at the moment she darted into the yard. It may have been that the quarrel between the Bergenheims and Corandeuils had reached the canine species; it may have been at the instigation of the footmen, who all cordially detested the beast—the sad fact remains that she was pounced upon in a moment as if she were a deer, snatched, turned topsy-turvy, rolled, kicked about, and bitten by the forty four-legged brigands, who each seemed determined to carry away as a trophy some portion of her *café-au-lait* colored blanket.

The person who took the most delight in this deplorable spectacle was Père Rousselet. He actually clapped his hands together behind his back, spread his legs apart in the attitude of the Colossus of Rhodes, while his coat-skirts almost touched the ground, giving him the look of a kangaroo resting his paws under his tail. From his large cockatoo mouth escaped provoking hisses, which encouraged the assassins in their crime as much as did Marillac's racket.

"Constance!" exclaimed Mademoiselle de Corandeuil a second time, frozen with horror at the sight of her poodle lying upon its back among its enemies.

This call produced no effect upon the animal section of the actors in this scene, but it caused a sudden change among the servants and a few of the hunters; the shouts of encouragement ceased at once; several of the participants prudently tried to efface themselves; as to Rousselet, more politic than the others, he boldly

darted into the *mêlée* and picked up the fainting puppy in his arms, carrying her as tenderly as a mother
would an infant, without troubling himself whether or
not he was leaving part of his coat-tails with the savage hounds.

When the old lady saw the object of her love placed
at her feet covered with mud, sprinkled with blood,
and uttering stifled groans, which she took for the
death-rattle, she fell back in her chair speechless.

"Let us go," said Bergenheim in a low voice, taking his guest by the arm. Gerfaut threw a glance
around him and sought Clémence's eyes, but he did
not find them. Without troubling herself as to her
aunt's despair, Clémence had hurried to her room; for
she felt the necessity of solitude in order to calm her
emotions, or perhaps to live them over a second time.
Octave resigned himself to following his companion.
At the end of a few moments, the barking of the dogs,
the joking of the hunters, even the wind in the trees
and the rustling leaves, had bored Octave to such
an extent that, in spite of himself, his face betrayed
him.

"What a doleful face you have!" exclaimed his host,
laughingly. "I am sorry that I took you away from
Madame de Bergenheim; it seems that you decidedly
prefer her society to ours."

"Would you be very jealous if I were to admit the
fact?" replied Octave, making an effort to assume the
same laughing tone as the Baron.

"Jealous! No, upon my honor! However, you are
well constituted to give umbrage to a poor husband.

But jealousy is not one of my traits of character, nor among my principles."

"You are philosophical!" said the lover, with a forced smile.

"My philosophy is very simple. I respect my wife too much to suspect her, and I love her too much to annoy her in advance with an imaginary trouble. If this trouble should come, and I were sure of it, it would be time enough to worry myself about it. Besides, it would be an affair soon settled."

"What affair?" asked Marillac, slackening his pace in order to join in the conversation.

"A foolish affair, my friend, which does not concern you, Monsieur de Gerfaut, nor myself any longer, I hope; although I belong to the class exposed to danger. We were speaking of conjugal troubles."

The artist threw a glance at his friend which signified: "What the deuce made you take it into your head to start up this hare?"

"There are many things to be said on this subject," said he, in a sententious tone, thinking that his intervention might be useful in getting his friend out of the awkward position in which he found himself, "an infinite number of things may be said; books without number have been written upon this subject. Every one has his own system and plan of conduct as to the way of looking at and acting upon it."

"And what would be yours, you consummate villain?" asked Christian; "would you be as cruel a husband as you are an immoral bachelor? That usually happens; the bolder a poacher one has been, the

more intractable a gamekeeper one becomes. What
would be your system?"

"Hum! hum! you are mistaken, Bergenheim; my
boyish love adventures have disposed me to indulgence.
Debilis caro, you know! Shakespeare has translated
it, 'Frailty, thy name is woman!'"

"I am a little rusty in my Latin and I never knew
a word of English. What does that mean?"

"Upon my word, it means, if I were married and my
wife deceived me, I should resign myself to it like a
gentleman, considering the fragility of this enchanting
sex."

"Mere boy's talk, my friend! And you, Gerfaut?"

"I must admit," replied the latter, a little embarrassed, "that I have never given the subject very much
thought. However, I believe in the virtue of women."

"That is all very well, but in case of misfortune
what would you do?"

"I think I should say with Lanoue: 'Sensation is for
the fop, complaints for the fool, an honest man who is
deceived goes away and says nothing.'"

"I partly agree with Lanoue; only I should make a
little variation—instead of *goes away* should say *avenges
himself*."

Marillac threw at his friend a second glance full of
meaning.

"*Per Bacco!*" said he, "are you a Venetian or a
Castilian husband?"

"Eh!" replied Bergenheim, "I suppose that without
being either, I should kill my wife, the other man, and
then myself, without even crying, 'Beware!' Here!

Brichou! pay attention; Tambeau is separated from the rest."

As he said these words the Baron leaped over a broad ditch, which divided the road from the clearing which the hunters had already entered.

"What do you say to that?" murmured the artist, in a rather dramatic tone, in his friend's ear.

Instead of replying, the lover made a gesture which signified, according to all appearance: "I do not care."

The clearing they must cross in order to reach the woods formed a large, square field upon an inclined plane which sloped to the river side. Just as Marillac in his turn was jumping the ditch, his friend saw, at the extremity of the clearing, Madame de Bergenheim walking slowly in the avenue of sycamores. A moment later, she had disappeared behind a mass of trees without the other men noticing her.

"Take care that you do not slip," said the artist, "the ground is wet."

This warning brought misfortune to Gerfaut, who in jumping caught his foot in the root of a tree and fell.

"Are you hurt?" asked Bergenheim.

Octave arose and tried to walk, but was obliged to lean upon his gun.

"I think I have twisted my foot," said he, and he carried his hand to it as if he felt a sharp pain there.

"The devil! it may be a sprain," observed the Baron, coming toward them; "sit down. Do you think you will be able to walk?"

"Yes, but I fear hunting would be too much for me; I will return to the house."

"Do you wish us to make a litter and carry you?"

"You are laughing at me; it's not so bad as that. I will walk back slowly, and will take a foot-bath in my room."

"Lean upon me, then, and I will help you," said the artist, offering his arm.

"Thanks; I do not need you," Octave replied; "go to the devil!" he continued, in an expressive aside.

"*Capisco!*" Marillac replied, in the same tone, giving his arm an expressive pressure. "Excuse me," said he aloud, "I am not willing that you should go alone. I will be your Antigone—

Antigone me reste, Antigone est ma fille.

"Bergenheim, I will take charge of him. Go on with your hunting, the gentlemen are waiting for you. We will meet again at supper; around the table; legs are articles of luxury and sprains a delusion, provided that the throat and stomach are properly treated."

The Baron looked first at his guests, then at the group that had just reached the top of the clearing. For an instant Christian charity struggled against love of hunting, then the latter triumphed. As he saw that Octave, although limping slightly, was already in a condition to walk, especially with the aid of his friend's arm, he said:

"Do not forget to put your foot in water, and send for Rousselet; he understands all about sprains."

This advice having eased his conscience, he joined

his companions, while the two friends slowly took the
road back to the château, Octave resting one hand
upon the artist's arm and the other upon his gun.

"The *bourgeois* is outwitted!" said Marillac with a
stifled laugh, as soon as he was sure that Bergenheim
could not hear him. "Upon my word, these soldiers
have a primitive, baptismal candor! It is not so with
us artists; they could not bamboozle us in this way.
Your strain is an old story; it is taken from the *Mariage
de raison*, first act, second scene."

"You will do me the favor to leave me as soon as we
reach the woods," said Gerfaut, as he continued to
limp with a grace which would have made Lord Byron envious; "you may go straight ahead, or you may
turn to the left, as you choose; the right is forbidden
you."

"Very well. Hearts are trumps, it seems, and, for
the time being, you agree with Sganarelle, who places
the heart on the right side."

"Do not return to the château, as it is understood
that we are together. If you rejoin the hunting-party,
say to Bergenheim that you left me seated at the foot
of a tree and that the pain in my foot had almost
entirely gone. You would have done better not to accompany me, as I tried to make you understand."

"I had reasons of my own for wishing to get out of
Christian's crowd. To-day is Monday, and I have an
appointment at four o'clock which interests you more
than me. Now, will you listen to a little advice?"

"Listen, yes; follow it, not so sure."

"O race of lovers!" exclaimed the artist, in a sort of

transport, "foolish, absurd, wicked, impious, and sacrilegious kind!"

"What of it?"

"What of it? I tell you this will all end with swords for two."

"Bah!"

"Do you know that this rabid Bergenheim, with his round face and good-natured smile, killed three or four men while he was in the service, on account of a game of billiards or some such trivial matter?"

"*Requiescat in pace.*"

"Take care that he does not cause the *De Profundis* to be sung for you. He was called the best swordsman at Saint-Cyr: he has the devil of a lunge. As to pistol-shooting, I have seen him break nine plaster images at Lepage's one after another."

"Very well, if I have an engagement with him, we will fight it out with arsenic."

"By Jove, joking is out of place. I tell you that he is sure to discover something, and then your business will soon be settled; he will kill you as if you were one of the hares he is hunting this moment."

"You might find a less humiliating comparison for me," replied Gerfaut, with an indifferent smile; "however, you exaggerate. I have always noticed that these bullies with mysterious threats of their own and these slaughterers of plaster images were not such very dangerous fellows to meet. This is not disputing Bergenheim's bravery, for I believe it to be solid and genuine."

"I tell you, he is a regular lion! After all, you will admit that it is sheer folly to come and attack him in

his cage and pull his whiskers through the bars. And
that is what you are doing. To be in love with his
wife and pay court to her in Paris, when he is a hundred leagues from you, is all very well, but to install
yourself in his house, within reach of his clutches!
that is not love, it is sheer madness. This is nothing
to laugh at. I am sure that this will end in some
horrible tragedy. You heard him speak of killing his
wife and her lover just now, as if it were a very slight
matter. Very well; I know him; he will do as he
says without flinching. These ruddy-faced people are
very devils, if you meddle with their family affairs!
He is capable of murdering you in some corner of his
park, and of burying you at the foot of some tree and
then of forcing Madame de Bergenheim to eat your
heart fricasseed in champagne, as they say Raoul de
Coucy did."

"You will admit, at least, that it would be a very
charming repast, and that there would be nothing *bourgeois* about it."

"Certainly, I boast of detesting the *bourgeois;* I am
celebrated for that; but I should much prefer to die
in a worsted nightcap, flannel underwear, and cotton
night-shirt, than to have Bergenheim assist me, too
brusquely, in this little operation. He is such an out-
and-out Goliath! Just look at him!"

And the artist forced his friend to turn about, and
pointed at Christian, who stood with the other hunters
upon the brow of the hill, a few steps from the spot
where they had left him. The Baron was indeed a
worthy representative of the feudal ages, when physical

strength was the only incontestable superiority. In spite of the distance, they could hear his clear, ringing voice although they could not distinguish his words.

"He really has a look of the times of the Round Table," said Gerfaut; "five or six hundred years ago it would not have been very agreeable to find one's self face to face with him in a tournament; and if to-day, as in those times, feminine hearts were won by feats with double-edged swords, I admit that my chances would not be very good. Fortunately, we are emancipated from animal vigor; it is out of fashion."

"Out of fashion, if you like; meanwhile, he will kill you."

"You do not understand the charms of danger nor the attractions that difficulties give to pleasure. I have studied Christian thoroughly since I have been here, and I know him as well as if I had passed my life with him. I am also sure that, at the very first revelation, he will kill me if he can, and I take a strange interest in knowing that I risk my life thus. Here we are in the woods," said Gerfaut, as he dropped the artist's arm and ceased limping; "they can no longer see us; the farce is played out. You know what I told you to say if you join them: you left me at the foot of a tree. You are forbidden to approach the sycamores, under penalty of receiving the shot from my gun in your moustache."

At these words he threw the gun which had served him as crutch over his shoulder, and darted off in the direction of the river.

CHAPTER XVIII

T the extremity of the sycamore walk, the shore formed a bluff like the one upon which the château was built, but much more abrupt, and partly wooded. In order to avoid this stretch, which was not passable for carriages, the road leading into the principal part of the valley turned to the right, and reached by an easier ascent a more level plateau. There was only one narrow path by the river, which was shaded by branches of beeches and willows that hung over this bank into the river. After walking a short distance through this shady path, one found himself before a huge triangular rock covered with moss, which nature had rolled from the top of the mountain as if to close up the passage.

This obstacle was not insurmountable; but in order to cross it, one must have a sure foot and steady head, for the least false step would precipitate the unlucky one into the river, which was rapid as well as deep. From the rock, one could reach the top of the cliff by means of some natural stone steps, and then, descending on the other side, could resume the path by the river, which had been momentarily interrupted. In this case, one would reach, in about sixty steps, a place where the river grew broader and the banks projected, forming here and there little islands of sand covered with bushes. Here was a ford well known to shepherds and to all persons who wished to avoid going as far as the castle bridge.

Near the mossy rock of which we have spoken as being close to the sycamore walk, at the foot of a wall against which it flowed, forming a rather deep excavation, the current had found a vein of soft, brittle stone which, by its incessant force, it had ended in wearing away. It was a natural grotto formed by water, but which earth, in its turn, had undertaken to embellish. An enormous willow had taken root in a few inches of soil in a fissure of the rock, and its drooping branches fell into the stream, which drifted them along without being able to detach them.

Madame de Bergenheim was seated at the front of this grotto, upon a seat formed by the base of the rock. She was tracing in the sand, with a stick which she had picked up on the way, strange figures which she carefully erased with her foot. Doubtless these hieroglyphics had some meaning to her, and perhaps she feared lest the slightest marks might be carelessly forgotten, as they would betray the secret they concealed. Clémence was plunged into one of those ecstatic reveries which abolish time and distance. The fibres of her heart, whose exquisite vibrating had been so suddenly paralyzed by Christian's arrival, had resumed their passionate thrills. She lived over again in her mind the *tête-à-tête* in the drawing-room; she could hear the entrancing waltz again; she felt her lover's breath in her hair; her hand trembled again under the pressure of his kiss. When she awoke from this dream it was a reality; for Octave was seated by her side without her having seen him arrive, and he had taken up the scene at the piano just where it had been interrupted.

She was not afraid. Her mind had reached that state of exaltation which renders imperceptible the transition from dreaming to reality. It seemed to her that Octave had always been there, that it was his place, and for a moment she no longer thought, but remained motionless in the arms which embraced her. But soon her reason came back to her. She arose trembling, and drew away a few steps, standing before her lover with lowered head and face suffused with blushes.

"Why are you afraid of me? Do you not think me worthy of your love?" he asked, in an altered voice, and, without trying to retain or approach her, he fell upon his knees with a movement of sweet, sad grace.

He had analyzed Madame de Bergenheim's character well enough to perceive the least variation in her capricious nature. By the young woman's frightened attitude, her burning cheeks and the flashes which he saw from her eyes through her long, drooping lashes, he saw that a reaction had taken place, and he feared the next outburst; for he knew that women, when overcome with remorse, always smite their lover by way of expiation for themselves.

"If I let this recovered virtue have the mastery, I am a lost man for a fortnight at least," he thought.

He quickly abandoned the dangerous ground upon which he had taken position, and passed, by an adroit transition, from the most passionate frenzy to the most submissive bearing. When Clémence raised her large eyes, in which was a threatening gleam, she saw, instead of an audacious man to be punished, an imploring slave.

There was something so flattering in this attitude of humility that she was completely disarmed. She approached Octave, and took him by the hand to raise him, seated herself again and allowed him to resume his position beside her. She softly pressed his hand, of which she had not let go, and, looking her lover in the eyes, said in that deep, penetrating voice that women sometimes have:

"My friend!"

"Friend!" he thought; "yes, certainly. I will raise no dispute as to the word, provided the fact is recognized. What matters the color of the flag? Only fools trouble themselves about that. 'Friend' is not the throne I aspire to, but it is the road that leads to it. So then, let it be 'friend,' while waiting for better. This word is very pleasant to hear when spoken in these siren's accents, and when at the same time the eyes say 'lover!'"

"Will you always love me thus?" Octave asked, whose face beamed with virtuous pledges.

"Always!" sighed Clémence, without lowering her eyes under the burning glance which met hers.

"You will be the soul of my soul; the angel of my heaven?"

"Your sister," she said, with a sweet smile, as she caressed her lover's cheek with her hand.

He felt the blood mount to his face at this caress, and turned his eyes away with a dreamy air.

"I probably am one of the greatest fools that has ever existed since the days of Joseph and Hippolytus," thought he.

He remained silent and apparently indifferent for several moments.

"Of what are you thinking?" asked Madame de Bergenheim, surprised by Octave's silence and rather listless air.

He gave a start of surprise at this question.

"May I die if I tell her!" he thought; "she must think me ridiculous enough as it is."

"Tell me, I wish you to speak out," she continued, in that despotic tone which a woman assumes when sure of her empire.

Instead of replying, as she demanded, he gave her a long, questioning glance, and it would have been impossible at that moment for her to keep a single secret from her lover. Madame de Bergenheim felt the magnetic influence of his penetrating glance so deeply that it seemed to her these sharp eyes were fathoming her very heart. She felt intensely disturbed to be gazed at in that way, and, in order to free herself from this mute questioning, she leaned her head upon Octave's shoulder, as she said softly:

"Do not look at me like that or I shall not love your eyes any more."

Her straw hat, whose ribbons were not tied, slipped

and fell, dragging with it the comb which confined her
beautiful hair, and it fell in disorder over her shoulders. Gerfaut passed his hand behind the charming
head which rested upon his breast, in order to carry
this silky, perfumed fleece to his lips. At the same
time, he gently pressed the supple form which, as it
bent toward him, seemed to ask for this caress.

Clémence made a sudden effort and arose, fastening
her hair at the back of her head with an almost shamed
haste.

"Will you refuse me one lock of your hair as a
souvenir of this hour?" said Octave, stopping her
gently as she was about to replace her comb.

"Do you need any souvenir?" she replied, giving
him a glance which was neither a reproach nor a refusal.

"The souvenir is in my heart, the hair will never
leave my bosom! We live in an unworthy age. I
can not boast of wearing your colors in everybody's
eyes, and yet I should like to wear a sign of my bondage."

She let her hair fall down her back again, but seemed
embarrassed as to how to execute his wish.

"I can not cut my hair with my teeth," she said,
with a smile which betrayed a double row of pearls.

Octave took a stiletto from his pocket.

"Why do you always carry this stiletto?" asked the
young woman, in a changed voice; "it frightens me
to see you armed thus."

"Fear nothing," said Gerfaut, who did not reply to
her question, "I will respect the hair which serves you

as a crown. I know where I must cut it, and, if my ambition is great, my hand shall be discreet."

Madame de Bergenheim had no confidence in his moderation, and, fearing to leave her beautiful hair to her lover's mercy, she took the stiletto and cut off a little lock which she drew through her fingers and then offered to him, with a loving gesture that doubled the value of the gift. At this moment, hunting-horns resounded in the distance.

"I must leave you now!" exclaimed Clémence, "I must. My dear love, let me go now; say good-by to me."

She leaned toward him and presented her forehead to receive this adieu. It was her lips which met Octave's, but this kiss was rapid and fleeting as a flash of light. Withdrawing from the arms which would yet retain her, she darted out of the grotto, and in a moment had disappeared in one of the shady paths.

For some time, plunged in deep reflection, Gerfaut stood on the same spot; but at last arousing himself from this dreamy languor, he climbed the rock so as to reach the top of the cliff. After taking a few steps he stopped with a frightened look, as if he had espied some venomous reptile in his path. He could see, through the bushes which bordered the crest of the plateau at the top of the ladder cut in the rock, Bergenheim, motionless, and in the attitude of a man who is trying to conceal himself in order that he may watch somebody. The Baron's eyes not being turned in Gerfaut's direction, he could not tell whether he was the object of this espionage, or whether the lay of the land allowed him to see Madame de Bergenheim, who must be under the sycamores by this time. Uncertain as to what he should do, he remained motionless, half crouched down upon the rock, behind the ledge of which, thanks to his position, he could hide from the Baron.

CHAPTER XIX

THE REVELATION

FEW moments before the castle clock struck four, a man leaped across the ditch which served as enclosure to the park. Lambernier, for it was he who showed himself so prompt at keeping his promise, directed his steps through the thickets toward the corner of the Corne woods which he had designated to Marillac; but, after walking for some time, he was forced to slacken his steps. The hunting-party were coming in his direction, and Lambernier knew that to continue in the path he had first chosen would take him directly among the hunters; and, in spite of his insolence, he feared the Baron too much to wish to expose himself to the danger of another chastisement. He therefore retraced his steps and took a roundabout way through the thickets, whose paths were all familiar to him; he descended to the banks of the river ready to ascend to the place appointed for the rendezvous as soon as the hunting party had passed.

He had hardly reached the plateau covered with trees, which extended above the rocks, when, as he entered a clearing which had been recently made, he

saw two men coming toward him who were walking
very fast, and whom to meet in this place caused him a
very disagreeable sensation. The first man was Mademoiselle de Corandeuil's coachman, as large a fellow
as ever crushed the seats of landau or brougham with
his rotundity. He was advancing with hands in the
pockets of his green jacket and his broad shoulders
thrown back, as if he had taken it upon himself to
replace Atlas. His cap, placed in military fashion
upon his head, his scowling brows, and his bombastic
air, announced that he was upon the point of accom-
plishing some important deed which greatly interested
him. Leonard Rousselet, walking by his side, moved
his spider legs with equal activity, carefully holding
up the skirts of his long coat as if they were petticoats.

Lambernier, at sight of them, turned to enter the
woods again, but he was stopped in his retreat by a
threatening shout.

"Stop, you vagabond!" exclaimed the coachman;
"halt! If you take a trot, I shall take a gallop."

"What do you want? I have no business with you,"
replied the workman, in a surly tone.

"But I have business with you," replied the big
domestic, placing himself in front of him and balancing himself first on his toes then on his heels, with a
motion like the wooden rocking-horses children play
with. "Come here, Rousselet; are you wheezy or
foundered?"

"I have not as good legs as your horses," replied
the old man, who reached them at last, breathless,
and took off his hat to wipe his forehead.

CHARLES DE BERNARD

"What does this mean, jumping out upon one from a corner in the woods like two assassins?" asked Lambernier, foreseeing that this beginning might lead to some scene in which he was threatened to be forced to play a not very agreeable *rôle*.

"It means," said the coachman: "first, that Rousselet has nothing to do with it; I do not need anybody's help to punish an insignificant fellow like you; second, that you are going to receive your quietus in a trice."

At these words he pushed his cap down over his ears and rolled up his sleeves, in order to give freer action to his large, broad hands.

The three men were standing upon a plot of ground where charcoal had been burned the year before. The ground was black and slippery, but being rather level, it was a very favorable place for a duel with fists or any other weapons. When Lambernier saw the lackey's warlike preparations, he placed his cap and coat upon an old stump and stationed himself in front of his adversary. But, before the hostilities had begun, Rousselet advanced, stretching his long arms out between them, and said, in a voice whose solemnity seemed to be increased by the gravity of the occasion:

"I do not suppose that you both wish to kill each other; only uneducated people conduct themselves in this vulgar manner; you ought to have a friendly explanation, and see if the matter is not susceptible of arrangement. That was the way such things were done when I was in the twenty-fifth demi-brigade."

"The explanation is," said the coachman, in his gruff voice, "that here is a low fellow who takes every opportunity to undervalue me and my horses, and I have sworn to give him a good drubbing the first time I could lay my hands upon him. So, Père Rousselet, step aside. He will see if I am a pickle; he will find out that the pickle is peppery!"

"If you made use of such a vulgar expression as that," observed Rousselet, turning to Lambernier, "you were at fault, and should beg his pardon as is the custom among educated people."

"It is false!" exclaimed Lambernier; "and besides, everybody calls the Corandeuils that, on account of the color of their livery."

"Did you not say Sunday, at the Femme-sans-Tête, and in the presence of Thiedot, that all the servants of the château were idlers and good-for-nothings, and that if you met one of them who tried to annoy you, you would level him with your plane?"

"If you used the word 'level,' it was very uncivil," observed Rousselet.

"Thiedot had better keep in his own house," growled the carpenter, clenching his fists.

"It looks well for a tramp like you to insult gentlemen like us," continued the lackey, in an imposing tone. "And did you not say that when I took Mademoiselle to mass I looked like a green toad upon the box, thus trying to dishonor my physique and my clothes? Did you not say that?"

"Only a joke about the color of your livery. They call the others measles and lobsters."

"Lobsters are lobsters," replied the coachman, in an imperative tone; "if that vexes them, they can take care of themselves. But I will not allow any one to attack my honor or that of my beasts by calling them screws—and that is what you did, you vagabond! And did you not say that I sent bags of oats to Remiremont to be sold, and that, for a month, my team had steadily been getting thin? Did you ever hear anything so scandalous, Père Rousselet? to dare to say that I endanger the lives of my horses? Did you not say that, you rascal? And did you not say that Mademoiselle Marianne and I had little private feasts in her room, and that was why I could not eat more at the table? Here is Rousselet, who has been a doctor and knows that I am on a diet on account of my weak stomach." At these words, the servant, carried away by his anger, gave his stomach a blow with his fist.

"Lambernier," said Rousselet, turning up his lips with a look of contempt, "I must admit that, for a man well brought up, you have made most disgusting remarks."

"To say that I eat the horses' oats!" roared the coachman.

"I ought to have said that you drank them," replied Lambernier, with his usual sneer.

"Rousselet, out of the way!" exclaimed the burly lackey at this new insult; the old peasant not moving as quickly as he desired, he seized him by the arm and sent him whirling ten steps away.

At this moment, a new person completed the scene, joining in it, if not as actor at least as interested spectator. If the two champions had suspected his presence they would have probably postponed their fight until a more opportune moment, for this spectator was no other than the Baron himself. As he saw from a distance the trio gesticulating in a very animated manner, he judged that a disorderly scene was in preparation, and as he had wished for a long time to put an end to the quarrelsome ways of the château servants, he was not sorry to catch them in the very act, so as to make an example of them. At first, he stooped and concealed himself in the thickets, ready to appear for the *dénouement*.

As Lambernier saw the giant's fist coming down upon him, he darted to one side and the blow only struck the air, making the coachman stumble from the force of his impetuosity. Lambernier profited by this position to gather all his strength, and threw himself upon his adversary, whom he seized by the flank and gave such a severe blow as to bring him down upon his knees. He then gave him a dozen more blows upon the head, and succeeded in overthrowing him completely.

If the coachman had not had a cranium as hard as iron, he probably could not have received such a storm of fisticuffs without giving up the ghost. Fortunately for him, he had one of those excellent Breton heads that break the sticks which beat them. Save for a certain giddiness, he came out of the scramble safe and sound. Far from losing his presence of mind by the disadvantageous position in which he found himself, he supported himself upon the ground with his left hand, and, passing his other arm behind him, he wound it around the workman's legs, who thus found himself reaped down, so to speak, and a moment later was lying on his back in front of his adversary. The latter, holding him fast with his strong hands, placed a knee, as large as a plate, upon his chest and then pulled off the cap that his enemy had pushed down over his eyes, and proceeded to administer full justice to him.

"Ah! you thought you'd attack me treacherously, did you?" said he, with a derisive chuckle as if to slacken the speed of his horses. "You know short reckonings make good friends. Oh! what a fine thrashing you are going to receive, my friend! Take care! if you try to bite my hand, I'll choke you with my two fingers, do you hear! Now, then, take this for the green toad; this, for my horses' sake; this, for Mademoiselle Marianne!"

He followed each "this" with a heavy blow from his fist. At the third blow the blood poured out of the mouth of the carpenter, who writhed under the pressure of his adversary's knee like a buffalo stifled by a boa-constrictor; he succeeded at last in freeing one hand, which he thrust into his trousers' pocket.

"Ah! you rascal! I am killed!" howled the coachman, giving a bound backward. Lambernier, profiting by his freedom, jumped upon his feet, and, without troubling himself as to his adversary, who had fallen on his knees and was pressing his hand to his left thigh, he picked up his cap and vest and started off through the clearing. Rousselet, who until then had prudently kept aside, tried to stop the workman, at a cry from his companion, but the scoundrel brandished his iron compass before his eyes with such an ugly look that the peasant promptly left the way open for him.

At this tragic and unexpected *dénouement*, Bergenheim, who was getting ready to make his appearance from behind the trees and to interpose his authority, started in full pursuit of the would-be murderer. From the direction he took, he judged that he would try to reach the river by passing over the rock. He walked in this direction, with his gun over his shoulder, until he reached the foot of the steps which descended into the grotto. Christian crouched behind some bushes to wait for Lambernier, who must pass this way, and it was at this moment that Gerfaut, who was forty feet below him, saw him without suspecting the reason for his attitude.

Bergenheim soon found out that he had calculated correctly when he heard a sound like that made by a wild boar when he rushes through the thickets and breaks the small branches in his path, as if they were no more than blades of grass. Soon Lambernier appeared with a haggard, wild look and a face bleeding from the blows he had received. He stopped for a moment to catch his breath and to wipe off his compass with a handful of grass; he then staunched the blood streaming from his nose and mouth, and after putting on his coat started rapidly in the direction of the river.

"Halt!" exclaimed the Baron, suddenly, rising before him and barring his passage.

The workman jumped back in terror; then he drew out his compass a second time and made a movement as if to throw himself upon this new adversary, out of sheer desperation. Christian, at this threatening pantomime, raised his gun to his cheek with as much coolness and precision as he would have shown at firing into a body of soldiers.

"Down with your weapon!" he exclaimed, in his commanding voice, "or I will shoot you down like a rabbit."

The carpenter uttered a hoarse cry as he saw the muzzle of the gun within an inch of his head, ready to blow his brains out. Feeling assured that there was no escape for him, he closed his compass and threw it with an angry gesture at the Baron's feet.

"Now," said the latter, "you will walk straight ahead of me as far as the château, and if you turn one step to the right or left, I will send the contents of my gun into you. So right about march!"

As he said these words, he stooped, without losing sight of the workman, and picked up the compass, which he put in his pocket.

"Monsieur le Baron, it was the coachman who attacked me first; I had to defend myself," stammered Lambernier.

"All right, we will see about that later. March on!"

"You will deliver me up to the police—I am a ruined man!"

"That will make one rascal the less," exclaimed Christian, repelling with disgust the workman, who had thrown himself on his knees before him.

"I have three children, Monsieur, three children," he repeated, in a supplicating tone.

"Will you march!" replied Bergenheim imperiously, as he made a gesture with his gun as if to shoot him.

Lambernier arose suddenly, and the expression of terror upon his countenance gave place to one of resolution mingled with hatred and scorn.

"Very well," he exclaimed, "let us go on! but remember what I tell you; if you have me arrested, you will be the first to repent of it, Baron though you are. If I appear before a judge, I will tell something that you would pay a good price for."

Bergenheim looked fixedly at Lambernier.

"What do you mean by such insolence?" said he.

"I will tell you what I mean, if you will promise to let me go; if you give me into the hands of the police, I repeat it, you will repent not having listened to me to-day."

"This is some idle yarn, made to gain time; no matter, speak; I will listen."

The workman darted a defiant glance at Christian.

"Give me your word of honor to let me go afterward."

"If I do not do so, are you not at liberty to repeat your story?" replied the Baron, who, in spite of his curiosity, would not give his word to a scoundrel whose only aim probably was to escape justice.

This observation impressed Lambernier, who, after a moment's reflection, assumed a strange attitude of cool assurance, considering the position in which he found himself. Not a sound was to be heard; even the barking of the dogs in the distance had ceased. The deepest silence surrounded them; even Gerfaut, in the place where he was concealed, could no longer see them, now that Bergenheim had left the edge of the cliff; from time to time their voices reached him, but he could not distinguish the meaning of their words.

Leaning with one hand upon his gun, Christian waited for the carpenter to begin his story, gazing at him with his clear, piercing eyes. Lambernier bore this glance without flinching, returning it in his insolent way.

"You know, Monsieur, that when the alterations were made in Madame's apartment, I had charge of the carving for her chamber. When I took away the old woodwork, I saw that the wall between the windows was constructed out of square, and I asked Madame if she wished that the panel should be fastened like the other or if she preferred it to open so that it would make a closet. She said to have it open by means of a secret spring. So I made the panel with concealed hinges and a little button hidden in the lower part of the woodwork; it only needs to be pressed, after turning it to the right, and the woodwork will open like a door."

Christian had now become extremely attentive.

"Monsieur will remember that he was in Nancy at the time, and that Madame's chamber was completed during his absence. As I was the only one who worked in this room, the other workmen not being capable of carving the wood as Madame wished, I was the only person who knew that the panel was not nailed down the length of the wall."

"Well?" asked the Baron, impatiently.

"Well," Lambernier replied, in a careless tone, "if, on account of the blow which I gave the coachman, it is necessary for me to appear in court, I shall be obliged to tell, in order to revenge myself, what I saw in that closet not more than a month ago."

"Finish your story," exclaimed Bergenheim, as he clenched the handle of his gun.

"Mademoiselle Justine took me into this room in order to hang some curtains; as I needed some nails, she went out to get them. While I was examining the woodwork, which I had not seen since it had been put in place, I saw that the oak had warped in one place because it was not dry enough when it was used. I wished to see if the same thing had happened between the windows, and if the panel could open. I pressed the spring, and when the door opened I saw a small package of letters upon the little shelf; it seemed very singular to me that Madame should choose this place to keep her letters, and the thought came to me that she wished to conceal them from Monsieur."

Bergenheim gave the workman a withering glance, and made a sign for him to continue.

"They were already talking about discharging me from the château's employ; I do not know how it happened, but the thought entered my head that perhaps one of these letters would be of use to me, and I took the first one in the package; I had only time to close the panel when Mademoiselle Justine returned."

"Very well! what is there in common between these letters and the criminal court that awaits you?" asked Christian, in an altered voice, although he tried to appear indifferent. .

"Oh! nothing at all," replied the carpenter, with an air of indifference; "but I thought that you would not like people to know that Madame had a lover."

Bergenheim shivered as if he were taken with a chill, and his gun dropped from his hand to the ground.

As quick as thought Lambernier stooped over to seize the gun, but he did not have time to carry out his intention, for he was seized by the throat and half choked by an iron hand.

"That letter! that letter!" said Christian to him, in a low, trembling voice, and he put his face down close to the carpenter's, as if he feared that a breath of wind might carry away his words and repeat them.

"Let me alone first, I can not breathe——" stammered the workman, whose face was becoming purple and his eyes starting out of his head, as if his adversary's fingers had been a rope.

The latter granted the prayer by loosening his hold of the carpenter's neck and seizing him by his vest in such a way as to take away all chance of escape while leaving him free to speak.

"This letter!" he repeated.

Frightened by the shaking he had just received, and not in a condition to reflect with his usual prudence, Lambernier mechanically obeyed this order; he hunted in his pockets for some time, and at last took a carefully folded paper from his vest-pocket, saying with a stunned air:

"Here it is. It is worth ten louis."

Christian seized the paper and opened it with his teeth, for he could not use his hands without releasing his prisoner. It was, like all notes of this kind, without address, seal, or signature. It did not differ from most of its kind save in the natural beauty of its style and its simple eloquence. Ardent protestations, sweet and loving complaints, those precious words that one bestows only upon the woman he loves and which betray a love that has yet much to desire but as much to hope. The handwriting was entirely unknown to Bergenheim, but Clémence's name, which was repeated several times, did not permit him to doubt for a moment that this note was written to his wife. When he had finished reading, he put it in his pocket with apparent serenity, and then looked at Lambernier, who, during this time, had remained motionless under the hand that detained him.

"You are mistaken, Lambernier," said he to him; "it is one of my letters before my marriage." And he tried to force himself to smile; but the muscles of his lips refused to act this falsehood, and drops of cold perspiration stood upon his forehead and at the roots of his hair.

The carpenter had watched the change in the Baron's countenance as he read the letter. He was persuaded that he could turn the capital importance of his revelations into profit for himself; he believed that

the time had come when he might gain advantage by
showing that he understood perfectly well the value of
the secret he had just imparted. So he replied with a
glance of intelligence:

"Monsieur's handwriting must have changed greatly,
then; I have some of his orders which do not resemble
this any more than a glass of water does a glass of
wine."

Christian tried to find a response but failed. His
eyebrows contracted in a manner that betokened a
coming storm, but Lambernier was not disturbed by
this symptom; he continued in a more and more assured voice:

"When I said that this letter was worth ten louis,
I meant that it was worth that much to a mere stranger,
and I am very sure I should not have to go very far
to find one; but Monsieur le Baron is too sensible not
to know the value of this secret. I do not wish to set
a price upon it, but since I am obliged to go away on
account of this coachman, and have no money——"

He did not have time to finish; Bergenheim seized
him in the middle of the body and made him describe
a horizontal half-circle without touching the ground,
then threw him upon his knees on the edge of the path
which descended almost perpendicularly alongside the
rocks. Lambernier suddenly saw his haggard face reflected in the river fifty feet below. At this sight, and
feeling a powerful knee between his shoulders which
bent him over the abyss, as if to make him appreciate
its dangers, the workman uttered a terrified cry; his
hands clutched wildly at the tufts of grass and roots of

plants which grew here and there on the sides of the rocks, and he struggled with all his might to throw himself back upon the ground. But it was in vain for him to struggle against the superior strength of his adversary, and his attempts only aggravated the danger of his position. After two or three powerless attempts, he found himself lying upon his stomach with half his body hanging over the precipice, having nothing to prevent him from falling over but Bergenheim's hand, which held him by the collar and at the same time hindered him from rising.

"Have you ever said one word about this?" asked the Baron, as he took hold of the trunk of a tree to steady himself upon this dangerous ground that he had chosen as the field of discussion.

"To nobody!—ah!—how my head swims!" replied the carpenter, closing his eyes in terror, for the blood rushing to his brain made him dizzy, and it seemed to him that the river was slowly reaching him.

"You see that if I make one gesture, you are a dead man," replied the Baron, leaning upon him harder yet.

"Give me up to the police; I will say nothing about the letters; as sure as there is a God, I will say nothing. But do not let me fall—hold me tight—do not let go of me—I am slipping—oh! holy mother of God!"

Christian taking hold of the tree near him, leaned over and raised Lambernier up, for he really was incapable of doing so himself; fright and the sight of the water had given him vertigo. When he was upon his legs again, he reeled like a drunken man and his feet nearly gave way beneath him. The Baron looked at him a moment in silence, but at last he said:

"Go away, leave the country at once; you have time to fly before there will be any pursuit. But remember that if I ever hear one word of what has passed between us from your lips, I shall know how to find you and you will die by my hand."

"I swear by the Holy Virgin and by all the saints—" stammered Lambernier, who had suddenly become a very fervent Catholic.

Christian pointed with his finger to the stone steps beneath them.

"There is your road; pass over the rock, through the woods, and reach Alsace. If you conduct yourself well, I will assure your living. But remember; one single indiscreet word, and you are a dead man."

At these words he pushed him into the path with one of those quick movements which very powerful men can not always calculate the effect of. Lambernier, whose strength was almost exhausted by the struggles he had undergone, had not vigor enough left to stand, and he lost his balance at this violent as well as unexpected push. He stumbled over the first step, reeled as he tried to regain his footing, and fell head first down the almost vertical declivity. A ledge of the cliff, against which he first struck, threw him upon the loose rocks. He slowly glided downward, uttering lamentable cries; he clutched, for a moment, a little bush which had grown in a crevice of the rocks but he did not have strength enough to hold on to it, his arm having been broken in three places by his fall. He let go of it suddenly, and dropped farther and farther down uttering a last terrible shriek of despair; he rolled over twice again—and then fell into the torrent below, that swallowed him up like a mass already deprived of life.

CHAPTER XX

MARILLAC TELLS A STORY

UESTS were seated that evening around the oval table in the dining-room of the castle of Bergenheim. According to custom, the ladies were not present at this repast. This was a custom which had been adopted by the Baroness for the suppers which were given by her husband at the close of his hunting parties; she dispensed with appearing at table on those days; perhaps she was too fastidious to preside at these lengthy séances of which the ruses of the hare, the death of the stag, and the feats of the hounds, formed the principal topics of conversation. It is probable that this conduct was duly appreciated by those who participated in those rather boisterous repasts, and that they felt a certain gratitude, in spite of the regrets they manifested on account of Madame's absence.

Among the guests was Marillac, whose sparkling eye, and cheeks even more rosy than usual, made him conspicuous. Seated between a fat notary and another boon companion, who were almost as drunk as he Marillac emptied glass after glass, red wine after the white, the white after the red, with noisy laughter, and jests of all kinds by way of accompaniment. His head became every moment more and more excited by the libations destined to refresh his throat, and his neighbors, without his perceiving the conspiracy, thought it would be good fun to put a Parisian dandy under the table. However, he was not the only one who was gliding over the slippery precipice that leads to the attractive abyss of drunkenness. The majority of the guests shared his imprudent abandon and progressive exaltation. A bacchic emulation reigned, which threatened to end in scenes bordering upon a debauch.

Among these highly colored cheeks, under which the wine seemed to circulate with the blood, these eyes shining with a dull, fictitious light, all this disorderly pantomime so contrary to the quiet habit of the gesticulators, two faces contrasted strangely with the careless mirth of the others. The Baron fulfilled his duties as master of the house with a sort of nervous excitement which might pass for genuine merriment in the eyes of those of his guests who were in no condition to study his countenance; but a quiet observer would soon have discerned that these violent efforts at good-humor and bantering concealed some terrible suffering. From time to time, in the midst of a sentence or a laugh, he would suddenly stop, the muscles of his face would twitch as if the spring which set them in motion had broken; his expression became sombre and savage; he sank back in his chair motionless, a stranger to all that surrounded him, and gave himself up to some mysterious thought against which resistance seemed powerless. Suddenly he appeared to wake from some perplexing dream, and by another powerful effort aroused himself and joined in the conversation with sharp, cutting speeches; he encouraged the noisy humor of his guests, inciting them to drunkenness by setting the example himself; then the same mysterious thought would cross his face anew, and he would fall back into the tortures of a revery which must have been horrible, to judge by the expression of his face.

Among his guests, one only, who was seated almost opposite Bergenheim, seemed to be in the secret of his thoughts and to study the symptoms with deep attention. Gerfaut, for it was he, showed an interest in this examination which reacted on his own countenance, for he was paler than ever.

"When I saw that the hare was reaching the upper road," said one of the guests, a handsome old man about sixty years of age, with gray hair and rosy cheeks, "I ran toward the new clearing to wait for its return. I felt perfectly sure, notary, that he would pass through your hands safe and sound."

"Now, notary," said Marillac, from the other end of the table, "defend yourself; one, two, three, ready!"

"Monsieur de Camier," replied the hunter whose skill had been questioned, "I do not pretend to have your skill. I never have shot as large game as you did at your last hunt."

This reply was an allusion to a little misadventure which had happened to the first speaker, who, on account of near-sightedness, had shot a cow, taking it for a buck. The laugh, which had been at the notary's expense first, now turned against his adversary.

"How many pairs of boots did you get out of your game?" asked one.

"Gentlemen, let us return to our conversation," said a young man, whose precise face aspired to an austere and imposing air. "Up to this time, we can form only very vague conjectures as to the road that Lambernier took to escape. This, allow me to say, is more important than the notary's hare or Monsieur de Camier's cow."

At these words, Bergenheim, who had taken no part in the conversation, straightened up in his chair.

"A glass of Sauterne," said he, suddenly, to one of his neighbors.

Gerfaut looked at him stealthily for a moment, and then lowered his eyes, as if he feared his glance might be noticed.

"The public prosecutor scents a culprit, and there is no fear he will drop the trail," said the notary.

"The case will doubtless come up at the next session of the Assizes."

M. de Camier put his glass, which was half filled, upon the table, angrily exclaiming:

"The devil take the jury! I am called to the next session, and I will wager my head that I shall be drawn. How agreeable that will be! To leave my home and business in the middle of winter and spend a fortnight with a lot of fellows whom I do not know from Adam! That is one of the agreeable things supplied by constitutional government. The French have to be judged by their peers! Of what use is it to pay for judges if we, land-owners, are obliged to do their work. The old parliaments, against which so much has been said, were a thousand times better than all this bedlam let loose in a court of assizes."

Marillac, who during this speech was amusing himself with singing his low "G" while peeling an apple, interrupted his song, to the great relief of a hound who lay at his feet, and whose nerves seemed to be singularly affected by the strain.

"Monsieur de Camier," said he, "you are a large land-owner, an eligible citizen and a Carlist; you fast on Fridays, go to mass in your parish, and occasionally kill cows for bucks; I esteem and respect you; but allow me to say that you have just uttered an old, antediluvian platitude."

"Gentlemen," said the public prosecutor, punctuating each word with his first finger, "I have the greatest respect for the old parliaments, those worthy models of our modern magistracy, those incorruptible defenders of national freedom, but my veneration is none the less great for the institutions emanating from our wise constitution, and it prevents me from adopting an exclusive opinion. However, without pretending to proclaim in too absolute a manner the superiority of the old system over the new, I am in a certain sense of Monsieur de Camier's opinion. In my position, I am better able than any other person to study the advantages and disadvantages of a jury, and I am forced to admit that if the advantages are real, the disadvantages are none the less indisputable. One of the great vices of juries consists in the habit that a great number of its members have of calling for material proofs in order to form their opinions. They must almost see the wounds of the victim before agreeing on a verdict. As to Lambernier, I hope that they will not contest the existence of the main evidence: the victim's still bleeding thigh."

"Tra-de-ri-di-ra," exclaimed the artist, striking alternately with his knife a glass and a bottle, as if he were playing a triangle. "I must say that you choose madly gay subjects for conversation. We are truly a joyous crowd; look at Bergenheim opposite us; he looks like Macbeth in the presence of Banquo's ghost; here is my friend Gerfaut drinking water with a profoundly solemn air. Good gracious, gentlemen! enough of this foolish talk! Let them cut this Lambernier's throat and put an end to the subject! The theatre for dramatic music, the church for sacred!

> Le vin, le jeu, les belles,
> Voilà mes seuls amours."

A general protestation rose from the whole table at this verse, which was roared out in a lugubrious voice. Noisy shouts, rapping of knives upon tumblers and bottles, and exclamations of all kinds called the orator to order.

"Monsieur Marillac," exclaimed the public prosecutor, in a joking tone, "it seems to me that you have wandered from the subject."

The artist looked at him with an astonished air.

"Had I anything in particular to say to you?" he

asked; "if so, I will sustain my point. Only do me the kindness to tell me what it was about."

"It was on the subject of this man Lambernier," whispered the notary to him, as he poured out a glass of wine. "Courage! you improvise better than Berryer! If you exert yourself, the public prosecutor will be beaten in no time."

Marillac thanked his neighbor with a smile and a nod of the head, which signified: "Trust me." He then emptied his glass with the recklessness that had characterized his drinking for some time, but, strangely enough, the libation, instead of putting the finishing stroke to his drunkenness, gave his mind, for the time being, a sort of lucidity.

"The accusation," he continued, with the coolness of an old lawyer, "rests upon two grounds: first, the presence without cause of the accused upon the spot where the crime was committed; second, the nature of the weapon used.—Two simple but peremptory replies will make the scaffold which has been erected upon this double supposition fall to the ground. First, Lambernier had a rendezvous at this place, and at the exact hour when this crime with which he is accused took place; this will be proved by a witness, and will be established by evidence in a most indisputable manner. His presence will thus be explained without its being interpreted in any way against him. Second, the public prosecutor has admitted that the carrying of a weapon which Lambernier may have been in the habit of using in his regular trade could not be used as an argument against him, and for that same reason could not be used as an argument in favor of premeditation; now, this is precisely the case in question. This weapon was neither a sword, bayonet, nor stiletto, nothing that the fertile imagination of the public prosecutor could imagine; it was a simple tool used by the accused in his profession, the presence of which in his pocket is as easily understood as that of a snuff-box in the pocket of my neighbor, the notary, who takes twenty pinches of snuff a minute. Gentlemen, this weapon was a pair of carpenter's compasses."

"A compass!" exclaimed several voices at once.

"A compass!" exclaimed the Baron, gazing fixedly at the artist. Then he carried his hand to his pocket, and suddenly withdrew it, as he felt the workman's compass there, where it had been ever since the scene upon the rocks.

"An iron compass," repeated the artist, "about ten inches long, more or less, the legs of it being closed."

"Will you explain yourself, Monsieur?" excitedly exclaimed the public prosecutor, "for it really seems as if you had witnessed the crime. In that case you will be called out as a witness for the defence. Justice is impartial, gentlemen. Justice has not two pairs of scales."

"To the devil with justice! You must have come from Timbuctoo to use such old-fashioned metaphors."

"Make your deposition, witness; I require you to make your deposition," said the magistrate, whose increasing drunkenness appeared as dignified and solemn as the artist was noisy.

"I have nothing to state; I saw nothing."

Here the Baron drew a long breath, as if these words were a relief.

"But I saw something!" said Gerfaut to himself, as he gazed at the Baron's face, upon which anxiety was depicted.

"I reason by hypothesis and supposition," continued the artist. "I had a little altercation with Lambernier a few days ago, and, but for my good poniard, he would have put an end to me as he did to this fellow to-day."

He then related his meeting with Lambernier, but the consideration due Mademoiselle Gobillot's honor imposed numberless circumlocutions and concealments which ended by making his story rather unintelligible to his auditors, and in the midst of it his head became so muddled that he was completely put out.

"*Basta!*" he exclaimed, in conclusion, as he dropped heavily into his chair. "Not another word for the whole empire. Give me something to drink! Notary, you are the only man here who has any regard for me. One thing is certain about this matter—I am in ten louis by this rascal's adventure."

These words struck the Baron forcibly, as they brought to his mind what the carpenter had said to him when he gave him the letter.

"Ten louis!" said he, suddenly, looking at Marillac as if he wished to look into his very heart.

"Two hundred francs, if you like it better. A genuine bargain. But we have talked enough, *mio caro;* you deceive yourselves if you think you are going to make me blab. No, indeed! I am not the one to allow myself to become entangled. I am now as mute and silent as the grave."

Bergenheim insisted no longer, but, leaning against the back of his chair, he let his head fall upon his breast. He remained for some time buried in thought and vainly trying to connect the obscure words he had just heard with Lambernier's incomplete revelations. With the exception of Gerfaut, who did not lose one of his host's movements, the guests, more or less absorbed by their own sensations, paid no attention to the strange attitude of the master of the house, or, like Monsieur de Camier, attributed it to the influence of wine. The conversation continued its noisy course, interrupted every few moments by the startling vagaries of some guest more animatedly excited than the rest, for, at the end of a repast where sobriety has not reigned, each one is disposed to impose upon others the despotism of his own intoxication, and the idle talk of his peculiar hallucinations. Marillac bore away the prize among the talking contingent, thanks to the vigor of his lungs and the originality of his words, which sometimes forced the attention of his adversaries. Finally he remained master of the field, and flashed volleys of his drunken eloquence to the right and left.

"It is a pity," he exclaimed, in the midst of his triumph, as he glanced disdainfully up and down the table, "it really is a pity, gentlemen, to listen to your conversation. One could imagine nothing more commonplace—prosaic or *bourgeois*. Would it not please you to indulge in a discussion of a little higher order?

Let us join hands, and talk of poetry and art. I am thirsting for an artistic conversation; I am thirsting for wit and intelligence."

"You must drink if you are thirsty," said the notary, filling his glass to the brim.

The artist emptied it at one draught, and continued in a languishing voice as he gazed with a loving look at his fat neighbor.

"I will begin our artistic conversation: 'Knowest thou the land where the orange-flower blooms?'"

"It is warmer than ours," replied the notary, who was not familiar with Mignon's song; and, beginning to laugh maliciously, he gave a wink at his neighbors as if to say:

"I have settled him now."

Marillac leaned toward him with the meekness of a lamb that presents his head to the butcher, and sympathetically pressed his hands.

"O poet!" he continued, "do you not feel, as I do at the twilight hour and in the eventide, a vague desire for a sunny, perfumed, southern life? Will you not bid adieu to this sterile country and sail away to a land where the blue sky is reflected in the blue sea? Venice! the Rialto, the Bridge of Sighs, Saint Mark! Rome! the Coliseum and Saint Peter—But I know Italy by heart; let us go instead to Constantinople. I am thirsting for sultanas and houris; I am thirsting——"

"Good gracious! why do you not drink if you are thirsty?"

"Gladly. I never say no to that. I scorn love in a nightcap; I adore danger. Danger is life to me.

GERFAUT

I dote on silken ladders as long as Jacob's, on citadels worth scaling; on moonlight evenings, bearded husbands, and all that sort of thing—I would love a bed composed of five hundred poniards; you understand me, poet——"

"I beg of you, do not make him drink any more," said Gerfaut to the notary.

"You are right not to wish to drink any more, Octave, I was about to advise you not to. You have already drunk to excess to-day, and I am afraid that it will make you ill; your health is so weak—you are not a strong man like me. Fancy, gentlemen, Monsieur le Vicomte de Gerfaut, a native of Gascony, a *roué* by profession, a star of the first magnitude in literature, is afflicted by nature with a stomach which has nothing in common with that of an ostrich; he has need to use the greatest care. So we have him drink seltzer-water principally, and feed him on the white meat of the chicken. Besides, we keep this precious phenomenon rolled up between two wool blankets and over a kettle of boiling water. He is a great poet; I myself am a very great poet."

"And I also, I hope," said the notary.

"Gentlemen, formerly there were poets who wrote only in verse; nowadays they revel in prose. There are some even who are neither prose nor verse writers, who have never confided their secret to anybody, and who selfishly keep their poetry to themselves. It is a very simple thing to be a poet, provided you feel the indescribable intoxication of the soul, and understand the inexpressible afflatus that bubbles over in your large brain, and your noble heart throbs under your left breast——"

"He is as drunk as a fool," said M. de Camier, loud enough for him to hear.

"Old man," said he, "you are the one who is drunk. Besides the word drunk is not civil; if you had said intoxicated I should not have objected."

Loud shouts of laughter burst forth from the party. He threw a threatening glance around him, as if he were seeking some one upon whom to vent his anger, and, placing his hand upon his hip, assumed the pose of a bully.

"Softly, my good fellows!" said he, "if any of you pretend that I am drunk, I declare to him that he lies, and I call him a misantrophe, a vagabond, an academician!" he concluded, with a loud burst of laughter; for he thought that the jesters would be crushed by this last heavy weapon.

"By Jove! your friend is hilariously drunk," said the notary to Gerfaut; "while here is Bergenheim, who has not taken very much wine, and yet looks as if he were assisting at a funeral. I thought he was more substantial than this."

Marillac's voice burst out more loudly than ever, and Octave's reply was not heard.

"It is simply astounding. They are all as drunk as fools, and yet they pretend that it is I who am drunk. Very well! I defy you all; who among you wishes to argue with me? Will you discuss art, literature, politics, medicine, music, philosophy, archæology, jurisprudence, magnetism——"

GERFAUT

"Jurisprudence!" exclaimed the thick voice of the public prosecutor, who was aroused from his stupor by this magic word; "let us talk jurisprudence."

"Would you like," said Marillac, without stopping at this interruption, "that I should improvise a discourse upon the death penalty or upon temperance? Would you like me to tell you a story?"

"A story, yes, a story!" they all exclaimed in unison.

"Speak out, then; order what story you like; it will cost you nothing," replied the artist, rubbing his hands with a radiant air. "Would you like a tale from the Middle Ages? a fairy, an eastern, a comical, or a private story? I warn you that the latter style is less old-fashioned than the others."

"Let us have it, then, by all means," said all the drunken voices.

"Very well. Now would you like it to be laid in Spain, Arabia, or France?"

"France!" exclaimed the prosecutor.

"I am French, you are French, he is French. You shall have a French story."

Marillac leaned his forehead upon his hands, and his elbows upon the table, as if to gather his scattered ideas. After a few moments' reflection, he raised his head and looked first at Gerfaut, then at Bergenheim, with a peculiar smile.

"It would be very original," said he, in a low voice as if replying to his own thoughts.

"The story!" exclaimed one of the party, more impatient than the rest.

"Here it is," replied the artist. "You all know,

gentlemen, how difficult it always is to choose a title. In order not to make you wait, I have chosen one which is already well known. My story is to be called 'The husband, the wife, and the lover.' We are not all single men here, and a wise proverb says that one must never speak——"

In spite of his muddled brain, the artist did not finish his quotation. A remnant of common-sense made him realize that he was treading upon dangerous ground and was upon the point of committing an unpardonable indiscretion. Fortunately, the Baron had paid no attention to his words; but Gerfaut was frightened at his friend's jabbering, and threw him a glance of the most threatening advice to be prudent. Marillac vaguely understood his mistake, and was half intimidated by this glance; he leaned before the notary and said to him, in a voice which he tried to make confidential, but which could be heard from one end of the table to the other:

"Be calm, Octave, I will tell it in obscure words and in such a way that he will not see anything in it. It is a scene for a drama that I have in my mind."

"You will make some grotesque blunder, if you go on drinking and talking," replied Gerfaut, in an anxious voice. "Hold your tongue, or else come away from the table with me."

"When I tell you that I will use obscure words," replied the artist; "what do you take me for? I swear to you that I will gloss it over in such a way that nobody will suspect anything."

"The story! the story!" exclaimed several, who

were amused by the incoherent chattering of the artist.

"Here it is," said the latter, sitting upright in his chair and paying no heed to his friend's warnings. "The scene takes place in a little court in Germany— Eh!" said he, looking at Gerfaut and maliciously winking his eye—"do you not think that is glossed over?"

"Not in a German court, you said it was to be a French story," said the public prosecutor, disposed to play the critic toward the orator who had reduced him to silence.

"Well, it is a French story, but the scene is laid in Germany," he replied, coolly.—"Do you desire to teach me my profession? Understand that nothing is more elastic than a German court; the story-teller can introduce there whoever he likes; I may bring in the Shah of Persia and the Emperor of China if I care to. However, if you prefer the court of Italy, it is the same thing to me."

This conciliating proposal remained without response. Marillac continued raising his eyes in such a way that nothing but the whites could be seen, and as if he were searching for his words in the ceiling.

"The Princess Borinski was walking slowly in the mysterious alley on the borders of the foaming torrent——"

"Borinski! she is a Pole, then?" interrupted M. de Camier.

"Oh! go to the devil, old man! Do not interrupt me," exclaimed the artist, impatiently.

"That is right. Silence now."

"You have the floor," said several voices at once.

"—She was pale, and she heaved convulsive sighs and wrung her soft, warm hands, and a white pearl rolled from her dark lashes, and——"

"Why do you begin all your phrases with 'and?'" asked the public prosecutor, with the captiousness of an inexorable critic.

"Because it is biblical and unaffected. Now let me alone," replied Marillac, with superb disdain. "You are a police-officer; I am an artist; what is there in common between you and me? I will continue: And he saw this pensive, weeping woman pass in the distance, and he said to the Prince: 'Borinski, a bit of root in which my foot caught has hurt my limb, will you suffer me to return to the palace? And the Prince Borinski said to him, 'Shall my men carry you in a palanquin?' and the cunning Octave replied——"

"Your story has not even common-sense and you are a terrible bore," interrupted Gerfaut brusquely. "Gentlemen, are we going to sit at the table all night?"

He arose, but nobody followed his example. Bergenheim, who for the last few minutes had lent an attentive ear to the artist's story, gazed alternately at the two friends with an observing eye.

"Let him talk," said the young magistrate, with an ironical smile. "I like the palanquin in the court of Germany. That is probably what novelists call local color. O Racine, poor, deserted Racine!"

Marillac was not intimidated this time by Gerfaut's withering glance, but, with the obstinacy of drunkenness, continued in a more or less stammering voice:

"I swore that I would gloss it over; you annoy me. I committed an error, gentlemen, in calling the lover in this story Octave. It is as clear as day that his name is Boleslas, Boleslas Matalowski. There is no more connection between him and my friend Octave than there is between my other friend Bergenheim and the prince Kolinski—Woginski—what the devil has become of my Prince's name? A good reward to whoever will tell me his name!"

"It is wrong to take advantage of his condition and make him talk any more," said Gerfaut. "I beg of you, Marillac, hold your tongue and come with me," said he, lowering his voice as he leaned toward the headstrong story-teller and took him by the arm, trying to make him rise. This attempt only irritated Marillac; he seized hold of the edge of the table and clung to it with all his might, screaming:

"No! a thousand times no! I will finish my story. President, allow me to speak. Ah! ha! you wish to prevent me from speaking because you know that I tell a story better than you, and that I make an impression upon my audience. You never have been able to catch my *chic*. Jealous! Envious! I know you, serpent!"

"I beg of you, if you ever cared for me, listen!" replied Octave, who, as he bent over his friend, noticed the Baron's attentive look.

"No, I say no!" shouted the artist again, and he added to this word one of the ugliest-sounding oaths in the French language. He arose, and pushing Octave aside, leaned upon the table, bursting into a loud laugh.

"Poets all," said he, "be reassured and rejoice. You shall have your story, in spite of those envious serpents. But first give me something to drink, for my throat is like a box of matches. No wine," he added, as he saw the notary armed with a bottle. "This devilish wine has made me thirsty instead of refreshing me; besides, I am going to be as sober as a judge."

Gerfaut, with the desperation of a man who sees that he is about to be ruined, seized him again by the arm and tried to fascinate him by his steady gaze. But he obtained no response to this mute and threatening supplication except a stupid smile and these stammering words:

"Give me something to drink, Boleslas—Marinski—Graboski—I believe that Satan has lighted his heating apparatus within my stomach."

The persons seated near the two friends heard an angry hiss from Gerfaut's lips. He suddenly leaned over, and taking, from among several bottles, a little carafe he filled Marillac's glass to the brim.

"Thanks," said the latter, trying to stand erect upon his legs; "you are an angel. Rest easy, your love affairs will run no risk. I will gloss it all over—To your health, gentlemen!"

He emptied the glass and put it upon the table; he then smiled and waved his hand at his auditors with true royal courtesy; but his mouth remained half open as if his lips were petrified, his eyes grew large and assumed a haggard expression; the hand he had stretched out fell to his side; a second more, and he reeled and fell from his chair as if he had had a stroke of apoplexy.

GERFAUT

Gerfaut, whose eyes had not left him, watched these different symptoms with unutterable anxiety; but in spite of his fright, he drew a sigh of relief when he saw Marillac mute and speechless.

"It is singular," observed the notary, as he aided in removing his neighbor from the table, "that glass of water had more effect upon him than four or five bottles of wine."

"Georges," said Gerfaut to one of the servants, in an agitated voice, "open his bed and help me carry him to it; Monsieur de Bergenheim, I suppose there is a chemist near here, if I should need any medicine."

The greater part of the guests arose at this unexpected incident, and some of them hastened to Marillac's side, as he remained motionless in his chair. The repeated bathing of his temples with cold water and the holding of salts to his nose were not able to bring him to consciousness.

Instead of going to his aid with the others, Bergenheim profited by the general confusion to lean over the table. He plunged his finger into the artist's glass, in which a part of the water remained, and then touched his tongue. Only the notary noticed this movement. Thinking this rather strange, he seized the glass in his turn and swallowed the few drops that it contained.

"Heavens!" he exclaimed, in a low voice, to Bergenheim, "I am not surprised that the bumper asphyxiated him on the spot. Do you know, Baron, if this Monsieur de Gerfaut had taken anything but water during the evening, I should say that he was the drunker of the two; or that, if they were not such good friends, he wished to poison him in order to stop his talk. Did you notice that he did not seem pleased to hear this story?"

"Ah! you, too!" exclaimed the Baron angrily, "everybody will know it."

"To take a carafe of kirsch for clear water!" continued the notary, without paying any attention to the Baron's agitation. "The devil! the safe thing to do is to give him an emetic at once; this poor fellow has enough prussic acid in his stomach to poison a cow."

"Who is talking of prussic acid and poisoning?" exclaimed the public prosecutor, running with an unsteady step from one extremity of the table to the other, "who has been poisoned? I am the public prosecutor, I am the only one here who has any power to start an investigation. Have they had an autopsy? Where did they find it? Buried in the fields or the woods, or floating on the river?"

"You lie! there is no dead body in the river!" exclaimed Bergenheim, in a thundering voice, as he seized the magistrate by the collar in a bewildered way.

The magistrate was incapable of making the least resistance when held by such a vigorous hand and he received two or three shakings. Suddenly the Baron stopped, and struck his forehead with a gesture common to persons who feel that their reason has given way under a paroxysm of rage.

"I am crazy," said he, with much emotion. "Monsieur," he added, "I am very sorry. We really have all taken too much wine. I beg your pardon, gentlemen. I will leave you a moment—I need some fresh air."

GERFAUT

He hurriedly left the room, almost running against the persons who were carrying Marillac to his room. The public prosecutor, whose ideas had been somewhat mixed before, was now completely muddled by this unheard-of attack upon his dignity, and fell back exhausted in his chair.

"All poor drinkers!" said the notary to Monsieur de Camier who was left alone with him, for the prosecutor, half suffocated with indignation and intoxication, could no longer be counted as one of them. "Here they are, all drunk, from just a few glasses of wine."

The notary shook his head with a mysterious air.

"These things, though, are plain enough to me," said he at last; "first, this Monsieur Marillac has not a very strong head and tells pretty tedious stories when drunk; then his friend has a way of taking kirsch for water which I can understand only in extreme cases; but the Baron is the one who astonished me most. Did you notice how he shook our friend who has just fallen on the floor? As to the Baron pretending that he was drunk and thus excusing himself, I do not believe one word of it; he drank nothing but water. There were times this evening when he appeared very strange indeed! There is some deviltry underneath all this; Monsieur de Camier, rest assured there is some deviltry underneath it all."

"I am the public prosecutor—they can not remove the body without me," stammered the weak voice of the magistrate, who, after trying in vain to recover his equilibrium, lay flat upon the floor.

CHAPTER XXI

A STRATAGEM

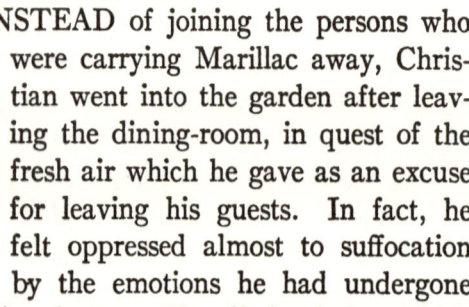NSTEAD of joining the persons who were carrying Marillac away, Christian went into the garden after leaving the dining-room, in quest of the fresh air which he gave as an excuse for leaving his guests. In fact, he felt oppressed almost to suffocation by the emotions he had undergone during the last few hours. The dissimulation which prudence made a necessity and honor a duty had aggravated the suffering by protracted concealment.

For some time Christian walked rapidly among the paths and trees in the park. Bathing his burning brow in the cool night air, he sought to calm the secret agitation and the boiling blood that were raging within him, in the midst of which his reason struggled and fought like a ship about to be wrecked. He used all his strength to recover his self-possession, so as to be able to master the perils and troubles which surrounded him with a calm if not indifferent eye; in one word, to regain that control over himself that he had lost several times during the supper. His efforts were not in vain. He contemplated his situation without weakness, exaggeration, or anger, as if it concerned another. Two facts

rose foremost before him, one accomplished, the other
uncertain. On one side, murder, on the other, adultery. No human power could remedy the first or prevent its consequences; he accepted it, then, but turn his
mind away from it he must, in the presence of this
greater disaster. So far, only presumptions existed
against Clémence—grave ones, to be sure, if one added
Lambernier's revelations to Marillac's strangely indiscreet remarks. It was his first duty to himself, as well
as to her, to know the whole truth; if innocent, he
would beg her forgiveness; if guilty, he had a chastise-
ment to inflict.

"It is an abyss," thought he, "and I may find as
much blood as mud at the bottom of it. No matter,
I will descend to its very depths."

When he returned to the château, his face had resumed its usual calm expression. The most observing
person would hardly have noticed any change in his
looks. The dining-room had been abandoned at last.
The victorious and the vanquished had retired to their
rooms. First of all, he went up to the artist's apartment, so that no singularity in his conduct should
attract attention, for, as master of the house, a visit
to one of his guests who had fallen dead, or nearly so,
at his own table was a positive duty. The attentions
lavished upon Marillac by his friend had removed the
danger which might have resulted from his imprudent
excesses in drinking, and the sort of poisoning with
which he had crowned the whole. He lay upon his
bed in the same position in which he had first been
placed, and was sleeping that heavy, painful sleep

which serves as an expiation for bacchic excesses. Gerfaut was seated a few steps from him, at a table, writing; he seemed prepared to sit up all night, and to fulfill, with the devotion of a friend, the duties of a nurse.

Octave arose at sight of the Baron, his face having resumed its habitual reserved expression. The two men greeted each other with equal composure.

"Is he sleeping?" asked Christian.

"But a few minutes only," replied the latter; "he is all right now, and I hope," Octave added, smilingly, "that this will serve as a lesson to you, and that hereafter you will put some limits to your princely hospitality. Your table is a regular ambush."

"Do not throw stones at me, I pray," replied the Baron, with an appearance of equal good-humor. "If your friend wants to ask an explanation of anybody it is of you, for you took some kirsch of 1765 for water."

"I really believe that I was the drunker of the two," interrupted Octave, with a vivacity which concealed a certain embarrassment; "we must have terribly scandalized Monsieur de Camier, who has but a poor opinion of Parisian heads and stomachs."

After looking for a moment at the sleeping artist, Christian approached the table where Gerfaut was seated, and threw a glance over the latter's writing.

"You are still at work, I see?" said he, as his eyes rested upon the paper.

"Just now I am following the modest trade of copyist. These are some verses which Mademoiselle de Corandeuil asked me for——"

"Will you do me a favor? I am going to her room

now; give me these verses to hand to her. Since the
misfortune that befell Constance, she has been terribly
angry with me, and I shall not be sorry to have some
reason for going to her room."

Octave finished the two or three lines which remained to be copied, and handed the sheet to Bergenheim. The latter looked at it attentively, then carefully folded it and put it in his pocket.

"I thank you, Monsieur," said he, "I will leave you
to your friendly duties."

There was something so solemn in the calm accent
of these words, and the polite bow which accompanied
them, that Gerfaut felt chilled, though not alarmed,
for he did not understand.

When he reached his room, Bergenheim opened the
paper which Gerfaut had just given him and compared
it with the letter he had received from Lambernier.
The suspicions which a separate examination had
aroused were confirmed upon comparing the two letters; no doubt was possible; the letter and the poetry
were written by the same hand!

After a few moments' reflection, Christian went to
his wife's room.

Clémence was seated in an armchair, near the fireplace, indulging in a revery. Although her lover was
not there, she was still under the charm of this consum-
ing as well as intellectual passion, which responded to
the yearnings of her heart, the delicacy of her tastes,
and the activity of her imagination. At this moment,
she was happy to live; there was not a sad thought
that these words, "He loves me!" could not efface.

CHARLES DE BERNARD

The noise of the opening door aroused her from her meditation. Madame de Bergenheim turned her head with a look of vexation, but instead of the servant whom she was ready to reprimand, she saw her husband. The expression of impatience imprinted upon her face gave way to one of fright. She arose with a movement she could not repress, as if she had seen a stranger, and stood leaning against the mantel in a constrained attitude. Nothing in Christian's manner justified, however, the fear the sight of him seemed to cause his wife. He advanced with a tranquil air, and a smile that he had forced upon his lips.

With the presence of mind with which all women seem to be gifted, Clémence fell back into her chair, and, assuming a languid, suffering tone, mixed with an appearance of reproach, she said:

"I am glad to see you for a moment in order to scold you; you have not shown your usual consideration to-night. Did you not think that the noise from the dining-room might reach as far as here?"

"Has it troubled you?" asked Christian, looking at her attentively.

"Unless one had a head of cast-iron—It seems that these gentlemen have abused the liberty permitted in the country. From what Justine tells me, things have taken place which would have been more appropriate at the Femme-sans-Tête."

"Are you suffering very much?"

"A frightful neuralgia—I only wish I could sleep."

"I was wrong not to have thought of this. You will forgive me, will you not?"

Bergenheim leaned over the chair, passed his arm around the young woman's shoulders, and pressed his lips to her forehead. For the first time in his life, he was playing a part upon the marital stage, and he watched with the closest attention the slightest expression of his wife's face. He noticed that she shivered, and that her forehead which he had lightly touched was as cold as marble.

He arose and took several turns about the room, avoiding even a glance at her, for the aversion which she had just shown toward her husband seemed to him positive proof of the very thing he dreaded, and he feared he should not be able to contain himself.

"What is the matter with you?" she asked, as she noticed his agitation.

These words brought the Baron to his senses, and he returned to her side, replying in a careless tone:

"I am annoyed for a very simple cause; it concerns your aunt."

"I know. She is furious against you on account of the double misfortune to her dog and coachman. You will admit that, as far as Constance is concerned, you are guilty."

"She is not content with being furious; she threatens a complete rupture. Here, read this."

He handed her a large letter, folded lengthwise and sealed with the Corandeuil crest.

Madame de Bergenheim took the letter and read its contents aloud:

"After the unheard-of and unqualifiable events of this day, the resolution which I have formed will doubtless not surprise you in the least, Monsieur. You will understand that I can not and will not remain longer in a house where the lives of my servants and other creatures which are dear to me may be exposed to the most deplorable, wilful injury. I have seen for some time, although I have tried to close my eyes to the light of truth, the plots that were hatched daily against all who wore the Corandeuil livery. I supposed that I should not be obliged to put an end to this highly unpleasant matter myself, but that you would undertake this charge. It seems, however, that respect and regard for women do not form part of a gentleman's duties nowadays. I shall therefore be obliged to make up myself for the absence of such attentions, and watch over the safety of the persons and other creatures that belong to me. I shall leave for Paris to-morrow. I hope that Constance's condition will permit her to endure the journey, but Baptiste's wound is too serious for me to dare to expose him. I am compelled, although with deep regret, to leave him here until he is able to travel, trusting him to the kind mercies of my niece.

"Receive, Monsieur, with my adieux, my thanks for your courteous hospitality.

"YOLANDE DE CORANDEUIL."

"Your aunt abuses the privileges of being foolish," said the Baron, when his wife had finished reading the letter; "she deserts the battlefield and leaves behind her wounded."

"But I saw her, not two hours ago, and, although she was very angry, she did not say one word of this departure."

"Jean handed me this letter but a moment ago, clad in full livery, and with the importance of an ambassador who demands his passports. You must go and talk with her, dear, and use all your eloquence to make her change her mind."

"I will go at once," said Clémence, rising.

"You know that your aunt is rather obstinate when she takes a notion into her head. If she persists in this, tell her, in order to decide her to remain, that I am obliged to go to Epinal with Monsieur de Camier to-morrow morning, on account of the sale of some wood-land, and that I shall be absent three days at least. You understand that it will be difficult for your aunt to leave you alone during my absence, on account of these gentlemen."

"Certainly, that could not be," said she, quickly.

"I do not see, as far as I am concerned, anything improper about it," said the Baron, trying to smile; "but we must obey the proprieties. You are too young and too pretty a mistress of the house to pass for a chaperon, and Aline, instead of being a help, would be one inconvenience the more. So your aunt must stay here until my return."

"And by that time Constance and Baptiste will be both cured and her anger will have passed away. You did not tell me about this trip to Epinal nor the selling of the wood-land."

"Go to your aunt's room before she retires to bed," replied Bergenheim, without paying any attention to this remark, and seating himself in the armchair; "I will wait for you here. We leave to-morrow morning early, and I wish to know to-night what to depend upon."

As soon as Madame de Bergenheim had left the room, Christian arose and ran, rather than walked, to the space between the two windows, and sought the button in the woodwork of which Lambernier had told him. He soon found it, and upon his first pressure the spring worked and the panel flew open. The casket was upon the shelf; he took it and carefully examined the letters which it contained. The greater part of them resembled in form the one that he possessed; some of them were in envelopes directed to Madame de Bergenheim and bore Gerfaut's crest. There was no doubt about the identity of the handwriting; if the Baron had had any, these proofs were enough. After glancing rapidly over a few of the notes, he replaced them in the casket and returned the latter to the shelf where he had found it. He then carefully closed the little door and reseated himself beside the fireplace.

When Clémence returned, her husband seemed absorbed in reading one of the books which he had found upon her table, while he mechanically played with a little bronze cup that his wife used to drop her rings in when she removed them.

"I have won my case," said the Baroness, in a gay tone; "my aunt saw clearly the logic of the reasons which I gave her, and she defers her departure until your return."

Christian made no reply.

"That means that she will not go at all, for her anger will have time to cool off in three days; at heart she is really kind!—How long is it since you have known English?" she asked, as she noticed that her husband's attention seemed to be fixed upon a volume of Lord Byron's poems.

Bergenheim threw the book on the table, raised his head and gazed calmly at his wife. In spite of all his efforts, his face had assumed an expression which would have frightened her if she had noticed it, but her eyes were fastened upon the cup which he was twisting in his hand as if it were made of clay.

"*Mon Dieu!* Christian, what is the matter with you? What are you doing to my poor cup?" she asked, with surprise mingled with a little of that fright which is so prompt to be aroused if one feels not above reproach.

He arose and put the misshapen bronze upon the table.

"I do not know what ails me to-night," said he, "my nerves are unstrung. I will leave you, for I need rest myself. I shall start to-morrow morning before you are up, and I shall return Wednesday."

"Not any later, I hope," she said, with that soft, sweet voice, from which, in such circumstances, very few women have the loyalty to abstain.

He went out without replying, for he feared he might be no longer master of himself; he felt, when offered this hypocritical, almost criminal, caress, as if he would like to end it all by killing her on the spot.

CHAPTER XXII

THE CRISIS

WENTY-FOUR hours had passed. The Baron had departed early in the morning, and so had all his guests, with the exception of Gerfaut and the artist. The day passed slowly and tediously. Aline had been vexed, somewhat estranged from her sister-in-law since their conversation in the little parlor. Mademoiselle de Corandeuil was entirely occupied in restoring her poodle to health.

Marillac, who had been drinking tea ever since rising, dared not present his face, which showed the effects of his debauch of the night before, to the mistress of the house, whose exacting and aristocratic austerity he very much feared. He pretended to be ill, in order to delay the moment when he should be forced to make his appearance. Madame de Bergenheim did not leave her aunt, and thus avoided being alone with Octave—who, on account of these different complications, might have spent a continual *tête-à-tête* with her had she been so inclined. Christian's absence, instead of being a signal of deliverance for the lovers, seemed to have created a new misunderstanding, for Clémence felt that it would be a mean action to abuse

[310]

the liberty her husband's departure gave her. She was thus very reserved during the day, when she felt that there were more facilities for yielding, but, in the evening, when alone in her apartment, this fictitious prudery disappeared. She spent the entire evening lying upon the divan in the little boudoir, dreaming of Octave, talking to him as if he could reply, putting into practice again that capitulation of conscience which permits our mind to wander on the brink of guilt, provided actions are strictly correct.

After a while this exaltation fell by degrees. When struggling earnestly, she had regarded Octave as an enemy; but, since she had gone to him as one passes over to the enemy, and, in her heart, had taken part with the lover against the husband, her courage failed her as she thought of this, and she fell, weak, guilty, and vanquished before the combat.

When she had played with her passion, she had given Christian little thought; she had felt it childish to bring her husband into an amusement that she believed perfectly harmless; then, when she wished to break her plaything, and found it made of iron and turning more and more into a tyrannical yoke, she called to her aid the conjugal divinities, but in too faint a voice to be heard. Now the situation had changed again. Christian was no longer the insignificant ally that the virtuous wife had condemned, through self-conceit, to ignorant neutrality; he was the husband, in the hostile and fearful acceptation of the word. This man whom she had wronged would always have law on his side.

CHARLES DE BERNARD

Religion sometimes takes pity on a wayward wife, but society is always ready to condemn her. She was his own, fastened to him by indissoluble bonds. He had marked her with his name like a thing of his own; he held the threads of her life in his hands; he was the dispenser of her fortune, the judge of her actions, and the master of their fireside. She had no dignity except through him. If he should withdraw his support for a single day, she would fall from her position without any human power being able to rescue her. Society closes its doors to the outcast wife, and adds to the husband's sentence another penalty still more scathing.

Having now fallen from the sphere of illusion to that of reality, Madame de Bergenheim was wounded at every step. A bitter feeling of discouragement overwhelmed her, as she thought of the impossibility of happiness to which a deplorable fatality condemned her. Marriage and love struggled for existence, both powerless to conquer, and qualified only to cause each other's death. Marriage made love a crime; love made marriage a torture. She could only choose between two abysses: shame in her love, despair in her virtue.

The hours passed rapidly in these sad and gloomy meditations; the clock marked the hour of midnight. Madame de Bergenheim thought it time to try to sleep; but, instead of ringing for her maid, she decided to go to the library herself and get a book, thinking that perhaps it might aid her in going to sleep. As she opened the door leading into the closet adjoining her parlor, she saw by the light of the candle which she held in her hand something which shone like a precious stone lying upon the floor. At first she thought it might be one of her rings, but as she stooped to pick it up she saw her error. It was a ruby pin mounted in enamelled gold. She recognized it, at the very first glance, as belonging to M. de Gerfaut.

She picked up the pin and returned to the parlor She exhausted in imagination a thousand conjectures in order to explain the presence of this object in such a place. Octave must have entered it or he could not have left this sign of his presence; it meant that he could enter her room at his will; what he had done once, he could certainly do again! The terror which this thought gave her dissipated like a dash of cold water all her former intoxicating thoughts; for, like the majority of women, she had more courage in theory than in action. A moment before, she had invoked Octave's image and seated it lovingly by her side.

When she believed this realization possible, all she thought of was to prevent it. She was sure that her lover never had entered the closet through the parlor, as he never had been in this part of the house farther than the little drawing-room. Suddenly a thought of the little corridor door struck her; she remembered that this door was not usually locked because the one from the library was always closed; she knew that Octave had a key to the latter, and she readily understood how he had reached her apartment. Mustering up all her courage through excessive fear, she returned to the closet, hurried down the stairs, and pushed the bolt. She then returned to the parlor and fell upon the divan, completely exhausted by her expedition.

Little by little her emotion passed away. Her fright appeared childish to her, as soon as she believed herself sheltered from danger; she promised herself to give Octave a good scolding the next morning; then she renounced this little pleasure, when she remembered that it would force her to admit the discovery of the pin, and of course to return it to him, for she had resolved to keep it. She had always had a particular fancy for this pin, but she would never have dared to ask him for it, and besides, it was the fact that Octave usually wore it that made it of infinite value to her. The desire to appropriate it was irresistible, since chance had thrown it into her hands. She tied a black satin ribbon about her white neck, and pinned it with the precious ruby. After kissing it as devotedly as if it were a relic, she ran to her mirror to judge of the effect of the theft.

"How pretty, and how I love it!" said she; "but how can I wear it so that he will not see it?"

Before she could solve this problem, she heard a slight noise, which petrified her as she stood before her glass.

"It is he!" she thought; after standing for a moment half stunned, she dragged herself as far as the stairs, and leaning over, listened with fear and trembling. At first she could hear nothing but the beating of her heart; then she heard the other noise again, and more distinctly. Somebody was turning the handle of the door, trying to open it. The unexpected obstacle of the bolt doubtless exasperated the would-be visitor, for the door was shaken and pushed with a violence which threatened to break the lock or push down the door.

Madame de Bergenheim's first thought was to run into her chamber and lock the door behind her; the second showed her the danger that might result if the slightest noise should reach other ears. Not a moment was to be lost in hesitation. The young woman quickly descended the stairs and drew the bolt. The door opened softly and closed with the same precaution. The lamp from the parlor threw a feeble light upon the upper steps of the staircase, but the lower ones were in complete darkness. It was with her heart rather than her eyes that she recognized Octave; he could distinguish Madame de Bergenheim only in an indistinct way by her white dress, which was faintly outlined in the darkness; she stood before him silent and trembling with emotion, for she had not yet thought of a speech that would send him away.

He also felt the embarrassment usual in any one guilty of so foolhardy an action. He had expected to surprise Clémence, and he found her upon her guard; the thought of the disloyal part he was playing at this moment made the blood mount to his cheeks and took away, for the time being, his ordinary assurance. He sought in vain for a speech which might first justify him and then conquer her. He had recourse to a method often employed in the absence of eloquence. He fell on his knees before the young woman and seized her hands; it seemed as if the violence of his emotions rendered him incapable of expressing himself except by silent adoration. As she felt his hands touch hers, Clémence drew back and said in a low voice:

"You disgust me!"

"Disgust!" he repeated, drawing himself up to his full height.

"Yes, and that is not enough," she continued, indignantly, "I ought to say scorn instead of disgust. You deceived me when you said you loved me—you infamously deceived me!"

"But I adore you!" he exclaimed, with vehemence; "what proof do you wish of my love?"

"Go! go away at once! A proof, did you say? I will accept only one: go, I order it, do you understand?"

Instead of obeying her, he seized her in his arms in spite of her resistance.

"Anything but that," he said; "order me to kill myself at your feet, I will do it, but I will not go."

She tried for a moment to disengage herself, but although she used all her strength, she was unable to do so.

"Oh, you are without pity," she said, feebly, "but I abhor you; rather, a thousand times rather, kill me!"

Gerfaut was almost frightened by the agonized accent in which she spoke these words; he released her, but as he removed his arms, she reeled and he was obliged to support her.

"Why do you persecute me, then?" she murmured, as she fell in a faint upon her lover's breast.

He picked her up in his arms and mounted the narrow stairs with difficulty. Carrying her into the parlor, he placed her upon the divan. She had completely lost consciousness; one would have believed her dead from the pallor of her face, were it not for a slight trembling which agitated her form every few seconds and announced a nervous attack. The most expert of lady's maids could not have removed the little ribbon from her neck, which seemed to trouble her respiration, more adroitly than did Octave. In spite of his anxiety, he could not repress a smile as he recognized the pin which he hardly expected to find upon Clémence's neck, considering the hostile way in which she had greeted him. He knelt before her and bathed her temples with cold water, making her also inhale some salts which he found upon the toilet table in the next room. Little by little, these attentions produced an effect; the nervous convulsion became less frequent and a slight flush suffused her pale cheeks. She opened her eyes and then closed them, as if the light troubled them; then, extending her arms, she passed them about Octave's neck as he leaned over her; she remained thus for some time, breathing quietly and to all appearances sleeping. Suddenly she said:

"You will give me your pin, will you not?"

"Is not all that I have yours?" he replied, in a low tone.

"Mine!" she continued, in a feebly loving voice; "tell me again that you belong to me, to me alone, Octave!"

"You do not send me away any longer, then? you like me to be near you?" he said, with a happy smile, as he kissed the young woman's brow.

[317]

"Oh! stay, I beg of you! stay with me forever!"

She folded her arms more tightly around him, as if she feared he might leave her. Suddenly she sat up, opened her eyes, and gazed about her in silent astonishment.

"What has happened?" said she, "and how is it that you are here? Ah! this is dreadful indeed; you have cruelly punished me for my weakness."

This sudden severity after her delicious abandon, changed Octave's pleasure into angry vexation.

"You are the one," he replied, "who are cruel! Why allow me so much bliss, if you intended to take it away from me so soon? Since you love me only in your dreams, I beg of you to go to sleep again and never awaken. I will stay near you. Your words were so sweet, but a moment ago, and now you deny them!"

"What did I say?" she asked, with hesitation, a deep blush suffusing her face and neck.

These symptoms, which he considered a bad augury, increased Octave's irritation. He arose and said in a bitter tone:

"Fear nothing! I will not abuse the words which have escaped you, however flattering or charming they may have been; they told me that you loved me. I do not believe it any longer; you are agitated, I can see; but it is from fear and not love."

Clémence drew herself up upon the divan, crossed her arms over her breast and gazed at him for a few moments in silence.

"Do you believe these two sentiments incompatible?" she asked at last; "you are the only one whom I fear. Others would not complain."

There was such irresistible charm in her voice and glance that Gerfaut's ill-humor melted away like ice in the sun's rays. He fell upon his knees before the divan, and tried to pass her arms about his neck as before; but instead of lending herself to this project, she attempted to rise.

"I am so happy at your feet," he said, gently preventing her. "Everybody else can sit beside you; I only have the right to kneel. Do not take this right away from me."

Madame de Bergenheim extricated one of her hands, and, raising her finger with a threatening gesture, she said:

"Think a little less of your rights, and more of your duties. I advise you to obey me and to profit by my kindness, which allows you to sit by my side for a moment. Think that I might be more severe, and that if I treated you as you merited—if I told you to go away, would you obey me?"

Gerfaut hesitated a moment and looked at her supplicatingly.

"I would obey," said he; "but would you have the courage to order it?"

"I allow you to remain until just half past twelve," said she, as she glanced at the clock, which she could see through the half-open door. Gerfaut followed her glance, and saw that she accorded him only a quarter of an hour: but he was too clever to make any observation. He knew that the second quarter of an hour is always less difficult to obtain than the first.

"I am sure," said she, "that you have thought me capricious to-day; you must pardon me, it is a family fault. You know the saying: *Caprice de Corandeuil?*"

"I wish it to be said: *Amour de Gerfaut*," said he, tenderly.

"You are right to be amiable and say pleasant things to me, for I need them badly to-night. I am sad and weary; the darkest visions come before my mind. I think it is the storm which makes me feel so. How doleful this thunder is! It seems to me like an omen of misfortune."

"It is only the fancy of your vivid imagination. If you exerted the same will to be happy that you do to imagine troubles, our life would be perfect. What matters the storm? and even if you do see an omen in it, what is there so very terrible? Clouds are vapor, thunder is a sound, both are equally ephemeral; only the blue sky, which they can obscure but for a moment, is eternal."

"Did you not hear something just now?" asked Madame de Bergenheim, as she gave a sudden start and listened eagerly.

"Nothing. What did you think it was?"

"I feared it might be Justine who had taken it into her head to come down stairs; she is so tiresome in her attentions——"

She arose and went to look in her chamber, which she carefully locked; a moment later, she returned and seated herself again upon the divan.

"Justine is sleeping by this time," said Octave; "I

should not have ventured if I had not seen that her light was out."

Clémence took his hand and placed it over her heart.

"Now," said she, "when I tell you that I am frightened, will you believe me?"

"Poor dear!" he exclaimed, as he felt her heart throbbing violently.

"You are the one who causes me these palpitations for the slightest thing. I know that we do not run any danger, that everybody is in his own room by this time, and yet, somehow, I feel terribly frightened. There are women, so they say, who get used to this torture, and end by being guilty and tranquil at the same time. It is an unworthy thought, but I'll confess that, sometimes, when I suffer so, I wish I were like them. But it is impossible; I was not made for wrong-doing. You can not understand this, you are a man; you love boldly, you indulge in every thought that seems sweet to you without being troubled by remorse. And then, when you suffer, your anguish at least belongs to you, nobody has any right to ask you what is the matter. But I, my tears even are not my own; I have often shed them on your account—I must hide them, for he has a right to ask: 'Why do you weep?' And what can I reply?"

She turned away her head to conceal the tears which she could not restrain; he saw them, and, leaning over her, he kissed them away.

"Your tears are mine!" he exclaimed, passionately; "but do not distress me by telling me that our love makes you unhappy."

"Unhappy! oh, yes! very unhappy! and yet I would not change this sorrow for the richest joys of others. This unhappiness is my treasure! To be loved by you! To think that there was a time when our love might have been legitimate! What fatality weighs upon us, Octave? Why did we know each other too late? I often dream a beautiful dream—a dream of freedom."

"You are free if you love me—It is the rain against the windows," said he, seeing Madame de Bergenheim anxiously listening again. They kept silent for a moment, but could hear nothing except the monotonous whistling of the storm.

"To be loved by you and not to blush!" said she, as she gazed at him lovingly. "To be together always, without fearing that a stroke of lightning might separate us! to give you my heart and still be worthy to pray! it would be one of those heavenly delights that one grasps only in dreams——"

"Oh! dream when I shall be far from you; but, when I am at your feet, when our hearts beat only for each other, do not evoke, lest you destroy our present happiness, that which is beyond our power. Do you think there are bonds which can more strongly unite us? Am I not yours? And you, yourself, who speak of the gift of your heart, have you not given it to me entirely?"

"Oh! yes, entirely! And it is but right, since I owe it to you. I did not understand life until the day I received it from your eyes; since that minute I have lived, and I can die. I love you! I fail to find words to tell you one-tenth of what my heart contains, but I love you——"

He received her in his arms, where she took refuge so as to conceal her face after these words. She remained thus for an instant, then arose with a start, seized Octave's hands and pressed them in a convulsive manner, saying in a voice as weak as a dying woman's:

"I am lost!"

He instinctively followed Clémence's gaze, which was fastened upon the glass door. An almost imperceptible movement of the muslin curtain was evident. At the same moment, there was a slight noise, a step upon the carpet, the turning of the handle of the door, and it was silently opened as if by a ghost.

CHAPTER XXIII

ADAME DE BERGENHEIM tried to rise, but her strength failed her, she fell on her knees, and then dropped at her lover's feet. The latter leaped from the divan without trying to assist her, stepped over the body stretched before him, and drew his poniard out of his pocket.

Christian stood upon the threshold of the door silent and motionless.

There was a moment of terrible silence. Only the eyes of the two men spoke; those of the husband were fixed, dull, and implacable; those of the lover sparkled with the audacity of despair. After a moment of mutual fascination, the Baron made a movement as if to enter.

"One step more and you are a dead man!" exclaimed Gerfaut, in a low voice, as he clutched the handle of his poniard.

Christian extended his hand, replying to this threat only by a look; but such an imperative one that the thrust of a lance would not have been as fearful to the lover. Octave put his poniard in its sheath, ashamed of his emotion in the presence of such calm, and imitated his enemy's scornful attitude.

"Come, Monsieur," said the latter, in a low voice, as he took a step backward.

Instead of following his example, Gerfaut cast a glance upon Clémence. She had fallen in such a dead faint that he sought in vain for her breath. He leaned over her, with an irresistible feeling of pity and love; but just as he was about to take her in his arms and place her upon the divan, Bergenheim's hand stopped him. If there is a being on earth to whom one owes regard and respect, it is the one whom our own wrong has rendered our enemy. Octave arose, and said, in a grave, resigned voice:

"I am at your orders, Monsieur."

Christian pointed to the door, as if to invite him to pass out first, thus preserving, with his extraordinary composure, the politeness which a good education makes an indelible habit, but which at this moment was more frightful to behold than the most furious outburst of temper. Gerfaut glanced at Clémence again, and said, as he pointed to her:

"Shall you leave her without any aid in this condition? It is cruel."

"It is not from cruelty, but out of pity," replied the Baron, coldly; "she will awake only too soon."

Octave's heart was intensely oppressed, but he managed to conceal his emotion. He hesitated no longer and stepped out. The husband followed, without giving a glance at the poor woman whose own words had condemned her so inexorably. And so she was left alone in this pretty boudoir as if in a tomb.

CHARLES DE BERNARD

The two men descended the stairs leading from the little closet. At the library door they found themselves in absolute obscurity; Christian opened a dark-lantern and its faint light guided their steps. They traversed, in silence, the picture-gallery, the vestibule, and then mounted the main staircase. They reached the Baron's apartment without meeting anybody or betraying themselves by the slightest sound. With the same outward self-possession which had characterized his whole conduct, Christian, after carefully closing the doors, lighted a candelabra filled with candles which was upon the mantel, and then turned to his companion, who was far less composed than he.

Gerfaut had suffered tortures since leaving the little parlor. A feeling of regret and deepest pity, at the thought of the inevitable catastrophe which must follow, had softened his heart. He saw in the most odious of colors the selfishness of his love. Clémence's last glance as she fell fainting at his feet—a forgiving and a loving glance—was like a dagger in his heart. He had ruined her! the woman he loved! the queen of his life! the angel he adored! This idea was like hell to him. He was almost unable to control his emotion, dizzy as he was on the brink of the abyss opened by his hand, into which he had precipitated what he counted as the dearest part of his own self.

Bergenheim stood, cold and sombre, like a northern sky, opposite this pale-faced man, upon whose countenance a thousand passionate emotions were depicted like clouds on a stormy day.

GERFAUT

When Bergenheim's eyes met Octave's, they were so full of vengeance and hatred that the latter trembled as if he had come in contact with a wild beast. The lover actually realized the inferiority of his attitude in the presence of this enraged husband. A feeling of self-pride and indignation came to his aid. He put aside remorse and regrets until later; these sad expiations were forbidden him now; another duty lay before him. There is only one reparation possible for certain offences. The course once open, one must go to its very end; pardon is to be found only upon the tomb of the offended.

Octave knew he had to submit to this necessity. He stifled all scruples which might have weakened his firmness, and resumed his habitual disdainful look. His eyes returned his enemy's glance of deadly hatred, and he began the conversation like a man who is accustomed to master the events of his life and forbids any one to shape them for him.

"Before any explanations take place between us," he said, "I have to declare to you, upon my honor, that there is only one guilty person in this affair, and that I am the one. The slightest reproach addressed to Madame de Bergenheim would be a most unjust outrage and a most deplorable error on your part. I introduced myself into her apartment without her knowledge and without having been authorized in any way to do so. I had just entered it when you arrived. Necessity obliges me to admit a love that is an outrage to you; I am ready to repair this outrage by any satisfaction you may demand; but in putting myself at your discretion, I earnestly insist upon exculpating Madame de Bergenheim from all that can in any way affect her virtue or her reputation."

"As to her reputation," said Christian, "I will watch over that; as to her virtue——"

He did not finish, but his face assumed an expression of incredulous irony.

"I swear to you, Monsieur," said Octave, with increasing emotion, "that she is above all seduction and should be sheltered from all insult; I swear to you— What oath can I take that you will believe? I swear that Madame de Bergenheim never has betrayed any of her duties toward you; that I never have received the slightest encouragement from her; that she is as innocent of my folly as the angels in heaven."

Christian shook his head with a scornful smile.

"This day will be the undying remorse of my life if you will not believe me," said Gerfaut, with almost uncontrolled vehemence; "I tell you, Monsieur, she is innocent; innocent! do you understand me? I was led astray by my passion. I wished to profit by your absence. You know that I have a key to the library; I used it without her suspecting it. Would to God that you could have been a witness to our *tête-à-tête!* you could then have not one doubt left. Can one prevent a man from entering a lady's room, when he has succeeded in finding the way to it in spite of her wishes? I repeat it, she——"

"Enough, Monsieur," replied the Baron coldly. "You are doing as I should do in your place; but this discussion is out of place; let this woman exculpate herself. There should be no mention of her between us now."

"When I protest that upon my honor——"

"Monsieur, under such conditions, a false oath is not dishonorable. I have been a bachelor myself, and I know that anything is allowable against a husband. Let us drop this, I beg of you, and return to facts. I consider that I have been insulted by you, and you must give me satisfaction for this insult."

Octave made a sign of acquiescence.

"One of us must die," replied Bergenheim, leaning his elbow negligently upon the mantel. The lover bowed his head a second time.

"I have offended you," said he; "you have the right to choose the reparation due you."

"There is only one possible, Monsieur. Blood alone can wipe away the disgrace; you know it as well as I. You have dishonored my home, you owe me your life for that. If Fate favors you, you will be rid of me, and I shall be wronged in every way. There are arrangements to be made, and we shall settle them at once, if you are willing."

He pushed an armchair toward Gerfaut, and took another himself.

They seated themselves beside a desk which stood in the middle of the room, and, with an equal appearance of *sang-froid* and polite haughtiness, they discussed this murderous combat.

"It is not necessary for me to say to you," said Octave, "that I accept in advance whatever you may decide upon; the weapons, place, and seconds——"

CHARLES DE BERNARD

"Listen to me, then," interrupted Bergenheim; "you just now spoke in favor of this woman in a way that made me think you did not wish her ruined in the eyes of the world; so I trust you will accept the proposition I am about to make to you. An ordinary duel would arouse suspicion and inevitably lead to a discovery of the truth; people would seek for some plausible motive for the encounter, whatever story we might tell our seconds. You know that there is but one motive which will be found acceptable by society for a duel between a young man who had been received as a guest of this house and the husband. In whatever way this duel may terminate, this woman's honor would remain on the ground with the dead, and that is what I wish to avoid, since she bears my name."

"Will you explain to me what your plan is?" asked Octave, who could not understand what his adversary had in mind.

"You know, Monsieur," Bergenheim continued, in his calm voice, "that I had a perfect right to kill you a moment ago; I did not do so for two reasons: first, a gentleman should use his sword and not a poniard, and then your dead body would have embarrassed me."

"The river is close by!" interrupted Gerfaut, with a strange smile.

Christian looked at him fixedly for a moment, and then replied in a slightly changed tone:

"Instead of availing myself of my right, I intend to risk my life against yours. The danger is the same for myself, who never have insulted you, as for you, who have offered me the deadliest insult that one man can offer another. I am willing to spill my blood, but not to soil my honor."

"If it is a duel without seconds that you desire, you have my consent; I have perfect confidence in your loyalty, and I hope you can say the same for mine."

Christian bowed his head slightly and continued:

"It is more than a duel without seconds, for the whole affair must be so contrived as to be looked upon as an accident; it is the only way to prevent the outbreak and scandal I dread so much. Now here is my proposition: You know that a wild-boar hunt is to take place to-morrow in the Mares woods. When we station ourselves we shall be placed together at a spot I know of, where we shall be out of the sight of the other hunters. When the boar crosses the enclosure we will fire at a signal agreed upon. In this way, the *dénouement*, whatever it may be, will be looked upon as one of those accidents which so frequently happen in shooting-parties."

"I am a dead man," thought Gerfaut, as he saw that the gun would be the weapon chosen by his adversary, and recalled his wonderful skill, of which he had had many and various proofs. But instead of showing the slightest hesitation, his countenance grew still more arrogant.

"This kind of combat seems to me very wisely planned," said he; "I accept, for I desire as much as you that this affair should remain an eternal secret."

"Since we are to have no seconds," continued Bergenheim, "let us arrange everything so that nothing can betray us; it is inconceivable how the most trifling circumstances often turn out crushing evidence. I think that I have foreseen everything. If you find that I have forgotten any detail, please remind me of it. The place I speak of is a narrow, well-shaded path. The ground is perfectly level; it lies from north to south, so that at eight o'clock in the morning the sun will be on that side; there will be no advantage in position. There is an old elm on the borders of the wood; at fifty steps' distance in the pathway, lies the trunk of an oak which has been felled this year. These are the two places where we will station ourselves, if you consent to it. Is it the proper distance?"

"Near or farther, it matters little. Breast to breast, if you like."

"Nearer would be imprudent. However, fifty steps with the gun is less than fifteen with a pistol. This point is settled. We will remain with heads covered, although this is not the custom. A ball might strike the head where the cap would be, and if this should happen it would arouse suspicion, as people do not hunt bareheaded. It only remains to decide who shall fire first," continued Christian.

"You, of course; you are the offended one."

"You do not admit the full offence to have been committed, and, since this is in doubt, and I can not be judge and jury together, we shall consult chance."

"I declare to you that I will not fire first," interrupted Gerfaut.

"Remember that it is a mortal duel, and such scruples are foolish. Let us agree that whoever has the first shot, shall place himself upon the border of the woods and await the signal, which the other will give when the boar crosses the enclosure."

He took a gold piece from his purse and threw it in the air.

"Heads!" said the lover, ready to acquiesce to the least of his adversary's conditions.

"Fate is for you," said Christian, looking at the coin with marked indifference; "but, remember, if at the signal given by me you do not fire, or only fire in the air, I shall use my right to shoot—You know that I rarely miss my aim."

These preliminaries ended, the Baron took two guns from his closet, loaded them, taking particular care to show that they were of equal length and the same calibre. He then locked them up in the closet and offered Gerfaut the key.

"I would not do you this injustice," said the latter.

"This precaution is hardly necessary, since, to-morrow, you will take your choice of those weapons. Now that everything is arranged," continued the Baron, in a graver tone, "I have one request to make of you, and I think you are too loyal to refuse it. Swear to me that whatever may be the result, you will keep all this a profound secret. My honor is now in your hands; speaking as a gentleman to a gentleman, I ask you to respect it."

"If I have the sad privilege of surviving you," replied Gerfaut, no less solemnly, "I swear to you to keep the secret inviolate. But, supposing a contrary event, I also have a request to make to you. What

are your intentions regarding Madame de Bergenheim?"

Christian gazed at his adversary a moment, with a
searching glance which seemed to read his innermost
thoughts.

"My intentions?" said he at last, in a displeased,
surprised tone; "this is a very strange question; I do
not recognize your right to ask it."

"My right is certainly strange," said the lover, with
a bitter smile; "but whatever it may be, I shall make
use of it. I have destroyed this woman's happiness
forever; if I can not repair this fault, at least I ought
to mitigate the effect as much as lies in my power.
Will you reply to me—if I die to-morrow, what will be
her fate?"

Bergenheim kept silent, his sombre eyes lowered to
the floor.

"Listen to me, Monsieur," continued Gerfaut, with
great emotion; "when I said to you, 'She is not
guilty,' you did not believe me, and I despair of ever
persuading you, for I know well what your suspicions
must be. However, these are the last words addressed
to you that will leave my mouth, and you know that
one has to believe a dying man's statement. If to-
morrow you avenge yourself, I earnestly beg of you,
let this reparation suffice. All my pride is gone, you
see, since I beg this of you upon my bended knees.
Be humane toward her; spare her, Monsieur. It is
not pardon which I ask you to grant her—it is pity for
her unsullied innocence. Treat her kindly—honorably.
Do not make her too wretched."

He stopped, for his voice failed him, and his eyes filled with tears.

"I know what I ought to do," replied the Baron, in as harsh a tone as Gerfaut's had been tender; "I am her husband, and I do not recognize anybody's right, yours least of all, to interpose between us."

"I can foresee the fate which you have in reserve for her," replied the lover, indignantly; "you will not murder her, for that would be too imprudent; what would become of your vaunted honor then? But you will slowly kill her; you will make her die a new death every day, in order to satisfy a blind vengeance. You are a man to meditate over each new torture as calmly as you have regulated every detail of our duel."

Bergenheim, instead of replying, lighted a candle as if to put an end to this discussion.

"Until to-morrow, Monsieur," said he, with a cold air.

"One moment!" exclaimed Gerfaut, as he arose; "you refuse to give me one word which will assure me of the fate of the woman whose life I have ruined?"

"I have nothing to say."

"Very well, then; I will protect her, and I will do it in spite of you and against you."

"Not another word," interrupted the Baron, sternly.

Octave leaned over the table between them and looked at him for a moment, then said in a terrible voice:

"You killed Lambernier!"

Christian bounded backward as if he had been struck.

"I was a witness of that murder," continued Gerfaut, slowly, as he emphasized each word; "I will
write my deposition and give it to a man of whom I
am as sure as of myself. If I die to-morrow, I will
leave him a mission which no effort on your part will
prevent him from fulfilling. He shall watch over your
slightest actions with inexorable vigilance; he will be
Madame de Bergenheim's protector, if you forget that
your first duty is to protect her. The day upon which
you abuse your position with her, the day when she
shall call out despairingly, 'Help me!' that day shall
my deposition be placed in the hands of the public
prosecutor at Nancy. He will believe its contents; of
that you may be certain. Besides, the river is an indiscreet tomb; before long it will give up the body you
have confided to it. You will be tried and condemned.
You know the punishment for murder! It is hard
labor for life."

Bergenheim darted toward the mantel at these
words and seized a hunting-knife which hung there.
Octave, as he saw him ready to strike, crossed his arms
upon his breast, and said, coldly:

"Remember that my body might embarrass you;
one corpse is enough."

The Baron threw the weapon on the floor with such
force that he broke it in two.

"But it was you," he said, in a trembling voice,
"you were Lambernier's assassin. He knew this infamous secret, and his death was involuntary on my
part."

"The intention is of little account. The deed is the

[336]

question. There is not a jury that would not condemn you, and that is what I wish, for such a sentence would bring a legal separation between you and your wife and give her her liberty."

"You are not speaking seriously," said Christian, turning pale; "you, a gentleman, would not denounce me! And, besides, would not my being sentenced injure the woman in whom you take so much interest?"

"I know all that," Gerfaut replied; "I too cling to the honor of my name, and yet I expose it. I have plenty of enemies who will be glad enough to outrage my memory. Public opinion will condemn me, for they will see only the action, and that is odious. There is one thing, however, more precious and necessary to me than the world's opinion, and that is peace for every day, the right to live; and that is the reason why, happiness having forsaken me, I am going to bequeath it to the one whom fate has put in your power, but whom I shall not leave to your mercy."

"I am her husband," Bergenheim replied, angrily.

"Yes, you are her husband; so the law is on your side. You have only to call upon society for its aid; it will come but too gladly at your call and help you crush a defenceless woman. And I, who love her as you have never known how to love her, I can do nothing for her! Living, I must keep silent and bow before your will; but dead, your absurd laws no longer exist for me; dead, I can place myself between you and her, and I will do it. Since, in order to aid her, I have no choice of arms, I will not recoil from the one weapon which presents itself. Yes, if in order to save her from your vengeance, I am obliged to resort to the shame of a denunciation, I swear to you here, I will turn informer. I will sully my name with this stain; I will pick up this stone from the mud, and I will crush your head with it."

"These are a coward's words!" exclaimed Christian, as he fell back in his chair.

Gerfaut looked at him with a calm, stony glance, while replying:

"No insults, please! One of us will not be living to-morrow. Remember what I tell you: if I fall in this duel, it will be to your interest to have this matter stop then and there. I submit to death myself; but I exact liberty for her—liberty, with peace and respect. Think it over, Monsieur; at the first outrage, I shall arise from my tomb to prevent a second, and dig a trench between you and her which never can be crossed —the penitentiary!"

CHAPTER XXIV

A FRIEND'S ADVICE

AFTER she came out of her faint, Madame de Bergenheim remained for a long time in a dazed condition, and did not realize, save in a confused manner, her real position. She saw vaguely, at her first glance, the curtains of the bed upon which she lay, and thought that she had awakened from an ordinary sleep. Little by little, her thoughts became clearer, and she saw that she was fully dressed, also that her room seemed brighter than it usually was with only her night-lamp lighted. She noticed between the half-open curtains a gigantic form reflected almost to the ceiling opposite her bed. She sat up and distinctly saw a man sitting in the corner by the fireplace. Frozen with terror, she fell back upon her pillow as she recognized her husband. Then she remembered everything, even the slightest details of the scene in the small parlor. She felt ready to faint again when she heard Christian's steps upon the carpet, although he walked with great precaution.

The Baron looked at her a moment, and then, opening the bed-curtains, he said:

"You can not pass the night thus, it is nearly three o'clock. You must go to bed as usual."

Clémence shivered at these words, whose accent, however, was not hard. She obeyed mechanically; but she had hardly risen when she was obliged to recline upon the bed, for her trembling limbs would not support her.

"Do not be afraid of me," said Bergenheim, drawing back a few steps; "my presence should not frighten you. I only wish that people should know that I have passed the night in your chamber, for it is possible that my return may arouse suspicion. You know that our love is only a comedy played for the benefit of our servants."

There was such affected lightness in these remarks that the young woman was cut to the very quick. She had expected an explosion of anger, but not this calm contempt. Her revolted pride gave her courage.

"I do not deserve to be treated thus," said she; "do not condemn me without a hearing."

"I ask nothing of you," replied Christian, who seated himself again beside the mantel; "undress yourself, and go to sleep if it is possible for you to do so. It is not necessary for Justine to make any comments tomorrow about your day clothes not having been removed."

Instead of obeying him, she went toward him and tried to remain standing in order to speak to him, but her emotion was so intense that it took away her strength and she was obliged to sit down.

"You treat me too cruelly, Christian," said she,

when she had succeeded to recover her voice. "I am not guilty; at least, not so much as you think I am—" said she, drooping her head.

He looked at her attentively for a moment, and then replied, in a voice which did not betray the slightest emotion:

"You must know that my greatest desire is to be persuaded of this by you. I know that too often appearances are deceitful; perhaps you will be able to explain to me what took place last evening; I am still inclined to believe your word. Swear to me that you do not love Monsieur de Gerfaut."

"I swear it!" said she, in a weak voice, and without raising her eyes.

He went to the bed and took down a little silver crucifix which was hanging above it.

"Swear it to me upon this crucifix," said he, presenting it to his wife.

She tried in vain to raise her hand, which seemed fastened to the arm of her chair.

"I swear it!" she stammered a second time, while her face became as pale as death.

A savage laugh escaped Christian's lips. He put the crucifix in its place again without saying a word, then he opened the secret panel and, taking out the casket, placed it upon the table before his wife. She made a movement as if to seize it, but her courage failed her.

"You have perjured yourself to your husband and to God!" said Bergenheim slowly. "Do you know what kind of woman you are?"

Clémence remained for some time powerless to reply; her respiration was so painful that each breath seemed like suffocation; her head, after rolling about on the back of the chair, fell upon her breast, like a blade of grass broken and bruised by the rain.

"If you have read those letters," she murmured, when she had strength enough to speak, "you must know that I am not as unworthy as you think. I am very guilty—but I still have a right to be forgiven."

Christian, at this moment, had he been gifted with the intelligence which fathoms the mysteries of the heart, might have renewed the bonds which were so near being broken; he could at least have stopped Clémence upon a dangerous path and saved her from a most irreparable fall. But his nature was too unrefined for him to see the degrees which separate weakness from vice, and the intoxication of a loving heart from the depravity of a corrupt character. With the obstinacy of narrow-minded people, he had been looking at the whole thing in its worst light, and for several hours already he had decided upon his wife's guilt in his own mind; this served now as a foundation for his stern conduct. His features remained perfectly impassive as he listened to Clémence's words of justification, which she uttered in a weak, broken voice.

"I know that I merit your hatred—but if you could know how much I suffer, you would surely forgive me—You left me in Paris very young, inexperienced; I ought to have fought against this feeling better than I did, but I used up in this struggle all the strength that I had—You can see how pale and changed I have become within the past year. I have aged several years in those few months; I am not yet what you call a—a lost woman. He ought to have told you that——"

"Oh, he has! of course he has," replied Christian with bitter irony. "Oh, you have in him a loyal cavalier!"

"You do not believe me, then! you do not believe me!" she continued, wringing her hands in despair; "but read these letters, the last ones. See whether one writes like this to a woman who is entirely lost——"

She tried to take the package which her husband held; instead of giving the letters to her, he lighted them at the candle and then threw them into the fireplace. Clémence uttered a cry and darted forward to save them, but Christian's iron hand seized her and pushed her back into her chair.

"I understand how much you care for this correspondence," said he, in a more excited tone, "but you are more loving than prudent. Let me destroy one witness which accuses you. Do you know that I have already killed a man on account of these letters?"

"Killed!" exclaimed Madame de Bergenheim, whom this word drove almost to madness, for she could not understand its real meaning and applied it to her lover. "Well, then, kill me too, for I lied when I said that I repented. I do not repent! I am guilty! I deceived you! I love him and I abhor you; I love him! kill me!"

She fell upon her knees before him and dragged herself along the floor, striking her head upon it as if she wished to break it. Christian raised her and seated her in the chair, in spite of her resistance. She struggled in her husband's arms, and the only words which she uttered were: "I love him! kill me! I love him! kill me!"

Her grief was so intense that Bergenheim really pitied her.

"You did not understand me," he said, "he is not the man I killed."

She became motionless, dumb. He left her then, from a feeling of compassion, and returned to his seat. They remained for some time seated in this way, one on each side of the fireplace; he, with his head leaning against the mantel; she, crouched in her chair with her face concealed behind her hands; only the striking of the clock interrupted this silence and lulled their gloomy thoughts with its monotonous vibrations.

A sharp, quick sound against one of the windows interrupted this sad scene. Clémence arose suddenly as if she had received a galvanic shock; her frightened eyes met her husband's. He made an imperious gesture with his hand as if to order silence, and both listened attentively and anxiously.

The same noise was heard a second time. A rattling against the blinds was followed by a dry, metallic sound, evidently caused by the contact of some body against the window.

"It is some signal," said Christian in a low voice, as he looked at his wife. "You probably know what it means."

"I do not, I swear to you," replied Clémence, her heart throbbing with a new emotion.

"I will tell you, then; he is there and he has something to say to you. Rise and open the window."

"Open the window?" said she, with a frightened look.

"Do what I tell you. Do you wish him to pass the night under your window, so that the servants may see him?"

At this command, spoken in a severe tone, she arose. Noticing that their shadows might be seen from the outside when the curtains were drawn, Bergenheim changed the candles to another place. Clémence walked slowly toward the window; she had hardly opened it, when a purse fell upon the floor.

"Close it now," said the Baron. While his wife was quietly obeying, he picked up the purse, and opening it, took the following note from it:

"I have ruined you—you for whom I would gladly have died! But of what use are regrets and despair now? And my blood will not wipe away your tears. Our position is so frightful that I tremble so speak of it. I ought to tell you the truth, however, horrible as it may be. Do not curse me, Clémence; do not impute to me this fatality, which obliges me thus to torture you. In a few hours I shall have expiated the wrongs of my love, or you yourself may be free. Free! pardon me for using this word; I know it is an odious one to you, but I am too troubled to find another. Whatever happens, I am about to put within your reach the only aid which it is possible for me to offer you; it will at least give you a choice of unhappiness. If you never see me again, to live with him will be a torture beyond your strength, perhaps, for you love me. I do not know how to express my thoughts, and I dare not offer you advice or entreat you. All that I feel is the necessity of telling you that my whole life belongs to you, that I am yours until death; but I hardly dare have the courage to lay at your feet the offering of a destiny already so sad, and which may soon be stained with blood. A fatal necessity sometimes imposes actions which public opinion condemns, but the heart excuses, for it alone understands them. Do not be angry at what you are about to read; never did words like these come out of a more desolate heart. During the whole day a post-chaise will wait for you at the rear of the Montigny plateau; a fire lighted upon the rock which you can see from your room will notify you of its presence. In a short time it can reach the Rhine. A person devoted to you will accompany you to Munich, to the house of one of my relatives, whose character and position will assure you sufficient protection from all tyranny. There, at least, you will be permitted to weep. That is all that I can do for you. My heart is broken when I think of the powerlessness of my love. They say that when one crushes the scorpion which has wounded him, he is cured; even my death will not repair the wrong that I have done you; it will only be one grief the more. Can you understand how desperate is the feeling which I experience now? For months past, to be loved by you has been the sole desire of my heart, and now I must repent ever having attained it. Out of pity for you, I ought to wish that you did love me with a love as perishable as my life, so that a remembrance of me would leave you in peace. All this is so sad that I have not the courage to continue. Adieu, Clémence! Once more, one last time, I must say: I love you! and yet, I dare not. I feel unworthy to speak to you thus, for my love has become a disastrous gift. Did I not ruin you? The only word that seems to be permissible is the one that even a murderer dares to address to his God: pardon me!"

After reading this, the Baron passed the letter to his wife without saying a word, and resumed his sombre attitude.

"You see what he asks of you?" he said, after a rather long pause, as he observed the dazed way in which Madame de Bergenheim's eyes wandered over this letter.

"My head is bewildered," she replied, "I do not understand what he says—Why does he speak of death?"

Christian's lips curled disdainfully as he answered:

"It does not concern you; one does not kill women."

"They need it not to die," replied Clémence, who gazed at her husband with wild, haggard eyes.

"Then you are going to fight?" she added, after a moment's pause.

"Really, have you divined as much?" he replied, with an ironical smile; "it is a wonderful thing how quick is your intelligence! You have spoken the truth. You see, each of us has his part to play. The wife deceives her husband; the husband fights with the lover, and the lover in order to close the comedy in a suitable manner—proposes to run away with the wife, for that is the meaning of his letter, notwithstanding all his oratorical precautions."

"You are going to fight!" she exclaimed, with the energy of despair. "You are going to fight! And for me—unworthy and miserable creature that I am! What have you done? And is he not free to love? I alone am the guilty one, I alone have offended you, and I alone deserve punishment. Do with me what you will; shut me up in a convent or a cell; bring me poison, I will drink it."

The Baron burst into sardonic laughter.

"So you are afraid that I shall kill him?" said he,

gazing at her intently, with his arms crossed upon his breast.

"I fear for you, for us all. Do you think that I can live after causing blood to be shed? If there must be a victim, take me—or, at least, begin with me. Have pity! tell me that you will not fight."

"But think—there is an even chance that you may be set free!" said he.

"Spare me!" she murmured, shivering with horror.

"It is a pity that blood must be shed, is it not?" said Bergenheim, in a mocking tone; "adultery would be pleasant but for that. I am sure that you think me coarse and brutal to look upon your honor as a serious thing, when you do not do so yourself."

"I entreat you!"

"I am the one who has to entreat you. This astonishes you, does it not?—While I live, I shall protect your reputation in spite of yourself; but if I die, try to guard it yourself. Content yourself with having betrayed me; do not outrage my memory. I am glad now that we have no children, for I should fear for them, and should feel obliged to deprive you of their care as much as lay in my power. That is one trouble the less. But as you bear my name, and I can not take it away from you, I beg of you do not drag it in the mire when I shall not be here to wash it for you."

The young woman fell back upon her seat as if every fibre in her body had been successively torn to pieces.

"You crush me to the earth!" she said, feebly.

"This revolts you," continued the husband, who

seemed to choose the most cutting thrust; "you are young; this is your first error, you are not made for such adventures. But rest assured, one becomes accustomed to everything. A lover always knows how to find the most beautiful phrases with which to console a widow and vanquish her repugnances."

"You are killing me," she murmured, falling back almost unconscious in her chair.

Christian leaned over her, and, taking her by the arm, said in a low tone:

"Remember, if I die and he asks you to follow him, you will be an infamous creature if you obey him. He is a man to glory in you; that is easy enough to see. He is a man who would drag you after him——"

"Oh! have pity—I shall die——"

Clémence closed her eyes and her lips twitched convulsively.

The first rays of the morning sun fell upon another scene in the opposite wing of the château. Marillac was quietly sleeping the sleep of the just when he was suddenly awakened by a shaking that nearly threw him out of his bed.

"Go to the devil!" he said, angrily, when he succeeded in half opening his heavy eyes, and recognized Gerfaut standing beside his bed.

"Get up!" said the latter, taking him by the arm to give more force to his command.

The artist covered himself with the clothes up to his chin.

"Are you walking in your sleep or insane?" asked

Marillac, "or do you want me to go to work?" he added, as he saw that his friend had some papers in his hand. "You know very well I never have any ideas when fasting, and that I am stupid until noon."

"Get up at once!" said Gerfaut, "I must have a talk with you."

There was something so serious and urgent in Gerfaut's accent as he said these words, that the artist got up at once and hurriedly dressed himself.

"What is the matter?" he asked, as he put on his dressing-gown, "you look as if the affairs of the nation rested upon you."

"Put on your coat and boots," said Octave, "you must go to La Fauconnerie. They are used to seeing you go out early in the morning for your appointments with Reine, and therefore——"

"It is to this shepherdess you would send me!" interrupted the artist, as he began to undress himself; "in that case I will go to bed again. Enough of that!"

"I am to fight with Bergenheim at nine o'clock!" said Gerfaut, in a low voice.

"Stupendous!" exclaimed Marillac, as he jumped back a few steps, and then stood as motionless as a statue. Without wasting any time in unnecessary explanations, his friend gave him a brief account of the night's events.

"Now," said he, "I need you; can I count upon your friendship?"

"In life and in death!" exclaimed Marillac, and he

pressed his hand with the emotion that the bravest of men feel at the approach of a danger which threatens one who is dear to them.

"Here," said Gerfaut, as he handed him the papers in his hand, "is a letter for you in which you will find my instructions in full; they will serve you as a guide, according to circumstances. This sealed paper will be deposited by you in the office of the public prosecutor at Nancy, under certain circumstances which my note explains. Finally, this is my will. I have no very near relative; I have made you my heir.

"Listen to me! I do not know a more honest man than you, that is the reason why I select you. First, this legacy is a trust. I speak to you now in case of events which probably will never happen, but which I ought to prepare for. I do not know what effect this may have upon Clémence's fate; her aunt, who is very austere, may quarrel with her and deprive her of her rights; her personal fortune is not very large, I believe, and I know nothing about her marriage settlement. She may thus be entirely at her husband's mercy, and that is what I will not allow. My fortune is therefore a trust that you will hold to be placed at her disposal at any time. I hope that she loves me enough not to refuse this service of me."

"Well and good!" said Marillac; "I will admit that the thought of inheriting from you choked me like a noose around my neck."

"I beg of you to accept for yourself my copyrights as author. You can not refuse that," said Gerfaut, with a half smile; "this legacy belongs to the domain of art. To whom should I leave it if not to you, my Patroclus, my faithful collaborator?"

The artist took several agitated turns about his room.

"To think," he exclaimed, "that I was the one who saved this Bergenheim's life! If he kills you, I shall never forgive myself. And yet, I told you this would end in some tragic manner."

"What business had he there? Is it not so? What can I say? We were seeking for a drama; here it is. I am not anxious on my own account, but on hers. Unhappy woman! A duel is a stone that might fall upon a man's head twenty times a day; it is sufficient for a simpleton if you stare at him, or for an awkward fellow if you tread upon his toes; but on her account —poor angel!—I can not think of it. I need the fullest command of my head and my heart. But it is growing lighter; there is not a moment to lose. Go to the stable; saddle a horse yourself, if there is no servant up; go, as I said, to La Fauconnerie; I have often seen a post-chaise in the tavern courtyard; order it to wait all day at the back of the Montigny plateau. You will find everything explained in detail in the note which I have given you. Here is my purse; I need no money."

Marillac put the purse in his pocket and the papers in his memorandum-book; he then buttoned up his redingote and put on his travelling cap. His countenance showed a state of exaltation which belied, for the time being, the pacific theories he had expounded a few days before.

"You can depend upon me as upon yourself," said he with energy. "If this poor woman calls for my aid, I promise you that I will serve her faithfully. I will take her wherever she wishes; to China, if she asks it, and in spite of the whole police force. If Bergenheim kills you and then follows her up, there will be another duel."

As he said these words, he took his stiletto and a pair of pistols from the mantel and put them in his pocket, after examining the edge of the one and the caps of the others.

"Adieu!" said Gerfaut.

"Adieu!" said the artist, whose extreme agitation contrasted strongly with his friend's calm. "Rest easy! I will look after her—and I will publish a complete edition—But what an idea—to accept a duel as irregular as this! Have you ever seen him use a gun? He had no right to exact this."

"Hurry! you must leave before the servants are up."

"Kiss me, my poor fellow!" said Marillac, with tears in his eyes; "it is not very manly I know, but I can not help it—Oh! these women! I adore them, of course; but just now I am like Nero, I wish that they all had but one head. It is for these little, worthless dolls that we kill each other!"

"You can curse them on your way," said Gerfaut, who was impatient to see him leave.

"Oh, good gracious, yes! They can flatter themselves this moment that they all inspire me with a deadly hatred."

CHARLES DE BERNARD

"Do not make any noise," said his friend, as he carefully opened the door.

Marillac pressed his hand for the last time, and went out. When he reached the end of the corridor, he stopped a moment, then went back.

"Above all things," said he, as he passed his head through the half-open door, "no foolish proceedings. Remember that it is necessary that one of you should fall, and that if you fail, he will not. Take your time —aim—and fire at him as you would at a rabbit."

After this last piece of advice, he went away; ten minutes after he had left, Gerfaut saw him riding out of the courtyard as fast as Beverley's four legs would carry him.

CHAPTER XXV

HE most radiant sun that ever gilded a beautiful September day had arisen upon the castle. The whole valley was as fresh and laughing as a young girl who had just left her bath. The rocks seemed to have a band of silver surrounding them; the woods a mantle of green draped over their shoulders.

There was an unusual excitement in the courtyard of the château. The servants were coming and going, the dogs were starting a concert of irregular barks, and the horses were jumping about, sharing their instinctive presentiment and trying to break away from the bridles which held them.

The Baron, seated in his saddle with his usual military attitude, and a cigar in his mouth, went from one to another, speaking in a joking tone which prevented anybody from suspecting his secret thoughts. Gerfaut had imposed upon his countenance that impassible serenity which guards the heart's inner secrets, but had not succeeded so well. His affectation of gayety betrayed continual restraint; the smile which he forced upon his lips left the rest of his face cold, and

[355]

never removed the wrinkle between his brows. An incident, perhaps sadly longed for, but unhoped for, increased this gloomy, melancholy expression. Just as the cavalcade passed before the English garden, which separated the sycamore walk from the wing of the château occupied by Madame de Bergenheim, Octave slackened the pace of his horse and lingered behind the rest of his companions; his eyes closely examined each of the windows; the blinds of her sleeping-room were only half closed; behind the panes he saw the curtains move and then separate. A pale face appeared for a moment between the blue folds, like an angel who peeps through the sky to gaze upon the earth. Gerfaut raised himself on his stirrups so as to drink in this apparition as long as possible, but he dared not make one gesture of adieu. As he was still endeavoring to obtain one more glance, he saw that the Baron was at his side.

"Play your *rôle* better," said he to him; "we are surrounded by spies. De Camier has already made an observation about your preoccupied demeanor."

"You are right," said Octave; "and you join example to advice. I admire your coolness, but I despair of equalling it."

"You must mingle with my guests and talk with them," Christian replied.

He started off at a trot; Gerfaut followed his example, stifling a sigh as he darted a last glance toward the château. They soon rejoined the cart which carried several of the hunters, and which Monsieur de Camier drove with the assurance of a professional coachman.

GERFAUT

There was a moment's silence, broken only by the trot of the horses and the sound of the wheels upon the level ground.

"What the devil ails your dogs?" exclaimed Monsieur de Camier suddenly, as he turned to the Baron, who was riding behind him. "There they are all making for the river."

Just at this moment the dogs, who could be seen in the distance, hurried to the water-side, in spite of all that their leader could do to prevent them. They almost disappeared behind the willows that bordered the river, and one could hear them barking furiously; their barks sounded like rage mingled with terror.

"It is some duck that they have scented," observed the prosecutor.

"They wouldn't bark like that," said Monsieur de Camier, with the sagacity of a professional hunter; "if it were a wolf, they could not make a greater uproar. Is it by chance some wild boar who is taking a bath, in order to receive us more ceremoniously?"

He gave the horses a vigorous blow from the whip, and they all rapidly approached the spot where a scene was taking place which excited to the highest pitch everybody's curiosity. Before they reached the spot, the keeper, who had run after the dogs to call them together, came out of a thicket, waving his hat to stop the hunters, exclaiming:

"A body! a body!"

"A body! a drowned man!" he exclaimed, when the vehicle stopped.

This time it was the public prosecutor who arose

and jumped from the cart with the agility of a deer.

"A drowned man!" said he. "In the name of the law, let nobody touch the body. Call back the dogs."

As he said these words he hastened to the spot which the servant pointed out to him. Everybody dismounted and followed him. Octave and Bergenheim had exchanged strange glances when they heard the servant's words.

It was, as the servant had announced, the battered body of a man, thrown by the current against the trunk of the tree, and there caught between two branches of the willow as if in a vise.

"It is the carpenter!" exclaimed Monsieur de Camier as he parted the foliage, which had prevented the head from being seen until then, for he recognized the workman's livid, swollen features. "It is that poor devil of a Lambernier, is it not, Bergenheim?"

"It is true!" stammered Christian, who, in spite of his boldness, could not help turning away his eyes.

"The carpenter!—drowned!—this is frightful!—I never should have recognized him—how disfigured he is!" exclaimed the others, as they pressed forward to gaze at this horrible spectacle.

"This is a sad way to escape justice," observed the notary, in a philosophical tone.

The Baron seized this opening with avidity.

"He must have crossed the river to escape," said he, "and in his haste he made a misstep and fell."

The public prosecutor shook his head with an air of doubt.

"That is not probable," said he; "I know the place. If he tried to cross the river a little above or a little below the rock—it doesn't matter which—the current would have carried him into the little bay above the rock and not here. It is evident that he must have drowned himself or been drowned farther down. I say, been drowned, for you can see that he has a wound upon the left side of his forehead, as if he had received a violent blow, or his head had hit against a hard substance. Now, if he had been drowned accidentally while crossing the river, he would not have been wounded in this manner."

This remark silenced the Baron; and while the others exhausted conjectures to explain the way in which this tragic event had taken place, he stood motionless, with his eyes fastened upon the river and avoiding a glance at the dead body. During this time the public prosecutor had taken from his pocket some paper and a pen, which he usually carried with him.

"Gentlemen," said he, seating himself upon the trunk of a tree opposite the drowned man, "two of you will do me the favor to act as witnesses while I draw up my official report. If any of you have a statement to make in regard to this affair, I beg of him to remain here, so that I may receive his deposition."

Nobody stirred, but Gerfaut threw such a penetrating glance at the Baron that the latter turned away his eyes.

"Gentlemen," continued the magistrate, "I do not wish any of you to renounce the sport on account of this untoward incident. There is nothing attractive about this spectacle, and I assure you that if my duty did not keep me here, I should be the first to withdraw. Baron, I beg of you to send me two men and a stretcher in order to have the body carried away; I will have it taken to one of your farms, so as not to frighten the ladies."

"The prosecutor is right," said Christian, whom these words delivered from a terrible anxiety.

After a deliberation, presided over by Monsieur de Camier, the *traqueurs* and the dogs left in silence to surround the thickets where the animal had been found to be hidden. At the same time the hunters turned their steps in the opposite direction in order to take their positions. They soon reached the ditch alongside of which they were to place themselves. From time to time, as they advanced, one of them left the party and remained mute and motionless like a sentinel at his post. This manœuvre gradually reduced their numbers, and at last there were only three remaining.

"You remain here, Camier," said the Baron, when they were about sixty steps from the last position.

That gentleman, who knew the ground, was hardly flattered by this proposition.

"By Jove!" said he, "you are on your own grounds; you ought at least to do the honors of your woods and let us choose our own positions. I think you wish to place yourself upon the outskirts, because it is always about that region that the animal first appears; but there will be two of us, for I shall go also."

This determination annoyed Christian considerably,

since it threatened to ruin the plan so prudently laid out.

"I am going to put our friend Gerfaut at this post," said he, whispering to the refractory hunter; "I shall be very much pleased if he has an opportunity to fire. What difference does one boar more or less make to an old hunter like you?"

"Well and good; just as you like," retorted Monsieur de Camier, striking the ground with the butt-end of his gun, and beginning to whistle in order to cool off his anger.

When the adversaries found themselves side by side and alone, Bergenheim's countenance changed suddenly; the smiling look he had assumed, in order to convince the old hunter of his cheerful disposition, gave place to deep gravity.

"You remember our agreement," he said, as they walked along; "I feel sure that the boar will come in our direction. At the moment when I call out, 'Take care!' I shall expect you to fire; if, at the end of twenty seconds, you have not done so, I warn you that I shall fire myself."

"Very well, Monsieur," said Gerfaut, looking at him fixedly; "you also doubtless remember my words; the discovery of this body will give them still more weight. The public prosecutor has already begun his preliminary proceedings; remember that it depends on me how they shall be completed. The deposition which I spoke to you about is in the hands of a safe person, who is fully instructed to make use of it if necessary."

"Marillac, I suppose," said Christian, in an evil

tone; "he is your confidant. It is a fatal secret that you have confided to him, Monsieur. If I survive to-day, I shall have to secure his silence. May all this blood, past, present, and future, be on your head!"

Deeply affected by this reproach, the Vicomte bowen his head in silence.

"Here is my place," said the Baron, stopping before the trunk of an old oak, "and there is the elm where you are to station yourself."

Gerfaut stopped, and said, in a trembling voice:

"Monsieur, one of us will not leave these woods alive. In the presence of death, one tells the truth. I hope for your peace of mind, and my own, that you will believe my last words. I swear to you, upon my honor and by all that is sacred, that Madame de Bergenheim is innocent."

He bowed, and withdrew from Christian without waiting for a response.

Bergenheim and Gerfaut were out of sight of the others, and stood at their posts with eyes fastened upon each other. The ditch was wide enough to prevent the branches of the trees from troubling them; at the distance of sixty feet, which separated them, each could see his adversary standing motionless, framed by the green foliage. Suddenly, barking was heard in the distance, partially drowned by the firing of a gun. A few seconds later, two feeble reports were heard, followed by an imprecation from Monsieur de Camier, whose caps flashed in the pan. The Baron, who had just leaned forward that he might see better through the thicket, raised his hand to warn Octave to hold himself in readiness. He then placed himself in position. An extreme indecision marked Gerfaut's attitude. After raising his gun, he dropped it to the ground with a despondent gesture, as if his resolution to fire had suddenly abandoned him; the pallor of death could not be more terrible than that which overspread his features. The howling of the dogs and shouts of the hunters increased. Suddenly another sound was heard. Low, deep growls, followed by the crackling of branches, came from the woods opposite our adversaries. The whole thicket seemed to tremble as if agitated by a storm.

"Take care!" exclaimed Bergenheim, in a firm voice.

At the same moment an enormous head appeared, and the report of a gun was heard. When Gerfaut looked through the smoke caused by his gun, at the farther end of the ditch, nothing was to be seen but the foliage.

The boar, after crossing the clearing, vanished like a flash, leaving behind him a trail of broken branches —and Bergenheim lay behind the trunk of the old oak, upon which large drops of blood had already fallen.

CHAPTER XXVI

N the same morning the drawing-room of the Bergenheim castle was the theatre of a quiet home scene very much like the one we described at the beginning of this story. Mademoiselle de Corandeuil was seated in her armchair reading the periodicals which had just arrived; Aline was practising upon the piano, and her sister-in-law was seated before one of the windows embroidering. By the calm attitude of these three ladies, and the interest they seemed to show in their several occupations, one would have supposed that they were all equally peaceful at heart. Madame de Bergenheim, upon rising, had resumed her usual habits; she managed to find the proper words to reply when spoken to, her dejection did not differ from her usual melancholy enough for it to become the subject of remark. A rather bright color in her cheeks heightened her beaujy; her eyes never had sparkled with more brilliancy; but if a hand had been placed upon her forehead, one would have soon discovered by its burning the secret of all this unwonted color. In fact, in the midst of this sumptuous room, surrounded by her friends, and bending over her embroidery with most exquisite grace, Madame de Bergenheim was slowly dying. A wasting fever was circulating like poison through her veins. She felt that an unheard-of sorrow was hanging over her head, and that no effort of hers could prevent it.

At this very moment, either the man she belonged to or the one she loved was about to die; whatever her widowhood might be, she felt that her mourning would be brief; young, beautiful, surrounded by all the privileges of rank and fortune, life was closing around her, and left but one pathway open, which was full of blood; she would have to bathe her feet in it in order to pass through.

"What is that smoke above the Montigny rock?" Aline exclaimed with surprise; "it looks as if there were a fire in the woods."

Madame de Bergenheim raised her eyes, shivered from head to foot as she saw the stream of smoke which stood out against the horizon, and then let her head droop upon her breast. Mademoiselle de Corandeuil stopped her reading as she heard Aline's remark, and turned slowly to look out of the window.

"That's some of the shepherds' work," said she; "they have built a fire in the bushes at the risk of setting fire to the whole woods. Really, I do not know what to think of your husband, Clémence; he takes everybody away to the hunt with him, and does not leave a soul here to prevent his dwelling from being devastated."

Clémence made no reply, and her sister-in-law, who expected she would say something to keep the conversation alive, returned and seated herself at the piano with a pouting air.

"Thanks, that will do for to-day!" exclaimed the old lady at the first notes; "you have split our heads long enough. You would do better to study your history of France."

Aline closed the piano angrily; but instead of obeying this last piece of advice, she remained seated upon the stool with the sulky air of a pupil in disgrace. A deep silence reigned. Madame de Bergenheim had dropped her embroidery without noticing it. From time to time she trembled as if a chill passed over her, her eyes were raised to watch the smoke ascending above the rock, or else she seemed to listen to some imaginary sound.

"Truly," said Mademoiselle de Corandeuil, as she laid her journal down in her lap, "good morals have made great progress since the July revolution. Yesterday a woman twenty years of age ran away to Montpelier with her lover; to-day, here is another, in Lyons, who poisons her husband and kills herself afterward. If I were superstitious, I should say that the world was coming to an end. What do you think of such atrocious doings, my dear?"

Clémence raised her head with an effort, and answered, in a gloomy voice:

"You must pardon her, since she is dead."

"You are very indulgent," replied the old aunt; "such creatures ought to be burned alive, like the Brinvilliers."

"They often speak in the papers of husbands who

[366]

kill their wives, but not so often of wives killing their
husbands," said Aline, with the partisan feeling natural
to the fair sex.

"It is not proper that you should talk of such horrid
things," said the old lady, in a severe tone; "behold
the fruits of all the morals of the age! It is the effect
of all the disgusting stuff that is acted nowadays upon
the stage and written in novels. When one thinks of
the fine education that is given youth at the present
time, it is enough to make one tremble for the future!"

"*Mon Dieu!* Mademoiselle, you may be sure that I
shall never kill my husband," replied the young girl,
to whom this remark seemed particularly addressed.

A stifled groan, which Madame de Bergenheim could
not suppress, attracted the attention of the two ladies.

"What is the matter with you?" asked Mademoiselle
de Corandeuil, noticing for the first time her niece's
dejected air and the frightened expression in her eyes.

"Nothing," murmured the latter; "I think it is the
heat of the room."

Aline hastily opened a window, then went and took
her sister-in-law's hands in her own.

"You have a fever," said she; "your hands burn and
your forehead also; I did not dare tell you, but your
beautiful color——"

A frightful cry which Madame de Bergenheim uttered made the young girl draw back in fright.

"Clémence! Clémence!" exclaimed Mademoiselle de
Corandeuil, who thought that her niece had gone insane.

"Did you not hear?" she cried, with an accent of

terror impossible to describe. She darted suddenly toward the drawing-room door; but, instead of opening it, she leaned against it with arms crossed. Then she ran two or three times around the room in a sort of frenzy, and ended by falling upon her knees before the sofa and burying her head in its cushions.

This scene bewildered the two women. While Mademoiselle de Corandeuil tried to raise Clémence, Aline, still more frightened, ran out of the room to call for aid. A rumor which had just begun to arise in the courtyard was distinctly heard when the door was thrown open. A moment more, and a piercing shriek was heard, and the young girl rushed into the parlor; throwing herself on her knees beside her sister-in-law she pressed her to her breast with convulsive energy.

As she felt herself seized in this fashion, Clémence raised her head and, placing her hands upon Aline's shoulders, she pushed her backward and gazed at her with eyes that seemed to devour her.

"Which? which?" she asked, in a harsh voice.

"My brother—covered with blood!" stammered Aline.

Madame de Bergenheim pushed her aside and threw herself upon the sofa. Her first feeling was a horrible joy at not hearing the name of Octave; but she tried to smother her hysterical utterances by pressing her mouth against the cushion upon which her face was leaning.

A noise of voices was heard in the vestibule; the greatest confusion seemed to reign among the people outside. At last, several men entered the drawing-room; at their head was Monsieur de Camier, whose ruddy face had lost all its color.

"Do not be frightened, ladies," said he, in a trembling voice; "do not be frightened. It is only a slight accident, without any danger. Monsieur de Bergenheim was wounded in the hunt," he continued, addressing Mademoiselle de Corandeuil.

At last, the folding-doors were thrown open, and two servants appeared, bearing the Baron upon a mattress.

When the servants had deposited their burden in front of one of the windows, Aline threw herself upon her brother's body, uttering heartrending cries. Madedame de Bergenheim did not stir; she lay upon the sofa with eyes and ears buried in the cushions, and seemed deaf and blind to all that surrounded her. Mademoiselle de Corandeuil was the only one who preserved her presence of mind. Controlling her emotion, she leaned over the Baron and sought for some sign of life.

"Is he dead?" she asked, in a low voice, of Monsieur de Camier.

"No, Mademoiselle," replied the latter, in a tone which announced that he had little hope.

"Has a physician been sent for?"

"To Remiremont, Epinal, everywhere."

At this moment Aline uttered a cry of joy. Bergenheim had just stirred, brought to life, perhaps, by the pressure of his sister's arms. He opened his eyes and closed them several times; at last his energy triumphed over his sufferings; he sat up on his improvised cot and, leaning upon his left elbow, he glanced around the room.

"My wife!" said he, in a weak voice.

Madame de Bergenheim arose and forced her way through the group that surrounded the mattress, and silently took her place beside her husband. Her features had changed so terribly within a few moments that a murmur of pity ran through the group of men that filled the room.

"Take my sister away," said Christian, disengaging his hand from the young girl, who was covering it with kisses and tears.

"My brother! I can not leave my brother!" exclaimed Aline, as she was dragged away rather than led to her room.

"Leave me for a moment," continued the Baron; "I wish to speak to my wife."

Mademoiselle de Corandeuil gave Monsieur de Camier a questioning glance, as if to ask if it were best to grant this request.

"We can do nothing before the doctors arrive," said the latter, in a low voice, "and perhaps it would be imprudent to oppose him."

Mademoiselle de Corandeuil recognized the correctness of this observation, and left the room, asking the others to follow her. During this time, Madame de Bergenheim remained motionless in her place, apparently insensible to all that surrounded her. The noise of the closing door aroused her from her stupor. She looked around the room as if she were seeking the others; her eyes, which were opened with the fixed look of a somnambulist, did not change their expression when they fell upon her husband.

"Come nearer," said he, "I have not strength enough to speak loud."

She obeyed mechanically. When she saw the large red stain which had soaked Christian's right sleeve, she closed her eyes, threw back her head, and her features contracted with a horrified expression.

"You women are wonderfully fastidious," said the Baron, as he noticed this movement; "you delight in causing a murder, but the slightest scratch frightens you. Pass over to the left side; you will not see so much blood—besides, it is the side where the heart is."

There was something terrible in the irony of the voice in which he spoke at this moment. Clémence fell upon her knees beside him and took his hand, crying:

"Pardon! pardon!"

The dying man took away his hand, raised his wife's head, and, looking at her a few moments attentively, he said at last:

"Your eyes are very dry. No tears! What! not one tear when you see me thus!"

"I can not weep," replied she; "I shall die!"

"It is very humiliating for me to be so poorly regretted, and it does you little honor—try to shed a few tears, Madame—it will be remarked—a widow who does not weep!"

"A widow—never!" she said, with energy.

"It would be convenient if they sold tears as they sell crape, would it not? Ah! only you women have a real talent for that—all women know how to weep."

[371]

"You will not die, Christian—oh! tell me that you will not die—and that you will forgive me."

"Your lover has killed me," said Bergenheim, slowly; "I have a bullet in my chest—I feel it—I am the one who is to die—in less than an hour I shall be a corpse —don't you see how hard it is already for me to talk?"

In reality his voice was becoming weaker and weaker. His breath grew shorter with each word; a wheezing sound within his chest indicated the extent of the lesion and the continued extravasation of blood.

"Mercy! pardon!" exclaimed the unhappy woman, prostrating herself upon the floor.

"More air—open the windows——" said the Baron, as he fell back upon the mattress, exhausted by the efforts he had just made to talk.

Madame de Bergenheim obeyed his order with the precision of an automaton. A fresh, pure breeze entered the room; when the curtains were raised, floods of light illuminated the floor, and the old portraits, suddenly lighted up, looked like ghosts who had left their graves to witness the death agonies of the last of their descendants. Christian, refreshed by the air which swept over his face, sat up again. He gazed with a melancholy eye at the radiant sun and the green woods which lay stretched out in front of the château.

"I lost my father on such a day as this," said he, as if talking to himself—"all our family die during the beautiful weather—ah! do you see that smoke over the Montigny rock?" he exclaimed, suddenly.

GERFAUT

After opening the windows, Clémence stepped out upon the balcony. Leaning upon the balustrade, she gazed at the deep, rapid river which flowed at her feet. Her husband's voice calling her aroused her from this gloomy contemplation. When she returned to Christian, his eyes were flaming, a flush like that of fever had overspread his cheeks, and a writhing, furious indignation was depicted upon his face. "Were you looking at that smoke?" said he, angrily; "it is your lover's signal; he is there—he is waiting to take you away—and I, your husband, forbid you to go—you must not leave me—your place is here—close by me."

"Close by you," she repeated, not understanding what he said.

"Wait at least until I am dead," he continued, while his eyes flashed more and more—"let my body get cold—when you are a widow you can do as you like—you will be free—and even then—I forbid it—I order you to wear mourning for me—above all, try to weep——"

"Strike me with a knife! At least I should bleed," said she, bending toward him and tearing open her dress to lay bare her bosom.

He seized her by the arm, and, exerting all his wasting strength to reach her, he said, in a voice whose harshness was changed almost into supplication:

"Clémence, do not dishonor me by giving yourself to him when I am dead—I would curse you if I thought that you would do that——"

"Oh! do not curse me!" she exclaimed; "do not drive me mad. Do you not know that I am about to die?"

CHARLES DE BERNARD

"There are women who do not see their husband's blood upon their lover's hands—but I would curse you——"

He dropped Clémence's arm and fell back upon the mattress with a sob. His eyes closed, and some unintelligible words died on his lips, which were covered with a bloody froth. He was dying.

Madame de Bergenheim, crouched down upon the floor, heard him repeating in his expiring voice:

"I would curse you—I would curse you!"

She remained motionless for some time, her eyes fastened upon the dying man before her with a look of stupefied curiosity. Then she arose and went to the mirror; she gazed at herself for a moment as if obeying the whim of an insane woman, pushing aside, in order to see herself better, the hair which covered her forehead. Suddenly a flash of reason came to her; she uttered a horrible cry as she saw some blood upon her face; she looked at herself from head to foot; her dress was stained with it; she wrung her hands in horror, and felt that they were wet. Her husband's blood was everywhere. Then, her brain filled with the fire of raving madness, she rushed out upon the balcony, and Bergenheim, before his last breath escaped him, heard the noise of her body as it fell into the river.

Several days later, the *Sentinelle des Vosges* contained the following paragraph, written with the official sorrow found in all death-notices at thirty sous per line:

[374]

GERFAUT

"A frightful event, which has just thrown two of our best families into mourning, has caused the greatest consternation throughout the Remiremont district. Monsieur le Baron de Bergenheim, one of the richest land-owners in our province, was killed by accident at a wild-boar hunt on his own domains. It was by the hand of one of his best friends, Monsieur de Gerfaut, well known by his important literary work, which has given its author a worldwide reputation, that he received his death-blow. Nothing could equal the grief of the involuntary cause of this catastrophe. Madame de Bergenheim, upon learning of this tragic accident, was unable to survive the death of her adored husband, and drowned herself in her despair. Thus the same grave received this couple, still in the bloom of life, to whom their great mutual affection seemed to promise a most happy future."

Twenty-eight months later the Parisian journals, in their turn, inserted, with but slight variations, the following article:

"Nothing could give any idea of the enthusiasm manifested at the Théâtre-Français last evening, at the first representation of Monsieur de Gerfaut's new drama. Never has this writer, whose silence literature has deplored for too long a time, distinguished himself so highly. His early departure for the East is announced. Let us hope that this voyage will turn to the advantage of art, and that the beautiful and sunny countries of Asia will be a mine for new inspirations for this celebrated poet, who has taken, in such a glorious manner, his place at the head of our literature."

Bergenheim's last wish had been realized; his honor was secure; nobody outraged by even an incredulous smile the purity of Clémence's winding-sheet; and the world did not refuse to their double grave the commonplace consideration that had surrounded their lives.

[375]

CHARLES DE BERNARD

Clémence's death did not destroy the future of the man who loved her so passionately, but the mourning he wears for her, to this day, is of the kind that is never put aside. And, as the poet's heart was always reflected in his works, the world took part in this mourning without being initiated into its mystery. When the bitter cup of memory overflowed in them, they believed it to be a new vein which had opened in the writer's brain. Octave received, every day, congratulations upon this sadly exquisite tone of his lyre, whose vibrations surpassed in supreme intensity the sighs of René or Obermann's *Reveries*. Nobody knew that those sad pages were written under the inspiration of the most mournful of visions, and that this dark and melancholy tinge, which was taken for a caprice of the imagination, had its source in blood and in the spasms of a broken heart.

www.ingramcontent.com/pod-product-compliance
Lightning Source LLC
Chambersburg PA
CBHW032140010726
47494CB00002B/297

* 9 7 8 1 4 3 4 4 3 1 6 2 2 *